Adrienne Vaughan

Secrets of the Heart © Adrienne Vaughan 2014

www.adriennevaughan.com

First Edition

Printed Edition

This book is a work of fiction. The characters and incidents are either fictitious or are used fictitiously. Any resemblance to any real person or incident is entirely coincidental and not intended by the author.

ISBN 978-0-9573949-8-8

Other books by Adrienne Vaughan

The Hollow Heart

A Change of Heart

Hocus Pocus – short story anthology – various authors

Praise for Adrienne Vaughan

Beautifully written, the characters are so well drawn, the descriptions are vivid and colourful, and the Irish background shines through. I loved it!
June Tate, author.

There is romance, drama, heartache and trauma, you will be wiping a tear away one minute and smiling the next.
Elaine G, Amazon Top 50 Reviewer.

I only put The Hollow Heart down to sleep and go to work.
K.Wyatt, Amazon Review.

I absolutely loved this - with beautifully crafted characters, it's an emotional roller-coaster of a read. I really didn't want it to end and can't wait to get my hands on the next book in the series.
Jennie Findley, journalist.

Talk about Maeve Binchy meets Jackie Collins – this is another lovely book in the series - just superb - romped through it - couldn't put it down - great story - fabulous writing and so pleased there was a happy ending. Light the fire, get on the sofa, open a nice bottle of something and away you go .... the characters are so wonderful you will be immersed from the outset and won't want to stop for anything at all.
Anna Bergmann, Scotland

It is a very good read that you can get totally lost in and certainly it kept me turning pages wanting to know what happened next. It is a book that had me smiling quite a lot and even crying a little at one point. I have to say this really is a first class read.
Elaine Gall, Goodreads and Amazon Top 50 Reviewer

A most enjoyable tale. The characters came to life in such a way that I felt I was living amongst them. Will be looking for more from this author.
Wendy Poole – Amazon Review

Secrets of the Heart

This book is dedicated to the memory of two fantastic men and one great horse.

My grandfathers; Joseph Houlihan, his rosary beads are powerful voodoo when needed, and Henry Wrafter, whose words of wisdom I lend to Franco Rossini.

And finally, to Scala Milan aka Marco, after ten wonderful years, spurs now well and truly hung up - gallop on, my knight, gallop on.

Secrets of the Heart

Prologue

T he rug was spread with the entire contents of a battered, over-large hatbox; a random scattering of disparate clutter. To an onlooker, the mismatch of photographs; scraps of paper; flutter of ribbon; torn ticket stubs and lone glove would mean little. Yet, this was a treasure trove, a precious collection which told, the secret story of her life. Marianne Coltrane knelt before these fragments of memorabilia and smiled. The heat from the hearth warmed her face, as the litter of memories warmed her heart. This was to be a labour of love.

A most unusual situation had brought her to this task. Her parents were to be married. Not the parents she had grown up with, but two people she did not even know existed until recently, who because of the sad story surrounding her birth and subsequent adoption, had been separated by ignorance, prejudice and a wide stretch of ocean for over thirty years.

Reunited at last, Kathleen MacReady, postmistress and spinster of the island parish of Innishmahon, and Brian Maguire, newly-returned from the USA, were finally to be wed; their long-lost daughter, attending the bride; her movie star partner, best man to the groom. Now, all she had to do was fill the pages of this newly-purchased, beautiful leather-bound book with her story thus far, a fitting wedding gift for these two people she hardly knew, yet already loved.

Marianne set about her job, arranging things chronologically, editing out the bad, smoothing over the ragged and highlighting the best. Each element carefully designed to present her new mother and father with a snapshot of their daughter's past; her now, what seemed so long ago, life. A precious gift to have and to hold, as they were joined on their special day, taking the next step into the future, together.

Chapter One – Dublin Can Be Heaven

It had been a stupendous occasion. Emotional, solemn and hilarious, every second of it bursting with love; the whole day filled to the brim with the rich, deep, happiness only a human heart can hold and share at the same time. A truly lovely wedding and a marriage made in heaven. So everyone said.

It was the lust for life kind of wedding that could only happen on Innishmahon. This rock solid, jewel of an island, flung into the Atlantic off Ireland's west coast. This gem where glinting cliffs towered above beaches like the walls of a fortress, protecting its little community, battling the elements, the malevolent influences of the outside world, and, occasionally each other. An eccentric, eclectic mix; joined together for one fabulous day of celebration, uniting two of their own, who were finally sharing their dream after over thirty years apart.

A magical story, the type that forges bonds, strengthens ties and deep-roots loves and loyalties. Which was just as well, because in the months ahead every single living creature at that wedding was going to be called upon to dig deep inside themselves and hold onto everything they believed in, for better or worse.

No battles today though; this was a truly momentous milestone, a red-letter day, to be marked forever on the calendar with a big red X. Today was the day Miss Kathleen MacReady opened her eyes to discover she was finally who she had wanted to be all her life. Today, with bright winter sun streaming through the huge, Georgian window, and the hum of traffic murmuring pleasantly below, she was at last Mrs Brian Maguire. Oh yes, that's exactly who she was.

She closed her eyes and, turning in the vast hotel bed, reached out for her husband of barely forty-eight hours. He was fast asleep, a faint smile on his lovely mouth. She slid towards him, brushing his lips with hers. He wiggled his nose, a good nose she thought, a manly nose. She traced the outline of his eyebrows with the tip of her finger, still dark, like his eyelashes. She pushed her fingers through his hair, a silver halo around his tanned face. She sighed. *God, you're a lucky woman, Kathleen,* she thought, *to have this fine looking fella here in your big, hotel bed and you a married woman and he a married man, and the best of it all, married to each other.* She moved closer. He opened an eye.

"I know what you're thinking, Kathleen, so stop it right now," he said firmly.

"What, what am I thinking?" She looked into his face.

"You're thinking, I wish that fine fella of a husband of mine would wake up and devour every inch of me with his fabulous lovemaking like he has done every night of our married life."

"Right on the button." She grinned at him, slipping her fingers under his t-shirt.

"Stop!" He clamped her hands to his chest.

"Ah, Brian," she tried a seductive tone. There was a knock on the door. Brian checked his watch, leapt from the bed and crossed the room. She heard him open the door …voices. He reappeared, carrying a tray laden with breakfast and a champagne bucket, fresh juice, glasses. He poured a *Buck's Fizz*, taking it back to where she sat up in bed, smiling. She pulled on a marabou-trimmed bed jacket, letting it fall lasciviously off one shoulder. She arranged her hair, russet against the crisp, white pillow. He opened the curtains a little. She could see he was aroused. She felt a flutter deep inside her.

"Breakfast first, Mrs Maguire, we need to build up our strength," he lifted the silver cover to reveal scrambled egg with smoked salmon, grilled tomatoes, mushrooms, "don't we?"

"Do we?" she laughed, sipping her drink, the bubbles tickling.

"Oh we do, because once we've eaten this, I'm going to eat you, every last morsel of you," he told her in his melting Irish-American lilt. It made her toes curl.

"Lovely, that's just lovely," she twinkled at him over her glass.

The well-dressed couple strolling hand in hand through St Stephen's Green could have been any age, from anywhere. The one thing an onlooker would have been absolutely sure of - they were totally in love.

They walked down the path towards the lake, across the bridge and, finding a quiet bench nestling in a small spinney, they sat, watching sunlight play on the water. Parents and children laughed as ducks vied for food; executives late for appointments hurried past, and Christmas shoppers, taking a short cut through the park to the Luas, waddled by, laden.

"I just love Dublin, don't you?" she asked, unnecessarily. She knew he loved Dublin; they both did.

"When were you last here?" He put his arm around her, pulling her to him, the extravagant fur of her coat, soft against his skin.

"The time Ryan invited us to the premiere of his movie. We went to the TV show too. We had a ball. Mind you, there was a bit of bother, but Dermot sorted it out, good man that he is."

"Dermot was with you?" Brian had a lot to catch up on.

"No, that's how we met him. There was a punch-up in a bar between Ryan and a journalist, things got a bit bloody, and we had to be at RTE for the Late, Late Show. So we patched the boys up and Dermot gave us a police escort. We made it with only minutes to spare." She was matter-of-fact.

"Really? That sounds quite an adventure." Sometimes Kathleen did get a little carried away.

"It was," she looked wistfully into the distance, "seems like a lifetime ago. Totally true though, honest to God." He raised an eyebrow. "Come on, I'll take you to the very bar. Someone there will confirm it, if you don't believe me."

"What makes you think I don't believe you?" Brian laughed, taking her arm as they headed towards Grafton Street. Kathleen stopped as a flotilla of swans glided towards them.

"Oh look," she exclaimed, "I adore swans, so regal, so loyal, they mate for life, you know."

A young man was taking pictures; the pretty girl with him laughed. "It looks like a wedding procession," she said in heavily-accented English. Brian took a camera from his pocket.

"Would you?" he asked the girl, wrapping his arms around Kathleen, standing on the bridge. They beamed into the lens, the stream of swans on the lake behind them.

"We're just married," Kathleen remarked, as she handed the camera back.

"Really?" the girl smiled. "We're engaged. My mother, she is pleased I marry an Irishman."

"Wise woman, they're very good in bed," Kathleen stage whispered, making Brian and the young man laugh. The girl blushed.

Coming through the gates of the park onto Grafton Street, Kathleen patted the horses, standing before gleaming traps awaiting a fare, before braving the swathe of Christmas shoppers, bustling beneath lavish decorations draped building to building across the thoroughfare. The wind had a bite to it. They stopped to sway to the street musicians' rendition of *Last Christmas* and then stood to admire the *Brown Thomas* window, ornately decorated as *The Snow Queen's House Party*, with a throne made of ice and a handsome prince bearing diamonds in a crystal cask, complete with frosted eyelashes. Kathleen squeezed Brian's arm, eyes glittering with excitement.

"Appeals to children of all ages," he said, grinning, guiding her into the exclusive bar she declared was the scene of the brawl.

Secrets of the Heart

A few early diners were having lunch, sitting with soup and sandwiches at small round tables dotted about the place, a couple of men were at the bar with pints of stout. The outside world hushed away as the heavy glass door closed behind them. They stood, taking it in, warm wooden panels, walls the colour of moss, pale gold shades defusing soft light and, centre stage, gently dominating the whole place a huge, shiny bar, marble on polished mahogany. Velvet covered stools stood proudly before it and behind, rows of glass shelves, stacked to the ceiling with glittering bottles, every brew, hue and concoction known to man displayed for all to see. Legend ran, if you asked for a drink they did not stock, you could drink all night for free of anything else. To date – and the bar had been in the same spot for nearly two hundred years – no one had ever been obliged to imbibe their second choice.

"Mac? Good Lord, if it isn't Mac!" exclaimed the bartender, pumping Brian's hand. "When did you get in? Are you here on business?" The man grinned at Brian, giving Kathleen the once-over.

"Not this time, Jimmy. Meet Mrs Maguire. We're on honeymoon," Brian told him, smiling broadly.

"Well, I never, isn't that great news? Congratulations, and to you, too, Missus. Honeymoon? Well, I'll be ... always thought you were a confirmed bachelor."

"Came back to marry the love of my life, childhood sweethearts, you see," Brian said, proudly. Kathleen hopped onto a stool. Brian ordered drinks, the barman busied himself.

"I didn't know you knew this place. Are you often here?" Kathleen asked.

"Kathleen, it *is* one of the most famous pubs in Dublin. I modelled the bar in New York on it, visited a few times over the years, and before you start, I never came to Innishmahon or anywhere near when I was in Ireland. Dublin and then straight back to JFK. As far as I knew you never wanted to see me again." He laid his hand over hers; she softened.

"And the other business," she kept her voice low, "is that over with?"

He raised a finger to his lips. "No names, no pack-drill."

"You're not still involved though, tell me that much?" She looked earnestly into his face. She was referring to his role as a fundraiser for a subversive political party. They had opposing and passionate opinions, but their views had never prevented them from falling in love.

"Not so's you'd notice." He gave her a grin.

"It's not me noticing you need to worry about. But seriously, Brian, that side of things does not sit happily with me, not happily with me at all." She took a sip of the Bloody Mary the bartender put before her.

"Let's not talk about it now. This is our honeymoon, no arguments, not one word of disagreement – agreed?"

She thought for a moment, remembering their passionate lovemaking after breakfast that very morning.

"Agreed." She touched the tip of his nose with her gloved finger. "We have the rest of our lives to argue."

"Indeed," Brian nodded. "Now, tell me all about the shenanigans that happened the last time you were here. What was that all about?"

Taking tiny sips of the delicious cocktail as she spoke, Kathleen explained how Ryan, currently playing the legendary superspy *Thomas Bentley* in the latest Hollywood blockbuster, sent a helicopter for Marianne, their dear friend Oonagh, and herself, bringing the three women to Dublin for the movie premiere. He had organised for them to attend the TV studios, where he was a guest on the nation's favourite chat show, stay in a fabulous hotel and generally have the time of their lives.

"But why was there a brawl here?" asked Brian, bemused as he cut into his toasted sandwich, dunking it in the steaming seafood chowder the bartender had delivered.

"Well, Paul Osborne is the type of journalist who would sell his own grandmother for a by-line. He'd worked with Marianne in the past, and if I'm not mistaken had quite a yen for her. Anyway, he was always having a go at Ryan in the press, digging dirt and generally making a nuisance of himself, but we had no idea he was here, in Dublin, reporting on the premiere. He ran into Ryan and Marianne having a quiet drink here and decided to make their private moment as public as he could. Ryan punched him on the nose and the whole place erupted!"

Brian looked up, the bartender was listening.

"There was a hell of a row, alright," he agreed, "fists and chairs flying. I took hold of the young lady and pulled her in behind the bar out of harm's way. The film star fella took a hell of a puck in the eye and then he really went for that English reporter, and he got a right seeing to as well."

Kathleen coughed. "As I was saying ..."

"Sorry Mrs ..." the bartender moved to serve another customer.

"Oonagh and I showed up here about the same time as Dermot, sure the place was in tatters."

Brian put his pint down. "Dermot was with you, too?"

"Well, not exactly." Kathleen removed her lavender gloves, one finger at a time. "He was with the Gardaí. Inspector Dermot Finnegan of the Garda Siochana turns up at the door, the whole place falls silent, everyone terrified he'd arrest the lot of them and there'd be a bigger scandal than any Paul Osborne could have invented. Turns out, in another life, Dermot and Ryan knew each other."

"You mean Ryan has a criminal record?" Brian was aghast. He, too, knew Ryan, they had been friends in New York.

"Not at all," Kathleen flicked him with her glove, "they were young actors together, treading the boards. It appears Dermot traded the footlights for a flashing light – a blue one." Cutting her sandwich into little squares, so she could pop them into her mouth without smudging her *Coral Kiss* lipstick, Brian waited patiently until she had eaten and dabbed the edges of her mouth with a lace hanky. He gestured she continue.

"Well, the sight of Dermot standing there, resplendent in his uniform – he really is a fine figure of a man – seemed to soothe the troubled waters and once everyone was cleaned up, he gave us a police escort to the studio, in time for Ryan to appear on the show."

"No bad press, then?" Brian asked her, finishing the chowder by wiping his bowl clean with a crust of soda bread.

"Not a bit of it, the movie was a smash hit, Ryan and Paul put their differences behind them and the rest, as they say, is history." Kathleen gazed into the middle distance. "We'd a great night, the whole show turned into a huge party, dancing, singing, the craic was mighty, alright."

Brian pictured the scene; if there is one thing the Irish know how to do well, it is party and the natives of Innishmahon know how to party, better than most. Maybe it was because they lived life on the edge, flung out in the ocean, clinging to a bit of farming and tourism, on the brink of civilisation in many ways. He suddenly felt the many years he and Kathleen had been separated, weigh on him, guilty for not being there for her, while she had forged her own way, making a career, a place for herself. Fighting for a position of respectability, lest anyone denigrate her for being an unmarried mother, abandoned by her family and the father of her child … himself. He took her hand. She gave him a beguiling smile.

"Isn't it great here? The whole city buzzing by outside the door and here we are in a little haven, a time-slip, back in the day, like when we were young." She nestled into her chair, the fraudulent fox draped around her shoulders, mixed with her hair. She looked just the same to him.

"And was that the first time you'd been back in our hotel since …"

"Since we consummated our love affair and I became pregnant with our child?" she said in a soft tone, relishing the memory, all bitterness dissolved. She glanced at the Claddagh ring on her wedding finger. "It upset me in one way, yet thrilled me in another, you see, it brought it all back to me. I felt you close to me in some way, almost as if that fabulous building still held the spirit of us within its walls, our love was still alive and so it proved to be."

He leaned across and planted his lips firmly on her forehead.

"You're an incredible woman, Kathleen," he said, voice thick with emotion.

"You can call me Mrs Maguire," she chided, gathering her things together. "I have to be wary of young men like yourself becoming too familiar. Now come on, let's get out of here and immerse ourselves in all that glorious, Christmas-ness. I've loads of shopping to do before I get you back to that hotel and shag you senseless!" She stood and twirled the amber velvet coat, pulling the luxuriant fur about her ears. Brian finished his pint, following her through the door and out into the happy hoardes.

"Last chance to get your squeezy Santie," called a street vendor, "only five euros; look he even lights up when you squeeze him." *I'll just have to buy her one of those,* Brian thought to himself, as Kathleen disappeared into a glittering department store.

Brian had business to attend to the following morning; his lawyer was based in Dublin and he had papers to sign. Kathleen had been left to bathe and dress at leisure, sort through the many parcels and packages they had acquired the previous day, before finally descending the sweeping Art Nouveau staircase to the lobby. The hotel was packed, busy businessmen, noisy tourists and polished South Dublin ladies who pushed through the rotating doors, brimming with the frivolity of festivity. Excitement was building.

The new Mrs Maguire stopped halfway down the stairs. A magnificent Christmas tree had been erected in the foyer, the scent of spruce tingled her nose, red baubles glinted beneath the huge *Waterford* crystal chandelier. She rested her hand on the brass balustrade, admiring her manicure, nails the colour of the baubles, she was pleased to note. Scanning the milieu for Brian's return, she saw a man, tall, slim, fair-haired, stride confidently past the concierge, the blazing peat fire, and into the bar. There was something about his walk that was vaguely familiar. She spotted Brian, on a sofa, reading a newspaper. Her hand went to her hair; she took a compact out of her bag to check her make-up. Her eyes were shining, reflecting perfectly, the vintage crystals hanging from her ears. She loved the way the very sight of him made her sparkle.

She walked slowly, willing him to look up and watch the elegant woman in the burgundy velvet trouser suit descend the stairs. Let him see the other admiring glances upwards and realise this gorgeous creature was his and his alone. But Brian continued to read the paper until Kathleen was upon him and tapped him on the shoulder.

"Brian, you missed my grand entrance," she teased. He pulled her onto his knee. She squealed, and people turned, smiling at the playful middle-aged couple. "What had you so engrossed?"

"Big article about the new *Thomas Bentley* movie, locations, cars, yachts, gadgets, fascinating."

Kathleen scanned the paper. "That PR machine never sleeps." She eyed a photo of the movie's famous producer, Franco Rossini, a handsome, powerful man, who had unknowingly played a significant role in her life over the past couple of years. "Ever met him?" she asked Brian, as he took her arm. Having owned one of New York's most exclusive bars, it would not surprise her. New York was much like Dublin, a native could rarely traverse a thoroughfare without running into someone they knew.

"Once or twice, but in Cesare's, you know, the Italian restaurant. Cesare and I are old friends. I'll take you there on our next trip, Mrs Maguire, you'll love it," he promised.

But Kathleen did not hear the invitation. She had recognised the by-line, the thumbnail portrait of the writer. She gripped Brian, unwittingly digging *Chanel's Rouge Noir* into his arm.

"What is it?" he asked. She gave her head a little shake.

"Nothing, nothing at all," she reassured him, "let's have a drink. I'd like a very dry Martini." She was suddenly eager to visit the hotel's famous horseshoe bar.

"Very well," Brian said, as Kathleen folded the newspaper and tucked it into her bag.

"I think that belongs to the hotel." Brian indicated the coffee table, strewn with reading material.

But she was gone, striding away surprisingly quickly, considering her heels. Brian had to trot to catch up.

Kathleen scanned the room as they entered. A man in a long tweed coat offered her his seat, but she did not want to sit, not yet. Pushing past people, jostling bags and packages, she made it to the bar. Brian was there before her, tall, self-assured, the type of man who always caught a waiter's eye straight off. He handed her a drink. She knocked it back.

"What is it?" he mouthed above the hubbub, searching her face as she craned her neck, looking around. She climbed onto a newly vacated stool, and perching on the bar-rail, thought she saw him. Was it him? The far door swung open and another gaggle of pre-Christmas revellers appeared. She saw the man turn, wrap a scarf about his ears. She strained to see, and he was gone.

"What?" Brian demanded.

"I thought it was someone I recognised; probably not." She arranged her face in a smile. "Have you booked us a nice lunch somewhere?"

"I have."

"Good, let's go, and you can tell me how you got on with your lawyer."

He laughed, taking her arm.

"No, Kathleen, no business talk today, we're on honeymoon, remember?"

"How could I forget?" She beamed at him, stopping to run a dark fingernail across the outline of his mouth. "Are we having a lie down after lunch?"

He raised an eyebrow. "You're insatiable, Mrs Maguire."

"A lot to make up for," she replied.

Adrienne Vaughan

Chapter Two – Bah, Humbug!

Marianne was in the attic of the Georgian mansion that she was turning into a holiday home for young carers; children responsible for seriously ill or disabled parents, who rarely had time to be children at all. She was dedicating the project to the late Oonagh Quinn, her dearest friend and one of the most caring people on the planet. Marianne felt it would be a fitting tribute, to her at times, outrageous, but always kind-hearted friend.

The house, a fine gated property with at least a dozen bedrooms, galleried landing, four reception rooms, massive kitchen and butler's pantry, had been beautifully restored to its former glory by the previous owner, a London stockbroker who had lost everything in the last recession. Marianne had bought it for a good price and renamed it *The Oonagh Quinn Foundation*, putting a smart brass plaque at the portico entrance, but the locals just called it *Oonagh's Project* and, despite her best efforts, Marianne knew the name would stick.

Sorting through innumerable boxes and trunks, long pre-dating the hapless stockbroker, she had come across little of interest; faded curtains, moth-eaten blankets and a collection of broken picture frames. She sighed. Not much to stir the imagination.

Looking up, at the sound of scuffling in the corner, she pushed auburn locks behind her ears to focus on the white bottom and wagging tail of her beloved companion, Monty, the West Highland terrier. He made a grumbling noise and, wriggling backwards, appeared with a piece of tinsel in his mouth. She laughed. He trotted towards her, a long trail of fading glitter sliding behind him in the dust. He dropped the end at his mistress' feet, looking up expectantly, eyes' bright with playful anticipation. She smiled; his perfect pedigree looks even more appealing since a near-fatal accident left him with a scar above one eye and a seriously lopsided ear.

"Good work, boy," she told him, and the velocity of his tail increased. "How did you know to find Christmas decorations? We've hardly any at home. We can't have Joey's first Christmas without a bit of glitz now, can we? Let's see what else we have here ..."

She lifted the lid of the huge chest, and gasped. It was an Aladdin's cave, a cornucopia of trinkets and treasures. All kinds of trimmings and frippery were crammed into the box; a rainbow of colourful adornments. She started to unpack; first shamrocks and harps, then ornamental lanterns and hangings, a collection of exotic hats, it seemed unending. Brushing dust from her clothes, Marianne sat back to admire the fruits of her labour; a kaleidoscope of gaiety splayed all around, with herself and Monty marooned in the middle.

"Wow, these guys certainly knew how to party. No feast or festival left unmarked." She twirled a beautiful concoction of feathers and black lace; a jewel-encrusted mask that would have graced the grandest Viennese Ball in days gone by. Judging by the age of the contents, the trunk had been there for a very long time.

A loud clatter made her jump. Monty sprang to his feet, growling. Erin Brennan's head popped up through the trap door, facing the other way.

"We're here!" Marianne called.

"You could have told me you'd be gone for hours. I've been all over the place looking for you," Erin said. "What a mess. That lot needs skipping!"

"No way," Marianne embraced her haul protectively, "there's some amazing stuff here; antiques, curios, memorabilia."

Erin spat out a laugh. "Euphemisms for crap, just a load of old crap. Bin the lot, that's my advice."

Ignoring her, Marianne started sorting decorations into a basket.

"You're not actually going to take that stuff home and put it up, are you?"

"Come on, give me a hand, the pub could do with glitzing up a bit, too." Marianne started humming *Winter Wonderland.*

"I *hate* Christmas," Erin moaned. "Sentimental load of ole shite!"

Marianne was shocked.

"How can you hate Christmas? All the best things happen at Christmas ... parties, presents, delicious food, wine, romance." She lifted Monty into her arms, nuzzling the space between his ears with her nose. "Monty was a Christmas present, arrived with a ribbon around his neck and a proposal of marriage scrawled across a large brown label." She closed her eyes and was instantly back there, at the doorway of her little house in Chesterford. George, with his red scarf and big smiley face. Monty in a basket, the tiniest bundle of white fur she had ever seen. She took a deep breath, reaching out to steady herself, the rush of memory so strong.

"Talk about emotional blackmail. I suppose you had no choice but to say yes to the eejit. You're not married, so I'm guessing you got out of that particular situation as soon as." Erin was walking around the attic, turning things over with the toe of her boot.

"No, actually, he was a lovely man. He died in a car crash a few weeks before the wedding," Marianne said, quietly.

Erin looked up, shamefaced. "Sorry."

"Don't be. George turned my life around. I was a cold, lonely, workaholic. He showed me how to love again, live for now, not what might have been."

Erin buried her nose in a trunk. She was pulling out papers and files, old medical correspondence. It all needed to be burned, in her opinion.

"Besides, without George I wouldn't have Monty and we would never have come here to make a new life." Marianne gave the ball of white fur a squeeze.

"Yeah, yeah, whatever." A spider crawled out of a file Erin was holding. She let it fall to the floor. "Let's get out of here. This place gives me the creeps."

Having festooned a glittering bauble to Monty's collar, Marianne gathered up her findings and headed for the trap door. "If you ever want to talk about it, I'm here for you," she said, trying to look into Erin's brittle grey eyes.

"Talk about what?" the younger woman bit back.

"Whoever broke your heart."

"Bullshit. More sentimental claptrap. No one broke my heart. Now, come on, let's go." Erin clambered down the ladder.

'That's probably true. Who could get though all the barbed wire wrapped around it?' Marianne thought to herself. She called Monty, who was dragging a bulging envelope along by a piece of ribbon and, lifting him up, with his find still in his mouth, pulled the trap door behind them. They clattered to the landing and headed down the back staircase.

Glorious winter sunshine flooded the courtyard. Marianne stopped to gaze out to sea, taking deep breaths of sharp salt air to melt the attic dust from her lips. The rear of the house faced the ocean. The stone terrace stepped down to derelict flower beds, a strip of grass and then a tiny beach of shiny shale. At its edge, a lacy frill of wave trimmed the midnight blue; the vast Atlantic splayed out across the globe beyond. She closed her eyes to hold the image in.

"I could never tire of such a view. Could you?" she said, but Erin was already loading the 4x4.

"Like I've said before, Marianne, you blow-ins think it's great for a year or so. Get stuck here in a storm, you'll think twice about it." Erin pulled her door closed. Marianne let Monty in ahead of her, relieving him of his treasure. She gave the dusty package a cursory once-over and threw it in the basket with the rest of the haul. Monty still liked to tear things to shreds and she had just cleaned the car in time for Christmas.

"I've been here in a storm, don't forget. We'll be fine. The new bridge is well underway. We'll soon be connected to the mainland again." Sometimes Erin could be a real *Jonah.*

"Yeah, one way in and one way out. Really reassuring."

Marianne was just about to argue that could be true of many places, but she stopped herself. She was not in the mood to dispel Erin's depressing cynicism today. With Ryan and Joey in England, she was feeling pretty low herself. She started the engine, giving the fabulous view one last glance before pulling away.

"Any idea what you're doing for Christmas?" she asked, as she swung the truck across the gravel, passing an overgrown circle of lawn with a rusting fountain at its centre, and on through the huge wrought iron gates flanked either side by tall stone pillars. It was one of the most impressive buildings on the island, probably the whole area. Marianne zapped the gates. She loved the way the previous owner had kept all the traditional aspects of the property, but had modernised things so beautifully. It was going to make a fantastic holiday retreat for these deserving youngsters. They would make new friends, enjoy some precious downtime, forge happy memories that would stay with them for the rest of their lives. *Oonagh's Project* would be something the whole island could be proud of.

"What did you say?" Erin broke her reverie.

"Christmas, any plans?" Marianne said.

Erin sighed. "No. I don't like it. I'll be glad to be working."

Marianne thought for a minute.

"Anyone you'd like to spend it with?"

"Not really." Erin pulled her knees up to her chest and stared blankly out of the window.

"What about ...?"

"Can we drop it please, Marianne?" Erin sniped at her. "For godsake, this place doesn't change. Matchmaking, that's the national frigging sport in this fecking dump. Even the blow-ins are at it now," she grumbled.

"I'm not matchmaking," Marianne was wounded, "and I'm not a blow-in, either, as you so delicately put it."

"Really?" Erin replied. They drove back to Maguire's in silence. Monty looked from one to the other, chin on his paws. He could sulk too, if that was the order of the day.

Rattling towards the village, turning right at the church, with the cranes and dumper trucks working on the bridge, and new marina to the left, Marianne's mood brightened. Things were coming on. The structure for the bridge was in place, and she could see the marina walls jutting out of the water. They were on schedule. It was coming together; it would be ready, up and running in time for the new season. Progress ... she did like a bit of progress. They trundled down the road, over the one and only, totally unnecessary pedestrian crossing on the island and into the car park.

Sean Grogan was leaning on his bicycle, parked in the entrance of the pub. His battered tweed cap rammed on his head, his one good eye - the other seemed to have a will of its own - glaring at them, thin lips drawn back over tombstone teeth in a snarl.

"Somebody's pleased to see us," Erin announced. She was hardly out of the vehicle when he railed on her.

"What hour of the day do you call this?" he roared, stabbing at a non-existent watch on his wrist.

"Keep your hair on," Erin replied, winking at Marianne. Sean touted the most famous comb-over in the Western World.

"If you're not going to keep civilised hours now Padar's emigrated and the new owner is gallivanting up above in Dublin, I will have to take my obviously undervalued custom elsewhere!"

"It's hardly opening time," Erin told him, unlocking the heavy oak door.

"Padar didn't have opening times. Padar was *always* open." Sean pushed the bike into the hallway.

"I'm only following instructions." Erin flicked lights, switching the electrics to start the pumps. Sean climbed onto his usual stool.

"I'll have to wait now ... not even ready to serve yet," he grumbled.

"I'm sure a large whiskey while you wait will keep your thirst at bay." Erin handed Sean a glass.

"Good enough, about time," came his gracious thanks.

Father Gregory was next through the door, dragging a couple of bulging bin liners behind him. He met Marianne unloading in the car park and was delighted to help bring a bit of the festive spirit into the local. Eyebrows had been raised when the new owner and his bride had promptly disappeared to the capital without so much as a fairy light left aglow in the island's favourite public house. The fact that Erin, the new manageress, had little time for the festival, was becoming more and more evident the nearer Christmas loomed.

Marianne followed the priest into the bar. She had been in a couple of times since her parents had set off on honeymoon, but between cleaning up after their hurried nuptials, then helping Ryan to prepare to fly to England for meetings ahead of the next movie in the *Thomas Bentley* franchise, there had been rather a lot going on to say the least.

Now, as she stood in what was, to her, a very familiar place, she let the bags and boxes drop to the stone-flagged floor. The brasses looked dull; the shine of the huge mahogany bar dimmed. There was no blazing peat fire in the grate, no smell of warm bread and tasty soup permeating from the kitchen. Sean sat there alone, the glass of whiskey in hand. Erin had disappeared and Father Gregory was putting up a poster on the community board.

Marianne felt a huge clump of sorrow squeeze at the base of her throat. She could almost hear the echo of Oonagh's gravelly voice, giving out to Padar for forgetting something she considered vitally important, like collecting her favourite magazine from the newsagents or running out of Grenadine the very day Miss MacReady had to have Tequila Sunrise or die. Or the worse crime of all, not remembering to tell her how gorgeous she was, and why was she dieting at all? *Sure, was she not perfect ...?* to him, anyway.

She remembered how they had welcomed her, taken her and Monty into their hearts, at a time – hardly realising it herself – she had no one in the world but a dog and a hell of a lot of baggage. Marianne swallowed hard. How, in only a matter of weeks, could this place, the centre of all she had known here, suddenly become so sad and soulless?

Erin reappeared from the cellar.

"That's sorted, we're all good to go now, Sean," she said, reaching for a pint glass.

"Too late!" Sean replied, leaping from his stool. "I can't stay here drinking all day. There's work to be done." And with that, he rushed from the bar, barely tipping his cap at Marianne as he passed.

"Well, I fell for that one." Erin stared down at the glass in her hand. "Bloody chancer."

Father Gregory hovered between the door and the bar.

"Gregory?" Erin waved the glass at him. Marianne frowned. Everyone knew the priest drank *Budweiser*, ice cold, straight out of the bottle.

"Not for me, thanks Erin. We're hunting tomorrow. I need to give Bessie a canter on the beach while the weather holds. There's a couple of Oblate fathers over from the mainland on retreat, think they can ride. Well, we're going to whip their townie arses, you see if we don't," he coughed. "Figuratively speaking, of course. See you later. God bless," he called, as he left.

Erin came out from behind the bar and flopped down in the armchair beside the fireplace. Marianne started unpacking the decorations.

"Come on, new manageress, let's get this place looking spick and span and shipshape in time for the honeymooners return. What do you say we deck the halls with boughs of holly?"

Erin started flicking through a magazine.

"I told you, I hate Christmas, it's a load of hype about nothing. Tacky tinsel, crappy music, people pretending they're having a great time with other people pretending they're having a great time. It's the pits."

Marianne folded her arms.

"Erin, you're in the entertainment business now, you know. You left insurance to take the job as manageress here, remember?"

"So?" Erin was being deliberately obtuse.

"So it's the biggest, single money-making opportunity of the year. Christmas keeps everything ticking along until the tourists arrive. Whatever you make this time of year has to pay for a lot of things and last a very long time. *Capiche*?" Marianne was unravelling fairy lights.

"I know, but it's so depressing," Erin groaned.

"You're in the wrong occupation to be depressed about Christmas. And if you don't mind my saying so, this place could do with a good clean. What's changed? You had it gleaming when Padar was here."

Erin checked her fingernails.

"I'm the manageress now. Cissy Beagle does the cleaning these days, but she's not brilliant."

Marianne rolled her eyes.

"She's not brilliant because she won't get her cataracts seen to and she can't clean below waist level with the arthritis in her knees. Besides, there's not enough for a manageress to do and *not* do the cleaning."

Erin was just about to fight her corner when the door swung open and Dermot Finnegan blew in. He spotted the baubles immediately.

"Aha, brilliant," he boomed. "You'll need a hand with those. Erin throw me on a pint there, will you, and Marianne and I will start getting the decs up. You're pushing it aren't you, time-wise? Have you put up the calendar of events yet? Are you doing a candlelight supper at all?"

"Why?" Erin was surly as she went to pull Dermot a pint.

"I was thinking of organising some Carol singing, maybe getting a bit of a choir together."

"That's a lovely idea," Marianne said, giving Dermot an armful of crystal stars to hang from the ceiling. Erin plonked Dermot's pint on the bar.

"If you want another one I'll be down in the cellar, the electrics are playing up," she said, sharply.

"Fair enough, so," Dermot replied. "Tell you what, I've time on my hands today, waiting for materials to be delivered. Will I give the place a really good clean before I put these up?"

Marianne beamed at him; she did like Dermot.

"Good man. I'll light the fire and get some soup and sandwiches on the go. What do you think, Erin?"

"Ah, please yourselves," she said narkily, pushing open the cellar door, "you always do anyway." And promptly left them to it.

Dermot shrugged at Marianne.

"Bad hair day?" he offered.

"She does seem a bit tetchy, alright. Maybe needs a bit of male company, you know, night out, romantic meal, that kind of thing?"

Dermot scratched his chin, green-grey eyes darkening in concentration.

"Trouble is, there aren't many single men her age around here. She's met all the building lads up at the marina.

It doesn't look like any of them have caught her eye," he said.

Marianne pretended to think for a while.

"What about you, take you both out of yourselves, what do you say?"

"No," he said quickly, "if I'm taking anyone out, it's you."

"What?"

"While Ryan's away, he said I'm to mind you. I could take *you* out to dinner if you'd like, cheer you up and keep you amused. I'm sure that's what he meant."

"Really?" Marianne was incredulous. She had hoped Dermot's crush on her had long waned.

"Really!" Dermot replied.

"I tell you what," Marianne was determined, "let's have a get together, make sure no one is on their own over Christmas. What do you think?"

"When will Ryan be back?" Dermot was disappointed not to be taken up on his offer.

"In time for our little do, no worries." Marianne said, confidently.

"There's a storm brewing. Do you think he'll bother coming if it kicks off? Be a bit much for Joey, and they'll be nice and cosy in a five star hotel in London, hot and cold running starlets, the lot." Dermot immediately regretted his crassness. Marianne looked as if she had been punched in the stomach.

Chapter Three – Weather Or Not?

Ryan O'Gorman had achieved his wildest ambition. He was world famous for his role as the suave and incredibly sophisticated superspy, *Thomas Bentley*. His alter ego led a dramatic and charmed existence, foiling dastardly villains hell bent on global domination; a role many of his contemporaries would kill for. Yet Ryan had been offered it at precisely the point he decided he was going to change career, try something different, become someone else, someone with a far less loveless and lonely lifestyle. It had been an offer he could not refuse, and now the crown weighed heavy on his head. His world had been so turned upside down by the constant media pressure focusing on his turbulent private life, that from the moment he decided to make Innishmahon his home and, one day, Marianne his wife, he was prepared to overcome every obstacle to achieve this new dream.

He was pondering this ever closer ambition, as he sat on the vast king-size bed in the five star London suite the movie company had rented for his sojourn in the capital. He had been dozing gently, his young son Joey in his arms, having watched a particularly colourful DVD, featuring a soothing lullaby as the credits rolled. The two were happily at one with the world.

Ryan pulled a cushion to his head, blocking the ringing in his ears, until he realised the persistent trill would not be stilled.

"Ryan, is that you?!" A man's voice, New York accent, anxiety rippling down the line.

"This is a private number. Of course it's me," Ryan whispered, not wishing to disturb Joey.

"Oh yeah, sorry. Anyways, I have news, good news, or bad news, I've yet to decide, but news, anyways." The voice calmed a little.

"Okay, shoot." Ryan lifted the sleepy little boy onto his shoulder, walking through to the adjacent room. He laid him in his cot.

"Big press conference day after tomorrow in London, so you ain't gotta go nowhere. The boss wants to announce the replacement *Thomas Bentley*, give the public a chance to come to terms with a new guy in the role."

Far away in New York, Ryan could picture his agent, Larry Leeson, sitting on a stool at the gleaming bar in the corner of his penthouse apartment. It was far too early for a drink in his time zone, but Larry sounded as if he could do with a very large bourbon right now. He pondered the news.

"Ryan?"

"Still here, just thinking. I was under the impression I'm to do the next movie, then manage the handover as part of the storyline in number three." Ryan knew an earlier get out would suit him better, but there had been much deliberation about maximising the return on the franchise and, Franco Rossini, the movie mogul in charge of the whole shebang, was adamant Ryan remain in the role for as long as possible. Ryan's interpretation of the elegant *Bentley* had been the most lucrative ever.

"Yeah, still the plan, but the young blood is coming in as a bit of a sidekick in number two. He's got more girly appeal, apparently."

Ryan laughed, checking his greying temples in the mirror.

"I suppose I span yummy-mummy to 'still got it' granny, but that's about it. Who's my understudy? Anyone I know?"

Larry paused. This would not sit happily with Ryan; the new *Thomas Bentley* was an actor they both knew well. A brilliant, dazzling, talented star with more problems than you could shake a stick at.

"Steven Saggito," Larry said.

"What?! Tell me this is a joke? Surely, after all we've been through, this has to be a joke," Ryan bit back.

"Sorry, Ryan, I wouldn't joke about something like this."

"But he's a total fuck up. Larry, didn't you make that clear to Rossini? Surely Lena freaked?" Ryan was referring to Larry's partner and terrifying elder sister, Lena, who definitely wore the trousers when it came to running their successful theatrical agency. "Surely she told Rossini and all his hangers-on, what a big mistake Saggito would be."

Larry sighed. "Sorry, Ryan, for whatever reason the deal's been done!"

"Undo it!" Ryan demanded.

"I can't. Besides, things change. Lena assures me he's clean, good as gold, no monkey business at all. He just wants to get on with his career, thrilled about landing the role and working with you. So give it a go, hey, Ryan, it's worth a shot?"

"But that's all just so much bullshit!" Ryan spat down the phone. Joey stirred.

"You're the one who wants out. None of this would be happening if you hadn't resigned." It was early. Larry was grouchy; he never slept well and, knowing he had to transmit this message on this particular morning, had kept him awake most of the previous night.

"For fuck's sake, Larry," Ryan yelled, and slammed the phone down, wakening Joey.

In New York, the conversation continued.

"Good, good, I knew once you gave it a bit of thought it would all make sense. I mean, you're a match made in heaven." Larry was strolling over to the far side of the room. "You're gonna look great on the screen together. Is that Joey I hear in the background? Everything okay with him? Enjoying his visit? Great news, good, yeah, yeah. No problem, will do. Speak soon, okay?" He replaced the receiver, moving to open a window. The smoke from the other man's cigar was filling the room, cloying at his chest.

"How'd it go down?" the man seated on the sumptuous white sofa asked.

"Just peachy," Larry replied, coughing delicately into a tissue.

"He'll soon get used to it. They'll be best buddies, you see if they don't." Franco Rossini's warm brown eyes crinkled, he blew a smoke ring.

"Mr Rossini, I'm not sure if you're aware ..."

The great man lifted a hand to silence him.

"He can handle it," he replied. Larry was not sure to which star he was referring.

"Now, shall we watch a movie?" Mr Rossini started to remove his coat. Larry fumbled at the console on the arm of the sofa. The painting above the fireplace slid back to reveal a massive screen.

"One of the classics," his guest told him, making himself comfortable. It had started to snow outside. He would be there for some time.

Larry quickly scrolled his collection, arranged in genre, then sub-divided into release date order.

"That one!" Rossini ordered, pointing at the title on the screen. Larry hit play and the opening credits of *Miracle on 34th Street*, started to roll.

'If we get this next movie made without world war three breaking out, it will be another miracle,' Larry thought to himself, hurrying to the kitchen to make popcorn and pour soda for one of the most powerful producers in the world.

If the atmosphere in Larry's New York apartment had turned decidedly frosty, quite the opposite was happening on Innishmahon. Preparations for the forthcoming festivities were in full swing, and Maguire's was aglow with fairy lights and candles. The scent of spicy cinnamon mixed with smouldering peat greeted customers as, buffeted by the wind, the villagers heaved in through the huge oak doors, the ambiance a delicious attack on their senses, as they divested themselves of dripping jackets and muddy boots.

Erin had grudgingly come round to the idea that it made sense to give customers what they wanted and, whether she liked it or not, Christmas and New Year could not be ignored. Marianne had also pointed out as these were early days of her tenure-ship, it would not harm to score some brownie points with her boss, Brian Maguire, when he and his bride arrived off the ferry that very lunchtime. The pub was packed and buzzing, which pleased him immensely. The previous landlord was forever bemoaning the lack of trade. Marianne was busy serving pheasant casserole and mustard mash, while Erin ladled mulled wine into glasses at the bar. Kathleen pointed at the blackboard.

"Festive Shopper Special," she said, approvingly. "Isn't that a great idea altogether, sure nearly everyone goes to the mainland this week to stock up for Christmas. Dropping in for a meal and a glass of wine as they land off the ferry, rounds the whole trip off nicely. Good work, Erin," she told her, as she hopped onto a stool at the bar.

"Will you have a mulled wine, Mrs Maguire?" Erin used Kathleen's new name, declining to enlighten her that the 'Festive Special' was Marianne's idea.

"I'll have the works. That casserole looks delicious," Kathleen replied, removing the Russian fur hat she was wearing, and arranging her hair in the mirror advertising stout behind the bar. "I see you've been very busy, fair play to you, the place looks lovely." Kathleen's laser-like eyes swept the room.

It was a far cry from the run-up to last Christmas, when Padar Quinn, the previous landlord, had been struggling following the loss of his wife, in what was referred to as a 'tragic boating accident' while trying to make a living and care for his infant daughter. No one could jolly him along and even Marianne, who was definitely one of the best things that had ever happened to the island as far as Kathleen was concerned, retreated to her own cottage with Monty, the terrier. At the time, Kathleen considered this understandable. Marianne and her lover, the movie star Ryan O'Gorman, had parted and the poor girl seemed to be wishing the whole world would get a move on, rush towards

New Year and a fresh start. What a difference a year had made.

"Any news of Ryan?" Kathleen called across to her daughter. "Are they alright over there in England?"

Marianne was just completing an order; she totted up the bill and passed it to a waiting customer.

"They're great. All done and dusted. He and Joey will be home tomorrow. I'm waiting till they get back to put up our tree." Her eyes were sparkling.

"Like a real family." Kathleen beamed back at her.

"Nearer the *Addams Family* than the *Von Trapps,* I'd have said." Sean Grogan slipped onto his stool. The women ignored him.

Father Gregory breezed in, rubbing his hands together as he strode towards the bar, cassock swishing against the stone flags.

"I see the happy couple are back among us. Welcome home," he said, in his big, reassuring voice. Kathleen made a fuss of kissing him on both cheeks, leaving the inevitable imprint of Revlon's *Sugar Plum Fairy*.

"This looks more like it," he pronounced.

"Indeed it does and I hear there's a Candlelight Supper planned for Christmas Eve. I know it's a busy time for you, Gregory, but would you be joining us for that?" Kathleen asked.

The priest took the bottle of *Budweiser* Marianne offered.

"I'll do what I can. I was thinking I'd do an early Midnight Mass if that suited everyone, and come to dinner after that." He took a grateful slurp of the beer.

"That makes perfect sense," Kathleen sipped her mulled wine, "have it about eight?"

Sean tutted loudly.

"Something wrong, Sean?" the priest kept the exasperation out of his voice.

"If it's all the same to you, Father, I'll have my Midnight Mass at midnight, if you don't mind," he grumbled. "I don't like this lackadaisical approach to religion. I'll do this bit if it suits me, I'll change that bit if it doesn't!"

"Would you not give the man a bit of social life, Sean? He works very hard for all of us all year round, the Candlelight Supper might be the only chance we all get together as a family over Christmas." Kathleen glared at Sean.

Sean downed his pint.

"We're not a family, Miss MacReady, or Mrs Maguire, or whatever you want to call yourself. And he," he stabbed a finger towards Father Gregory, "made his choice when he took his vows. He has no family, either. He's a job to do at Christmas, let him get on with it." He plonked his glass on the bar, dragging on his shabby tweed coat as he left.

"It was only a suggestion," Kathleen said. "Is Sean always at Midnight Mass, then?" she asked the priest; everyone knew her own attitude to religion was all-embracing and highly flexible.

"Never seen him at it in all the years I've been here," replied the priest, thoughtfully, turning the beer bottle in his large hands. Brian appeared behind the bar.

"I've put all the bags and purchases upstairs," he told Kathleen, "I'm not sure what you'll want where."

Kathleen looked up, startled.

"Oh Brian, that's not right, I hadn't thought. I mean with everything going on, it all happened so quickly. I can't stay here. I'm needed up at the Post Office, I only had temporary cover while we were away. I have to be there at my post. You'll have to come and live with me." She finished her drink, reaching for her hat.

"I'm sorry, love, that's not going to work. I own the pub now, I'm needed here, we're coming into a very busy time. I assumed my wife would live here with me." Brian was smiling, but his tone was unyielding.

"You have Erin, haven't you? She's the manageress. Besides, the postmistress' position is a state appointment, far too important not to live on the job." Kathleen gathered her gloves, her bag. "You'll have to fetch everything down. I've to go and make sure all is well. You think you're coming into a busy time, well what about me? I won't be able to move up above with all the parcels and cards I'll have to deal with."

"Kathleen," Brian leaned across and touched her hand, "you're Mrs Maguire now. Your home is with me. You will have to give up the Post Office. I'll need you here."

Kathleen shook her hand free. Erin stopped polishing glasses. Marianne put her tray down. The wind howled around the building.

"I'll sort the luggage out, we'll discuss this later," Brian said, throwing a smile around the room.

"Very well." Kathleen bared her teeth at him before heading for the door. She ran straight into Dermot.

"Miss MacReady, you're back! Great to see you. Did you have a ball up there in me old home town?" He gave her a grin. "Oh, sorry, my mistake, Mrs Maguire it is now, of course."

Kathleen was pulling on her gloves.

"No, Dermot, you were right the first time. I may be married to Brian Maguire, but I am still Miss MacReady, the postmistress. That's my professional name and I have had a profession a lot longer than I've had a husband."

Mildly confused, Dermot propped open the door for her. The wind was building. It had started to squall as she set out towards the Post Office at the top of the town.

Marianne placed the tray of steaming food her mother had ordered on the bar.

"Is that, for me?" grinned Dermot, taking up the newly vacated stool.

"It can be, of course," Marianne smiled back at him.

"You're a wonder, you know that Marianne. No one looks after me like you." Dermot fell on the food. Marianne raised her eyebrows at her father, as her mother departed.

"It'll be alright, we'll work it out." He put a hand on her shoulder. "I keep forgetting we've been single all our lives. It's going to take time."

"Quite a bit of it by the sounds of things," she said, looking into his eyes.

"We've the rest of our lives," he replied.

"Yeah, looks like you'll need it," Erin chipped in. "Have you paid for that?" she demanded of Dermot, who had nearly finished the unwanted casserole.

Marianne made it, just before the ancient phone in the hallway rang off.

"Hello, hello."

Monty slipped in behind her, giving himself a good shake as she closed the door with her bottom.

"It's me, you okay?" The line was crackly but it was so good to hear his voice.

"Only out of breath, because we ran back from the pub. There's a hell of a storm brewing. You?"

"Listen, I don't think we're going to make it back tomorrow."

"Oh no, flight cancelled?" she was crestfallen.

"It might well be, but that's not the reason. I've to stay for a press conference. My replacement is being announced, we're doing the publicity together here in London. I'll be home after that." He had his business-like 'Ryan O'Gorman – movie star, public property' voice on. She slumped against the wall, sliding down to where Monty sat patiently watching her. She pulled him to her, the handset cradled against her shoulder.

"Sooner than expected?" she asked.

"Yes, Rossini wants him in the next movie as a bit of a sidekick for *Bentley*, so the fans get used to him, I suppose," Ryan explained.

"Anyone we know?" She tried desperately to hide her disappointment. They had never spent Christmas together, she so wanted it to be special. She wanted all of them to enjoy as much of it as they could.

"Saggito," he said, flatly.

"Really, Steven Saggito? I'm thinking he wouldn't be your first choice." Marianne knew they had history and there had been rumours of Saggito's penchant for the 'high' life. Illegal substances were anathema to Ryan, even more so since Joey's mother had died of an overdose earlier that year.

"Hmm," was all he said. They were always circumspect on the telephone. Ryan was paranoid about being tapped or hacked, and with good reason. He lived his professional life in a goldfish bowl. Innishmahon was his safe haven; Marianne his port in a storm. The sooner he could return there with his son for good, the better.

"How's Christmas coming on?" He changed the subject.

"Good. Loads to tell and lots to do." Monty started wagging his tail. Marianne was perking up. "Come home soon, we'll pick a tree and decorate it together. Is Joey excited?"

Ryan laughed. Marianne always had masses to do, and made sure she kept everyone else busy too. Tireless schemes, endless lists, unforgiving deadlines; she always had some sort of project on the go.

"Yes, he definitely knows something's going on and seems to have decided Santa is one of the good guys. His face lights up every time he sees a red suit or a white beard," Ryan told her.

"Does he know what he wants from Father Christmas yet?"

"I think whatever it is, the wrapping will be more interesting to him at this stage. What about you? What would you like Father Christmas to bring you?" he asked gently, his delicious Irish-American lilt melting her, as always.

"I don't need anything, thanks."

"No Christmas wishes?" he pressed.

"Just one, just us, all together, that's all I need," she told him.

"Me too," he whispered, "don't worry we'll be home for Christmas."

"Perfect." She could hear someone calling him in the background. Lisa, his PA, no doubt, rushing him to get ready for a photo-call or media interview. "Oh, and Ryan … no surprises."

"Surprises? Me?" The line went dead, as it often did.

It clicked twice. A familiar voice asked, "Marianne, do you want me to try to reconnect you?"

"No, thanks Kathleen, they'll be home for Christmas, that's all I need to know." Marianne replaced the receiver and hugged Monty, unaware the airport was closed, and the ferry was not going to risk another sailing. By the time the next weather forecast was announced, the island would need to be preparing for the worst.

Chapter Four – A Safe Harbour

Dermot was in a huddle with Brian in the corner of the bar. He had left shortly after finishing Kathleen's abandoned meal, only to return dressed from head to toe in high visibility wet weather gear, his mobile phone in one hand, two-way radio in the other. The new man running the construction team and a couple of the other lads were with him. Erin knew something was wrong when she hovered behind the pumps for nearly five minutes and none of them asked her for a pint.

She took a glass and poured herself a shot of vodka, it nearly made her gag but she swallowed hard and it hit the spot, warming her cheeks and calming her slightly. Brian was frowning as Dermot talked into the radio.

"What's *Robin Hood* and his band of *Merry Men* doing here not drinking?" she asked Brian.

"Some of the landlines are down. He's saying we need to evacuate the pub." Brian took her behind the bar, away from customers, keeping an eye on Dermot.

"How bad is it?" she whispered, sensing a stampede was best avoided. Customers were looking up at the men, an odd sight, a group of men not drinking, not even talking.

"It's pretty wild out there and getting worse. The main crane is listing, they don't know how secure it is."

Brian was calm. "No need to alarm anyone though. Dermot and the boys are on the case."

"Is it dangerous?" Erin was nonplussed. She had been brought up on the island, she knew how volatile the weather could be.

"The crane's listing out to sea at the moment, but if the wind changes or the current turns, or it breaks its moorings and drifts down the coast, who knows?"

Erin flashed him a look. The new harbour wall was just finished, the structure for the bridge in place, but there were at least four or five months' work left until completion. If the massive piece of equipment broke free, hundreds of tonnes of steel could smash into the bridge like a carefully targeted wrecking ball. With rising seas and hurricane winds turning the bay into a tsunami, all the work of the past year could be lost.

Dermot stood at the fireplace. He raised his hands for quiet.

"Ladies and gentlemen, friends, as you are aware, the storm is building outside and we have just heard the weather forecast. We're in for a bad one. The airports on the mainland have been closed and the ferry port shut down. Anyone who can get home quickly should leave now and sandbag their properties. Anyone who can't get home quickly, is advised to stay here."

Father Gregory stood up.

"I have a list of all the elderly on the island. I'll head up to the rectory for it, they need calling to prepare themselves. Some of them don't have television, they won't have heard the news."

"Email it to me," Erin cut in. "I can do that."

"Thanks, Erin." said the priest. Dermot was barking into the handset again. "I think I'll be needed elsewhere."

There was a scrabble as people started to bundle themselves out of the pub. Brian was helping with coats and bags, homes and livelihoods were at risk, they needed to act quickly.

"What's the plan?" Erin asked Dermot when she finally heard him say 'over' into the radio.

He fixed her with a look.

"The worst plan of all," he said, tonelessly, "wait and see."

"You mean there's nothing we can do?" Erin was dismayed.

"No, this really is in the lap of the gods," Dermot replied, grimly.

"We're all stuffed then," Erin said into his face. "None of those gods have ever been on duty when I needed them!"

Dermot had no idea what she was on about. Erin was a complete mystery to him, charming and flirtatious one minute, usually when she had a drink in her hand, and cuttingly blunt the next. He was just about to leave when two elderly sisters, laden with Christmas shopping, struggled to their feet.

"Can a nice young man take us home, please?" one of them asked. "Tabitha will be beside herself, above in the cottage on her own. She hates a storm."

Two of the building lads leapt to their aid.

"Come on, missus, let's get you back and safely hunkered down. How old is she?" one enquired, expecting Tabitha to be an infirm, older relative.

"Only four," replied the other woman, heaving her bag onto her shoulder.

"You left a four-year-old on her own while you went shopping?" the man was horrified. The women, both fairly deaf, had already pulled on hats, wrapping scarves around themselves.

"Tabitha's a cat," explained Erin.

Just after they left, Father Gregory flew through the door. He was dressed in waterproofs and ready for action.

"I've written out the list, no electricity at the rectory, can you ring them now?" he ordered Erin, then, turning to Dermot, "The crane has broken free, we've no lights up there, no idea where it's heading, can't see a thing."

"We've spots on site, I'll fire up the generator," one of the building team shouted, galvanising the rest of the men.

"If it's headed for the bridge, I could take the boat out and try to push it in another direction," Dermot said.

"How?" Brian was bemused.

"Lash it with chains?"

"Hundreds of tonnes in a hurricane, are you nuts?" Brian shook his head.

"Not this time, Dermot, no superhero stuff, the best we can hope for is not to lose anybody," Father Gregory said.

"If it breaks through the harbour wall, it could drift down the coast, might even be washed ashore," Brian was looking at Father Gregory, he had come from his house, close to the marina, he was grey with fear.

"Could it crash into buildings along the sea edge?" Father Gregory pondered. "Well, the pharmacy and the Post

Office are the nearest, but it would have to really whip up
…"

A loud crack, crash, the lights went out. A blast of
icy wind rushed in. Erin looked down. She felt a weight on
her leg, a sharp pain. The metal edge of the pub sign, which
had emblazoned the side of the building since time
immemorial, had sliced through her calf. The MA of
Maguire's was covered in bright, red blood, she could see by
the moonlight through the window — except the window
was no longer there. The sign had burst through, landing on
her, shattering the glass into a thousand pieces, spraying the
bar like diamond confetti.

"The Post Office … Kathleen!" Brian roared,
charging for the door. The men followed. Dermot stopped,
Erin was clutching her leg.

"Did that get you? Are you hurt?" he asked.

"No, go. I'm fine. I'll call Marianne, she'll give me
hand," she barked at him.

Weathervane nestled behind Maguire's, with the pub's other
holiday cottages, April and May, along the lane. It was well
sheltered from the elements, the eccentric glass garden room
turned into a hothouse unless the doors were flung open and
folded back. But tonight the whole place rattled, the
grandiose Spanish chandelier tinkling as it trembled.

Monty was restless, pacing the kitchen, his claws
tapping against the quarry tiles as he trotted round and
round. Marianne was just about to bolt the door and pour
herself a nightcap when the phone rang again.

"Marianne, can you come? The storm's blown the
window in. We need to board it up and get the sandbags
from the cellar," Erin's husky voice sounded distant, weak.

"Anyone hurt?" Marianne asked.

"Not really, but can you come now?" Erin said, urgently.

"On my way." Marianne banged the phone down. Racing into the kitchen, she scooped Monty up, taking the stairs two at a time to deposit him on his rug at the end of the huge double bed. Sharp, black eyes watched as she pulled heavy duty wet weather gear and serious boots from the wardrobe.

"Stay here and keep watch!" she told him sharply. Monty immediately took up sentry duty at the window. Marianne checked outside, she could just make out a couple of high-vis jackets disappearing towards the top of the town. She kissed Monty on the nose, closed the bedroom door and fled, grabbing a flashlight, gloves, string. She quickly sandbagged the door, before racing down the path, through the gate and into Maguire's side entrance, the wind beating her back every step of the way.

The whole place was in darkness, except for the faint glow of fading embers. She flicked on the flashlight. Half the large plate window to the front of the building was smashed in, chairs and stools were scattered, tables upended, there was glass everywhere and in the middle, half in, half out, was the sign, the huge sign that had hung on the side of the building for decades. The gale had ripped it off the wall and smashed it through the window.

"Erin!" Marianne called out. She thought she heard something. The cellar door was open. Flicking the torchlight down the steps, Erin was at the bottom, struggling to carry sandbags up. Marianne fixed the beam on her. One leg of her jeans was ripped away, she was covered in blood. She looked up, grey frightened eyes in a grey face.

"Good, you made it. I need a hand."

"You're hurt!" Marianne started down the steps.

"The sign blew in, landed on my leg."

Marianne could not see how deep the wound was, there was so much blood.

"Is there water coming in?" Erin asked.

"Not yet," Marianne took the sandbag from her, "can you make it into the kitchen? We need to try and stop the blood." She reached out for Erin to take her arm. They struggled up to the cellar door and fell into the kitchen. Marianne found candles and lit them quickly. She set the torch on the counter, directing the beam at Erin's leg, now propped on a chair. Part of the team at Maguire's more or less since her arrival on the island, Marianne knew where everything was, including the first aid kit. She started to clean the wound.

"If you're going to fiddle around with that," Erin winced, "you can pour me a large vodka and sling me a couple of painkillers."

Marianne smiled, remembering Erin's similar first aid tactics when she had scalded her hand in this very kitchen. "I was just about to."

The new bridge and marina project was a major investment for Innishmahon. Agreed by the government at the height of the *Celtic Tiger's* economical prowess, the project had teetered between grants since the recession. The residents had fought long and hard to ensure it went ahead, raising much of the funding themselves. No one could say the little community lacked gumption, the islanders were trying to protect their future, without tourism, more and more local families would leave to find work further afield.

Dermot fired up the powerful megawatt lights the construction team used to illuminate the site, training them out to sea. The crane was still visible, listing wildly from side to side. The marina wall, creating the harbour, remained intact. The steel structure for the bridge, also still in place. If the crane broke free and smashed the marina wall, the sea would come spilling in. The newly constructed flood defences would take an almighty hammering and the beach behind the buildings along Innishmahon's main street could be hit with a tidal wave. One of these buildings was the Post Office, where Kathleen MacReady had lived and worked for over twenty-five years. Her new husband, Brian Maguire, was beating on the door.

"Kathleen, open up, open up for godsake," he yelled. He squinted through the window, the driving rain beating at the glass like a drum. "Kathleen, it's me, Brian," he roared in through the letterbox. He saw a glimmer of light. If there was one thing Kathleen would never be short of, it was candles, well, candles and whiskey, to be fair. The front door opened a sliver. Kathleen was wary. Not that long ago, the Post Office had been subjected to a terrifying burglary, she was not taking any chances; she hid the poker behind her back. She saw it was Brian. Relieved, she opened the door and he dived in, grabbing her by the wrist.

"Quickly, get your boots and mac, shove a few things in a bag, you're in danger Kathleen. We've to leave now."

She blinked at him, holding the candelabra closer to check he had not taken leave of his senses.

"What? It's a filthy old storm is all, have you been that long away you've forgotten how we get a good few batterings here, especially during the winter?"

He shook his head, water sprayed off his hat.

"It's more than a storm, the big crane's broken free up above, could smash through the harbour wall, bringing a tidal wave down the beach," he spoke so quickly she could hardly understand him. It was her turn to grip him by the wrist.

"Are you panicking because you've not seen a storm like this in a long time, or is it really bad?" she asked. He looked scared alright, and the Brian Maguire she knew and loved did not scare easily. Even she, at her most vociferous, barely caused him to raise an eyebrow. "I'm all sandbagged, plugged up and sorted. I'm sure I'll be fine," she told him, trying to remember if she had ever replaced the sandbags that had been washed away the last time.

"No, you can't risk it. The coastguard has been onto Dermot, there's a tsunami heading in this direction, we're going now!" he said, severely.

"I can't leave my post, this is the communication centre, what will happen if the emergency services can't get through," she insisted.

"Kathleen, half the phone lines on the island are already down. Let's go," Brian was pulling her towards the door.

"But what will happen to Christmas if I'm flooded?" she beseeched.

"What?"

She walked back into the room, taking the light with her. There were piles of envelopes everywhere, a small mountain of packages.

"Christmas will be ruined. All this has yet to be delivered." She spoke slowly, hoping the weight of her words would be felt. There was a loud thud. Voices.

"Kathleen, Brian, open up, it's coming."

Brian opened the door. An icy draught hit them, blowing out the light. Dermot swept his flashlight around the hallway.

"It's coming," he said, monotone.

By now Kathleen was struggling into her wax coat. Brian handed her the wellingtons by the door.

"Have you men with you?" Kathleen asked. Dermot nodded. "Good, grab those mail bags and shove all those envelopes and packages in them."

"There's no time," Dermot replied.

"If I'm going to lose my home, young man, we will do what we can to save Christmas. We'll have little enough left to celebrate when this is over." She was busy filling one of the bags. Brian shrugged at Dermot and started to do the same. Dermot shouted to the men outside. They were knocking doors, checking other properties. Luckily, the pharmacy next door was empty, and the Redmund family had decamped to the priest's house on higher ground.

Half a dozen sack loads later, the men looked like Santa's little helpers, carrying bags across to the presbytery. Kathleen insisted on remaining until the end, pulling the door behind her and locking it. She carried a small leather case with valuables from the safe and a *Louis Vuitton* weekend bag, stuffed full of her most precious belongings.

60

As she reached the top of the steps to follow the men, there was a deep, far boom. The air seemed to still, before another sound, like thunder, rolled through the night sky. But it was not thunder, it was water, millions of gallons of it, hurtling towards the beach. Kathleen ran as fast as she could, as the biggest wave the island had ever seen, hit the crane, depositing it on the harbour wall. The wall broke apart like *Lego*. The ocean crashed free, throwing waves taller than buildings along the coast. The tempest railed against the inadequate flood defences, sweeping all before it. The men pulled Kathleen in over the pile of sandbags, slamming the presbytery door behind her, as the sea spilled between buildings and onto the road, instantly turning Innishmahon's main thoroughfare into an angry river.

Back in Maguire's, Erin was propped on a stool, passing tacks to Marianne who was hammering pieces of wood across the gaping hole in the window. They had found some old packing cases in the storeroom which had broken up easily. The wind had changed and the rain was beating horizontally across the street. Marianne worked as quickly as she could, the patchwork of wood did not look pretty but at least it made the building secure and kept the water out for the time being. She was banging the last piece into place as a torrent of sea water started to sweep down Main Street. She jumped back as it whooshed past, cutting a trench along the far side of the road as it went.

Her mind flashed back to the last time she had seen Main Street awash. Piling into a 4x4 with Oonagh and Sinead as they had sped down to the old harbour wall, to watch with bated breath as an elderly neighbour was airlifted to hospital, the men in boats bobbing beneath the helicopter, like corks in the ocean. She remembered Father Gregory and

Ryan racing their vessels up the street like schoolboys at a regatta, back to the pub and the sanctuary it was to become over the coming weeks.

'*Ryan!*' she thought, '*does he know? Has he heard about the storm? Are he and Joey okay? Safe? Out of harm's way?*' She swallowed. Tears pricked her eyes. She had said a soft goodnight to him only hours ago. He promised he would be home for Christmas. She looked back at the room. Decorations scattered, tinsel and baubles strewn about the place, the wind howling like a banshee outside. What home? What Christmas?

Erin hobbled behind the bar, now lit with a selection of candles.

"Two large brandies coming up," she said cheerily. "You've done a great job there, Marianne, we'll have this place shipshape in no time."

Marianne stared at her. '*She really is a funny onion,*' she thought, '*whenever we're in a sticky situation she comes into her own. Love's a fight, that one, even if it's against nature itself.*'

"Not for me, thanks," Marianne replied, pulling on another fleece. It was cold now she had stopped working.

"Ah, have one," Erin insisted. "It's medicinal. Most alcohol is around here, it would need to be, only way anyone can stand the place is, if they're half-cut."

Marianne took a sip as Erin lifted the telephone. She listened.

"Dead as a dodo," Erin told her, "no contact with the outside world, again."

Marianne sighed. As much as she loved the island, Innishmahon really was the pits at times, but she decided to keep that particular opinion to herself, especially with Erin in earshot.

Chapter Five – Beam Me Up, Scottie

The terrestrial channels were hopeless. All the news and weather reports too local. There were gale force winds and torrential rain in the South West, blizzards in Scotland and warnings of flooding in the Thames Valley. Ryan was pacing up and down in front of a large television, pointing the remote control in agitated jerks at the screen, channel-hopping like a bored teenager. The only time he stopped was when a forecast displayed the whole of the British Isles and Ireland, and he would peer to the far left, desperate to pick out Innishmahon amid the tightly packed isobars and swirling thermals. Fearing it had dropped off the map altogether.

He tried to phone, email, *Skype*. Nothing. He fired up the RTE App on his *iPad*, watching the news anxiously. An airborne camera crew flew precariously over Knock Airport, the car park underwater, all aircraft grounded. The helicopter flittered out towards the coast, turbulence causing the camera to bounce nauseatingly.

"The storm here has been relentless. The worst the area has experienced in over ten years. Even at its height, last year's storm, which washed away the bridge to the nearby island of Innishmahon, was not as fierce. So far no loss of life has been reported, although one fishing boat with a crew of five is still missing," the reporter shouted into his microphone, trying to be heard above the blades and the wind. "Most communications are down, latest from the Coastguard reports damage to the new harbour and the main town has been flooded. With the island only just recovering, it's bad news, only days before everyone is looking forward to their Christmas break." There was a crash, the picture on the screen blurred.

"We're heading back," the reporter continued shakily, "this wind is building. No longer safe for us to be airborne. This is Kieran O'Flynn for RTE news, off the coast of Westport."

Ryan stared blankly at the *iPad,* long after the report had flipped back to the studio and film footage of floods in Cork and the Shannon bursting its banks. Joey, who had been playing happily, started to grizzle. Ryan lifted his son, who gripped him like a spider monkey. He kissed him distractedly as he pulled his leather jacket around the boy. Joey liked it under there, resting his head against his father's chest.

After a few attempts, Ryan was finally patched through to Dermot on the radio.

"Marianne?"

"Holed up in Maguire's with Erin. Over." Dermot's voice was crackly but he sounded strong.

"You?" Ryan was brief, not sure how long they would stay connected.

"At the marina with some of the men. Over."

"Need a hand?" Stupid question, Ryan thought, immediately he said it.

"We will. Main crane has smashed the harbour wall. There'll be work to do. Over."

"Best place to land a helicopter?" Ryan asked.

"What?" Dermot snapped back, forgetting 'over'.

"Helicopter, where?" Ryan demanded. It went quiet. Dermot was thinking.

"Field behind the churchyard. Over."

"Doable?" Ryan asked.

"Only if there's a lull. It's bad, Ryan. Over," Dermot said.

"Next lull?"

"Who knows? Over," Dermot replied.

"We're on our way," Ryan told him.

"Who?" Dermot shouted.

"The cavalry. Over." Ryan answered.

A crackle, hiss, silence. Ryan was pushing things into a bag, his mobile on speaker, ringing urgently.

"Scott?"

"Aye, is that you, O'Gorman?"

"Yeah, you working at the moment?"

"Finishing a job. Your movie's my next big project, why?" The voice was warm; soft Scottish accent.

"Can you get myself and my son over to Ireland?" Ryan hotched Joey up on his hip, the boy still clinging to him.

"Where exactly?"

"Innishmahon, off the west coast."

"I know it," Scott replied. "When?"

"In time for Christmas." Ryan held his breath.

"Don't see why not," the other man replied.

"Bit of a storm blowing."

"Seen worse," Scott said, and Ryan imagined that indeed he had.

"I've a press conference, here in London tomorrow, can we leave straight after that?"

"Sure, weather permitting," Scott laughed. Ryan knew that was a joke. Nothing prevented Scott Wallace from doing anything, ever.

Rossini's PR team were making the most of the announcement that the wild and unpredictable movie actor, Steven Saggito, would be joining the world's favourite superspy in the next *Thomas Bentley* blockbuster.

In keeping with the franchise's image, the ballroom of a top London hotel was seconded for the event. Nothing too flashy, this was old school, elegant, understated, top drawer.

The BBC's most popular chat show host had been booked to present the event, featuring footage of previous *Thomas Bentley* movies, interspersed with interviews with some of the stars who had appeared in them over the years. Rossini was particularly keen for any members of the *Royal Shakespeare Company*, who had been in the movies, to have a few moments in the spotlight, too, giving the whole show added gravitas.

Lisa, Ryan's PA, was busying herself with final arrangements. Most of the invited media were availing themselves of the free bar. Rossini's PR team were good, making sure the most influential journalists were looked after, ensuring powerful movie reviewers and gossip columnists had the best seats, giving each an exclusive, an angle which, perfectly fitted the media they represented. Everyone would go away happy, diligently reporting what they had been steered to write, building the anticipation ahead of the next movie; the one destined to break all box office records.

Ryan was in make-up when Lisa finally caught up with him. They had worked together since he first joined the franchise. They liked each other, mutual respect, but Lisa was paid by Rossini. Ryan knew to keep her on side, she could make things very difficult if she had to, and Ryan had endured a bellyful of 'difficult' in recent times. Now, he just wanted the quickest route to a quiet life.

Lisa lifted Joey out of his baby seat beside Ryan. She smoothed his hair, smiling at him. Ryan caught her eye in the mirror.

"You're doing a good job," Lisa said to his reflection.

"Hey, don't sound so surprised," Ryan retorted, secretly pleased his freshly laundered, well-fed, beautiful son was down to him. He had refused the studio's offer of a nanny. He was in the UK for a few days, visiting his grown-up son, introducing Joey to the rest of his family. He wanted everything low-key and as normal as possible. It was important Joey became used to normal.

"Five minutes!" a voice called along the corridor.

"Many here?" Ryan asked, dodging face powder.

Lisa nodded, "and some."

"Seen Saggito yet?" Ryan watched her.

"Yep. Looks fine. He *is* fine." She kissed Joey as she strapped him back in. "He was asking after you, too, said it's a long time since he's seen you."

"Not long enough, in my opinion." Ryan took a tissue, pressing it to his mouth, sealing the lip rouge.

"We're on!" shouted the voice along the corridor.

Ryan ruffled Joey's hair.

"Back in a wee while," he told him.

"Shall I put him to bed?" Lisa asked. She had already volunteered to take care of him while the press conference was underway.

"I didn't think we were scheduled for longer than an hour?" Ryan was at the door.

"Cocktail party afterwards. Rossini has invited a select few to stay behind," she said.

"Is Rossini expected to show?" Ryan was surprised. He heard his boss was engulfed in a legal wrangle over film rights back in the States; he could not remember the last time the great man had been to Europe.

"He can't make it, expects you and Saggito to entertain, be charming, you know the sort of thing," Lisa confirmed.

"No can do," Ryan told her.

"But I can take care of Joey, I'd like to."

"Sorry, we're leaving straight after the press conference. Can't miss our flight," Ryan explained.

"What flight?" The storms were widespread. Lisa could not think of an airport still operational.

"Scott's picking us up, as soon as we're done." Ryan had to go.

"From where?" Lisa was dismayed.

"The roof, where else?" Ryan called back.

Lisa plonked herself on the sofa. "Should have guessed." She turned to the make-up girl. "Do you know Scott Wallace?"

"Sure," said the girl, "tried to do his make-up a few times. Never sits still long enough. Cheeky, too." She turned pink.

"Don't I know it!" Lisa confirmed, kicking off her heels to settle down to some serious colouring in with Joey.

The PR took Ryan into the Green Room. The chat show host was already there, checking his notes, sipping water nervously. He greeted Ryan warmly, they had worked together before.

"Have you seen Saggito yet?" he asked Ryan in hushed tones.

"Not yet." Ryan smiled, full Hollywood beam; it really was quite dazzling. Time to go into *Thomas Bentley* mode, he told himself, suave, sophisticated, debonair.

"You nervous about working with him?" the host asked, checking over his shoulder.

"Not at all. He's a good actor, he'll be perfect in the role. The ideal understudy for *Bentley*, I'm sure," Ryan spoke soothingly, *Bentley's* seductive voice.

The door burst open, the PR rushed in.

"Is he here?" he asked, glancing anxiously around the room.

"You've lost him?" squeaked the host.

"Never seen him; his assistant said he jumped in a taxi and headed here hours ago. I've looked everywhere."

The host checked his watch. "We're already running late, what should we do?"

"We'll go on, say he's been unavoidably detained and will be with us as soon as possible," Ryan said in his calm, do not worry, the-mad-evil-villain-will-not-take-over-the-world, *Bentley* voice. But his pulse had started to race. He had his own deadline to meet. Besides, Lisa had seen Saggito, spoken to him, he was probably just on the wrong floor, signing autographs in the lobby. He had to show, it was all part of the deal.

Cameras flashed and the hubbub stilled, as world-famous movie star, Ryan O'Gorman and one of the UK's most respected TV hosts strolled into the room; taking their seats on a raised dais before rows of red velvet banqueting chairs, bearing the weight of some of the most powerful columnists on the planet. Scanning the faces as best he could, Ryan suddenly missed Marianne desperately. The super confident person he always managed to portray so successfully, stripped bare in an instant. The pain of insecurity rubbed raw like a wound. Where was his rock, his harbour wall, when he needed her?

"And how are you preparing for the new *Thomas Bentley*, Ryan?" the TV host asked. Ryan gave himself an internal shake. He smiled at the host, crossed his legs, sat back in his chair.

"Pretty much the way *Thomas Bentley* would expect me to, gambling, late nights, plenty of alcohol, fast cars and even faster women," his mouth twitched. You could hear a pin drop. He leaned across and slapped the host on the back. "Just joshing." He gave the camera his famous twinkle and patted his flat stomach. "Working out, plenty of fresh air, wholesome food, clean living, you know the kind of thing."

There was a communal release of breath. Bad boy actors were one thing, but full-blown movie stars really did have to be squeaky clean to stay on top. It was a tough job.

Rossini and the publicity machine had done a brilliant job keeping Ryan's image intact, through his turbulent relationship with the beautiful but dangerous actress, Angelique de Marcos, their short-lived marriage – which had resulted in the birth of their son Joey – and Angelique's tragic, but not unexpected, early demise.

Throughout all this, pick and poke as much as they liked, the media could find little to berate him about. Even when the paparazzi turned up on the island to dig dirt about his relationship with Marianne, Ryan survived. The over-hyped articles, the out-of-focus photographs did little to dent his popularity. In fact, when Angelique arrived in Innishmahon, no one could have faulted the welcome she received from everyone, including Ryan and Marianne. And their appearance at her funeral, supporting the actress' doting uncle, was reported all over the world. It had all been well handled, and Ryan, aka *Thomas Bentley*, was as adored as he had always been. So, he had to kill a few baddies, sleep with a beautiful spy or two, it was all in the script and Ryan always stuck to the script.

The host cut to footage of the last movie. A text message flashed on Ryan's phone. *Saggito AWOL. Fill in, please. Lisa x.* The VTR finished. Ryan dropped the phone back in his pocket.

"What can you tell us about the new movie? And what of your new co-star? Will sparks fly?"

"I'm very sorry," he turned to the phalanx of press, "but my co-star Steve Saggito is unable to be here today. Bad weather conditions, I believe most of the airports are closed."

From where he was watching at the back of the room, a tall, well-groomed young man nodded. '*Impressive,*' he thought to himself, *'he hasn't lied, he hasn't even linked Saggito's non-arrival with the weather, but everyone else has.'*

Ryan raised a hand, waiting for the murmurs of disappointment to subside.

"I'm sure he'll get here if he can. In the meantime, I hope I'll be able to answer any questions you may have, he's only going to be *Bentley's* understudy, after all, we all know who the main man is," Ryan said, with his tongue firmly shoved in his cheek. The presenter and the audience laughed, a smattering of applause, and then wearing his full Hollywood smile, Ryan handled the press conference alone, skilfully steering any sensitive or controversial questions back to the job in hand, promoting the new movie, keeping the franchise in the limelight, ensuring the cash-cow would keep everyone replete.

Pushing through the barrage of cameras and microphones much later than he had planned, a security guard was guiding Ryan to the rooftop after show cocktail party, when the movie star gave him the slip. Ryan checked his phone again. Scott was on his way. He needed to grab Joey and go. He jumped into the lift heading down to his suite. His phone started to vibrate. Racing along the corridor, a door opened, and a man, he vaguely recognised, stumbled into the corridor, dragging on a dinner jacket, shoes in his hand. He swayed a bit. Ryan drew closer. At least two pairs of arms reached out and tried to haul the man back into the room. There was much pleading and giggling. The man pushed the flailing arms away and slammed the door. He fell back. Ryan caught Steven Saggito just in time.

"Cheers pal," the half-dressed actor slurred.

"Wondered what happened to you," Ryan said.

73

Saggito struggled upright.

"Hey, Ryan," he blinked into his face, "ran into an old friend, is all. Press conference?"

Ryan checked him out. He had seen him look better, he had seen him look worse.

"Too late for that," Ryan told him, fixing his colleague's tie. "But they need you at the cocktail party. Take the lift to the roof."

Saggito gave him a confused look. Ryan turned him around.

"The elevator. To the top. There'll be plenty of your old friends there."

"Good work, pal. A bit of a party, feel like partying, know what I mean?" He gave Ryan a wink, staggering in the direction of the lift.

Ryan's phone rang urgently. He burst into the suite. Lisa was pacing the floor, pushing Joey ahead of her, asleep in his travel buggy.

"All good to go?"

"It's a terrible night. Do you really want to risk it?" She watched as he pulled his sailing jacket over his DJ. "We could do with you here, especially with your co-star missing. Rossini's been on, ready to hit the roof. He said you did a great job, by the way."

"Gee, thanks." Ryan was zipping Joey into an infant carrier, fixing the straps, securing the boy to him. "Sorry, Lisa, it's Christmas Eve tomorrow, what if Santa Claus doesn't know where to leave this little fella's presents." He kissed her furrowed brow. "By the way, Saggito's showed up."

"What?" Lisa gasped.

"I literally caught him coming out of a room a few floors away. I think he'd been entertaining some journalists, well that's what we should probably tell Rossini."

"Oh dear." Lisa started punching numbers into her phone.

"Merry Christmas," Ryan called, as he left.

Minutes later, the glitterati sipping cocktails in the Glasshouse - the fabulous nightclub nestled in the roof garden of one of London's most famous hotels - became aware of a thundering noise, far louder than the storm which had been rattling the crystal structure since dusk. A large military-style helicopter hovered outside, attempting to land on the H on the roof, but the wind kept pushing it back over the edge of the building, despite the pilot's valiant efforts. A door on the roof opened, and a man wearing a balaclava ran across the tarmac to where the helicopter shuddered, feet above the surface. There was a bundle strapped to his chest.

"My God, is that what I think it is?" shrieked a woman.

The door to the aircraft opened, as the man reached it. He leapt into the air. Another man inside the helicopter leaned out, grabbing him, as he clambered aboard. The door shut.

"What?" asked the woman's male companion, now squinting at the commotion on the roof.

"A terrorist," she hissed.

The man seated next to the pilot pulled off his hat. He lifted the bundle away from his chest, checking it.

"Nope, that's Ryan O'Gorman and he has his young son Joey with him." The man had put his glasses on at this

75

stage. They were all straining to get a good view, cameras and phones at the ready.

"Jeez, that was a dangerous thing to do. Is he quite sane?" the woman asked.

The man did not reply, lifting his phone to follow the helicopter as it drew away from the roof.

"Rossini shouldn't really let him retire, you know. Still does all his own stunts, by the looks of things." Steven Saggito, glass in hand, had joined the throng gazing out as the lights of the disappearing aircraft melded with the city's sparkling canvas below.

"Bloody show off," laughed the man. "Now, where are those very friendly fans you were telling me about, Steven? I hope they didn't take any pictures of you having too much fun. We have the worldwide rights, don't forget," he said sweetly, steering the dishevelled, but still devilishly handsome actor back to the bar.

Chapter Six – Super Troopers

The next morning dawned on another planet. The air soft and calm as the first streaks of silver seeped into the eastern edge, just above where the sky met the ocean. Sea birds emerged from cliff crevices. A straggle of livestock on the hills were taking tentative steps out of field shelters and from behind hedgerows, shaking damp coats, picking over sodden ground.

Soon the humans would stir too, well, any who had managed to sleep. Marianne dragged the duvet over her head, pulling her knees up to her chest. Monty wriggled to be free. She had held him clamped to her through what remained of the night, having fought her way back from Maguire's once Erin was comfortable and the pub was as secure as they could make it. She needed to put off waking for as long as she could, not wanting to face any element of reality until she had to, because she knew whatever lay beyond the sanctuary of her little cottage, would be horrific, and she had no desire to face it, not yet, not ever.

The wind had dropped. She drifted back to sleep. Through the layers of her dreams, she felt a ripple, a tremor of sound, a deep rumble. She pushed it away. It came again, grumbling. *No, no more*, she begged. The grumble became a growl, it reverberated up from the depths. It was Monty, now howling in full cry. Someone was banging on the door, trying to break it down. The knocking grew louder, more fervent. Monty was running round in circles, yapping wildly. Marianne opened the door a crack, eyes half-closed. But she could sense him before she saw him. Ryan pushed the door gently with his foot, his arms were full. For the first time in over twenty-four hours, the little boy turned away from his father.

"Mar-yan," the child uttered, throwing his arms out to the white-faced, red-eyed spectre. Ryan felt his heart tighten. He had never seen anything look so good.

"Thank God," a sob caught in her throat. She reached out, her knees gave way. Ryan filled the space, catching her in his embrace. Monty was wild with excitement. She wrapped her arms around Ryan's neck, crushing the little boy between them. She looked up into his face, and for a moment ... all was still. Slate blue eyes glittered down at her. He planted his soft mouth on her forehead, then lifting her chin, kissed her lips.

"Happy Christmas," he said.

Kathleen lifted the receiver. The ancient telephone took pride of place on the antique desk in the presbytery study. The luxury of book-lined walls, a replica Adams fireplace and a crunchy leather *Chesterfield* gave her little comfort on a morning such as this ... seven a.m. on Christmas Eve. She had not slept a wink, tossing and turning in the old brass bed which dominated the small, second guest room in the priest's house. She was not in her own home, she was away from her post and this did not sit happily with her. Fine to be away on holiday, visiting friends or relations, but not fine to be home and not home at all.

Besides, the illuminated portrait of the Sacred Heart glowing at her from an alcove would give anyone nightmares. She had never understood the bizarre depiction of Christ, chest ripped open, displaying a bloodied heart, pierced with a sword, and bearing a crown of thorns. What was it supposed to mean? What purpose did this representation serve, but to scare the living daylights out of children? Having nightmares enough trying to conjure up sins they may or may not have committed, to appease a priest, head bowed, behind a grille, doling out Hail Mary's to beat the band, a Rosary in one hand and the *Racing Post* in the other, she ranted to herself, trying to sleep.

She was well rattled, alright. Even Brian's warm embrace and low murmurings for her to 'sleep now', 'rest awhile' made not a jot of difference. What state had the storm left the place in? How was her home, her place of work? Where was her child? What remained of the village? As soon as watery light filtered through the heavy velvet drapes, she slid out of bed, tiptoeing along the landing and downstairs to the study.

She pressed the button in the cradle, clicking it impatiently. No dial tone. Nothing. A creak, the door opened. Father Gregory in tee shirt and jogging bottoms, gave her a tired smile.

"Coffee?" he asked.

"All the lines are down."

"Terrible night," he said.

"I've never known anything like it." She replaced the receiver, it made a hollow clunk.

"Could have been worse," he told her.

"I don't think we know that yet." She gave him a steely glare over her spectacles.

"We do, we're alive, aren't we?" He headed off in the direction of the kitchen. Kathleen scowled at his back and followed him. The house had stirred, Joy Redmund, three little ones, and a puppy were at one end of the long refectory table. Dermot was stirring porridge in a saucepan.

"Alright?" The priest touched the other woman's shoulder.

"Paul's gone to help Sean save the sheep. The field's turned into a lake," Joy said, as one of the younger children climbed onto her lap.

"Daddy's going to save the sheep, he couldn't save Mitzy, isn't that right, Mammy? Mitzy couldn't swim, so she went to heaven instead." The child turned huge, blue eyes up at the priest.

"Our cat," Joy explained, "she was in the garden, ran into the shed when the wave burst up from the beach …washed away, I didn't see ..." Joy swallowed. The priest squeezed her hand.

"Today will be better," he said, "we'll get going after breakfast, sort out what we can, sure we're all able enough to get on with the job in hand, thank God." Gregory blessed himself. Kathleen watched him, guessing he was willing an extra dose of superpower be gifted with the blessing. She hoped it worked. They were going to need a fair bit of superpower, alright.

By the time Ryan appeared in the doorway of Maguire's with Joey fed and fast asleep in his buggy and Monty at his heels, the women were busy. Marianne had shovelled and swept away glass and debris, and Erin had water heating on the stove, to wash floors and clean surfaces; everywhere was covered in a fine layer of silt, and a rank stench hung in the air. The Hollywood movie star wrinkled his nose.

"What can I do?" he asked, pouring water into a bucket Erin had just produced.

"We're thinking if we sort this place out, anyone needing somewhere to sleep would be welcome." Erin was taking bottles off the shelf and wiping them. She stopped. "I've just realised it's you!" She gave Ryan a hug. "Good God, how on earth did you make it through?"

"I have a friend who makes *Superman* look weedy!" Ryan told her, giving her a cheesy grin.

"Luckily the storeroom is quite dry but there's a metre of water in the cellar, so we'll move any perishables in there, then start bailing the cellar out," Marianne told him, checking her handiwork at the broken window. She stood for a moment looking out across the road, the river of water had subsided to a stream and if she stood on tiptoe, she could see a chunk of beach between the buildings, less beach than usual, but it meant the sea was receding, the tide was taking the water away. She heard a clatter of boots at the door, sandbags being dragged back. The door opened and Brian and Dermot stepped into the bar. Ryan was on them immediately.

"What's the story?" he asked.

"Did you get any sleep?" Dermot asked, his usually immaculate friend looked a little worn around the edges. Ryan shrugged and Dermot cast his mind back to the events of the previous night. Scott had radioed that he was bringing Ryan and Joey in as quickly as the forecasted lull would allow. He would land at Knock and then take a calculated risk to make the hop across to Innishmahon. Scott said he hoped to make it just before dawn. Dermot and Brian had struggled up to the field beyond the churchyard, planting flares in four corners to guide the landing. As soon as his precious cargo had disembarked, Scott set the blades, waved and took off, making the most of the only respite they had witnessed in nearly forty-eight hours. Brian was impressed, as later, Dermot explained Scott Wallace was probably the most admired stunt professional in the business.

"It must have cost Ryan a fortune to book him for just one flight, coming straight from London and everything," Brian said, sharing the last drop of whiskey between them.

"Old friends," Dermot knocked the shot back, "Ryan's always been there for Scott, he's been through some rough times."

"Sure, haven't we all?" Brian smiled. "You and Ryan go way back, too, don't you?"

"Yeah, we do." Dermot was momentarily wistful. "He's a good bloke, you know. Shame he's so fucking ugly, he could have made something of himself."

Now, the three were huddled, deep in discussion. Elderly people needed checking on, young families too, medicine might be required.

Marianne interrupted. "Brian, the pub sign flew in through the window, slicing Erin's leg. I did what I could but would you mind taking a look?"

Erin, sheet-white, was propping herself up while she went about her task along the optics. Marianne laid the fire, as Erin, protesting loudly, was taken into the kitchen to be examined by a professional.

"It's a shame he bought this place," Dermot told Ryan, as they stood the huge Christmas tree upright, fixing it in a pail of sand.

"Why's that?" Ryan was surprised. They had all been relieved the New York entrepreneur had secured the future of the pub.

"He's a doctor, a proper GP. There isn't one on the island, if there's an emergency, we have to rely on the ferry or the air ambulance. The ferry won't sail if the weather's bad, and the air ambulance is always stretched to breaking point along this coastline." Dermot rubbed his chin. "Now the pharmacy is closed, we need someone medical. Sure, there isn't even a vet within shouting distance."

"You're right," agreed Ryan. "Maybe when he and Kathleen are a bit more settled, he'll reconsider. I've only ever known him run a bar though, he gave up practising medicine a long time ago."

Dermot laughed. "He's been pretty busy on the medical front since he got here. It's fairly obvious we need someone qualified."

"We do if you're going to continue pursuing every bad ass criminal that ventures within a hundred miles of the place and blowing them to Kingdom Come!"

"Don't worry, I've retired. Besides, I still have a bit of a limp." He pointed at his foot, the bullet wound from his encounter with an escaped convict healing nicely. Ryan lifted his arm, the one he had broken capturing gunrunners on the high seas. The 'little job' Dermot said would be a piece of cake and very nearly went tragically wrong.

"Glad to hear it," Ryan told him. "I'm only just getting my strength back."

Brian emerged from the kitchen.

"Good work, you did a professional looking job there, Marianne, just need to make sure it doesn't become infected. Should be fine."

"Must be in the genes. Speaking of genes, how's my mother?"

Brian smiled. He did love to hear Marianne refer to Kathleen that way, even though it was usually when his new wife was out of range.

"Up and raring to go this morning. She had us bring all the parcels and cards across from the Post Office last evening, insisting if we saved anything it needed to be Christmas. We left her with Joy and the children, sorting mail on the kitchen table up at the priest's house."

"How badly damaged is the Post Office?" Marianne asked.

"Don't know yet. She wouldn't let me go and check, said there were other things needed attention first."

Marianne laughed. "I know, the mail first, then it'll be the phones. She's in charge of communications, it's her life's work."

"Don't I know it," Brian replied, remembering Kathleen's indignation when he suggested she should give up the Post Office and reside in Maguire's with him.

By now, Marianne had lit the fire, and candles glowed on tables and along the bar. She was just heading to the kitchen, when the door crashed open and Father Gregory burst in, carrying a large bundle. A gaggle of people trudged in behind.

"A couple of barns have collapsed over beyond," he looked toward Croghan, the island's highest mountain, "taken half the roof off a cottage and most of the livestock lost." He knelt, unwrapping the wriggling bundle, two tiny lambs, squirmed before the fire. They bleated piteously, wobbling on spindly legs, cold and weak with hunger.

Ryan recognised the family who had come in with the priest, two elderly brothers and their ancient father, complaining bitterly they had forgotten his walking frame. A young, collie bitch pushed between their legs to the fire, much to Monty's chagrin. She shook herself and started licking the lambs vigorously, warming them with her rough tongue.

"Isn't there another farm further up the mountain?" Ryan asked, as Erin and Brian poured tea laced with whiskey for the men.

"Two. Sean Grogan's place and Mrs O'Brien's stud. It's very exposed up there, dread to think what state they're in." It was not like the priest to be defeatist. Ryan guessed the carnage he had already witnessed was taking hold.

"Let's go in convoy," Dermot said, "safer that way and we'll have more capacity for anything or anyone we need to bring back."

Ryan agreed. Brian had bought the island's entire fleet of hire vehicles – six ancient 4x4s when he purchased the pub. Taking keys off hooks behind the bar, he tossed a set to each of the men. The priest stood up and gave Erin one of the lambs he had been cradling. She pulled a face.

"Okay troops, let's go," he called.

"We're heading up the mountain," Ryan poked his head round the door, Marianne was busy in the kitchen, "it's bad up there."

She stopped stirring soup, staring into space. They had been here before. A terrible storm, livelihoods, property, people, left devastated and desperate. Last time, she had been helping Oonagh; Oonagh was the one the islanders had come to; the one who fed and watered them; kept their spirits up and warmed their hearts. Here she was, standing in Oonagh's place, in front of the old range, making soup and sandwiches again. Suddenly exhausted, she felt a sham, a facile interloper, with neither the strength nor the will to carry on.

She watched Ryan, hauling on his sailing jacket. Her handsome movie star, the love of her life, having given everything up, all because she was determined to be here, live out her dream, the dream that was becoming more of a nightmare every day. What was she even thinking? She was out of her depth, drowning. He caught the anguish in her eyes.

"Hey?" he said, softly. "Come on, it'll be okay." He went to her. She raised her hands, blocking him. If he touched her, she would break down, beg him to stay, stay and be safe.

The door opened. Erin stood with a bleating, wiggling, lamb under each arm. Joey, squealed in delight, eyes lighting up. Erin looked at her blankly, the lambs squirming in her grasp. It was her turn to bleat.

"How're we going to feed these two on top of everything else?"

The collie pushed in and went straight to Marianne, looking at her with pleading brown eyes, swishing its feathery tail. Marianne cast about. She spotted the rubber gloves at the sink.

"Make an udder out of those," she said, "prick holes in the fingers, fill the gloves with milk and let them feed that way."

"Can they have cow's milk?" Erin asked, askance.

"Good thinking, see if there's any baby formula in the store cupboard." Marianne's goddaughter Bridget had been born in the pub only eighteen months ago. Erin placed the lambs on the floor, much to Joey's delight, who immediately started talking to them in his gibberish. Monty gave them an indolent sniff, far more interested in the pretty collie with the long legs. Erin reappeared triumphantly bearing a tin of *Cow & Gate*. She placed it on the side.

"Can you see to them? I'm rather busy," Marianne said. The humans needed fuel too.

Erin stayed where she was. "I'm not mad on animals." Monty lifted an eyebrow. "Especially baby ones, helpless yokes, squawking at you for food, then just crapping everywhere."

One of the lambs collapsed, a piteous bleat rang out as it hit the stone flags. Erin sighed and picked up the tin.

"I've food for this one," Marianne said, pointing her spoon at the collie dog. "Monty won't mind sharing."

Ryan grinned. There she was, with her 'can do' attitude right back. She flicked him a look. "And you can get lost, we're busy," she smiled. The engines were revving up outside, the convoy of 4x4s preparing to leave.

"Save some of that soup for us," he called as he left.

As the vehicles shuddered along Main Street and up towards the marina, with Brian leading the convoy in the newest model, he spotted the women standing outside the priest's house; mail sacks piled beside them. He stopped. Kathleen opened the door, and she and Joy started throwing bags into the car.

"They're all labelled and sorted, should be easy enough to drop off," she told him. She was wearing a full length wax coat. He spotted tartan trews beneath, tucked into pearlescent red wellington boots. He eyed a couple of packages. The labels read, *Mrs O'Dowd, Carrigcross, Innishmahon,* the other, *Bernie Dowd, Carrig, Ireland.* Only someone in the know would realise they were for the same person.

"I'd have no idea where these are to go," he said.

"I know, that's why I'm coming with you. I'm the only person on the island who understands the nuances and foibles of the system. Don't worry, we'll have this lot delivered in no time. There'll be no cancelling Christmas on my watch. If *Wells Fargo* and *The Pony Express* can do it, so can we!"

She hopped into the seat beside him, taking a crimson Santa hat out of her pocket. As she pulled it on, he noticed her earrings, dangling, replica Christmas trees, complete with candles. She gave him a grin.

"They light up," she said, waving at Joy as they pulled away.

"I bet they do," laughed Brian. God, he had missed her, missed her for over thirty years.

Chapter Seven – Santa Baby

B y four o'clock, as light was fading and the night was drawing in, the pub was buzzing. The men had returned bringing good news. Miraculously, all the farms and cottages they visited were still intact, and apart from a few trees down and some fencing whipped away with the wind, everything was more or less safe; the islanders had learned lessons from the last savage beating nature had bestowed, and were better prepared this time.

The village of Innishmahon had borne the brunt of it, with the freak wave crashing through the harbour wall, taking most of the rear of the waterside buildings with it. Thankfully, the weather warning had been heeded, and the whole street had been evacuated in the nick of time. So it was mainly townspeople who gathered in Maguire's for an impromptu and most welcome Christmas Eve dinner party.

Father Gregory had stuck to his plan and offered Midnight Mass early so he could join the rest of the villagers in the pub. He had been pleased with the turnout in church, with a number of new faces in the pews, obviously hoping that keeping on God's good side was wise, considering recent events. It was still only December, plenty of weather to come yet. He had been especially delighted to see Ryan, Marianne, Joey and Monty slip into the church as he belted out *I Saw Three Ships,* one of his favourite carols. He beckoned them to the front. The priest was totally relaxed about guests in God's house, Monty was as welcome as the next creature; leg count never exempted any living thing from this building.

Once the replica crib had been carried in and laid in the makeshift manger to the side of the altar, and everyone was well and truly blessed, the priest announced the team at the pub had organised hot food, warm company and the chance to start some semblance of celebration of this most festive of seasons, following which the majority of the congregation made their way down the hill to Maguire's.

With fire blazing and candles glowing, the initial subdued murmur began to build, with people having proper conversations, making the odd quip, even joking. By the time Erin and Marianne had ladled scoops of thick Guinness and beef stew into bowls, passing around platefuls of soda bread, slathered with golden butter to dunk in the rich sauce, there was a merry buzz to the place, the atmosphere helped along with a few bottles of wine sponsored by Brian, a contribution, as this was his first Christmas as the new landlord.

"I don't drink wine," whinged Sean Grogan, sitting in his usual spot at the bar.

"Yes, but the pumps don't work without electricity, so no stout," Erin told him.

"I know, but there's bottles, look …" He pointed at the glass fronted fridge behind her.

"Mr Maguire has put wine on the tables," she told him.

"Oh, so here I am, one of the pub's regular customers and I don't get a drink at Christmas because I can't stomach that foreign muck!" He jumped off the stool. "I think I'll take my business elsewhere."

"Please yourself." Erin gave a thin smile. "You're hardly a big spender."

Marianne in search of wine glasses, overheard.

"I don't think Brian would mind if Sean had a bottle of stout instead," she said quietly to Erin. "We've all had a long day." She widened her eyes at her colleague, beseeching a more charitable stance.

"Yes, we have," Erin replied, glaring at her, "but I'm the new manageress here, so I'll handle this, thank you, Marianne."

Sean climbed back on his stool. If there was going to be a row, he did not want to miss it. Marianne stood her ground.

"I was just saying ..."

"It might be Christmas but that's no reason to be giving drinks away willy-nilly to all and sundry, this is a business, after all. None of us will have a job if that's how we're going to carry on." Erin folded her arms.

"It's one bottle of beer," Marianne said, bending to take one out of the fridge.

"Put that back," Erin ordered.

"What?" Marianne snapped. "Don't be ridiculous."

Brian, who was tending the fire, noticed the room growing quiet. He hastened over to the women.

"Anything wrong?"

"Erin won't give Sean a bottle of stout. He doesn't drink wine, I thought he could have a beer instead," Marianne told him.

"And I said we can't give drinks away, and it's nothing to do with her anyway, she's just a part-time cook. I'm the manageress."

"Now, now ladies," Brian said smoothly, "you've both done an amazing job here today, let's chill, have some food, a glass of wine. Sean can have a bottle of beer, though you're right, we don't want to be giving drinks away, this is our livelihood, after all, but hey, it's Christmas, what do you say?" He gave them his big, warm smile.

Marianne shrugged. Erin had always been prickly, but she hoped, when Erin revealed she had been made redundant from her job as an insurance investigator for a big firm in Dublin, that coming to work as the manageress of Maguire's might help smooth the edges a bit, give her a place to call home, somewhere where she was valued and loved. Marianne felt a twinge of guilt. As far as she could tell, Erin was not loved, she was not sure many even liked her.

As if reading her mind, Erin flicked Marianne a look and, unfolding her arms, took the bottle and plonked it down in front of Sean.

"Happy Christmas," she said, through gritted teeth.

"I wasn't undermining you," Marianne told Erin. "You're the manageress."

Erin's turn to shrug.

"Thought you'd have enough on your plate with Ryan and the young fella landed back in time for Christmas, seeing you were telling me how much you wanted to be together, like a proper family."

"I want everyone to be together, really. Before this bloody storm kicked off, I was going to invite you, Dermot,

Brian, my mother, and Father Gregory, everyone, round to Weathervane for a proper Christmas lunch."

"Not for me thanks," Erin started folding tea towels.

"Ah, come on, it'll be fun. I don't know how or what I'll be able to cook, but anything we have, we'll share." Marianne tried to catch her eye, show it was a genuine invitation.

"I'm needed here," Erin told her.

"But the bar will only open for a couple of hours, if that, without any pints to pull. I won't serve lunch until everything is done and dusted here, then you can come to us for a bit of a break, how does that sound?" she cajoled.

"Look Marianne, I'm not fond of Christmas, everyone pretending to like each other, all that forced jollity really winds me up, so if you don't mind I'll spend my few hours off doing something that suits me," Erin said, not looking her in the eye.

"Please change your mind," Marianne tried.

"Please leave me alone," Erin responded.

Marianne sighed and pushed her hands into her jeans, as Dermot stomped up from the cellar.

"Nearly all bailed out down there." He wiped his hands on one of Erin's neatly folded, tea towels.

"You'll be ready for a bowl of stew, then?" Marianne asked, as Ryan appeared behind him, jeans rolled up, shapely calves streaked green with slime and seaweed. "You look like you've had fun," she observed.

"It ain't gonna quite make the spa resort we hoped, so thought it best we get it back to a working cellar," Ryan grinned, wriggling his toes.

"Good, we don't want it wet down there when the power comes back on, it'll fuse everything." Erin pulled the tea towel off Dermot.

"Did someone mention stew?" Ryan cut in.

"Yeah, Marianne's made a vat of it," Erin replied.

"You're an angel, Marianne, what would this place be without you?" Dermot said, folding her in a huge, soggy hug. Erin threw the tea towel down on the bar with such force it upended Sean's glass, crashing it to the floor.

"Ah, me Christmas drink," Sean whined.

"Just an accident. I'll get you another one, and some stew, how's that sound?" Brian offered.

"Jeez, there's always something eating that one." Dermot nodded after Erin's disappearing back.

"She's just tired," Marianne said.

"And she hates Christmas," Ryan supplied.

"How do you know?" Dermot was curious.

"That's all she's been saying since we got back," Ryan told him.

"It's not everyone's cup of tea," Marianne said.

Dermot fell on the food as soon as it appeared.

"I've never been much for it, if I'm honest," said Ryan, dipping his bread in the stew, "always terrified I'd end up one of those ageing *Lotharios* and Christmas would mean pantomime in some provincial wilderness, with just a bottle of whiskey and a mince pie for company."

Marianne looked at him, pulling her mouth down at the corners to make him smile.

"I was never much for it, myself," she agreed, "not until now, that is." She ruffled Ryan's hair and he gave her a big, soppy grin.

"I love it," boomed Dermot, "you get pissed, eat loads of food, kiss everyone in sight and if you're lucky, someone, somewhere, will take pity on you and give you a Christmas shag! Sure it's a great time, full of opportunity. Just drift along like that until New Year, get hammered again and this time have a massive punch up. It's totally, the best time of year if you ask me."

Marianne stared at him. "Dermot, you don't ..."

"He does, it's all true, hasn't a Christian bone in his body, always been the same, raping and pillaging his way through the holidays," Ryan confirmed.

"I'm not a total heathen," Dermot said with his mouth full, Viking hair standing on end, as he downed a glass of wine in one big swallow.

"Great," Marianne said weakly. She spotted Kathleen divesting herself of her wax coat at the doorway. Watching her glide through the melee, she noticed the blinking, candlelit earrings; even in the height of a crisis, her mother ensured standards were maintained at all times. Brian rushed to greet her, sweeping her into his arms, he twirled her to face those gathered.

"Ladies and gentlemen, I give you the real heroine of the hour, Innishmahon's very own Madame Santa Claus, my lovely wife, Kathleen."

"Ah, stop Brian," she laughed. "Sure, I was only doing my job."

"Are you joking me? You've just hand-delivered every last card and parcel about to be swept away by the tidal wave that's just whipped through here like a dose of salts."

"She did," Ryan told the onlookers, "and she made sure any of the children expecting presents from Lapland did not see what she was up to."

"I bet you're starving, will you have some stew?" Marianne was touched by Kathleen's kindness, as she whispered she had hidden Joey's gifts in Weathervane's porch.

"I'll take a drink first. Brian, make me one of those bourbon and rye yokes, will ye? And let me in by the fire, I'm chilled to the bone." Kathleen pushed through the crowd who were clapping her on the back and thanking her for delivering Christmas.

"Give us a song, Kathleen," someone called out.

"Something festive, sure it's Christmas Eve, after all," Brian reminded everyone.

She placed her drink on the mantelpiece, "One minute, I'll be right with you," and disappeared into the ladies.

Ryan arrived at Marianne's side.

"Erin gone off in a huff?" he asked her.

"I looked in a minute ago, she's curled up on the sofa with Joey, Monty, the collie, and the two baby lambs are all fast asleep in front of the range."

"I didn't think she liked children?" Ryan observed.

"Or animals." Marianne gave him a sad smile.

"She'll come round," Ryan assured her. "Christmas doesn't last forever," Ryan smiled into her eyes, pulling her closer, "but we will. Good job I didn't mail your gift, even when it looked touch and go whether we'd get back or not."

"I thought we said no presents, we've enough going on." She pushed a finger at his chest. He grabbed her hand.

"Careful, don't want you guessing what it is before Christmas morning." He patted a bump in his breast pocket. "There's no way my best girl's not having a present, especially as this is our first Christmas together, here, at home."

Marianne swallowed. That small bump in his pocket, she really hoped it was not ...the door burst open to a loud jangling of bells. Two Santa Claus' appeared in the room, followed by an elf in a glittering red cloak and telltale Christmas tree earrings. The elf sat on the piano stool with a Father Christmas either side. The opening bars of *Santa Baby* filled the room, as Brian and Dermot, Santa hats pulled over their ears, accompanied Kathleen pounding the ivories, earrings swinging recklessly, the red wellingtons beating time against the stone flags.

"This is going to be the best Christmas ever," Ryan called above the music to Marianne, pulling her into the space before the fire to dance.

As Kathleen reached the final line, the whole building shook, glass rattled, walls groaned, there was a flash and the lights came on. A huge cheer went up, the power was back, electricity had been restored; Christmas could start properly at last.

Arriving back in Weathervane in the early hours of the morning, having enjoyed a good, old-fashioned hooley in the pub, Marianne tucked Joey and Monty up in their respective beds, before sliding under the sheets and wrapping her arms around a now totally exhausted Ryan. He gave a deep sigh as she snuggled into him, drawing her knees up. She nestled tightly, pushing her nose on the silky skin behind his ear, so she could savour the essence of him, breathing in the deep, musky scent she so missed, whenever he was away for any length of time.

She closed her eyes, trying to quieten the pictures in her brain, as she lay silent in the darkness. The violence of the storm, the sheer superhuman effort of pulling together against a mighty, unstoppable force, and in the midst of it all, just when she felt the smallest and loneliest she had felt in so long a time, she had opened the door and there he stood. White-faced, eyes boring into her and, as the wind howled around them, at the very core, instantly all was well. She pressed her lips against the nape of his neck. He murmured.

"I love you," she whispered into his skin.

"Sure, why wouldn't you?" he replied, a smile in his voice.

"You bastard, you're not asleep." She smacked his shoulders. He spun round, pinning her arms against her. Her eyes had adjusted to the moonlight seeping in through the drapes. His eyes were half-closed, but she saw the glint of lust and could feel he was aroused.

"Thought you were exhausted," she teased, turning her head so he could not kiss her.

"Never!" he exclaimed, "take more than a tsunami to cool my ardour, my lovely," he grinned, trying out his pirate voice. It made her chuckle. He found her lips and pressed his mouth against hers, taking her laughter into him. When he broke off and she caught her breath, she smoothed his hair back, looking into his eyes.

"Thank you for hitching a ride on a passing helicopter, pulling out all the stops so you could be home for

Christmas." She had watched the video on *You Tube* through her fingers, horrified at the crazy stunt he had concocted to get back.

He smiled down at her.

"It's I who should thank you."

"What for?" she asked.

"For giving me a home to come back to."

She frowned.

"Really," he continued, "this is the first real home I've ever had."

"Are you serious?" She was surprised. Ryan had been a successful actor for many years, she imagined his past homes had been in fabulous locations. He knew what she was thinking.

"I've had houses, apartments, condos ... but never a home, this is home, you're home."

He started to nuzzle her throat, tickling her skin, pulling the straps of her nightdress off her shoulders with his teeth. The silk slipped down, exposing her breasts, soft cream skin shone in the moonlight. He made a growl and fell on her flesh, caressing her, licking and sucking at her flesh, pulling at her nipples, tweaking and teasing them between his fingers. She moaned as he pressed his lips between her breasts and ran his tongue downwards, her flesh rippled with pleasure, she lifted her hips.

"Oh Ryan, I can't wait," she whispered. He slipped out of his pants, rubbing himself along her wetness. "Please," she said.

He spread her thighs, pushing his fingers gently inside her, and then taking his weight on his elbows, straddled to enter her, a little at first, and then as she relaxed, he plunged deeper and deeper inside. She wrapped her legs around him, burying her fingers in his hair, her tongue in his mouth.

No one had ever made love to her like Ryan; she had never felt so completely and utterly fulfilled in any other man's arms. If he was at home, she was in heaven, and she intended to stay there, for as long as she could.

Chapter Eight – All I Want For Christmas

Erin was feeding the animals while Kathleen made coffee, dressed in a pale pink Kimono, splashed with sea-green dragons, and little else.

"What state is the Post Office in?" asked Erin, rinsing out the rubber gloves, the makeshift udder for the lambs.

"Not sure, if I'm honest I don't want to look yet. It's mine and Brian's first Christmas together in many a year, I want to try and have a few special memories at least." Kathleen stopped spooning the freshly ground beans into the cafetière, and gazed dreamily out of the window. Erin hurrumphed a bit, bringing her back to reality. "I tell you what, shall I make us all Buck's Fizz to have with our salmon and scrambled egg? It's traditional, after all."

"Whose tradition?" Erin asked, lifting the bowl to fill it with water for the collie dog, swishing its tail and gazing at her with huge brown eyes.

"Mine, I'm introducing lots of new ones now Brian and I are married and he's making the island his home. I want him to feel as settled as possible. Little rituals and traditions are part of being a couple, aren't they?" Kathleen already had a bottle of champagne in one hand, as she ferreted about in the fridge for the juice.

Erin rolled her eyes. The kitchen door opened and a farmer who had taken shelter from the storm, stood, bleary-eyed, rubbing his chin. Kathleen, smiling, swirled towards him.

"Merry Christmas, Joseph," she trilled, and plonked a scarlet kiss on his lips. He jumped back, startled. Kathleen's enthusiasm was not to everyone's taste. "Will you stay and have breakfast, we're having Buck's Fizz?" She waved the bottle at him. Her gown fell open. The man raised his hands, visibly shocked.

"No thanks Mrs," he baulked. "I need to head back and check everything's alright now the storm has passed."

"Will you come back and have Christmas lunch with us?" Kathleen batted her eyelashes at him, the poor man was a bachelor, he could do with some female company.

"No, no I have food enough at home, with the electric back on, I'll be grand."

"Ah, don't be on your own on Christmas day, Joseph," Kathleen cajoled.

"Thanks for the thought, but I really would rather be home," he insisted.

Erin pointed at the lambs; the collie had herded them under the table.

"You can take your livestock with you." She told him.

"Not mine," he replied, "who brought them in?"

"The men, when they came back after being up on Croghan. They were trapped on a bank with the water rising. The ewe didn't make it."

The farmer shrugged.

"I'll take them with me, they're probably Sean Grogan's, he's very forgetful lately, stock left out when it should be in, fences down all over the place."

"Spends too much time here, if you ask me." Erin unceremoniously dumped the lambs in the farmer's arms.

"It's only a bit of company he's needing." Kathleen was full of the milk of human kindness as she set out the champagne glasses. Sean Grogan usually got right up her nose.

"Do you want a rope for the dog?" Erin had the collie by the scruff.

"That's not mine, either." The man was halfway out the door.

"Well, who does it belong to?" Erin whined. The collie was licking her hand.

"That thing's a stray, goes from farm to farm for scraps," the man said.

"Take it with you, it's a sheep dog, isn't it?"

The man shook his head. "Hasn't got the brain for working, a few people have tried. I don't want it, I've enough mouths to feed."

The champagne cork popped.

"Happy Christmas," Kathleen grinned at them.

"Same to you," the man said, letting the door slam behind him.

"Bloody hell," Erin cursed, looking down at the dog, unblinking brown eyes staring back at her. "We've enough mouths to feed around here, too," she told it.

Kathleen handed her a glass.

"You can't turn it out, not today."

"But a dog is for life, not just for Christmas," Erin retorted.

"Fair enough," Kathleen said, bending to pat the collie's mangy head. "She may be a better guard dog than she is a sheep dog, a pub needs a good guard dog."

"We have an alarm," Erin grumbled, not touching her drink.

"Not terribly reliable, all the power cuts we get round here," Kathleen said gently. The dog swished its tail, looking from one to the other. Brian came downstairs. He was wearing an old style smoking jacket over striped pyjama bottoms, the tag swung from the sleeve as he greeted the women with hugs and season's greetings. He noticed the dog and kissed her, too.

"She's a stray, seems to like it here," Kathleen told him.

"Isn't she lovely, a bar needs a dog, maybe we can keep her, what d'ya think?" Brian said.

"Great idea!" beamed Kathleen.

"Bloody hell," Erin said again, and, handing Brian her drink, left them to it.

Not twenty yards away in Weathervane, Christmas morning was in full swing. Carols blared from the radio, while Joey sat happily amidst boxes and wrapping paper, and Ryan busied himself assembling the mini railway Father Christmas had delivered for his son. Monty was trying to bury his new bone under the tree, now twinkling centre stage in the sitting room.

Marianne stood at the back door, a mug of coffee in her hand, gazing across the scrap of lawn, down to the gate and out across the road to the sea beyond. A cloudless, brittle blue sky domed the beach, navy waves broke gently on the sand, bubbling softly over driftwood and debris, the only clue the island had been in the grip of a monumental storm less than twenty-four hours ago.

She took a deep, calming breath of sea air, smiling as she sipped her drink. She could hear Joey's squeals of delight above *Bowie and Bing* singing *Little Drummer Boy,* while Ryan whooped as the miniature engine trundled around the track. She would leave the boys to play happily for a while. Contentedly preparing lunch in the kitchen, she wondered who would turn up, having invited nearly everybody she knew. If only half of them came, the cottage would be full to bursting.

It was going to be perfect, everyone together, having a fabulous time. Everyone except Erin. Christmas was forced and false, according to the caustic Miss Brennan. Marianne remembered a time when she, too, had felt that way. Taking on extra shifts at the newspaper, working through the holiday, batting away all invitations with her work schedule, pretending not to be lonely. Ryan brought her back to the present; he had Joey in his arms.

"This is great, isn't it?" he beamed. "I'm playing with the train set, he's crazy about the wrapping paper, Monty's knocked the tree over burying his bone ... what time are we expecting guests?"

She laughed. "I don't know. I just told everyone to come and eat with us."

Ryan was surprised. Marianne was highly organised, always a deadline.

"How many are coming?" he asked her.

She laughed again. "Haven't a clue. Not sure what I'm going to feed them, either."

"Are you alright?" Ryan gave her a look.

"I just want everyone here, in our home. Who cares about the other stuff?" she lifted Monty and kissed him. He wriggled in her arms, wagging his tail. She squeezed him to her, she had nearly lost him last autumn, they had all nearly lost each other. Ryan wrapped them in a huge hug.

"Love you," he told her.

"Love you right back," she said.

"Will you ever reconsider the marriage thing?" he whispered into her hair. She pulled back, looking him in the eye.

"Ryan, don't." Marianne and marriage plans had never been a good mix, she and Ryan were not teenagers, they both had their fair share of failed relationships, lost love.

"Just checking." He smiled. "One day you will. You'll beg me to marry you." She flicked his nose with her finger.

"Yeah, and Rudolph landed on the roof last night," she said.

"'Course he did. I believe, even if you don't." He gave her his crooked smile. The phone rang. "Saved," he told her. She released herself and went to answer it.

"That's good, the line's been down since the storm," she said.

"It's me, Dermot," a man's voice bellowed at her. "I've fixed it, jeez I'm a genius, I fecking well, fixed it."

"It's Dermot," she shouted back to Ryan. "He's fixed the phone."

Ryan burst out laughing. "Dermot? Now I really do believe in miracles." He gave her his best Hollywood smile.

Three hours later Weathervane was full of laughter, music and the smell of delicious, home-cooked food, just the way Marianne liked it. Her mother had raided Maguire's ample freezer and they were soon sitting down to spiced apple and parsnip soup, a fragrant turkey curry with walnut and pear chutney, served with fluffy jacket potatoes.

It was while Ryan was serving Christmas pudding and custard laced with brandy, that Dermot recounted how he had seconded a scaffold, and with a couple of the building lads, had scaled it to reconnect the phones. They had also managed to reposition the satellite dish. Kathleen was impressed with his determination to reconnect the island to the outside world.

Brian disappeared into the kitchen to help Marianne slice fruit for the cheeseboard, as Father Gregory arranged an assortment of glasses on a tray for liqueurs. Joey and a vagarie of Redmund youngsters were playing in the sitting room. Monty, replete with far too much ham, had waddled off to his basket, which had been placed beside the fire in honour of the occasion; the first, full on, family Christmas he had ever experienced.

"No Erin, then?" Marianne asked Brian as they served the last course.

"I went to her room before we left, but no sign of her. She's keen to keep fit, I wonder if she went for a run?"

"Not with that gash in her leg," Marianne reminded him.

"Maybe she's just taking some air then, she insisted she wanted to be on her own. I know lots of people, who

107

don't like Christmas, lots of people who don't like other people come to that." Brian was wistful.

"She's in the wrong job if that's how she feels," Marianne told him.

"She does blow hot and cold," Brian confirmed, "funny and flirty when she's on form, a bit of a grump when she isn't."

"I wonder if she'll stay. She does complain about the island, and this storm might have put the cap on it," Marianne said, sadly.

Kathleen looked up from a pile of CDs she was sorting through.

"Known her since she was a child, always the same. Oonagh was the sunny one, Erin a bit on the dark side. Would she be happy anywhere?"

"She said she was only back here by accident, a coincidence that the insurance company sent her to report on the jewellery that went missing," Marianne confirmed.

"Or did she jump at the chance of coming back here? A port in a storm, perhaps?" Kathleen asked. Marianne looked at her, Kathleen always seemed to know more than she let on.

"You think she was running away from something?" Marianne pressed.

"Or someone," Kathleen replied, folding her napkin. "Now, surely it's time for a song. Brian's brought his fiddle, pull up that rug and he'll give us a jig."

With the decanter empty and everyone dancing and singing and looking like they were in for the night, Dermot offered to go back to Maguire's and purloin a bottle of whiskey and a litre of Red Lemonade; that uniquely Irish concoction many favoured to dilute the hard stuff. Slightly intoxicated, he had not thought to ask for a key, but was unsurprised the door opened easily. The whole place was in darkness, the fire long died out.

Dermot flicked on the lights, making his way across the pub to fish behind the bar for a couple of bottles of Brian's stock, when he heard a low moaning, a sort of dirgey singing. He turned his head to listen, it was coming from upstairs. He moved to the stairwell. It was definitely singing, coming from a room above. Maybe it was Erin, deciding to enjoy herself, after all. Maybe she was celebrating Christmas, perhaps someone was with her, maybe that was why she had not wanted to join them, she was entertaining someone alone, having a private party.

Dermot put the bottles down and started up the stairs, tiptoeing slowly, taking one step at a time. The music became clearer, an old pop song, *Wham's Last Christmas, George Michael* singing plaintively about how he gave his heart to someone, who just gave it away. Dermot hated *George Michael*, another good-looking bastard, with more luck than talent, in his opinion. He stood on the landing, listening, he could hear someone half-singing, half-snivelling. 'It can't be Erin,' thought Dermot, 'not she of the hard nose and cold shoulder.'

It was coming from the room Erin's sister, the former landlady, had turned into a boudoir for herself and her longed-for baby daughter. Her grieving husband Padar had left it untouched after a yachting accident resulted in his wife's tragic death, and finally unable to make ends meet, he and his new partner had left the island, taking his baby daughter with them. Dermot had always been curious about this sad, family story. He turned the handle of the door as quietly as he could. Maybe he would find Erin crying over her dead sister, or worse, conjuring up her ghost, speaking in tongues, draped in a cloak daubed with demonic symbols. She was probably drinking blood.

The door creaked open. The room was dark, candles scattered about, flickered in the draught. There was a hooded creature, bent, huddled in the corner. It was stroking and crooning at something. Dermot felt every hair on his body rise, his throat tightened, his heart beat hard in his chest. He was right, on this most Holy night, demons were being summoned, the dead were being called to walk among the living …

"There!" the creature said loudly, and stood up.

Dermot jumped backwards, bashing his head off the door jam, his arm off the wall, accidently hitting the light switch.

It screamed, a bloodcurdling, banshee wail. He screamed back.

"Jeez, Dermot, you fecking eejit, you frightened me half to death!" Erin barked at him, pushing the hood of her towelling robe back, black curls dripping onto her shoulders. The bundle before her was also dripping wet. It wriggled free from the towel she had wrapped around it. The collie blinked huge, brown eyes, swishing its tail at the intruder.

"What are you doing?" squeaked Dermot, finally finding his voice.

"She needed a bath. By the time I'd finished, so did I." Erin laughed, her eyes twinkled, the smile completely changing her face. "You okay?" Dermot's pallor was pricked with pink blotches.

"Fine," he laughed too, "just checking you're okay." He suddenly realised she was naked beneath the robe. His gaze lingered a little too long. The collie let out a low grumble. Erin pulled the gown across her chest.

"Sorry," Dermot said. "Would you not get dressed and join us? It's just a party, everyone's in great form."

"No, thanks." She was brittle again.

"Ah, come on." He swayed in the doorway.

"I'm grand, having my own party." She indicated a bottle of vodka and a glass.

"Just you and the bitch, here?" Dermot asked.

"You talking to me, or the dog?" Erin gave him a flinty look. He squirmed, and she burst out laughing. Relieved, he laughed too.

"Why don't you join us? Have one before you go back." She smiled again. He liked her smile. What harm would it do? They had both had a couple of drinks, they might even get to know each other better, become a bit friendlier towards each other; it was Christmas, after all.

Two thirds of a bottle of vodka later, Erin, now more respectably dressed in jeans and a rugby shirt, and Dermot divested of his sailing jacket, were discussing the merits of eighties pop music versus seventies heavy metal. Dermot's real heroes were *Led Zeppelin*, Erin was passionately in love with *Paul Young*. They were exchanging song lyrics.

"I like this one, too," she said. He had chosen something upbeat, rocking, while she sat on the floor brushing the dog's coat in time with the music.

"Now you've washed her, she's an awful, scrawny runt, isn't she?" Dermot confirmed.

"I thought that, I can feel every bone, poor thing," Erin said.

"You're not mad about animals though, are you?" Dermot asked her.

"No, but I wouldn't harm one, just don't see the point of getting attached to something that doesn't live very long, costs you a fortune, and then goes and dies on you."

"That's a very cynical way of looking at things." Dermot ruffled the collie's fringe.

"Fact though." She drained her glass. "I'll go and fetch us another bottle."

While she was gone, Dermot fiddled about with the *iPod* and found some *Queen*. He turned out the light, leaving the candles glowing, and was swaying about to one of the band's ballads, when Erin reappeared with more vodka and a few slices of pizza on a plate. He grinned at her as she handed him the food.

"Ah, me long lost youth, this reminds me of my student days," he said.

"You listened to *Queen* when you were a student? Christ how old *are* you?" Erin teased.

"I have electric taste in music," he replied, "love the classics."

"Eclectic," she corrected, "but we've finally found something we agree on, *Freddie Mercury* was sublime." Erin closed her eyes as the opening bars of *You're My Best Friend* began. Dermot drifted towards her, soon they were swaying together, singing the lines softly. It was a song in praise of having someone who loved you no matter what, who stuck with you through thick and thin, who loved you for yourself, despite yourself. Dermot placed an arm tentatively around her shoulders. The collie growled, but Erin did not resist. Instead she moved closer, she put her arms around his waist and rested her head on his chest as they danced. He breathed her in, fragrant, freshly washed hair, soft like damp silk. She stopped dancing, stepped back, looked up at him, her grey eyes shone with tears.

"Imagine having a best friend like that," she said softly. Dermot could not hold back any longer. He wrapped his arms around her and, pulling him to her, crushed her in a huge bear hug, only releasing her slightly to find her mouth, quickly kissing away any protest. For the merest moment she melted against his lips, and then like a snowflake, was gone.

"Dermot, you're such a caveman. Why do fellas always have to spoil everything?" she sniped.

"It was only a Christmas kiss," he said.

She turned the music off abruptly. The moment lost. Embarrassed, Dermot sat down. The dog joined him.

"This one can come and stay with me on the boat, if you like? I could do with the company." He stroked the collie's velvety ears, she turned adoring eyes at him.

"She's alright here for a while, her owner might turn up, they need to know where to find her." Erin stretched out beside the beast on the floor.

"She's a stray." Dermot followed suit, stretching out on the chaise, hands behind his head.

"Not ness … ness … really," Erin said, slurring slightly. "Has a name now."

"What name?" Dermot was suddenly sleepy.

"Eve … geddit … Christmas Eve … s'good name, isn't it not?" The dog thumped its tail on the floor. Dermot replied with a slight snore. Erin smiled, burying her arms in the soft fur. "Nite, nite, Eve," she said, closing her eyes, unconsciously synchronising her snores with Dermot, now out for the count.

Chapter Nine – A Ring Of Truth

It was late morning when Dermot stirred on the narrow chaise. Twisting stiffly, he landed unceremoniously on the floor beside a still-sleeping Erin, arms wrapped around the body of the collie in a vice-like grip. Turning to face her, Dermot's mouth nearly touched her lips. They were nose to nose. He held his breath, but her eyes remained closed. He blinked, his eyelashes hurt, he knew then that he was in for one hell of a hangover. He tried to speak, but his mouth was full of something fat and spongy. It was his tongue. He tried again.

"I suppose a Christmas shag is out of the question?" he slurred at his companion. The collie thumped her tail against Erin's chest. "I meant the human," he said, sure Erin would leap up any second and blast him with a full-on barrage of feminist rage. But she remained comatose and silent.

Dermot propped himself up on an elbow, examining her face. Fine black eyebrows, quizzically arched; a long elegant nose that gave a haughtiness when she looked down it; her mouth, pale lips, half-turned in a smile as she slept. He looked at her mouth again, remembering that stolen kiss. He noticed how grey she was, a thin film of perspiration covered her skin. Dermot looked again. Was she even breathing?

"Erin." He shook her by the shoulders. "Erin, wake up now, come on, wake up."

The collie opened its eyes, and grumbled, then, watching Dermot trying to wake her new mistress, wriggled free, licking Erin's hands, snuffling, nudging her body. Dermot touched her skin. It was icy. He shook her again, hard this time. He tried pulling Erin's eyelids open with his thumb, there was no response. She was out of it. He felt for her pulse, Christ, she was barely alive. Adrenalin kicked in, he had witnessed scenes like this before, having worked Drugs and Vice during his time in the Dublin police force.

For all her big, brash talk Erin felt like a small child in his arms as he carried her into the bathroom. He had no idea what she had taken. Was this reaction alcoholic poisoning, or had she taken something else? His brain was buzzing, he had no idea what Erin had been up to before he arrived. Her head flopped back, her lips were parched white. The one thing he did know was, he had to empty her stomach, as quickly as possible.

He propped her on the loo, while he ran to the kitchen to concoct a nauseating mixture of mustard and salt water, telling the collie to keep nagging her while he was gone. She was slipping away, he needed her back; back, so he could help ... help her from ever wanting to do such a thing again.

It was dawn by the time Weathervane's mammoth, impromptu Christmas party was breaking up. Brian Maguire had exhausted his repertoire of jigs and reels, twice. The world famous, Hollywood movie star, Ryan O'Gorman, had sung everything from swing to soul, finishing with his now traditional grand finale of *Good Looking Woman,* a perfect impersonation of the late, great *Joe Dolan*. Not to be outdone, Father Gregory did a credible impersonation of *Elvis* singing *Jailhouse Rock*, followed by a very similar interpretation of *Mud's, Lonely This Christmas*.

Marianne had laughed so hard, her face ached and her throat was sore. She was unsure which had been the most entertaining, Kathleen's cocktail tasting competition, or Joy Redmund's dancing, a bizarre mix of traditional Irish and go-go, as far as she could tell.

As Ryan waved the last guest goodbye, and Marianne carried another tray of dirty glasses into the kitchen, they had no idea that not a hundred yards away, Erin was vomiting and crying out so loudly that Dermot did not hear Brian and Kathleen return, until the bathroom door burst open and they stood there, horrified.

"What's going on?" shrieked Kathleen, convinced Dermot was murdering or raping the half-naked, unconscious woman in his arms. Brian was in the room like a shot.

"I loosened her clothes to push on her stomach," Dermot told him, "she needed to be sick."

"Kathleen, fetch my bag," Brian ordered. "Do you know what she's taken?"

Dermot shrugged. "We only had a few drinks, vodka, that's all." Brian gave him a look. "That's all while I was here, anyway," Dermot said.

Kathleen returned with the bag.

"What is it?" she asked her husband.

"Not sure, allergic reaction, anaphylactic shock? I'll give her a shot, see if we can stabilise her."

Erin groaned.

"What on earth's been going on here, Dermot?" Kathleen demanded. "And you a former officer in the guards."

"Nothing, I swear it, a few drinks only, honest."

Kathleen's gaze swept over him, unconvinced. Dermot was a young, virile man. He liked to party, he could easily obtain certain substances if he felt so inclined. And, what of Erin, lonely and depressed, alone on Christmas night, an easy target for a predatory male.

"It's not what you're thinking, Kathleen." Dermot was affronted. Erin coughed, rolling over in his arms. Her eyes flickered open.

"Here she is," Brian said, patting and rubbing Erin's hands and wrists, checking all the time for needle marks. "Come on, Erin, back you come, love," he cajoled.

"Gawd, I feel crap," she muttered, and turning her head, vomited copiously onto Dermot's designer shirt. He stroked her hair.

"That's better," he told her. "You'll be grand now."

"Yeah, merry fecking Christmas," she replied.

It was not until everyone had left and Joey was tucked up in bed, the shiny engine in pride of place on his bedside table, that Ryan and Marianne finally sat down. She snuggled under his arm, finding his hand and entwining fingers. The only light, the glow of embers and sparkle of the tree.

"Good day?" she asked.

"Great day," he replied, "the best."

She wriggled out of his grasp, pulling a large soft parcel from beneath the fir. She handed it to him.

"We said no gifts," he teased, tearing open the wrapping paper. A beautiful soft, Arran sweater sprang free, dark teal flecked with amber and turquoise. He held it to his face, burying his fingers in the rich wool.

"One of the women on the far side of the island knitted it, the wool is from local sheep, too," she said.

"It smells of peat." He passed it to her.

"I wanted you to have something from here, something you can take with you wherever you go." She watched as he pulled off his rugby shirt. His new jumper was perfect. He twirled so she could check him out, striking a pose. She laughed and he wiggled his bottom.

"You look like you're starring in a classic Irish film," she smiled, it suited him.

"*The Quiet Man*, the remake," he said. They often talked about movies they loved. The nineteen fifties film starring *John Wayne* and *Maureen O'Hara* being one of their favourites. It told the story of a handsome Irish American returning to find his roots, and falling for a feisty, Irish colleen. Their story, in many ways.

"Thank you, I'll wear it until it falls apart," he said, and kissed her, wrapping his arms and the soft, peaty wool around her. "Have you found your gift? It's here on the tree." He reached up and plucked out a small gold box nestling deep in the pine needles. He placed it in his palm, holding it out to her. She looked at the box and then into his eyes. An odd look. A look that said, 'I'm not sure about this, whatever it is."

"Go on, it'll be alright," he assured her.

Carefully she unpicked the edges and peeled back the gold foil. It revealed a gleaming, perfectly tooled leather box. She could see it had a lid and at its base, a small gold handle. Ryan pointed to it. "Open the drawer first."

She took the handle between finger and thumb and drew open the drawer. A sparkling chain of links lay glinting on dark velvet. She lifted it out, a single charm, a golden key, hung from it. She gave him a quizzical look. He touched a panel on the box, it slid across to reveal a miniature lock.

"Try it," he told her.

She turned the key in the lock and the lid slowly lifted. She watched as it rose, to reveal a band of brilliance, which even in the muted light, danced sparkles up at her. She lifted it out of the box, holding it up. It was a deep band of gold, set all round with baguette-cut stones, placed side by side. She turned it, sapphire, citrine, tourmaline, turquoise and diamond, the precious gems repeated so the ring was a solid band of jewels. Marianne gasped. It was stunning, a work of art, one of the most spectacular pieces of jewellery she had ever seen. The gems were set deep in the gold, to lay flat against the finger, bewitchingly beautiful, highly wearable. It was exquisite.

"That's the loveliest thing, I've ever seen," she whispered, beguiled yet unsure of how to react. She went to put the ring on her right hand.

"It won't fit that finger," he told her.

"Oh …" She tried, but the ring was too small.

"The coloured stones are the island, a symbol of our home, where we fell in love. The diamonds, dual purpose, the sparkling sun on the water, and the rock … that means forever." He gripped her hand. "It's an engagement ring, a wedding ring and an eternity ring – it's everything combined. It's my heart and soul." His voice caught in his throat. "You gave me an ultimatum once, Marianne. Come back this time for good, or never come back again. Leave me here to live my life, that's what you said. My turn for the ultimatum. If you're not ready, no problem, lock the ring away, but I won't wait forever. You know what I want."

She stopped trying to make the ring fit the wrong finger. It had been made for her left hand, she could see that now, although she dare not even try it on. She held it out to him. He gave a stern look. She put it back in the box. He closed the lid, she locked it.

"Thank you, Ryan, it is truly beautiful," she said.

"I'm pleased you like it." He bent and kissed her nose. "Don't make me wait too long, now." And he laughed, a cold, brittle laugh she had never heard before. She took the box and placed it in her desk, clipping the chain with the charm around her wrist.

"Don't forget I have the key." She tried to make a joke.

"To so much it would seem." He smiled, hiding his pain. She had no idea how much he had wanted her to agree to be his wife that night, no idea it was the most important thing in the world to him right now. She was totally unaware, that she had just locked the rest of his life away.

"Coming to bed?" she asked, putting the guard against the fire.

"I'll be up in a while. I want to get the wear out of my jumper." He went to pour himself a nightcap, the room had turned quite cool, right enough.

Chapter Ten – Fairytale Of New York

A few days earlier in New York, there was a storm brewing of an altogether different kind. Larry Leeson always and without exception, spent the holidays with his sister Lena. The Leesons had enjoyed an unorthodox childhood. Lena, the adored little girl, closely followed by Larry, a totally spoiled baby boy, were the only offspring of their glamorous parents' tempestuous showbiz marriage. Although Lena had come close a few times, neither of them were married nor had children of their own. So, despite arguing where they were going to spend a couple of precious days without their noses to the grindstone, Larry, complaining bitterly, always headed west to his elder sibling's sprawling Los Angeles beach house.

Lena loved to entertain, filling the house with stars of stage and screen, producers, directors, writers and any amount of wannabes. Larry, although less keen on schmoozing and razzmatazz, appreciated the importance of good PR, so always braced up and threw himself into the melee.

Lena threw a '*Dress to Kill*' formal dinner party on Christmas Eve, followed by a laid-back open-house on Christmas Day, with guests enjoying a vintage movie show, followed by supper. Up to a dozen guests could be comfortably catered for at the house, with at least another ten in bungalows and apartments scattered around the grounds, which led down to a private beach. This year, Lena excelled even her demandingly high standards and ensured every room and every moment was filled with celebrity and celebration. She and Mimi, Larry's long-suffering personal assistant, had been working on the guest list and itinerary for months.

Larry groaned as yet another email bearing his sister's unmistakable logo landed in his inbox. It was a list of 'must have' items from the very best New York had to offer. Purveyors of fine wines and liquor; top quality butchers and greengrocers; the most special of specialist delicatessens. *How on earth did they survive in that sleepy little backwater called Los Angeles without all this stuff?* he asked himself, dutifully printing the list. He would go to the stores, personally, order the produce, and ensure delivery was scheduled for precisely when Lena had requested it.

The one time he had given the task to someone else, they had delivered the wrong kind of caviar, and Lena had more or less accused him of ruining her entire holiday, due to his lack of care. No way was he ever going to suffer her chagrin over so petty a misdemeanour again, he considered, pulling on his full-length Donegal tweed. He ferreted in a drawer for his gloves and stood, gazing, at the snow-filled sky, a smut-stained cloak draping the towering New York skyline. He loved New York in the winter. He sighed. How he hated the heat and interminable sunshine of the west coast.

It was bitterly cold outside, yesterday's blizzard had frozen the streets in sheet-white ice, ensuring traffic slowed, trains and flights were disrupted. Of course, he reminded himself, the airports had been fogbound, maybe his flight would be cancelled, all seats on subsequent flights booked. He would call Lena, explain he had no choice, he was sorry, he had to stay in New York. He would shut off the computer, unplug the phone, eat pizza, watch movies, drink bourbon …

Leaving his high-rise, plate-glass apartment building, Larry pulled his hat over his ears, wrapping the scarf tightly around his throat, as cold air burned his cheeks. The day was looking altogether brighter, there was even a slight spring in his step as he decided to walk the few blocks to the first store on his list. He saw a trash can. It occurred to him to screw up the list and just throw it in with the trash; there, done, gone forever. But he stopped himself; that would have been a rebellion too far, even for the mood he was in, this brilliant December day.

Franco Rossini stomped snow off his boots in the porchway of the back kitchen to the rear of his home in upstate New York. He had been in the glasshouse, checking the soft fruit trees were properly protected from the cold. Roberto, his gardener, was not as young as he once was, he could be forgetful. Franco shrugged, could say the same about himself.

Peeling off his old waterproof jacket, he hung it on a peg, absent-mindedly patting the spaniel, waiting patiently for a treat at his side. He caught the look on the dog's face, and digging in his pocket for a biscuit, pulled out the battered piece of card which was Lena Leeson's formal invitation to join her and her brother Larry for the holidays. She had accompanied the gilt-edged card – a nice touch – with a small booklet, highlighting the agenda she had carefully and meticulously planned for the extended break, and although the world-famous Hollywood movie producer was pleased to be cited as the Leesons' guest of honour, he wondered if he could really be bothered to make the huge effort to buy gifts, book flights and travel all the way to Los

Angeles, to be both entertained and entertaining, and then travel all the way back again. He was so rarely at home these days, what harm would it do to luxuriate in his own company for a little longer, to enjoy some downtime before he had to get on with business? Come the New Year, he had a massive, potentially blockbusting movie to make, what harm would a few more days pottering around the farm do?

Franco lit the fire, poured himself a large glass of red wine, his own vintage he was proud to acknowledge, and, taking his usual seat in the den, slipped a small box out of his pocket and popped a pill under his tongue. He then took a pack of cigarettes off the table beside him and lit one with a slim gold lighter. He was just taking his first taste of the sweet tobacco, when Roberto - his gardener and old friend - burst into the room.

"For Christ's sake, where's the fire?" Franco demanded.

"No fire," puffed Roberto, who was a few years younger than his boss but far too partial to large cigars. "But check this out, c'mere." He held an electronic tablet in his hand. It fascinated Franco how his pal embraced all manner of new technology. It had started with a sensory heat system for the glasshouses, followed by solar powered irrigation for the vineyard and had escalated from there. Roberto was always emailing and *Skyping* people all over the world, asking questions, researching solutions. Franco wondered what he had found now. He punched the *You Tube* app. A hazy video flickered onto the screen. A man running, looked like he was on a roof. He was wearing a hoodie, with something strapped to his chest.

"A suicide bomber?" asked Franco, aghast, transfixed as the man leapt upwards, and was hauled on board a hovering helicopter. The package on his chest squirmed. It was a child.

"Oh my God, he's going to kill the baby," Franco roared. "I can't watch!"

The man in the video turned, looked back briefly and smiled. Franco froze.

"Play it again," he demanded. Only one man on the planet had a smile like that. Ryan O'Gorman, that crazy, never-give-a-frig, good-looking son-of-a-bitch. "What's he doing? I hope he's not making movies outside his contract. Is it an advertisement or something?"

"No," Roberto said, "look again, it's for real, he's hitching a ride on a helicopter."

"What? But it looks like he's on top of a building."

"He is."

"Is he mad? Shit, if the insurance company sees this." Franco hit his forehead with the heel of his hand. "Who's the kid?" But before he even asked the question, he knew the answer, who the child was. Not only Ryan's infant son, but the only living relative, he, the great Franco Rossini, had left on the planet. He sat down heavily.

"Great publicity," Roberto told him, "this thing's gone viral."

"Damn dangerous though, what was he thinking?" Franco asked.

"The report says there was a massive storm over there, airports shut down, that sort of thing. He wanted to be home for Christmas, he'd promised his girl."

"He could have killed himself, killed them both." Franco took a gulp of his drink. He could feel his blood pressure rising, he was starting to sweat. "Always was crazy, even for an Irish man."

"They're all okay, though. The island, what's it called? Was cut off for a while, but Ryan got there and everyone's okay. Great footage though, don't you think? Recorded on an *iPhone,* that's amazing, isn't it?" Roberto played it again. But Franco was not listening. He lit another cigarette, he needed time to think, he needed to make a plan.

"You doing anything special for the holidays?" he asked after a while.

"Same as always, spending it here with you, if you're staying. I'll miss Angelique though, she always made it back for Christmas, bringing a crowd of pals to stay, used to be fun."

Franco laughed. "Always such extravagant gifts, things we'd never use." He could picture her now, his beautiful, wayward niece, running down the vast staircase, dressed in silk pyjamas, shiny black hair swirling about her shoulders, as she flew into the library on Christmas morning, desperate to be the first to hand out gifts, loving the surprise and delight her wildly expensive presents evoked from all those gathered.

Roberto watched his friend, as his rheumy eyes misted over.

"Did you send the boy anything?" he asked.

Franco frowned. "I asked a couple of assistants to send something, a few of this year's best sellers from FAO Schwarz, no expense spared."

"Hmmm," Roberto replied.

"I've been so busy," Franco offered, "always so much to do." His voice trailed off as he looked out of the window, his gaze resting on the landscape, the lake and the hills beyond, swirling snowflakes adding to the already deep blanket of white.

"Does it snow much in Ireland?" he asked his companion.

"Dunno," Roberto said, 'but they have mountains and lakes, too, I know that much."

"No wine though, I don't think they can make wine."

"Whiskey, they make that," Roberto confirmed.

Franco pulled his mouth down in distaste.

"We could send them some wine," Roberto said, trying to read his boss' face.

"Or take some." Franco gave a slow smile.

"For the kid?" Roberto queried.

"No, stupido, for the grown-ups. I know exactly what I'm gonna buy the boy, a pony, a beautifully bred, well-mannered pony. The Irish breed great horses."

"Ah," Roberto nodded. "But ain't he a bit young?"

"Never too young to get on a horse, you should know that," Franco reminded him, they had both ridden all their lives, sitting beside their fathers as they inspected the fields and vineyards on horseback, in the old country.

"Yeah, but a horse, you ain't gonna let anyone else choose him a horse, you'd have to do it personal, and I know horseflesh better than you, you probably need someone like me with you." Roberto poked the logs on the fire. "And you ain't gonna be able to ship a horse in time for Christmas … unless you bought it in Ireland."

Franco finished his drink and went to the phone on his desk.

"How long will it take you to pack?"

Roberto shrugged. Franco always had bags packed and ready to go, any country, any climate, any time.

"We leave in half an hour," Franco told him, not waiting for an answer.

John F Kennedy airport was packed full of people waiting and wailing. Wailing because flights were cancelled, and with the forecast promising even more icy blizzards to come, there was little likelihood the majority would reach their destination in time for the holidays. They sat on suitcases, staring blankly at screens, perched cautiously on sofas, unsure whether to stay or cut their losses and battle back from whence they had come. Those arguing with airline staff were given short shrift. No one was in a position to be granted special treatment. The weather was the weather, end of.

Larry Leeson was perplexed, his normal condition at airports, but today he was even more stressed and anxious than usual. He had not checked in for his flight to Los Angeles, hoping the longer he left it, the more chance there was it would be cancelled, and he would have a legitimate reason to telephone Lena and explain why he could not come. He sat in the VIP lounge, flicking through a magazine with one hand, tapping the armrest of his chair with the other. There was a flurry at the doorway, some people came in, others went out. Larry looked up. Two men he thought vaguely familiar were at the refreshment counter.

"You want somethin' to eat?" he heard one ask the other.

"Nah, just coffee is good," came the reply.

Larry dropped the magazine. The voice was unmistakable, it was the heavy huskiness of Franco Rossini; he would recognise that commanding timbre anywhere. Larry immediately stood up, smoothed his hair, straightened the seam of his pants; Mr Rossini had been at his apartment only the other evening, but had still been unsure if he was flying to Los Angeles for the holiday. It would appear he had finally decided. Now Larry had a big problem. Did he grab his things and disappear back out into the airport, dissolving quickly into the crowd, or should he greet the great man, check in on the flight and travel with him, to somewhere he did not want to go, to spend time with people he did not even want to see. Too late. Roberto had spotted him.

"Hey, Larry, hey over here. Franco, look who it is?" The man waved and Larry had no choice but to join them. Franco looked mildly surprised as he kissed Larry on both cheeks.

"Nightmare, ain't it?" Larry said. "Flights cancelled all over the place." He had one eye trained on the monitor, still hoping.

"Where you headed?" Roberto asked.

"Same as you, I guess," Larry said, flatly.

"You going to Ireland?" Roberto widened his eyes.

"*You're* going to Ireland?" Larry was stunned. "Are you serious?"

"Change of plan," Franco said.

"Are you going to Innishmahon? To see Ryan and Joey?" Larry could not believe it.

"Hey, why not? The holidays, a good time to see family, catch up." Franco said evenly, but his eyes had lit up.

"Oh, how I envy you," Larry replied with feeling, "do they know?"

"Nah, a surprise visit only," Franco told him, enjoying the effect the news was having.

"Where are you headed then?" Roberto asked him.

"LA, Lena's house party. I thought maybe the flight would be cancelled, but not yet, anyways."

Franco eyed him over his coffee cup.

"Not keen?"

"Ah, you know me, not mad about LA." Larry hated the place.

"You crazy? Sunshine, parties, beautiful women?" Roberto nudged him.

Larry pulled a tight smile. "I'd change places with you in a blink of an eye," he said.

They were quiet for a minute.

"You been to Ireland before, haven't you?" Franco asked him.

"Yeah, a couple of times, you remember?" Larry had been twice. The first time to haul Ryan out of his 'spiritual home' because he had landed the role of *Thomas Bentley,* superspy. The second to explain to Ryan he had no choice but fulfil his movie contract, having just resigned live on a TV chat show in front of millions of viewers. That trip had ended badly though. Larry had offered to escort Franco's wayward niece, the actress Angelique de Marcos, back to the USA, but failed in his duty of care because she went into a coma and tragically died during the flight. Just thinking about it made Larry's armpits prickle with panic.

"Oh yes." Franco's eyes were hard. "I remember, I will never forget." Larry swallowed. From that day to this, they had never discussed it, a ghost in the corner of the room, whenever they were together. He felt a clamp tighten around his head. Franco was gazing at him, deep in thought. "Wanna swop with Roberto here? I could use some local knowledge, and he said it himself, he prefers sunshine and beautiful women."

Larry let the words hang in the air. He opened and closed his mouth.

"Come on, it'll be fun. You can tell me all about it on the airplane. Where to stay, what to eat, what d'ya say?" Franco was clearly warming to the idea. Roberto was, too. New York was freezing, a bit of sunshine warming his bones looked increasingly appealing.

"But ... but how would we do it, who would make the arrangements?" Larry asked, taking a Kleenex from his pocket, wiping non-existent perspiration from his brow. Mimi handled all this stuff. Franco's warm, brown eyes glittered with merriment.

"Easy, we go to the desk, substitute Roberto for you on your flight, and you for Roberto on mine." Franco may be a world-famous movie producer, but he was hands on, he got things done. He had his arms around both men. They started walking towards a very pretty airline supervisor. She knew exactly who Franco Rossini was, she was already willing to do everything she could to help.

"What about Lena?" Larry asked, plaintively.

"No problem. Roberto will explain we needed to see Ryan, chat through a few issues. I wanted to see the kid, it made sense to kill two birds." Sounded perfectly reasonable, especially coming from Franco's lips.

"Hey, what about the horse? You need me for the horse?" Roberto felt duty-bound to remind his friend.

"Nah, we'll be fine. Larry can help me with that, he's been to Ireland two times, practically a native, eh Larry?" Franco said, patting Larry on the back. Larry could feel the blood drain from his face, he was terrified of horses.

"Whatever you say, Mr Rossini. I'll do what I can."

"Could you do one thing?" the older man asked, turning to look Larry in the eye.

"Of course," Larry replied.

"Call me Franco."

"Mr Rossini, sir," the pretty supervisor gave her most sparkling smile, "you're in luck, both flights are cleared and ready for boarding." She handed over the paperwork. "You and Mr Leeson to Shannon, and you sir, to Los Angeles," she told Roberto. "They're among the first flights to take off today, so all good to go. Have a pleasant journey, gentlemen."

Chapter Eleven – The Magi

Joyce MacReady always decorated the house sumptuously for Christmas. A well-heeled spinster of a certain age, she loved the opportunity to bring out the *Waterford* crystal, polish the best silver and twist wreaths of berry-covered greenery around gleaming woodwork. Not, for her the tinsel and tat some others might favour, but fine Irish linen, good quality porcelain and only the very best of food and drink would grace her elegant Georgian dining table, lovingly crafted around the time the substantial and beautifully kept house was built.

As one of the most exclusive country guesthouses in the area, she had a couple of regulars to stay for the holidays, giving her enough reason to maintain standards, and enough revenue to make it worthwhile. Her two extra and unexpected guests, therefore, were not only a bonus, but a delight. One, the very pleasant and hugely successful, New York theatrical agent, Larry Leeson, the other, and this was a coup, the world renowned movie mogul, Franco Rossini. Joyce was absolutely thrilled to receive the call from Larry at Knock Airport, asking if she had any vacancies and was then totally frustrated that she had not been able to get through to her sister, the postmistress on Innishmahon, to tell her all about it.

It was Saint Stephen's Day morning, and breakfast was a leisurely affair, presented in time-honoured tradition in glass and silver dishes on the rosewood sideboard in the dining room. Guests could help themselves, before taking coffee and newspapers into the morning room, where the drapes were drawn back to give a glorious view of the mountains, and a fire of peat was laid waiting to be lit.

Joyce had taken extra care this morning, rolling her fine red hair, streaked with silver, into a French pleat and fixing it with a tortoiseshell comb. She inspected the good plaid skirt and gold cashmere cardigan before she put them on, finishing her ensemble with her best pearls. She made to leave her dressing room, and then darting back, dabbed *Chanel No 5* behind both ears. Well, if it was good enough for *Marilyn Monroe?*

Larry was chatting amicably with Joyce's other guests at the breakfast table. The men stood as she entered the room.

"Sit, sit, don't let me disturb you." She smiled warmly at them all. Her usual holiday guests comprised a smart, elderly couple from Dublin, he a retired judge, she formerly a surgeon; two widowed sisters from London, whose father, an Irish playwright, had been brought up in the next village, and an aging bachelor of indeterminable background, except to say he was widely travelled and had been a very personal assistant to a member of the British aristocracy. He was a particular favourite, as the more port he downed, the racier his tales of the swinging sixties became. Joyce always stayed up late into the night when he started storytelling, ensuring he erred on the side of discretion, bearing in mind with whom her other guests might be acquainted. Indeed, some of them might even know people in the media, heaven forfend!

The hostess took her seat beside Larry.

"No sign of Mr Rossini?" she queried, assuming the movie producer would not be an early riser. "Shall I send him up a tray?"

Larry was slathering a piece of toasted soda bread with Joyce's homemade thick-cut whiskey marmalade. Despite protestations of martyrdom to his stomach, his appetite always appeared to be enjoying a bout of robustness whenever he was at Joyce's table.

"No need, he was up early. I imagine he's out, taking a stroll, enjoying the view." Larry seemed far more relaxed than he had been on any of the other occasions Joyce had met him. Maybe having a travelling companion suited him better, or maybe the laid-back Irish lifestyle was beginning to rub off, just a little.

"So different from New York," Joyce said.

"Indeed, although he's not often in the city. He has a farm and vineyards upstate, but with so much business handled in LA, he's rarely there, either," Larry confirmed.

Joyce was surprised. She would never have guessed the movie producer was also a farmer, a wine maker, too, it appeared, how interesting. They had spoken only briefly at supper the previous evening, both men exhausted from the journey and extremely lucky to make it at all; arriving from Shannon on the last connection.

Joyce scanned the table, making sure her guests were replete. The hunt met at eleven, Joyce always attended, enjoying a catch up with neighbours before hounds set off. Her guests often went with her, the spectacle and a glass of damson gin with the locals, part of the charm of the place. It had been many years since she had ridden to hounds, but her retired hunters lived in the lap of luxury close by, and she kept a working pony and trap to ferry guests to and from the lake for picnics in the summer. She was a traditional countrywoman, after all.

Joyce found Franco in the stables chatting to one of the lads who came to help when he was home on holiday from agricultural college. The visitor was examining her pride and joy, a dark bay thoroughbred cross; a fine gelding who stood over sixteen hands and had won many rosettes in his day. Franco was running his hands along his back, stroking his gleaming, ebony flanks. The horse munched on his hay net, undisturbed by the stranger in his box, always a good sign.

"He must know there's a connection," Joyce said, surprising them. The horse snickered at the sound of her voice.

"How come?" Franco asked.

"He, too, has an Italian name, Scala Milan, breeder was an opera fan from Naas." She took a mint from her pocket, giving it to Franco to give to the horse.

"He certainly is a black beauty. How old?"

"In his twenties now, but a fantastic all-rounder in his day. Do you ride, Mr Rossini?" Joyce asked.

"Franco, please, if I may call you Joyce?"

"Of course," she fluttered, even a simple question in his rich, chocolate voice sounded like flirtation.

"Did quite a bit in my younger days, still keep a few horses, but only Roberto, my farm manager, rides out regularly. They are still the best mode of transport in certain areas."

Joyce nodded. "Indeed, if the mount is sure-footed and you ride with confidence, you can go anywhere." She kissed the horse's velvet muzzle; he seemed used to being showered with affection. "We're going to the Meet, the local hunt; not terribly smart, but what they lack in glamour, they make up for in enthusiasm. Will you join us?"

His face broke into a broad grin.

"I would love to, in fact I'm in the market for a good pony, perhaps you could help me?"

Joyce gave him a quizzical look; the penny dropped.

"For the little boy? Of course, a perfect gift, a great idea, get him in the saddle as soon as possible. You know, Father Gregory over on the island is a fine horseman. He'd love to take a youngster under his wing. Sure, he'd have the young lad galloping along the beach in no time."

"Sounds perfect. I wouldn't mind that, myself," he told her, patting Scala farewell. Franco took Joyce's arm as they strolled back to the house. What was the tallest mountain called? Could you fish in the lake? What did the Celtic cross on the lane mean? He was totally fascinated by the place.

"A lot like my homeland in many ways," Franco said, as they headed back to the house where vehicles were waiting to take them to the Meet. "Beautiful countryside, traditions, customs, it's good to hold onto the past."

"In some ways," Joyce said, thinking of her brother Pat, serving a long sentence for his part in a gunrunning escapade, supporting a breakaway gang of misguided freedom fighters. "But it's best to live in the present and let the future unfurl in its own time. No point clinging to what's gone, and rushing to embrace what might not happen at all."

Franco stopped and looked at her. If the accent had been different, he could have sworn those very words were spoken by his late wife Sophia; she always gave him a good hefty dose of reality when his romantic soul took flight.

"You don't agree?" Joyce hoped she had not offended her VIP guest.

"I do, I do," Franco squeezed her arm, "you just reminded me of someone. Someone beloved, who is no longer with us."

"I'm so sorry," Joyce said.

"Don't be, dear lady, made me feel even more at home. Now, where are we going? Another one of your unpronounceable places, no doubt. Bring it on," he laughed, watching her bustle efficiently away to check all was in order for their jaunt.

Although the reports claimed the weather was improving, Joyce grew concerned, she had still not spoken to her sister on Innishmahon. She checked with Larry if he had managed to contact Ryan and let him know that both his agent and his boss were on their way. Larry had just shrugged, saying between Ryan's infrequent use of his cell phone and the island's intermittent communications, connecting was always a bit hit and miss. He had left a voice mail just before boarding at JFK, and despite trying to call since landing, had heard nothing.

It was while she was in the kitchen, supervising lunch – cold cuts of meat with cider chutney, broccoli and blue cheese soup – that the shrill ring of the telephone cut through the pleasing hubbub of guests discussing the morning's events over sherry in the drawing room.

"Hello, hello, is that you, Joyce? Can you hear me?" her sister trilled down the line.

"Thank God." Joyce, tea towel in hand, clamped her fist to her chest. "We've been worried sick. Are you okay? How bad is it?"

"Ah, could have been a lot worse. A bit of a tidal wave seemed to swing round from Widow's Peak down into the harbour. One of the building cranes smashed the new marina wall and the sea burst through into the main street. We'd warning, and evacuated, but it was very sudden and thank goodness all is calm this morning, it seems to have passed."

"Dear Lord." Joyce blessed herself. "Any losses, much damage?"

"So far only livestock, though that's bad enough. I had to leave the Post Office though."

"Oh no." Joyce knew then how serious the situation was. Kathleen would never leave her post.

"Not before I delivered every last envelope. I've no idea yet how much damage there is there."

Joyce heard her sister take a large slurp of something. She automatically checked her watch, then reprimanded herself, she needed to cut Kathleen a bit of slack, considering what she had been through. It was Christmas, after all. She heard Franco's deep brown laugh echo into the hall.

"I have news," Joyce whispered into the handset, not sure if she should be spilling the beans. "Two visitors heading over to you."

"Oh." Kathleen was unfazed. Joyce ran a guesthouse, after all. "I'm not sure the ferry's back on yet, but Dermot has his boat in the water. I know, because he picked the vet up this morning."

"Well," Joyce had taken the phone into the morning room, "you'll be delighted to see one of them and very surprised to meet the other."

"Will I? Why's that, then?" Kathleen usually loved surprises, but only when she was instigating them. Besides, Joyce's idea of a surprise and her own were very different.

"Larry Leeson is here, and guess who's with him?"

"No way, Larry? How exciting." Kathleen adored Larry, in fact there had even been a hint of romance between them, and love might have bloomed, if Brian had not made such a dramatic reappearance back into her life recently. "What's wrong? Larry only turns up when something's wrong. And who's with him, not Lena? Now that is trouble."

"Calm yourself, Kathleen," the elder sister said, softly. "Everything's grand. No, not Lena, Mr Rossini, himself."

"What?" Kathleen barked. "The movie producer?"

"One and the very same." Joyce was enjoying this, she really had one over on her sibling this time.

"No one's mentioned they're coming, does anyone know? Is it meant to be a surprise?" Kathleen was both thrilled and put out. Why had Larry not been in touch; she thought they were close? Why no news of this from Ryan, or Marianne, her own daughter?

"I think it was a sudden decision to come," Joyce said, reading her mind. "Anyway, how would you have heard, you've been incommunicado over there?"

News that two of the most dominant personalities in his life were on their way to disturb his peace had just filtered through to Ryan. He was enjoying a leisurely morning at home with the family, padding around in bare feet and jog pants, serving coffee and juice to Marianne and Joey, who were building a fortress out of *Lego* on the kitchen table. It was to take pride of place in the middle of the model railway now circumnavigating the conservatory. He was delivering sausage and tomato sandwiches to the 'construction' team, when the shrill ring of the landline broke through the cosy calm. It was Dermot.

"What are you up to today?" he asked, sounding even more jaunty than usual.

"Just chilling, why? Is there a problem, need a hand with anything?" Ryan's offer of help was genuine, but reluctant. He longed for a day holed up in the cottage with his little gang. There was plenty of work to be done after the storm, he knew that, but he was hoping they would stick to the plan they had agreed, recharging their own batteries on Saint Stephen's Day, to regroup the day after and get out and about and inspect the damage.

"Expecting anyone?" Dermot asked, ignoring Ryan's questions. "Because we have visitors coming and they're friends of yours."

"Really?" Ryan relaxed, guessing a couple of fans had made it across to the island and were badgering Dermot to tell them where the famous movie star lived. That would really get on Dermot's nerves. As much as he loved Ryan, sometimes he loathed him too.

"Word has it a couple of Americans are staying with Joyce MacReady, on their way to visit for the rest of the holidays."

Ryan sighed. "Stop trying to be tantalising, Dermot, you always were a hopeless actor, who are these mysterious Americans then?"

"Only Larry Leeson and the top man, Franco Rossini," Dermot announced.

Ryan laughed. "That's not even funny, you trying to wind me up?"

"Nope, all true. A fella who does the airport run for a taxi firm told me. Dropped them off yesterday evening. Mr Rossini said they were visiting family here, staying a while. I guessed you didn't know." Ryan rarely used his cell phone, the signal was poor on the island and the battery was usually flat. Besides, one of the main reasons he had come back to the island was because it was so remote, cut off from all the pace and pressure that had been driving him to distraction, pushing him towards the decision to leave it all behind forever. Fate seemed to have other ideas, for now, anyway.

"Shit, that sounds like trouble," he told Dermot. "How are they going to get here? Is the ferry back on?"

"No, not yet, I can pick them up." Dermot's boat was always gleaming, primed and ready to go.

"Thanks," Ryan said, brain starting to whir. He rubbed his eyes, time to focus. "Okay, I'll ring Joyce, speak to them, see what's going on and call you back."

"No worries, not doing anything in particular today," Dermot replied. He was going to take a stroll down to Maguire's and see how Erin was. He was vaguely optimistic, now the festival she so despised, was over, she might be in a better, more approachable frame of mind. He remembered desperately wanting to kiss her last night. She looked so lonely, so fragile. Dermot gave himself a shake. This was Erin he was fantasising about, the rabid, she-bitch from hell when the mood took her. Dermot wondered if he was just desperate, full stop.

Only hours later, Marianne could not believe Weathervane was full again, and this time her guests had travelled much further afield than she could have imagined. Within minutes of arriving, one of the world's most famous movie producers, together with his leading man, were on their knees, shouting instructions at each other across the rattle of the model railway, as it whizzed around the room.

Larry was catching up on all the news over coffee with Dermot, when the door burst open and Kathleen, in a blur of Ocelot, swept in to kiss him lusciously on both cheeks, *Revlon's Tangerine Dream*, the redoubtable evidence of her visitation.

"Larry Leeson, if you ever do that to me again, I swear I'll cut you out of my Will," she joked, eyes glittering at the sight of him. Larry raised an eyebrow at her, then hugged her right back. He explained how he had been going to LA to visit his sister, to help host her glamorous party, when he had accidently ran into Franco at the airport, who was not going to LA at all, but to Ireland. The proposal to come to Innishmahon came out of the blue, and without giving it too much thought, he changed flights, and here they were.

"I believe you made Larry an offer he couldn't refuse?" Kathleen smiled at Franco under her eyelashes, as she offered him one of her special Martinis. She had brought the drinks ready-mixed in a cocktail shaker from the pub, explaining to Brian, as she measured out the concoction, *how could you have a couple of native New Yorkers in the place and not serve proper drinks?*

Franco checked his watch.

"I haven't caught up with the time zone. Tell me, pretty lady, is the sun over the yardarm yet?" He took the drink from her, his fingers lingering for just half a second on hers.

"Well, it is somewhere!" she declared, eyeballing him right back.

Marianne had to put her hand over her mouth for fear she would burst out laughing. Despite the fact her mother had married the love of her life only earlier that month, she was flirting outrageously with the men.

"Martinis?" Ryan asked, joining them. He had just put Joey down for his afternoon nap, although the little boy was far too excited to sleep. Rossini told him to call him Papa Franco, and that very soon he was going to give Joey a huge surprise, one he would treasure for many years.

Marianne had opened the doors to the garden. Franco was standing on the little stone terrace, looking out across the lawn and the lane towards the sea. Ryan went to join him. Franco indicated the ancient cane chairs and taking their drinks, they went to sit together.

"You don't seem surprised to see me," Franco said, pulling a pack of cigarettes out of his pocket. Ryan slid him a smile.

"I knew I'd see you soon, just wasn't sure where." He took a cigarette and waited till his boss lit it with his slim gold lighter. They smoked in companionable silence.

"I saw the video … you on the roof, Scott hauling you onto the helicopter," Franco said. "Big risk, thought you'd grown out of pranks like that, especially now, with the boy."

Ryan did not reply. He knew there was more to come.

"You did good at the press conference, though. I saw that too. Shame Saggito didn't make an appearance, I hear he was at the party, very entertaining by all accounts." Franco took a drag of his cigarette. "He wouldn't necessarily

144

be someone you would choose to work with, but you know why I had to bring him in, don't you?"

Ryan was not sure how much Franco knew, probably everything.

"I know you failed the medical, Ryan. I have to be advised about stuff like that. Do we know what the problem is yet? Have you been for tests?"

Ryan looked briefly behind, making sure no one else was in earshot.

"It'll be fine, it's just a blip, they're not even sure they can see anything. It could just be a fault with the scan."

"Have you been for tests?" Franco asked again.

"Yes, I was referred to a consultant in Dublin, I'll know soon enough."

"You haven't mentioned this to anyone?"

"What's the point, it's nothing, a mistake."

"And if it isn't? If it's life threatening … have you even considered that possibility?" Franco kept his tone even, but his eyes were boring into Ryan's.

"Look, I'm fine, I'll make the sodding movie and we can move on, okay? Saggito's an arse, but I'll work with him, and no more pranks, I promise no more pranks. Heaven forbid we upset the insurance company." Ryan dropped his cigarette to the ground and crushed it out.

"Hey, forget about them." Franco laughed as they stood to walk back to the house. He placed an arm around Ryan's shoulders. "Like I could ever get insurance for you, anyways?!"

"We're going to join Brian in Maguire's for an early supper," Marianne explained to Ryan as he closed the doors,

"Larry and Mr Rossini are staying there. *Joyce?*" Joyce was asleep in the armchair in front of the fire.

"Not surprised, fantastic woman, works her fingers to the bone in that beautiful house of hers," Franco said.

"She does," agreed Kathleen, "and we so rarely see each other. Let's make her stay, at least one evening, surely her girls can take care of things there for one night?"

Joyce opened an eye.

"I heard that," she said, smiling. "And yes, they can. I'll stay with you, Kathleen."

"Of course." Her sister beamed. "I'm in Maguire's too don't forget, plenty of room for everyone."

"It's hard to get used to you as Mrs Maguire," Larry said, sipping his drink, now satisfied he had polished the glass to his liking.

"I'm still Miss MacReady, the postmistress, to many. I'm only temporary at the pub. We need to assess the storm damage at the Post Office urgently though, the service must not be interrupted, whatever the circumstances." She gave Dermot and Ryan a steely look, hoping they understood where their priorities lay.

"Big job in a small community like this," Franco confirmed, and Kathleen batted her eyelids in appreciation of the understanding of the great man. "You're a pillar of the community, Signore." He raised his glass. "As is your sister, of hers." He nodded at Joyce, also enjoying an early cocktail. "Glorious, indomitable, and I might add, stunningly attractive matriarchs, salut."

Ryan shrugged at Dermot. The women, Marianne included, were gazing at the smallish, slightly rotund, middle-aged man in unabashed awe.

"A masterclass," Ryan whispered to his chum. "These Italians, we've no chance."

Chapter Twelve – The Gift Horse

The weather between Christmas and New Year was unseasonably pleasant on Innishmahon and whilst little could be done in terms of repairs, work could be assessed and plans drawn up; Marianne was very good at that sort of thing. The island had been here before and the team who had worked together to get things moving, seemed to fall naturally into place, meeting in Maguire's to discuss priorities and allocate tasks.

Father Gregory took the chair. Dermot, relatively new to the island, and destined to be the coxswain of the Lifeboat when it was delivered later that spring, was appointed operations co-ordinator. Dermot liked a title, it helped people know their place and who they were dealing with. Brian was happy to be supportive, but the previous landlord had been very short of cash, and reinvesting in the pub had not been a priority. With many essentials in dire need of attention, including the electrics and the roof, Brian's focus was required elsewhere.

"No wonder we're plunged into darkness every time there's the slightest blip in the weather," Brian told Kathleen, "this place hasn't been touched since the nineteen sixties, the wiring looks like a map of the *London Underground*!" She carried on writing in her notebook. "I think we'll need a team of builders here for the next few years, with all the work that's needed." No response. "Kathleen, are you listening to me?"

She looked at him over her glasses. "Sorry, I was just sorting out the schedules for the Post Office. I can work from the shop front, that's no problem. I'll need a new kitchen though, and some of my loveliest treasures are beyond saving, but if that's the worst of it, so be it. I often believe when things are broken or destroyed, it's for a reason, making way for something better or taking a bad vibe with it."

Brian sighed. "You have a perfectly good kitchen here, love."

"Ah, Brian, it's a pub kitchen, has to be disinfected within an inch of its life, daily, hardly the kitchen of a woman of style and substance." She gave him a beguiling smile. "No, I've great plans for the Post Office, good reason to make changes."

"But Kathleen, we live here." Brian was growing tired of telling his wife she belonged at his side.

"Sure, all this is ages off," she tapped the pad with her pen, "things will work out for the best, I'm sure of it. Now, what's happening with our guests today, I wonder? Dermot was talking about a fishing trip and Father Gregory wants to take Franco to see some ponies for Joey. Isn't it great they're staying until the New Year? I can't believe how Franco has taken to the place, he absolutely loves it, and Joyce seems quite taken with him, most unusual, she's promised to come back and celebrate New Year with us. Now, that is a first." She continued speaking, but Brian was no longer in the kitchen, he was up a ladder on the landing, peering through the loft hatch. He could see bright blue sky through the roof in places.

The millionaire movie mogul sat companionably next to
Sean Grogan in the back of Father Gregory's ancient truck.
The seat next to the priest had been ripped out by the
previous owner to accommodate the transport of livestock,
usually a sheep or a couple of lambs. It had never been
reinstated, as the priest found the space quite useful for what
he called his Emergency Sacristy Kit, comprising crucifix,
blessed water and the Holy Sacrament, necessary for giving
the Last Rites, urgent baptisms or a quick Mass. Gregory
was a priest of our times.

"Know a bit about horses, my friend?" Franco asked.
Sean, his battered tweed cap pulled down over his eyes, was
glaring grumpily at the glorious landscape, as they climbed
higher, leaving a golden bay and swirling, sparkling sea
below.

"Enough," he replied.

"Do you breed them?" Franco tried.

"No way, I leave that to the other eejits!" Sean said.

"He's more of a whisperer," the priest called back
over the rattle of the truck, grinding upwards along the
potholed mountain road.

"Can you learn how to do that, or is it a gift?" Franco
was genuinely fascinated. Sean took the match he was
chewing out of his mouth.

"Can't go to college for it, anyway," Sean said.

"And what do you think the horse we're going to see
will tell you?" Franco asked. Sean pushed his cap back and
looked the man up and down. Smart coat, silk scarf, waxed
hat and a decent pair of boots. He did not think the foreigner

150

a fool, but he did think he was a bit too foreign to be American.

"Sure it mightn't spake to me at all," was all Sean said, and pulled his cap back down.

Gregory was hauling on the wheel as he swung into a well-kept driveway lined with trees, sweeping down to a pretty cream cottage and large stable block just visible behind. They passed a sign, The Croghan Stud – An IHS approved equestrian establishment.

"Here we are," announced the priest, "Lily O'Brien's place. She keeps the best bloodstock on the island, in the whole area actually. I've told her what you're looking for, she has two or three for us to see. Don't worry, she won't let you buy anything that's not right; more than her reputation's worth."

"Sounds good," Franco said.

Sean slid out and stood beside him. "She's a horse dealer, just remember that," he hissed, as one of the most attractive women Franco Rossini had ever seen, appeared at the cottage door. Tall, with long slim legs, clad in pale blue jodhpurs, she was wearing a check shirt and leather gilet zipped up high to her throat, but the layers could not disguise her curves. She smiled and waved with one hand, twisting a pile of golden curls up into a hat with the other, as she walked towards them.

"I'd close your mouth if I were you," Sean advised the visitor, barely hiding his grin.

Three hours later, a deal had been struck. Sitting in Lily's dove-grey kitchen, drinking fresh coffee from a pot perched on the *Aga*, Franco had bought not one horse but two. A pony for Joey and a hunter for himself. Sean was keen on the pony; she was kind and sensible, old enough to have experience, young enough to have plenty of quality life left. The hunter he was less sure about. Good-looking alright, and at the peak of fitness, but there was something or maybe nothing.

"This fella is a bit closed off. Not keen to open up. Maybe a bit shy, timid. He's sharp anyway," was Sean's summing up of the beast.

But Franco was as smitten with the horse as he was with Lily, who Franco noticed, despite her youthful physique, had soft crinkles beneath her corn-flower blue eyes, and silver through the golden curls. She had remained totally relaxed throughout the whole process; allowing the animals to be thoroughly inspected, tacked up and ridden by a young stable lad, putting both horses effortlessly through their paces, before popping them over a couple of jumps to conclude an impressive display.

"Please don't feel obliged to make any sort of decision right now," Lily said, in a light Tipperary lilt. "Have a think, come back and sit on them yourself, you're a horseman, aren't you, Mr Rossini?"

Franco smiled. "Only, how you say, a bit of a hacker, nothing fancy, no rosettes, anyway."

"Mr Rossini is after the pony for his grandnephew. I'm hoping he's buying the hunter for me," laughed Gregory, sampling a slice of Lily's delicious porter cake. Franco shot him a look. That was not a bad idea. Gregory could keep the horse fit and happy, and Franco could come and ride out with the boy whenever he visited. Maybe even have a gallop along the beach. How many years was it since he had done that, back in his native Tuscany, when he, too, was only a boy?

"If you would take care of them for me, and I could ride whenever I'm here, that would be good. I'd be very happy with that arrangement," Franco told the priest.

"Are you serious?" Gregory beamed, "that would be amazing, count me in!"

"You'd have to teach the boy how to ride," Franco insisted.

"I could help there," Lily said, standing at the window, watching as the horses grazed contentedly in the paddock at the front of the cottage. "Perhaps we could ride out together one day, there's some spectacular hacks around the island," she said, to no one in particular.

As the truck waddled through the gateway and onto the road leading back to town, Franco allowed himself a soft, "mamma mia!"

Father Gregory nodded. "I know, two fabulous horses, what a fantastic deal."

"I meant her, one of the most beautiful women I've ever seen," Franco said.

"Do you not know her?" Gregory asked. "She was one of those supermodels, international catwalk stuff. Lilly La Salle, I think was her professional name, did all the haute couture stuff in Paris and the like."

"Is she married?" Franco asked.

"A widow, sadly. He was a lovely guy, much older than her," the priest confirmed.

"How did he die?"

"Heart attack. The air ambulance didn't make it in time, who knows if they could have helped. It was a good few years ago now." Gregory eyed Sean through the rear-view mirror, expecting him to comment. Lily was known locally as *The Merry Widow* but Sean looked distracted and said nothing.

"Has she family?" Franco pressed.

"No, they didn't have children. She runs the place pretty much on her own, takes youngsters from the agricultural college during the holidays, sells horses, breeds terriers. I think she was left very well off, but cash flow, you know how it is?"

"I've heard she's had a special wardrobe built, kept at a certain temperature, full of furs. A proper *Cruella de Vil* is what she is!" Sean finally interjected.

Gregory laughed. "She's a head-turner alright, but I've always found her fair, good to do business with," he confirmed.

"And no partner?" Franco found it hard to believe.

"She has friends come to stay from time to time, but no one special I don't think."

They were silent for a while.

"Do you think she'd come and have dinner with us on New Year's Eve, the meal Brian and Kathleen are hosting? Would it be okay to invite her?" Franco asked.

"I'm sure she'll come," Sean interrupted, "sure, you're a customer, aren't you? Doesn't miss a trick, that one."

"You're not enamoured?" Franco said.

"Leave that sort of nonsense to the rest of you," Sean gave him a squinty look, "but she's a bit like the horse she's selling … *sharp*." He tapped his nose with his forefinger. "If you take my meaning."

Franco was delighted when Lily O'Brien said she would come as his guest to Maguire's New Year's Eve party, unaware this would not be everyone's reaction.

"Be straight with me now, Larry, what are you really doing there?" Lena's voice was crystal clear across the line, all the way from Los Angeles. Larry was in the hall in May cottage, the little house he rented last time he stayed on the island. He looked round appreciatively, sunny yellow walls, brightly coloured rugs on the stone-flagged floor. In total contrast to the cool, blonde penthouse he called home in New York, yet he liked it, it felt familiar, homely.

"Honestly, Lena, there ain't nothing wrong. Everything's fine, better than fine, good even," he told her. "We've had a couple of meetings with Ryan, gone over the schedules, made a few changes, but everything's on track, gearing up to start filming in the spring, lots to do, a busy time, all good," Larry watched himself in the mirror by the door, bright eyes, colour to his cheeks, and despite eating extremely well since arriving in Ireland, he looked like he had lost weight. He turned sideways. He definitely had.

"How did the holidays go? Everything ok with you?" Larry felt obliged to ask, not really in the mood for one of Lena's lengthy, blow-by-blow accounts of her Hollywood soiree; who was there; which designer they were wearing; diet they were on; starlet they were sleeping with. Besides, it was New Year's Eve, he had promised Kathleen he would play tonight. Larry did a very passable turn on the piano and was planning a medley of *Barry Manilow*, with a sprinkling of *Randy Edelman*. He needed to practise.

Lena launched into her diatribe which required from him only the occasional, "Really?" "You don't say?" and "that's outrageous!" to keep her happy. Larry spied Kathleen tottering up the path towards the cottage, and beckoned her in.

"Steven was here, breaking hearts as usual, he is such a good-looking boy. I think he'll be perfect in the *Thomas Bentley* role, better than Ryan even," Lena was now saying.

Larry was not having that. He re-engaged his brain and took up the mantle for his long-time client.

"Nah, I can't see that. He ain't got Ryan's charm. I mean O'Gorman can be a pain in the ass in real life, but he's charismatic on screen, you gotta give him that."

Lena laughed. She liked Ryan but he was unpredictable. She was at the stage in her career where she wanted a stable of manageable stars, popular household names, earning her good, steady fees.

"Still a loose cannon," she said.

"And you think Saggito ain't? He can be wilder than Ryan ever was. Leaving that one to you, sis," he told her.

"Steven's turned over a new leaf, he's taking his career seriously, he'll make us all proud."

"Just so long as he makes us money," Larry responded, indicating to Kathleen they were nearing the end of the call.

"He had a really cool English guy with him, a writer. Said he knew you, was real disappointed you and Mr Rossini weren't here. He's working on a series of articles about the franchise, all lined up for syndication," Lena went on.

"Good PR," Larry agreed. "Name?"

"Hmm, Paul, Paul something, been out in South America for a while, award-winning, investigative stuff, that kinda thing."

Larry gripped the receiver.

"Not Paul Osborne?"

"Er, yeah, think so, yeah that was it," Lena replied.

Kathleen had been reapplying her lipstick; she stopped, turning slowly to face Larry, who was staring at the phone as if it had just bitten him.

"He's the bastard who splashed Ryan and Marianne all over the press when they first got together. Caused a lot of trouble. Remember?" Larry's voice was rising.

"Of course … yes … now I do remember. It all worked out in the end though. I got a great deal for the exclusive of Ryan and Angelique's wedding. Where would we have been without that at the time? Needed the money to pay the mad bitch off." Lena was cross, she hated being caught on the back foot.

"Hey, listen I gotta go," Larry told her. "Just be careful, no 'off the record' stuff with that guy. He ain't trustworthy, okay?"

"You don't have to tell me! Anyway, I'm here working my ass off, entertaining business contacts, while you're on vacation, so butt out," Lena barked down the line.

"Okay, okay, just saying."

"Yeah, anyway Happy New Year's," Lena said.

"And to you too," Larry bit back, and dropped the handset back in its cradle. Kathleen was leaning against the door, arms folded.

"Bad penny, eh?" she asked. Larry nodded. "I saw an article he wrote about *Thomas Bentley* when Brian and I were in Dublin. I meant to tell Marianne about it, but with everything going on, it slipped my mind. What's he up to? Causing trouble as usual?"

Larry took his coat off the hanger.

"Not sure. He's best buddies with Steve Saggito, you know, the actor taking over Ryan's role. Maybe he's genuine, and he is just working on a series of articles about the franchise." He tied his scarf tightly.

"Always hoping some stardust will rub off on him, seems to me," Kathleen said, fixing Larry's collar. "Not above a bit of blackmail, either, I recall." Her sharp eyes scanned Larry's face, checking to see how worried he really was.

Larry shrugged. "Very fond of Marianne, wasn't he? That should count for something." He opened the door. Kathleen pulled on her crimson evening gloves.

"Very fond of digging up dirt, too, if I remember correctly," she said, lips pursed.

Larry shuddered on the doorstep. It was colder today, the wind had turned bitter. He put his arm around Kathleen as they walked the short distance to Maguire's. She felt good beside him. He pushed the thought away.

Chapter Thirteen – Secrets Below Stairs

Kathleen passed Erin a glass of exotic punch. Erin put it back on the table. Kathleen's eyes followed her actions.

"Will you have a glass of wine instead?" she asked, reaching for the chilled Sauvignon Blanc. Erin was the manageress of the pub, she could find herself any drink she wanted, but this was Kathleen and Brian's private party, the Maguires wanted everyone to relax, have a good time.

"No, thanks," Erin replied, scanning faces, looking for someone.

"I know, a vodka, you'll take a vodka. What will you have with it?" Kathleen placed ice and a slice in a glass.

"I won't, thanks," Erin said.

"But you've no drink, how will you bring in the New Year?" Kathleen was bemused.

"You must have a drink, Erin, shall I get you a nice, cold glass of beer? Champagne, maybe?" Joyce had joined her sister at the bar, concerned there was a glitch in the hospitality department. One thing the MacReady sisters had been trained to do from an early age was to entertain guests, their house had always been full of visitors, usually men on their way to or from somewhere.

"Do you know what?" Erin saw Dermot arrive, he was escorting Lily O'Brien, the *Merry Widow*. "I'll make tea."

"Tea? At this hour?" Kathleen looked at Joyce, askance.

Franco had spotted Lily arriving, and left a group he had been regaling with tales of movie star antics, to greet her enthusiastically. Joyce raised an eyebrow at Kathleen.

"She's here, is she?" she said, unimpressed.

"He's bought horses off her, I believe," Kathleen replied.

"Well, I hope they weren't doped when he saw them, she hasn't the best reputation," Joyce confirmed, snootily.

Dermot Finnegan stood before them, they had never seen him look so smart. Blazer with shiny buttons, a cravat at this throat, freshly washed hair.

"Have you seen Erin?" Dermot asked. The women had to lean away, his aftershave was so strong.

They nodded towards the kitchen door, mouths tight shut.

"Is she okay?" he asked them, immediately concerned.

"She's ... making ... tea." Kathleen enunciated every word heavily.

They scowled at him.

"That's okay, isn't it?" Dermot was bemused.

"Well, not really, not on New Year's Eve," Kathleen told him.

"Who's the tea for?" Dermot asked, downing a glass of punch, in one.

"Herself," Joyce said.

"I don't think she's fully recovered from Christmas." Kathleen gave Dermot a sweeping look.

"I wonder do you know what ails her?" Joyce folded her arms, watching him scoop another measure of punch from the bowl.

Dermot shrugged. "No idea." And then putting his glass down, abruptly followed Erin into the kitchen.

Erin was not making tea, she was sitting at the kitchen table staring blankly ahead, Eve's chin was in Erin's lap; dolefully gazing at her mistress. Erin had made some effort with her appearance in acknowledgement of the party. Her midnight-blue dress showed off her figure, and the rhinestones around the neckline made her eyes glitter. Only it was tears that were making her eyes shine, Dermot realised when he sat down. She looked up, startled, she had not heard him come in. She turned quickly away, blowing her nose on kitchen towel, making to leave.

"Hey, don't go," Dermot said. "What's wrong?" She did not reply, but stayed where she was. "Look if it's about the other night, nothing happened. We were a bit drunk, you told me you found me irresistible and then you passed out, nothing to be upset about."

She gave him a watery smile. "You wish."

"What's that?" He pointed at something in her hand. It looked like a photograph, a holiday snapshot.

"Just something I found."

Dermot took it from her. Two girls, pretty teenagers in evening gowns, laughing into the camera, eyes shining with excitement.

"Myself and Oonagh. A New Year's Eve hop on the mainland, everyone used to go, Daddy took us all in a coach."

"You both look gorgeous," Dermot said. "You haven't changed a bit." He leaned across the table to take her hand. She drew back.

"I have changed, I've changed a lot." Erin looked at the photograph. "I never thought we were close, but lately I seem to miss her more and more, she was all I had in the world."

He was just about to say he understood, offer a shoulder to cry on, when the door opened and Brian came in, backwards, carrying a large tray, piled with crockery. It was a special occasion, Mr and Mrs Maguire's first party as husband and wife. Kathleen insisted on the good delph, not standard issue, pub crockery. He put the tray down carefully. He could feel the tension in the room.

"Give me a hand, Erin," he said, sorting dishes and bowls. They were serving onion soup with homemade crab pate to start. "Dermot, can you nip down to the cellar and bring me up another case of champagne? Mr Rossini's table has run out."

"I'll go," Erin said, and bolted. Dermot went to help Brian.

"Any news on the Lifeboat?" Brian asked him. They had been waiting to hear if a vessel would become available. The policy was for new Lifeboats to go to the busiest waterways, with existing ones refurbished and delivered to new areas. Dermot's campaign was relentless. He was a newcomer on the island, he wanted to make his mark. He had just finished recounting chapter and verse to Brian, who was sorry he asked, when they realised Erin had not returned with the champagne.

"I'll go, you have your hands full." Dermot popped a piece of pate-laden soda bread into his mouth as he left.

He flicked the switch a couple of times at the top of the cellar steps, but the light was not working. He could see a faint glimmer below. He called out.

"Erin, you down there? You okay?" No reply. He descended the steps, slowly, holding onto the rail. The steps were damp and slippery, it was going to take a long time for the cellar to dry out.

A cavernous room running the length of the building, Maguire's cellar was used to store anything and everything the pub needed. Shelves piled with boxes and bottles lined the walls, old cupboards and chests of drawers leaned against each other in corners, packed full to bursting with every imaginable item required to maintain a successful hostelry on a remote isle, flung out in the middle of the Atlantic.

Dermot kept his eyes fixed on the glimmer, feeling his way stealthily past boxes and discarded furniture. He turned a corner and could see a figure in the distance. Erin was sitting on a barrel, head lowered. She seemed to be rubbing something, it was her leg, he saw in the candlelight, it was bleeding.

"Wondered where you were. What happened?" He went to her.

"Caught it on something sticking out over there." Erin was holding a piece of sackcloth over the wound. "It's where the glass from the window dug in, beginning to think this place is out to get me."

"Good job you thought to bring candles. Lights fused again?" Dermot said.

"Nothing works for long around here, goes for a bit then gives up the ghost, always the same," Erin told him. It was dark and dank in the cellar, like Erin's mood. Dermot suddenly wanted to take her out of there, upstairs to the warmth and the light, and the happy chatter of people bringing in the New Year, looking forward, being optimistic.

"Come on," he took her arm, "I'll give you a hand." She tried to stand. "Don't forget the champagne, it's over there, and mind the wall."

"What's gone on here, half the plaster is off? What's this?" Dermot was ferreting about. He looked round and spotted a torch hanging from a nail. He grabbed it and switched it on. Light spilled into the corner. He waited a second for his eyes to adjust, running the beam slowly over the walls. Cement and rubble piled onto the floor, exposing what looked like a small doorway. He pulled at the plaster, it crumbled and fell away. Erin hobbled towards him.

"What's behind this?" Dermot asked, kicking the debris clear of the door.

"Probably nothing. Bet Customs and Excise had that boarded up a hundred years ago, smuggling was big business here back in the day."

Dermot was fiddling at the lock, pulling the door. It held fast. Erin hopped closer.

"Mind you," she said, running her fingers over the handle, "this looks like it's been used recently, it's quite new."

"And so is this plasterwork." Dermot confirmed, looking at the mess on the floor.

"Let's try this." She pulled what looked like a pointed chopstick out of her hair and bent down to poke at the lock, working the handle at the same time. She gave it a couple of turns, a quick flick and it clicked, springing open. Dermot trained the light into the space.

"Wow," he gasped. "Well, well, what do we have here?" The small room, with a door at the other end, was piled high with boxes. The boxes were all the same, white cardboard, bearing a logo. An open-winged heraldic phoenix rising from a burst of red flames, it looked like a royal crest. The wording looked eastern European, Russian or Polish, and the style was old script, the only word they could make out was *vodka*, and in small letters underneath, *premium quality*. While Dermot stood gazing at the rows of boxes, glaring in the flashlight, Erin split open a lid and lifted a bottle out to examine the find more closely. She held it aloft, turning it in the light. Clear white liquid, a label bearing the same logo and script as the boxes. She unscrewed the cap and smelled it. She looked at Dermot.

"Virtually odourless." She passed it to him.

"Vodka is, isn't it?" Dermot said, sniffing the liquid. He took a swig, swallowed. "Agh, vodka alright, but rough as a badger's arse, I'd say."

Erin shrugged and tried some.

"Hmm, not a brand I've ever come across, does taste rough. Quite a haul, though. Does Brian strike you as a smuggler?"

Dermot shook his head. "Looks like flooding from the storm brought this lot off." He indicated the plaster.

Dermot watched Erin thinking, going into professional mode. He braced up, this was serious, he had been in the Gardaí long enough to know that.

165

"What's the plan?" he asked her.

"I don't have one yet. But this could get some people into very serious trouble, this has organised crime written all over it."

Dermot agreed. "Should we bring the guards in?"

"No, not yet. We don't know what we're dealing with. Could be a perfectly logical explanation, genuine receipts, paperwork, the lot," she suggested.

They heard footsteps. "What's going on down here?" Brian's voice rang out, bouncing off the damp walls. He appeared at the bottom of the steps. Erin and Dermot stood side by side, hiding the secret room behind them.

"Just coming, Brian. Erin hurt her leg, that's what kept us." Dermot lifted her into his arms. He gave Erin the flashlight, she turned it on Brian.

"I'm okay, caught my bad leg on a box, is all. Just need a plaster. I'll be grand," she said.

"I'll take a look at it later." Brian was frazzled, everyone had run out of champagne by now. He stood back to let Dermot, carrying Erin, ascend the steps.

"Tell you what, I'll get the champagne, shall I?" He glared at their backs.

Chapter Fourteen - Sixth Sense

❝Come on Monty, race yer!" she yelled. The little dog turned from busily inspecting a rock pool and ran towards her.

It was a glorious morning, cold and bright with a brittle blue sky and a smooth sparkling sea. Marianne had pulled on a padded jacket and serious boots almost the moment she opened her eyes, and once she was sure Joey and Ryan were fast asleep, she let Monty out through the half door and quickly disappeared along the sandy track, swinging right along the coast road in front of Maguire's and then left to halt abruptly in front of a huge cliff. There was an opening nature had cleverly designed to look like solid rock, she and the terrier slipped through the crevice, following the natural stone steps down to scrub, which splayed out into a picture perfect arc of golden sand – Horseshoe Bay.

She stopped and put her hands on her hips, pulling the fresh, sea air into her lungs, her heart, her mind. A new year, a fresh start, a beginning. She charged off along the sand, whooping loudly, swinging her arms like a demented windmill.

Sean Grogan, anchored off the bay in his ancient *Boston Whaler*, spotted her. He tutted to himself, taking the butt out of his mouth and flicking it into the ocean.

"Can't even have a quiet smoke in peace," he moaned, pulling up anchor and pushing the engine into life. Sean was in a particularly bad mood. Maguire's had been closed to the public last night, apparently they were having a private party, only friends and family invited. He had knocked on the door, but it was bolted. He tapped on the window, no response. So for the first time in his entire adult life, he had not been able to enjoy a pint seeing in the New Year. He had been treated badly, ostracised from the inner circle. This was not good. He would never darken their door again. He would make other arrangements, see how they liked that, bastards and interlopers, the lot of them.

Marianne and Monty were playing chase with the sea, running along the shoreline, waiting for a wave to break, standing still for as long as they dare, before the water gushed over the sand, chasing them away. Monty was barking so loudly, and she was laughing so much, they did not notice the man until he was upon them. She had to look twice. He was strolling along the beach, hands shoved in pockets, yellow and blue sailing jacket zipped up. It was Brian's jacket, but Franco was wearing it.

They started to walk towards each other and as Marianne drew closer, she could see the expression on his face; mouth drawn down, a fixed frown ridged on his brow. She was immediately back in New York, Angelique's funeral, the private, painful burial at Franco's home. She remembered him asking her to forgive his beautiful, wayward niece the damage she caused. Marianne told him there was nothing to forgive, she felt only pity, such a waste of life, and made her peace. She remembered how bleak he had looked that day, a man with all the trappings of success, alone and lonely. He looked like that now.

"Having fun, I see," he said, bending to scratch Monty's sodden ears. Marianne raised her arms to encompass the bay.

"My hangover cure." She smiled. She was pleased she felt on top form after last night. They had had plenty of champagne, but with platefuls of delicious food and much dancing there were no ill effects. "All packed?" She knew Franco and Larry were leaving today and despite threatening last night to stay in Europe, going to London, then onto Italy, reality had kicked in this morning. They needed to get back. He looked surprised, as if he had only just remembered where he was.

"This place," he said, scanning the bay, the glittering cliffs either end of the beach, the infinite stretch of deep blue, America beyond. "Bewitching, beguiling, like a beautiful woman. I have never been here before, not to Ireland, even, and yet this is the last place my beloved Angelique was alive and laughing, the home now of her child, the only family I have left in the world. It feels foreign yet so familiar. Odd." He picked up a piece of driftwood and threw it for Monty to fetch; they walked on together.

"You okay about everything?" she asked.

"I feel much happier now I have been here, spent time with Joey, such a sweet child, and Ryan, looks better than ever, relaxed, enjoying life. No, it was good to come." He stopped and, looking into her face, pushed a tendril of windswept hair behind her ears with his peasant fingers, a fatherly gesture. "And you, bella signorina, what of you? There is so much work to do here and you have your own projects and schemes. I have read about the 'babies for sale'. You won an award for that expose, didn't you?"

Marianne was taken aback. This globally successful, world-famous businessman knew about her minor award, her career on a local newspaper.

"It is no small achievement," he told her, reading her mind. "You should be very proud. And now you run this as a charitable trust, admirable indeed, what is this called?"

"*The Lost Babies*. We know children have always been sold, especially those of unmarried mothers, but with attitudes changing and these women now able to say what happened to them, we can help them be reunited with the babies they lost. We've hundreds of happy stories, after years of pain," she told him.

"I know, I've looked at the website. But who is *we*?" he asked. She gave him a crooked smile. She was being interrogated. "And next the holiday home for young people who are carers, in honour of your dead friend. Admirable again, but so much work, and now there is Joey. Surely he needs all your time and attention, if you are to be a mother to him, too?"

Marianne stopped. His words were not said critically, but they were questioning.

"I adore Joey," she told him.

"But do you love him, Marianne? I see you love Ryan and he loves you, and you care for Joey, very much. But a mother's love? Can you give that?" Franco's tone was even, but his words were poking her. She looked him in the eye, warm brown eyes with steel behind them.

"Because I am not a mother?" she asked. "His mother wasn't much ..."

He raised a hand. "She's gone. Joey is here with you. Is this where he should stay? Is this the best for him?"

"Of course it is. We're his family now," she told him.

"Correction. Ryan is family and so am I. I leave today, Ryan in a few months. Will you have time for a child who is not yours?" She opened her mouth to protest. "I only ask, Marianne, because you are a very busy woman, busy being a mother to the whole world, and one little boy really needs you."

Her chest started to burn, anger, confusion building. "But …"

"Admirable, as I have said. But what if there is no Ryan, no me? What of Joey, then? You and Ryan aren't married, who would he belong to?" He put his hands behind his back and carried on walking. She ran to catch up with him, stopping him in his tracks.

"I won't let him down," she was brimming with temper, "I won't let anyone down!"

His shrewd eyes looked back into hers.

"Good, I am pleased to hear it. And now breakfast. I love breakfast here, sausage, bacon, that meat and spices roll, what is it? Yes, white pudding. Kathleen calls the meal a heart attack on a plate." He laughed out loud. "But to die happy, eh?" Franco took Marianne's arm as they headed back. Monty trotted sombrely at her heels, he heard laughter but did not feel it.

Kathleen, whose morning regime consisted of hot lemon juice and glugs of Aloe Vera, had disappeared to re-establish a routine at the Post Office, and with Brian busy laying the fire in the bar, Dermot found Erin hanging washing in the yard.

"How's the leg?" he boomed, making her jump.

"Grand," she said. "How's your head?"

"I didn't have much drink last night."

She checked him out.

"Are you after a pint?" she asked.

"No, myself and Ryan are taking Larry and Rossini to the airport, thought I'd get here early and start loading up."

"Mr Rossini's packed, he went for a walk. Larry's probably still at it, I imagine he wraps everything in tissue paper," she said, referring to Larry's OCD tendencies; they had all witnessed him cleaning the piano keys with an antiseptic wipe before he regaled them with show tunes the previous night.

"Any thoughts on, you know, the other thing?" he asked. She swung round.

"Shush, keep it down," she hissed. He stepped over the wall, and in a stride, stood beside her.

"Sorry, but did you come up with anything? We have to do something," he said, under his breath.

"I know, I've thought of nothing else, been awake all night. We'll have to do a bit of investigating, find out who it belongs to. If it's stolen."

"You definitely don't think it's anything to with Brian, then?" Dermot said, holding the basket of washing so Erin could reach it more easily.

"I was here before Brian and I've been here since, I'd have noticed, there's litres of it. And what about hiding it, plastering over the door, who did that?"

Dermot frowned. "It has smugglers written all over it."

"And here's another thing. I've been on the internet, the writing on the labels and the boxes, it looks made up. No language *Google* recognises anyway," Erin hissed.

"What do you think that means?" Dermot's police training was kicking in. He had been at the forefront of drug trafficking and gunrunning, this was more than a simple case of stolen vodka, and there was far too much in the secret hideaway, even for pub consumption. He looked at Erin, their gaze locked, eyes bright with excitement. They had reached the same conclusion.

"Hey, Dermot, give me a hand here," Larry called, wheeling his luggage towards them, the weather so uncommonly mild he carried his coat over his arm. Erin and Dermot sprang apart as if they had been electrocuted. "Any sign of Kathleen? I wanted to say goodbye."

"Up at the Post Office," Erin told him. "Sole responsibility for global communications weighs heavily, you know."

Larry checked his watch. "Have I time to call by?" he asked Dermot.

"Ten minutes, we leave in ten," Dermot replied, handing the washing back to Erin with a wink, as he went to load the car.

The bell on the Post Office door chimed when Larry pushed it open, but Kathleen did not appear. He peered over the counter, the mail was strewn haphazardly across the desk, but there was no sign of the postmistress. He went through to the back, the door to her inner sanctum, unlocked. The smell of damp, mixed with traces of sewage, grew stronger. Larry pulled a tissue from his pocket and pressed it to his nose.

The sitting room was relatively unscathed, carpets would have to be replaced, new floors and skirting, but most of the furniture was piled high in the corners, topped with heaps of treasures, silver picture frames, crystal candlesticks and porcelain figurines. Larry breathed a sigh of relief, her eclectic collection had not been washed away.

He walked through to Kathleen's brightly coloured Kasbah kitchen and was shocked at the devastation. Half the outside wall had been demolished, all the windows smashed, frames ripped to pieces, hanging in gaping holes where the glass had been. It was as if a giant from another world had reached in, grabbed the very guts of her home and torn them out, flinging them across a now derelict yard and down to the beach. It was a total mess. Scanning the debris, he spotted a figure, swathed in a scarlet shawl, sitting slouched on what remained of the garden wall. He called out to her. She quickly wiped her nose with the back of her hand, turning to give him the biggest smile, face streaked with mascara.

"I won't ask what's wrong," he said, taking her hands in his. "Be a damn stupid question."

"Ah, sure, no use crying over spilt milk, as they say." She gave his hands a squeeze.

"Not this, then?" He was curious, she had been weeping alright.

"Something worse," she told him, sharp eyes scouring his face. "I didn't see this coming. I'd no idea, a complete bolt out of the blue."

"Was to everyone, wasn't it? The weathermen said a storm, but nothing like this," Larry assured her.

"Yes, but I should have known. It's like my sixth sense switched off. Too busy indulging my other senses,

swanning about up in Dublin, eating, drinking, having sex."
Larry baulked at this, but Kathleen ignored his sensibility.
"No, my soul and the island's are connected. We shouldn't
have gone, I shouldn't have left."

"Hey, come on, Kathleen, you're too hard on
yourself, too hard by far."

She sighed. "Well, the worst of it is, now I've
returned and the sixth sense is switched back on, everything
feels terrible, worse than that, feels like there's more to
come."

"More storms?" Larry squeaked; she was stressing
him out as usual.

"I don't know, but something just as horrendous, and
maybe even more devastating. I can't stop thinking about it.
I'm worried sick." She looked into her friend's face. "I'm
sorry, Larry, and you've come to say goodbye, and here I am
rambling on like a mad ole witch. Forgive me, give me a hug
and tell me I'll see you again soon. I miss you Larry. We've
always been close, haven't we?" She touched his cheek with
her forefinger, and he surprised her by pressing her palm
with a kiss.

"Always, Kathleen," he said. "Try not to worry, it's
just your overactive imagination, is all." She went to speak.
A car horn honked loudly. "My ride to the airport, I'd better
go." Larry kissed her forehead. Pulling the shawl more
tightly about her tiny frame, she watched him hurry away, to
join the others heading for the airport. On the one hand, she
was sad they were leaving, these glamorous Americans who
had brightened their New Year celebrations. On the other,
she was glad. Pleased they could all return to normal, put life
back on an even keel. For whatever she could feel was
coming, they could all face it a lot better without any

external distractions, and that was the only positive spin, even she, Kathleen MacReady-Maguire, the most optimistic person on the planet, could put on it, so grave, was the clump of dread in her chest.

Chapter Fifteen – Soul For Sale

Despite urgent demands to repair storm damage in other more influential areas of the country, the government agreed to honour its commitment to the island community of Innishmahon and provide funding to reinstate the harbour wall and reinforce the structure of the new bridge. But the project had to meet its deadline. Nothing could be funded beyond that.

Newly appointed operations director, Dermot Finnegan, was relishing the challenge, striding down Main Street with charts and graphs rolled under his arm, assuring everyone he met, the bridge would be open and the new marina functioning in time for the season. They need have no concerns in that department.

The immediate and more pressing problem of repairing storm damage to homes and businesses, was undertaken by the *Island Task Force*, comprising the usual suspects, Father Gregory, Kathleen MacReady-Maguire and Joy Redmund, who had stepped into the breach after the dilapidated building where she had been running her little kindergarten had been completely swept away. As a stopgap, she had taken over a room in the priest's house, but some parents were not keen on the association with the church, and Joy was desperate for a more appropriate, permanent location.

It was a dark January evening, one of those days when the sky stayed the same pewter grey from dawn to dusk. They were all gathered in Maguire's, mulling over quotes and estimates for essential repairs, bemoaning the rapidly dwindling balance in the community kitty, when Kathleen came up with one of her bright ideas.

"Let's do what we've done in the past. Host a fundraiser, a great big party and invite the whole world to it," she exclaimed, surprised they had not come up with this sooner.

"A good idea, Kathleen, and I know it's worked in the past, but it would take an awful lot of organisation. Are we up to it, and who would come? The island's hardly an attractive holiday destination at the moment, is it?" Father Gregory was scanning faces for a response.

"Well, you all heard the Taoiseach on television the other evening, saying communities have to help themselves, there's no crock of gold up there in parliament waiting to be thrown at us. I say we do what we've always done, get our own house in order, our own way," Kathleen told him, tapping her pen against her clipboard to emphasise her words.

Dermot and Erin, behind the bar, remained deep in conversation. They seemed to have a lot to talk about these days, Kathleen had remarked to Marianne. The women were hopeful the friendship might develop into something more, but there never seemed to be much jollity when the pair were together, it had to be said. Kathleen tutted, there was a distinct lack of enthusiasm for her proposal. This would not do, not do at all.

"Ryan, surely you've any amount of Hollywood friends who would support an event like this? They have huge fundraisers every five minutes over in America, don't they?" she insisted. Ryan was holding a measuring tape along the bar. Brian was planning major refurbishment.

"It's a long way to come, there would have to be a good reason, more than just a fundraiser, I think," Ryan replied, but he had not dismissed the idea. Kathleen looked at her daughter. Marianne was thoughtful, she was sure she could hear cogs starting to whir.

"We had a good guest list when we hosted the *Bridge Too Far* festival, rock stars, politicians, celebrities ..."

"And a couple of Royals, don't forget," Kathleen threw in, although she had started that rumour at the time.

"If we could add to that, mix it up a bit, appeal to those with Irish roots, that gives us millions to go at, American, Australians and think of all the Irish just across the water in the UK." Marianne picked up her pen. "Heritage and history, people love that, tracing families back through the centuries, finding out where they came from, who they are." She was drawing on her notepad. "I've got it!" she announced, eyes glittering in triumph. "We'll have a Ball, a real Ball, up at the big house. We'll raise enough money to get all the repairs and renovations completed and be ready for the best season we've ever had."

Kathleen was grinning, she had seen Marianne like this before, fired with enthusiasm, raring to go, no challenge too ambitious, no feat a stretch too far.

"But what's the hook?" Father Gregory asked, staring at the mad squiggle on Marianne's notepad. Ryan frowned too. Had she been on the sherry? Sniffing felt-tip pens?

"The price of the ticket will include a slice of the island," Marianne announced, letting the words hang in the air.

"What?" Father Gregory rubbed his chin. Marianne could be over-zealous at times, but she was far from hare-brained.

"We'll give them what everyone with Irish roots really wants, a home in their homeland. Well, not exactly a home, but a piece of the island. We'll sell a sod of turf with each ticket." She scratched on the pad, finishing with a flourish. "See?" She held it up. It was a badly drawn map of the island, the bridge, the marina, the new lifeboat station, all marked. Behind a square representing the big house, she had drawn a flagpole bearing a huge sign. It said 'For Sale' in big, bold letters.

Silence.

"You're selling the island now, is it?" The inevitable whine from Sean Grogan drifted across to those gathered. "Mother of Divine God, here we go again! Is there no stopping this mad woman and her cracked-up ideas?" he exclaimed, glaring at them with his good eye. "Jesus, Mary and Holy Saint Joseph, she'll have us all homeless and in hock to every foreign shyster, that crowd up in Dublin lets into the country." He jumped down from his perch at the bar. "And you're no better, Mrs Maguire, MacReady, or whoever you think you are. Bringing your man back from America and all the bad luck in the world with him. No good ever came of this place while those Maguires were here, let me tell you that for nothing." Angrily, Sean pulled his jacket on and his cap down.

"Hey now," Ryan said, standing to calm things; the man had worked himself into one of his usual fuzzy, furies. Sean pushed past him.

"Don't 'hey now' me," Sean snarled. "I've lived here all my life. This is my home and I'm damned if a fuckwit like you and the rest of this shower of deranged interlopers are going to drive me out of it. Sell the island? May as well sell your souls. You'll sell it over my dead body, or yours, and I mean that!" And spitting on the floor to seal his curse, he gave them all a good scowl and stomped out.

"Well, we're onto a winner so," Kathleen grinned, "nothing like Sean damning an idea to ensure its success. Do you think Mr Rossini might want to be involved, Ryan? He'd be a huge attraction, loads of contacts, too, I shouldn't wonder. Probably bring lots of movie executives, particularly as he's planning on making a film here."

"Is he?" Ryan was surprised.

"He is now," laughed Father Gregory, well used to Kathleen's penchant for rumour-mongering, although she called it PR, he seemed to remember.

"Do you think we should tell Brian?" Erin asked, watching Dermot swab down the deck of the boat he had lived on since he came to the island less than a year ago.

"You still don't think it's anything to do with him?" Dermot asked her. After discovering the haul of vodka in the cellar, he and Erin had returned the next day and disguised the doorway to the hideaway with barrels and old furniture, waiting to see if someone disturbed the arrangement, or even mentioned it.

"Hasn't said a word. Mind you he hasn't been in the cellar much. He's changed the odd barrel of beer, but it's off season, we're not that busy, no need to replenish bottles of spirits, particularly now Christmas is over." She gave him a look under her fringe. She had not meant to mention the festive season, remind him of Christmas night, when she had fallen into a drunken stupor, and had been violently ill. After taking care of her, he had put her to bed to sleep it off. She did not want to remember how she had nearly kissed him, just before passing out, and how grateful she was that she had not. But she had wanted to … she could remember that, far too clearly.

"What do you think we should do then?" He stood up. Dermot was tall, broad shoulders, narrow waist, he kept himself fit. Erin imagined he looked very smart in his police uniform, chasing criminals and busting heists in Dublin's fair city. Quite a charmer too, when he wanted to be. He gave her a sidelong smile. "Well?"

"The only way we're going to find out who's behind it, is to leave it where it is until they come back for it," she said, dragging her gaze out to sea.

"But how will we know when that happens?"

"We'll have to set a trap." Erin was matter-of-fact. "So we know who it is as soon as it's been got at, touched, even. Once we have our suspect, we can carry out a proper investigation, bring in the guards, if we have to. Those two eejits on the mainland will only cock things up if we involve them too early, remember the last time?"

Dermot nodded. If there was ever any sort of trouble on the island, Sergeant Brody and Garda O'Riordan were the last two people to be notified, the least they knew about things, the better.

"Good plan," Dermot agreed, relieved there was one. He was so busy organising urgent work at the marina, while trying to co-ordinate the delivery of one very necessary, but extremely expensive Lifeboat, the discovery of a cache of what appeared to be smuggled liquor weighed heavily on him. After all those years in the police force, it rankled that someone was blatantly breaking the law, right under his nose, in the very pub he considered to be his local.

"So how do we set the trap?" he asked Erin, who was zipping up her jacket, ready to continue her daily run along the coast.

"I haven't a clue," she laughed. "You're the fecking detective!" And with that, she took off, hair blowing in the wind, leaving little footprints in the sand.

Chapter Sixteen – The Party Planner

Marianne had taken to planning the fundraising ball with gusto. The idea for the scheme had come at precisely the right time. Everything was in place to take the first tranche of young people at *Oonagh's Project* for the May bank holiday. She had appointed a project manager, with excellent references, an ex-school teacher re-trained as a counsellor. The new incumbent would join six weeks before the youngsters arrived, plenty of time to iron out any glitches and ensure their first season providing holidays for young carers went well.

It was dovetailing nicely with the *Lost Babies* campaign she had been running ever since, as a journalist, she had exposed a long-established illegal child trafficking scam, right on her doorstep. Photographs of smiling strangers, reunited, after nearly a lifetime, pleased Marianne most of all. These were the pictures that littered the pin board above her desk, covering the ones of red carpet events with Ryan and his movie star friends.

Everything was going remarkably well, a new project to get her teeth into was just perfect.

"I have news," Marianne called, pushing open the door to the Post Office. The bell sounded, but Kathleen did not appear. Marianne called out again, lifting the counter to go through to the inner sanctum.

"I'm up here," Kathleen called down from the landing. Marianne ascended, stepping precariously over boxes and bags, spilling clothes, shoes and other female paraphernalia over the stairs. It looked like a sort out of mammoth proportions.

Marianne followed the voice to a back room. There were three bedrooms at the Post Office, all turned into dressing rooms, filled with wardrobes and cupboards to contain Kathleen's opulent collection.

"I'm trying to be disciplined, rid myself of things I haven't worn in a while, but it's difficult. I get so attached, the memories come flooding back, it's like throwing away an old friend."

Marianne watched as the older woman, in a sea-green satin evening gown, turned to look at her reflection in a huge baroque mirror, screwed to the wall. The bed, the floor, an over-stuffed chair, were all piled with garments bursting with colour, it was as if a rainbow had exploded in the room. "And I found these." She lifted a small suitcase onto the bed, looking at Marianne before she raised the lid. "Don't be upset now."

It was full of wigs. A silky mix of short and long, curls and waves in every colour. Marianne reached out tentatively, taking a bright blonde ringlet in her fingers and pulling it gently free of the mass of tendrils crowded into the case.

"The *Dolly Parton*," she whispered, taking the extravagant pile of backcombed, swirly strands in both hands, instinctively bringing it to her nose, desperate for a tiny trace of Oonagh, a sliver of scent to remind her, bring her back, just for a millisecond. She closed her eyes and there they were, high on the cliff, remnants of picnic splayed on the rug, the sea smooth and sparkling in the sunshine. It was the day Oonagh told her the cancer had returned, and whatever happened she would trust Marianne to take care of things if she were gone. Marianne had shared a secret too, how losing a baby she did not even know she was carrying, meant she could never have a child of her own. How they had cried, then laughed together, Marianne pulling off Oonagh's crazy *Dolly Parton* wig, worn to hide her newly sprouting scalp; surely a sign all would be well, she would recover and they would be friends forever.

When Marianne opened her eyes, Kathleen had disappeared. She heard a cork pop down below.

"We're having champagne," Kathleen called up the stairs, "come and have a glass, it'll set you up."

Marianne, still clutching the wig, entered the kitchen. She had not been here since the storm. She was taken aback, it was hard to take in the destruction. The crumbled brickwork made safe with steel props, the gaping hole to the outside world, sheathed in heavy duty polythene; it moved in the breeze, like sails on a boat. Kathleen handed her daughter a glass of bubbles, waving a hand towards the beach and the cliffs beyond.

"Given me a whole new perspective," she beamed. "Can't think why it never occurred to me before, I'm going to do all the repairs in glass, two storeys, maybe even a roof garden. The entire place will look out to sea. It'll be fabulous, every season played out before me, a magnificent vista, don't you think?"

Marianne nodded, she was right, it would be spectacular.

"And the clearing out?" she asked.

"All part of it. Sweeping changes, a fresh start. Sometimes when something bad happens, something better comes out of it. Isn't that often the case?"

"You're staying here then, not going to live in Maguire's with Brian?" Marianne was not being facetious, she never assumed her parents' marriage would be conventional.

"We've come to an arrangement. He'll keep a room at the pub for when it's mad busy or he needs to stay, if Erin's away. But our home will be here. We've agreed my career is more important, vital to the island. I'm appointed by the State, that can't be taken lightly. Brian understands. Erin's a very capable girl, he has a good woman in charge, both at home and at his business. The best of all worlds, nothing to complain about. Now," she raised her glass. Marianne lifted hers, and noticed another, poured and ready on the table. She gave her mother a quizzical look. "Oonagh's," Kathleen said.

Marianne felt goose bumps prickle her skin, as surely as if her dead friend had touched her.

"We can't leave her out, now, can we?" Kathleen sipped her drink. "You've news, you said?"

Marianne frowned, then laughed, remembering. "Oh … yes. Mr Rossini, our favourite movie producer, he's coming … coming to the Ball. Sent me the biggest guest list by email, wall-to-wall A-listers, actors, singers, the lot. If only half of them come, we'll be full to bursting."

"That's wonderful news. I told you he liked it here." But Kathleen did not seem over-surprised. Not for the first time, Marianne suspected her mother knew more than she was letting on.

"Do they all have Irish connections? Will they be coming to buy a piece of the island?"

"I guess so, they're used to raising millions for good causes over there. I'm sure the novelty of owning a bit of the Emerald Isle will appeal." Marianne smiled, tasting her bubbles at last.

Kathleen was pouring more champagne. "Brian's New York contacts are already loving the idea. Desperate to know when it's happening so they can book flights and package it as part of a grand European tour. When are you planning to hold it? Have you fixed a date yet?"

Marianne nodded. "What about a Valentine's Masked Ball? Do you think that would work?" Marianne was beaming at her mother, she already knew she would adore the idea.

"Perfect, just perfect. I can see the slogan already, *Fall in Love with Ireland at the island's Valentine's Ball!*"

Marianne laughed, "I like it! But if we're going for it, there's no time to lose. So I wondered if you're not too busy over the next couple of days, we can get the invitations out and crank up the media campaign. Will you front it? You were so good with the media last time, you and Ryan, I thought, both appealing in different ways."

"Of course, I'd be delighted. Let's get right to it." Kathleen finished her drink, scrabbled around for her bag and raincoat and made to leave.

"But you were in the middle …" Marianne scanned the room. The whole house was littered with Kathleen's clearance project.

"It can wait," said Kathleen, heading for the door. "Brian won't mind, he knows to be patient, I need to make space for a husband in my life. We may have rushed our wedding – impulsive, mad passionate things that we are – but you can't rush a marriage. That takes time and effort, you mark my words." She pulled the door closed, ensuring the 'Back in 5' sign was firmly in place. The same sign everyone used, invariably it meant five hours, especially if the tide was right for fishing, or there was a hooley in Maguire's.

Marianne watched as she strode off ahead, a woman on a mission, totally unperturbed, it was not yet noon, and she was wearing a sea-green evening gown, complete with leopard print wellies.

"You'll have to bring a date." Marianne was glazing apple cakes with deep yellow egg yolks.

"Ah, no." Erin shrugged and opened the cellar door.

"Anyone in mind?" Marianne, ignoring Erin's reply, turned to face her, pastry brush aloft.

"Hmm …" Erin made to descend the stairs. Marianne moved swiftly to bar the way. It was the third time she had attempted this conversation. "Tell me to stop poking my nose in, if that's what I'm doing."

Erin raised her eyebrows.

"There's only a few weeks to go, seating plans to be arranged, accommodation allocated." Marianne brushed her hands on her apron. Erin sighed and closed the door.

"I'm not sure I'm coming," she said, flatly.

"Of course you're coming." Marianne walked back to the huge oak table, her clipboard and file on the far end. "Now, let's see." She started sorting through paperwork.

"I mean it," Erin said, "I really don't fancy it. I hate anything formal. I either end up getting pissed and making a fool of myself, or I sip mineral water and have a lousy time."

Marianne frowned; this was not the Erin she had come to know – the cocky, plain-speaking, hard-nosed professional she thought she was dealing with. She put her file down.

"Come on, Erin, it'll be a great night. Celebs, stars, red carpet, champagne and all in aid of everything good, getting the island sorted and shipshape in time for the season. You'd regret missing it, I'm sure."

Erin pushed the dark fringe out of her eyes.

"I'll be needed here, though. With everybody up at the big house, who'd run the pub?"

"We'll do what we always do, call in the troops, sure there's any amount of Padar's cousins around, glad of a bit of temporary bar work."

"I'm not keen, and I certainly don't have anything posh enough to wear to a Ball."

Marianne dropped her pen on the table.

"Erin Brennan that is the puniest excuse for not going to a Valentine's Ball I ever heard in my life." Even as she said it, Erin's wardrobe flashed through her mind. She either dressed like a tomboy; jeans, sailing jacket, baseball cap, or erring on the vaguely tarty side, low cut tops with slogans in glitter, shiny leggings, and black, always in black. She never changed her hairstyle either, a cloud of dark, angry frizz, crying out to be smoothed and tamed, much like herself.

Marianne softened her tone.

"Well, I can certainly help in that department, and we've plenty of time. I can do hair, and we could always have a good rummage through Kathleen's endless wardrobe ..."

Erin raised her hands in horror.

"Stop right now. I have no intention of going anywhere dressed as *Widow Twankey*!"

Marianne laughed.

"A bit unkind, Erin, she has some stunning vintage pieces, just depends on how things are put together. Now that's settled, who will you bring?"

"Bring?" Erin sounded surprised.

"As your date?" Marianne replied. Erin flinched. "Now, let's see, there must be someone suitable." She started sorting through paperwork.

"Now, that is an unfixable problem. I mean there's no one around here, is there? Even you have to admit that." Erin folded her arms, sounding a bit more like her old combative self. Marianne picked up her pen, she would not be beaten.

"Let's see ... who *is* single," she tapped her teeth, "Rory O'Toole?"

"O'Toole by name, and by nature," Erin replied.

Marianne wrote the name down.

"Declan Byrne, he's not a plonker."

"Wears a toupee."

"Does not." Marianne scratched on her pad.

"Joseph Finch, he has loads of hair."

"Up his nose!"

Marianne still wrote the name down.

191

"If you say Sean Grogan, I'll flatten you with that fecking file."

That was the next name on Marianne's lips, but she was building up to the punchline. Erin sat down and poured them both a glass of wine. Marianne took a sip, now at least she was entering into the spirit.

"Dermot Finnegan, don't tell me there's anything wrong with him, gorgeous, funny, good company."

"Not my type." Erin swallowed back her wine in one gulp.

"Really? That's a shame, did you not go on a date together once?"

"Not a date, as such." Erin's face closed up.

"I don't think he's going with anyone."

"He's been up at widow O'Brien's for 'dinner' a few times lately," Erin made the inverted comma sign with her fingers, "he'll probably take her."

"No way, who told you that?"

"Her place is on the way to Sean Grogan's cottage," Erin confirmed. Sean was one of the biggest gossips on the island. "He's only after one thing anyway. I couldn't stand all the mauling and groping at the end of the night, spoils everything," she said with feeling, pouring herself another drink. Marianne was disappointed.

"Tony O'Riordan, he has nice hair, his own teeth and he's single," she offered.

"He's ninety!" Erin yelled, slamming her glass down. "At least Dermot is the right side of forty."

"Tony's only eighty-eight. God, Erin, you can be really picky at times." Marianne pushed her glass across the table for a refill. She was getting somewhere, at last.

Chapter Seventeen – Sleeping Arrangements

L arry was not sure this was a good idea, in fact, he had grave doubts. Not about the Ball. The Ball was a brilliant idea, funds were badly needed before the storm, never mind now, in the ravaged aftermath. When he had first visited Innishmahon, in what seemed like a lifetime ago, he had been shocked how primitive it was: no infrastructure to speak of; street lights were scant; the roads had potholes the size of craters. Major investment was long overdue.

"A tiny speck of an island, off a slightly larger speck of an island has little hope of attracting sizable funding from official sources," Kathleen had told him on the telephone a few weeks ago. "We're going to do what we've always done, help ourselves. Raise the money we need and spend it the way we want. No questions asked and no one to answer to." It was Kathleen who had insisted he invite Lena, and it was the notion of Lena going to Innishmahon that was causing Larry to reach for every stress-busting remedy he could lay his hands on.

"The more the merrier," she told him, sounding every one of the thousands of miles away, talking into her vintage, two-tone *Trim-phone*. "I know she loves a party and has always wanted to come here. Sure, wasn't your grandmother from Roscommon?"

"I've no idea. Where on earth is Roz-commin?" he asked, bemused.

"Here, in Ireland." Kathleen reminded herself that Americans would not necessarily be that familiar with the counties of Ireland. Unlike the Irish, most of whom could name all fifty states, and the shires of England if required, a good convent education and the legacy of family working abroad, ensured that.

"I never knew that," Larry told her.

"Of course you did. Lena told me. You just forgot, silly man." Kathleen said, magnanimously. "So far, we have guests coming from the US, a mix of Ryan's contacts and quite a few of Brian's old clients, and more or less the same amount coming from the UK. Marianne's working on the media list, lots of locals have come up with hundreds of Irish families with connections to the island."

"Hundreds?" Larry was not sure the island would be up to that.

"Ah, a good few anyway," Kathleen confirmed. "I just wanted to check you were having your usual arrangements. Stop over at Joyce's and then May cottage here. I'm guessing you'll want the second bedroom and the sofa bed made ready in the house. Who's staying with you?"

Larry pulled at his turtleneck, had someone turned up the thermostat in the apartment? "With me?" He could barely get the question out. He had not considered this, sharing the cottage. Did he have to?

"Lena, I assumed, and I thought Roberto, or will he be in Maguire's with Mr Rossini? And Mr Rossini's personal assistant, male or female? I wasn't sure. And Steven Saggito? Mr Rossini's party, or a friend of Ryan's? Would he stay in Weathervane, I wonder?" Between the list of names and interference on the line, Larry's head was spinning. All this on top of a journey he was dreading. No matter how many times he boarded an aircraft, he still hated flying. He swallowed, he was not sure his nerves could cope.

"Jeez, Kathleen, I dunno. It all sounds a pretty explosive mix to me, anyways. What does Mimi say? She and Lena are best with this sorta thing. If I can be with as few people as possible that would suit me better," he said this loudly into the handset, he wanted to make sure she heard that bit.

Kathleen understood. Larry liked his own routine, he was fastidious about hygiene and always had to watch what he ate, having a most delicate digestion. After all they had been through, she considered him a close, personal friend. She would sort out the accommodation arrangements herself. He would be taken care of.

"Very well," she could tell he was stressing, "leave it with me. Lena's asked if we have a spa on the island, if there's one at the hotel. Made her laugh when I told her there's no hotel, we don't even have a beauty parlour. She thought that was a great joke."

Larry looked in the mirror. Was that a rash on his forehead?

Marianne was padding about the cottage in bare feet. Monty had hidden her slippers as usual, and she had no idea what she had done with her spare pair. The whole place had been turned upside down in preparation for the influx of VIP guests arriving in a couple of weeks for the Ball.

She was admiring Ryan's handiwork – he had finished painting the hall and stairs a beautiful, rich teal the day before – when he appeared at the back door, having been to meet the ferry and collect more supplies. He pushed his nose up to the glass, pulling a face at her. She opened the top half, he was so wet he could have been swimming. He grabbed her, rubbing his face and sopping hair into her warm, dry skin. She tried to beat him back, but he held her tightly. Even his lips were cold as he kissed her, but his mouth grew warm as he lifted her up on her toes to reach him, pulling her halfway through the door into the spilling rain.

"Get a room!" a voice boomed out. Dermot hopped over the garden gate, running up the path to where the lovers stood, still entwined.

"Ignore him, he might go away," Ryan stage whispered.

"I won't. I've been promised breakfast. I've a list of things to go through." Dermot patted the pocket of his sailing jacket, bulging with paperwork. "And then we're going up to the big house. I've to get the generator working. Will you give me a hand?" He pushed his big handsome face between theirs, kissing first Marianne and then Ryan. He had already lifted Monty into his arms, who immediately joined in the communal kissing game, as Eve, the collie, wriggled with excitement through their legs.

Marianne opened the bottom half of the door to let them in; the kitchen was suddenly full of wet men and even wetter dogs.

"I'll get the grub on the go, you get dressed," Dermot told Marianne bossily. She left them to it. Dermot and Ryan often went into full bachelor-mode in the kitchen, cooking anything and everything, what the humans could not finish, the dogs did, so everyone was perfectly happy with the arrangement.

She stepped over Monty and Eve, playing tug of war with her slippers, as she returned. Joey was in his high chair at the table, with egg in his hair, the men poring over plans spread out amidst remnants of bacon and toast.

"What's that?" She poured fresh coffee.

"The electrics. The whole place was rewired when it was refurbished, but last time I was there I couldn't get some of the lights to work. We're just seeing if there's a way of isolating certain areas, so we can test it," Dermot said.

"I'd no idea you were an electrician," Marianne told him, refilling their mugs. Dermot liked to think he was highly skilled in the handyman department. He passed Marianne an envelope.

"That's from Kathleen, it's her latest guest list. She says she'll meet you up there later so you can agree who's going where."

"Wow," she said, scanning the page, filled with her mother's curly writing in green ink. "So many people, crikey masses of O'Gormans and Finnegans, seems all your far-flung cousins are coming too!" She grinned at the men.

"I hope not," laughed Ryan. "The O'Gormans hate the Finnegans, there'll be a hell of a row."

Dermot licked his fingers clean, before refolding the plans.

"Sure, it wouldn't be a proper hooley without at least one dust-up, now, would it?"

"It's not a hooley." Marianne scowled, lifting Joey into her arms; he had added marmalade to the egg in his hair. "It's a Ball. A beautiful, elegant Ball, something to show the island off for the jewel it is. Any fighting and you'll have me to deal with." She flicked them a look. "Now, get out of my sight, this place looks like a bomb's hit it, and this fella needs a bath."

"Good Lord, I haven't been here in an age," exclaimed Kathleen, standing on the tiny shale beach, looking back at the vast Georgian mansion, window panes glinting in the sun, the *Juliet* balcony above the double doors, gleaming white against the creaminess of the walls. The rain had stopped and the sky had suddenly cleared to bright blue, making everything look freshly laundered.

Erin had brought the sisters to the rear of the house, on Dermot's boat. He phoned to say he had left some tools on it and as she was dying to give the launch a spin, she offered to bring the ladies by sea, picking them up at the marina.

"Oh, they've done a beautiful job, restored to a glory we never saw." Joyce was referring to the fact that the Maguires had let the house go. There always seemed to be money for trips and furs, but never enough to repair the roof or replace a broken window.

"But the parties, Joyce, remember the parties. The house full with people dressed up to the nines, a band in the ballroom, a pianist on the baby grand in the hall." Kathleen started to sing, *These Foolish Things, Noel Coward's* quintessential serenade of lost love and longing. She lifted her arms, twirling, her tweed cape flapping in the breeze. Joyce smiled at her indulgently.

"I remember there were lanterns and candles everywhere, hiding the damp patches on the walls. Newspapers with rugs on top, so you didn't fall through the holes in the floor," she reminded her romantic sibling.

"The cocktails, the shiny silver punchbowls," Kathleen continued, paying no heed.

"The rose-coloured glasses," Joyce retorted, offering a hand to Erin as she unloaded the toolbox and other essentials from the boat onto the little jetty at the end of the beach.

Erin stopped to take it in. She had never seen the house from this angle, even though she had been born and reared on the island. It had been abandoned by the time she and Oonagh were old enough to explore, and strictly off limits. Everyone said it was haunted and though the practical Brennan sisters knew this was just an island legend, they were not prepared to risk it. Besides, they were far too busy trying to head in the opposite direction, hoping to be escorted to the bright lights of Dublin by one of the rich, young men who came sailing in the summer.

"I'm impressed," she said, shielding her eyes with her hand. "Too good for a holiday home for deprived kids, though."

"It's in Oonagh's memory," Kathleen reminded her.

Erin shrugged. "She'd have said the same." And she strode off towards the front of the house, to where Dermot's battered 4x4 stood skew-whiff on the gravel.

"We can put up at least a dozen here very comfortably, en suites and bathrooms galore." Marianne trotted downstairs towards them.

"We'll need some help." Kathleen eyed her list. "If we put a group of VIPs up here, will you and Dermot play host?" She looked at Erin. Erin raised her hands.

"No way, I'll be needed in the pub." She glared at Kathleen for even suggesting such a thing.

"Brian will be in the pub, we'll have other help there too," Kathleen said.

"I've all the staffing sorted," Joyce interrupted. "My girls, their sisters and cousins. Leave all that to me, just tell me how many are sleeping where, we'll change linen, clean bathrooms, do breakfasts, all that kind of thing." She flicked through a leather organiser. "Who are the hosts?"

"Myself and Ryan, obviously, Kathleen and Brian, yourself and Father Gregory, and I was hoping we could count on Dermot and Erin." Marianne gave Erin one of her pointed looks. Erin hid behind her dark fringe. "Joy Redmund is having all the children to stay up at the presbytery, and her husband, bless him, is taking charge of the animals; dogs will need walking, cats feeding. A few of the lads are lined up to do security checks on properties and boats, with everyone up at the Ball, it's best to be on the safe side."

"If Dermot and I are here, we'd be using two rooms, one less for guests," Erin told them, relieved she had come up with a valid reason to remain in the pub.

"I don't mind sharing, if you don't," Dermot called out, coming in from the utility room where he and Ryan had been fiddling about for what seemed like hours. Erin rolled her eyes.

"Most people here will be friends of yours, Ryan, probably best if it's you and Marianne." Erin was firm.

"Fair enough, but technically we should have separate rooms too. I wouldn't want to offend anyone's sensibilities." They turned to look at him. "We're not married," he concluded, giving them his crooked grin.

"Oh, Ryan!" Marianne protested.

"I'm serious, what we do in our own home is our own business, but alongside people who may not be, shall we say, so liberally-minded, well," he was half-smiling at her but his eyes were flinty.

"I have to say, I will only have married people sharing a room at the guesthouse," Joyce interjected into the frost. "I can't risk offending some of my older guests, or some with strong faith traditions, it can be a minefield."

"What would you do if a married gay couple turned up?" Marianne was intrigued, the journalist in her thinking this would make a great article.

"Stick to the rules, they're married," Joyce replied.

"And civil partnerships?" Marianne pushed.

"Like I said, a total minefield. In this instance I think we check who needs to be together and then mix the groups up a bit. I find that often works with people, making contacts, meeting new friends," Joyce said.

"Even falling in love." Kathleen was wistful. "The Ball will be perfect for falling in love."

"Right," Marianne closed her notebook choosing not to look at Ryan who was still staring at her. "We've done as much as we can, until the final guest list is confirmed. Ladies, shall we go and check we've enough linen and towels. Boys, is that generator fixed?"

Ryan shrugged. "Haven't a clue."

"Nearly there," confirmed Dermot. "We'll give everything a proper run through way before anyone arrives."

"Good." Marianne was not one hundred per cent convinced. "And what about ...?"

Ryan raised a hand. "That's enough for today. I worked all day yesterday, we're done here for now. Joey's at kindergarten, so Dermot and I are going fishing, we've lobster pots to sink. Is the boat here, Erin?"

She handed him the keys.

"But ..." Marianne started to protest.

"Sorry, that's what we bachelors do whenever we get the chance." He lifted his hand in salute as they watched the men disappear.

"Cut him a bit of slack," Kathleen advised, as she and Joyce headed off to what was the butler's pantry. "Sure Brian's gone up to Dublin, we all need our space, makes the coming back together all the more special."

Joyce had the good grace to tut, but Kathleen was right, Marianne was a fierce slave-driver, even for a MacReady.

The men had crossed the bay and around to the other side of Widow's Peak in no time. The sea, flat as steel and hard as nails, as the launch powered through the water. Ryan admired the way Dermot was embracing island life, living on the boat, cooking whatever he caught, swimming regularly in Horseshoe Bay. In fact Dermot never looked so good, golden freckles blending to make his skin glow, his green eyes shining with health. He made the right decision to leave Dublin. Ryan, too, was hoping his permanent move to the island would bring just as many benefits, especially with a young son and hopefully a wife to care for. That would be the best of all worlds for him.

"What do you think of proposals?" Ryan asked. Dermot had just reappeared with a couple of cans, celebrating the successful sinking of the lobster pots.

"What kind of proposals, business proposals, marriage proposals, what?" He handed Ryan a can.

"Well, between you and me, I'd really like Marianne and I to be married. It's time, it feels right. You know, get to the end of this movie, make a few changes, hole up here for a hundred years, all looks good from where I'm standing." Ryan took a swig from his can.

"Ah, no, you don't want to be doing that. What if a gorgeous young bimbo, with huge boobs threw herself at you, you being a famous movie star and all, sure how could you help yourself and who would blame you?" Dermot joked. "Have you asked her? Has she said no?" Dermot found it hard to believe anyone would say no to Ryan. He was handsome, of that there was no doubt, and he liked women, he talked to them, about everything, fashion, feminism, feelings. So why was Marianne holding back? Admittedly Ryan's track record was not good. Maybe Marianne was right, maybe Ryan was not that much of a catch.

"She and I have not had the best of experiences where marriage is concerned. She's been engaged twice, first time a disaster, then George, it was only a few weeks before the wedding when he died. I sometimes wonder if she thinks it would be unfair to him, you know, demeaning his memory."

"Good old George." Dermot lifted his can. Ryan joined him. "God rest him, great fellow." They were silent for a moment, remembering their long ago, mutual friend.

"But you think it was George who actually brought you guys together?" Dermot said.

"I do, and I know he wants me to take care of her, the way he tried to, I really believe that. But every time I raise the subject, she closes it down. Backs away, won't even discuss it seriously, and some aspects of it are serious. For instance, if anything happens to me, what happens to Joey? If we're not married and he's not legally adopted, who knows what could happen. Technically, Rossini is his next of kin, so where does that leave everything? Getting the kid settled here to end up, God knows where?"

"What's going to happen to you? You're fit as a flea, man. Don't do any of the stuff you used to do."

"True, but who knows, anything can happen." Ryan was looking out to sea.

Dermot pushed his cap back, scratching his head.

"Bloody hell, so much to think about, it's giving me a headache."

Ryan agreed. "Imagine how I feel? I can't force her to marry me."

"You'll have to admit it's ironic, though," Dermot said. "Biggest movie star in the world and his girl won't marry him."

Ryan thought for a moment.

"Yeah, well whatever you're thinking, forget it, you've no chance, she might not want to marry me yet, but she's my girl, I'll get her in the end." Ryan crossed his legs, resting on the bow rail. The boat bobbed pleasantly in the water. "You do like to convince yourself you're in love with my women, Dermot. It's your safety net."

"That's a load of ole crap. I won't be baited, ha ha, get it!" Dermot said, pointing at the fishing lines. Ryan gave him a grin, he could be such a fecking eejit; sometimes knocking around with Dermot was like being back in the playground.

"Time to change the subject?" Ryan suggested. They watched the sea sparkling before them, the gentle sloshing of the water against the sides of the boat, restful, reassuring; very different from the last time they had been on board together. "We haven't been out on the boat since I gave you a hand bringing in a couple of crooks, and all hell broke loose."

"Yeah, hoped I hadn't put you off fishing for life!" Dermot grinned at him. "How's the arm, by the way?" Ryan had broken his arm in the foray as they had attempted to capture two part-time criminals trying to despatch a cache of armaments to a terrorist group in the North.

"Grand." Ryan flexed his arm, demonstrating its recovery. "And your foot?" Dermot had been shot and even Monty was seriously injured trying to defend his mistress.

"Ah, the doc says the limp will go eventually," Dermot assured him. "Interesting though, the way it was all smoothed over. Barely a mention in the press, a boating accident is all they said, a nod to you being involved, that was about it."

"Well, you were undercover. I'm guessing it was for our own protection. Best kept that way, I reckon. We were so lucky, Dermot, jeez when I think about it." Ryan looked at the tip of the cigarette he had just lit, burning hot in the breeze, the kind of sparky heat he felt deep in the night, the same nightmare playing and replaying in his head; how he had lost everything, everyone, and the other version, how they had all survived and he was the only one lost. "What about everything down there?" He pointed over the bow, at the deep dark ocean. "Will it stay there?"

Dermot shrugged. "Guess so. Who'd go down for it? Diving and dredging is an expensive business, especially looking for something that's not supposed to be there in the first place. It's good and lost now anyway. Could be anywhere." He looked out across the Atlantic.

"Yeah, best left dead and buried. A bit like your love life," Ryan poked, taking a swig of his drink.

"I'm okay on my own." Dermot was checking the lines.

"Seen Erin, lately?" Ryan asked.

"See her every day in the pub if I want to."

"You know what I mean, a date, dinner? You ended up together at Christmas, any progress on that?"

"No, that wasn't anything, she had a bit too much to drink. I put her to bed," Dermot told him. "That was it."

"Really?" Ryan was incredulous. "You always seem to be in a huddle when I see you together."

"Only talking about boats, she's mad about them, she's so not my type, Ryan, so not. Think she's a lezzer, anyway." He gazed out to sea.

"Feck off, she is not, anyway, what if she is? You still fancy the pants off her," Ryan told him.

"I do not, she's hard work, I tell you. Nah, not for me." Dermot pulled his hat down over his eyes.

"What about sex? Apart from taking care of certain urges yourself, what about an old-fashioned romp with a good-looking female?" Ryan pressed.

"Hey, there's a few women on the island happy to show me a favour or two. I'm not short of offers." Dermot assured him.

"Take any of them up … on their offers?" Ryan asked. He had heard rumours about Dermot's car parked outside Lily O'Brien's cottage. Apparently, Sean had the number of times it was still there in the morning, marked on his calendar. "*Lily sells more than horses*," Sean was given to remark. But everyone ignored him. Sean was the biggest bad-mouther on the island. Even *Mother Theresa* would get a bad press off him, Father Gregory often said.

"One or two, nothing more than that, that's enough now, mind your own business," Dermot told his second in command. Ryan grinned, it was not like Dermot to be coy about his sexual exploits. Ryan was convinced he was right. Dermot had a huge crush on Erin, whether he recognised it or not, and was not dipping his toe in other waters in case he muddied the one he wanted to swim in, drown in, even.

Ryan looked at his friend. "You alright though, really?"

They opened another can each.

"Yeah, grand," Dermot said.

"It's just that, you know, you look a bit forlorn."

"Forlorn? *FORLORN*, jeez you've been in far too many shite mini-series, whoever uses a word like forlorn, I'm fucked if I even know what it means," Dermot told him.

Ryan watched him gulp his drink back. "You know what it means alright, and the sooner you do something about it the better. You ain't getting any younger and you weren't that good-looking to start with."

"Fuck off," Dermot told him, good-naturedly.

"Course I will," laughed Ryan, and threw his line back out to sea.

Chapter Eighteen – The Guest List

He pulled his collar up against the wind, it was not a cold day by London standards but he had grown used to warmer climes. The humidity had been hard to cope with at first. He had been what his mother had described as 'chesty' as a child, so any exertion in the vapid, airlessness rendered him gasping for breath. But he had been determined to not only survive, but thrive in this alien place.

He started to learn the language as soon as he went after the commission, blagging his way through his second interview with barely comprehensible Portuguese, that he had rehearsed parrot-fashion over, and over. He smiled to himself. Now he was almost fluent, even had an accent. He had no choice, there had been very little opportunity to speak English in the rainforest. When the natives tried to practise their English, immediately assuming because of his fair hair and blue eyes, that it was his mother tongue, he would feign foreignness, answering with a smattering of Danish. He looked like a Nordic prince, even more so, now his physical lifestyle had toned him. He checked his reflection in the window of *Harvey Nichols*. Not looking prone to chestiness these days, he thought, flashing the window-dresser a smile, causing the young man perched on steps to topple.

"Bullseye," he told his reflection, pointing an index finger and pulling an imaginary trigger. Then checking his watch, he grabbed a rival newspaper from a nearby vendor and headed to the global media centre that was his place of work.

He pushed through the steel and glass rotating door. The security guard nodded as he flicked his card at the electric eye and passed into the vast atrium, an oblong oasis of tinkling waterfalls, frothy palms and clusters of well-heeled media types, sipping energy drinks.

His office was on the tenth floor. There was a lift, a bubble of glass that swished up what had been, in Victorian times, an exterior brick wall. He took the stairs, part of his fitness programme; after all he had been through, ten flights of a building, in the British capital would hardly make him sweat. Paul Osborne was super-fit in both mind and body. He had worked hard to become the media group's most highly-prized, investigative journalist. He had recently returned from two years in the Columbian rainforest, flitting between the hottest cities in the Southern Hemisphere and the wildest jungle. Filing reports, interviews and features which were the lifeblood of Sunday supplements and late night television. Paul Osborne was fast becoming one of the most celebrated journalists on the planet. Paul Osborne was in his prime.

"Check this out," Cilla said, slinging a gold envelope at the work station. Feted or not, he had the same set up as everyone else, a 'hot desk', no place to call home. "An invitation, a real live invitation, nothing so crass as an email to this gig."

Paul held the square of bronze up to the light. How did she know what it was?

"It's a weird one," she told him, pushing blonde dreadlocks behind her ears. "A superstar, Hollywood fundraiser ... check. Guest list to die for ... check. Venue, some godforsaken island, get this … off the west coast of Ireland."

Paul was quiet.

"Did you hear me?" Cilla asked. "What's that all about?"

He pulled a face, non-committal. He could see the invitation had been opened and resealed, his intern was learning.

"Is the island called Innishmahon?"

Cilla shrugged.

"Well, if it is, it's going to be one, big fat Hollywood party in the back of beyond," he told her.

She read the invitation over his shoulder. "Wow, a masked ball, sounds amazing," she laughed, a lovely throaty laugh. "Need a date?"

"Sorry, junior, this is one gig where I need to go it alone," Paul said seriously, tapping the envelope against the desk; his plan was coming together. "I have a meeting in Dublin first, and then I'm on my way."

"What'll I tell the boss?" she asked him.

"Tell him I'm on the inside, tell him it's gonna be big!" Paul grinned, firing up his laptop to book his flight.

Plans for the Ball were going well. Supplies were arriving; lists were being checked; excitement was building. News that one of the many areas of the country, battered by yet another vicious storm, was organising a huge and rather ambitious fundraiser, was reported on national television. One minister commented it was admirable the way the small population of Innishmahon always seemed to rise to the challenge of whatever was thrown at it. His counterpart on

210

the opposition said it was an absolute disgrace there was no funding in the national coffers to help these poor people, who had paid taxes and contributed to the economy of the country, the same as everybody else. The populace of Innishmahon adopted its usual stoical stance. What had the government ever done for them, whichever party was in power?

"You were joking, weren't you?" Marianne asked Ryan. She was just finishing a blog post about the latest superstars attending the Ball.

"Joking about what?" Ryan was stretched out on the sofa in faded jeans, wearing the Arran the colour of his eyes, glasses on the end of his nose, reading the script. He was thinking he would need one heck of a stunt double for some of the antics *Thomas Bentley* was undertaking in this, his final foray into international espionage.

"Us, sharing a room at the big house, hosting the Ball. You made a bit of a song and dance about us not being married." She turned off the computer, threw another couple of lumps of peat on the fire, watching as the purple flame turned to a bright orange glow. She went to the decanter she had inherited with the house, and poured the amber liquid into her favourite whiskey glasses. Lifting two cubes of ice out of the little silver bucket, she dropped them into the liquid. They cracked on contact.

"It wasn't a song and dance." He joined her in the extravagant glass conservatory. There was just enough light to catch a glimmer of sea beyond the lane. He took his glass. Standing behind her, he put his arms around her shoulders, his chin on her head. She had opened the doors, the evening air seeped in, still and cold. She nestled into him. He was solid and warm.

"I want us to be married," he whispered into her hair. "I want that ring on your finger and you to be my wife." There was no edge to his voice, he was stating a fact. She was quiet. She sipped her drink. He kissed her neck, the velvet spot behind her ears. She turned and, reaching up, wrapped her arms around his neck, pulling him to her. She kissed his mouth. A long, hard kiss. When she released him, she looked him straight in the eye.

"Don't spoil this. We can't spoil this," she told him.

He pressed his lips together in a straight smile. Then downed his drink.

"Bed or in front of the fire?" he asked, eyes twinkling.

"Decisions, decisions," she said, unbuckling the belt of his jeans.

"Well?" he teased.

"Both, of course," she replied, and he scooped her up in one movement, carrying her back to where the peat was blazing and the goatskin rug was waiting.

They had all finally agreed which guests were staying where and who was hosting whom, when a call to Maguire's sent them all into a tailspin, putting plans majorly awry. It was Padar Quinn. He and his partner, Sinead, both recent residents of the island, had found someone to stand in for them, minding their new business in Cork, so they could come back to Innishmahon and give the Ball their full support.

"I never thought I'd say it, but I think we're both a bit homesick," Sinead told Marianne later that day, when she telephoned to say they would be bringing baby Bridget with them.

"Not so much a baby now," Sinead laughed. "She's talking like crazy, so much energy, like a whirlwind, and funny, she has us in fits of laughter." Marianne smiled to hear the pride in Sinead's voice. Bridget sounded as if she was indeed fulfilling her early promise, as one of the most charming children on the planet.

"I'm longing to see all of you," Marianne said, watching Joey as he sat on the floor, reading one of his favourite story books, half in English and half in gibberish, to Monty. Monty had, of course, heard it many times before, but he indulged Joey with his undivided attention; he loved the little boy. "Now, the big problem is, with hundreds turning up, and everything a bit makeshift, where are we going to put you?"

"Ah, no need to put us anywhere," Sinead replied, "sure I have the keys to the pharmacy, we'll stay in the flat, it's not sold yet, and if I'm honest, there's been very little interest." Sinead had put the chemist's shop on the market not long after losing her husband, and when her friendship with Padar, also widowed, turned into more than that, they both decided a fresh start was needed, and he put Maguire's up for sale, too. With Brian Maguire newly returned from New York after many years, and in need of an occupation, it seemed perfect timing to match him with the public house that also bore his name. Leaving Padar, Sinead and baby Bridget, free to start a new life together on the mainland.

Marianne lifted Joey into her arms and did a little dance around the kitchen, Monty running between her legs.

"They're coming home, they're coming home," she said in a singsong voice. Joey's eyes widened. "Padar,

Sinead and Bridget." Joey immediately twisted in her arms to look out of the window.

"Where Briggie?" he asked, craning his neck to get a better view along the lane. Marianne was instantly sorry for her outburst. It is hard to ask a toddler to wait a couple of weeks to see again someone he missed so much, someone who had left a huge hole in his, so far, short life.

"Soon," Marianne said. "Coming soon, in a while." Joey's eyes lit up.

Marianne sighed, annoyed with herself for not handling this better. Now Joey would be constantly asking where Bridget was, becoming fractious with anxiety, unable to grasp the concept of time having to pass before his favourite playmate arrived. Maybe that's why Santa Claus was invented, Marianne thought fleetingly, an exercise in anticipation, a formula to demonstrate days and nights passing.

She caught sight of herself in the mirror. She was clutching Joey tightly, as if protecting him. She did not want Joey's childhood to be like hers. Waiting for someone to come; collect her from school and take her somewhere exciting in the holidays. Rudderless, occasionally scooped up by one of her friend's families and bundled off with a gaggle of brothers and sisters to be summered somewhere sunny, sandy and shriekingly noisy. Sometimes she would catch a look of pity in the eyes of the grown-ups, and her heart would sag, like air being let out of a balloon. Disappointment.

"Come on," she called out, to no one but herself, really. "Let's go and see Kathleen, finalise the table plan now we have our guest list. Shall we have hot chocolate in Maguire's?" she asked the little boy, pulling on a fleecy jacket, before strapping him into his all-terrain buggy. But Joey was not the type to be distracted with promises of treats. Too ethereal by far. Monty, knowing an outing was on the cards, sat patiently beside the child, while Marianne hunted for her gloves.

"Briggy coming," Joey told the little dog, who pushed his nose excitedly at the child. "Soooon," Joey said slowly, indicating he had understood, and Monty would just have to be patient too.

"We're nearly there," Kathleen announced, sipping a Whisky Mac, wearing purple fingerless gloves that matched her nail varnish. "All tickets bought and paid for, sponsors for everything, food, wine, champagne reception." She was scanning the ubiquitous clipboard with sparkling eyes.

"Are you putting a fixed price on the sods of earth they're buying?" Brian asked, bringing hot chocolate and fudge in a plastic beaker for Joey, surreptiously slipping Monty a square of fudge, too.

"We considered that, but thought we'd start with a minimum, then if people wanted to bid more they could," Marianne told him. She had been impressed with Brian thus far, quietly calling upon his business contacts to sponsor this, donate that. They all appeared to be wealthy and powerful, and keen to do Brian a favour at the drop of a hat. Yet Brian came across as a modest, self-effacing kind of man, earnestly going about his work, genuinely helping whenever and wherever he could, no hint of the power he seemed to wield.

"Marianne," Kathleen tapped her paperwork, bringing her daughter back from speculating about her father's character. "The marquee will be here next week, the men are helping with that. We've musicians coming out of our ears, two bands, jazz and traditional with Noleen Casey, the harpist up at the big house for the reception, and then Irish dancing to launch the auction, and after dinner ..."

"Good old rock and roll!" declared Dermot, coming through the doors with Father Gregory. They were carrying a huge metal contraption, a pole with what looked like a basket on top. They propped it up in the centre of the room.

"What do you think?" he asked those gathered. It stood about six feet tall, covered in dirt and cobwebs, much of which was now on the floor.

"Ah, Dermot," Erin said testily, "this place was cleaned this morning." Father Gregory had the good grace to look sheepish, but Dermot was centre stage.

"Beacons," he announced, "I've found about a dozen of them, antiques I'm sure, they'll look amazing."

"Where?" Marianne was fascinated. She went to examine the structure, a massive torch.

"In the old boathouse. If we line them along the drive, with some either side of the marquee, it'll look spectacular," he said.

"But do they work?" Erin enquired, examining the poles for wires.

"Old school," Dermot confirmed, "fill the basket with fuel, wood, peat, anything, and light it. Once these are stuck in the ground and lit, they'll be seen for miles around, dramatic!"

"You are," Erin told him, wiping the rust off her jeans.

"Love it," declared Marianne. "They'll look amazing, very gothic, perfect with our masked Ball theme."

"I remember them," Brian said. "Don't you, Kathleen? My parents often had parties up at the house. The beacons would be lit along the beach so those coming by sea knew where to land."

"Not appropriate." Kathleen was frosty. "Decrepit old yokes, not right for our glamorous event. I'd dump them, Dermot, if I were you. Who's going to manage them, anyway? They have to be kept alight. No, some nice lanterns run off the generator will be far better," she dismissed the idea, and took herself off to the ladies.

"I'll talk her round," Brian said; he seemed to do a lot of that.

The discussions and debates surrounding outfits, hairstyles and footwear were far more convivial. The fact the event was billed as a 'Masked Ball' had debates running the length and breadth of the island, with rumours this spectacular, grandiose affair would be littered with intrigue and romance. Innishmahon's Grand Masked Ball, might not have quite the cache of the glamorous Venetians, but it was proving to be just as absorbing and exiting as anything those long ago Italians might have conjured up.

With so many volunteers offering to help over the Valentine's weekend, Erin had no choice but to bow to pressure and come to the Ball. She was officially escorting Brian, as Kathleen had decided the American VIPs needed herself and Joyce in attendance, with Marianne and Ryan as main hosts on the top table. Dermot was to take care of Larry's sister, Lena. He was instructed to be charming, and he scrubbed up very well, in fact they all did. But it was Franco Rossini who, true to form, put a spanner in the works.

"What do you mean, emailing me a table plan? We've done all the table plans." Kathleen was in the Post Office, on the phone. "I've three top tables, celebrities, aristocracy, politicians, representatives of faith communities, industrialists, locals and so forth, it's all been very carefully organised," she was speaking to Larry, who had telephoned on Lena's strict instructions.

"It's just that Rossini's entourage is a little bigger, is all," Larry was being his most cajoling, "a couple of backers, you know, the guys who help finance the movies, they've girlfriends and – you'll like this – Lena's bringing Steven Saggito. I mean, that's a coup, you'll have both *Thomas Bentleys* in the same room, that's bound to help the cause, surely?"

Kathleen pursed her lips, frowning at her reflection in the mirror. She pulled the turquoise bandana down to cover her temples. Her roots were coming through, she needed to leave having her hair done, until as close to the Ball as possible.

"Kathleen?" Larry pleaded gently.

"Very well, but do it this morning please, Larry," she was irritated. "It's Pension Day and there'll be a riot if I don't get out there and give the good burghers of the island their dues and demands."

"Is the money that badly needed?" Larry was shocked, imagining elderly folk wrapped in shawls with holes in their shoes, demanding a few measly euro to feed themselves and buy a bit of peat.

"It is." Kathleen was emphatic. "With the Ball nearly upon us, they need to get to the mainland, new outfits, the beauty parlour, that kind of thing. Anyway, between my duties, the Ball and you messing with the seating plan, I've enough to be doing. I'll have to get Marianne to give me a hand."

Larry was relieved. "Perfect, Kathleen, I knew I could rely on you," he told her.

"But that's the end of it, Larry, we're nearly there with everything, absolutely no more surprises, I mean it," she hung up. There was a banging on the door. The pensioners were growing impatient. "Honestly!" she drank her coffee, clipped on topaz earrings and refreshed her lipstick. "I don't get a minute's peace, honestly I don't!"

All the men were up at the big house, putting the finishing touches to the grounds. Kathleen had been overruled regarding the beacons, especially as Ryan's old chum Scott had volunteered his services, flying in VIPs by helicopter.

"The beacons are needed in the interests of health and safety," Brian reminded her, after Dermot phoned to announce the ace stuntman was making a welcome return. "We've no idea what the weather will be like, especially if one of our typical squalls blows in from nowhere."

It was early morning and he was distracting his wife with herbal tea and a neck massage. They had developed the routine of living at the Post Office during the week and staying over in Maguire's on Friday and Saturday. Kathleen had acquiesced, saying it was like going away for a romantic weekend, every week.

"Very well," she waved a hand. "Once they're managed properly. I just remember as a child, Joyce frightening the life out of me, telling me to stay well away from them, they were very dangerous."

"It'll be fine, you see," he kissed her. "Dermot has everything in hand."

"Now, I am worried," she laughed, wrapping her arms around his neck and pulling him back into bed.

Chapter Nineteen – Funny Valentines

February the fourteenth, Saint Valentine's Day. Marianne peeped cautiously through the bedroom curtains, as if coming upon the day too quickly might frighten it away. A soft, wispy mist hung in the air, swirling gently around the buildings; she looked east, the sun had slithered up as far as the horizon, pushing a clutch of cloud ahead of it. Fair to promising, she thought hopefully, but like most of the residents of Innishmahon, she had no clue what the day might bring weather-wise. Only the elder seafarers ever dare declare a prediction. 'The island has its own weather', the wisest would be heard to say.

She crossed her fingers and said a little prayer for a good day and a great party. Guests had started to arrive the night before, with the majority journeying in that morning, giving themselves a few hours to acclimatise and then prepare for the night ahead. In no time at all the island would be buzzing, people in the pub, the street, strolling on the beaches, nosing around the churchyard. Every room taken, anticipation building, excitement mounting, the whole place alive. Yet for now, before all she had planned, started to take shape and became an unstoppable bundle of full-on energy, she needed a moment, a precious sliver of time to be centred, focused, serene. Tiptoeing downstairs, she signalled Monty to follow and, slipping out of the back door, they picked up the pace, crossing the lane and on towards the sea.

The terrier scampered ahead, slipping through the opening in the cliff, trotting eagerly through the scrub to the beach and into the pearly mist clinging to the shore. Marianne pulled the scarf up to her ears against the chill, picking her way over the wet rocks until she stood at the water's edge; a frothy frill along the sand, grey in the dawn. Monty's outline had melded into the mist, but she could hear him paddling, sniffing along the shoreline, the air was so still. She closed her eyes, letting the rippling water ooze through her mind. All was calm.

First she felt it beneath her feet, a rumble. It grew stronger, she could hear it, as if the earth had a pulse. Monty was at her side, ears pricked, staring in the direction of the pounding noise, coming closer, louder. It was almost upon them. She cast about, where to run, hide? Her heart pounded in her chest. The sea mist held the sound, surrounding them.

Out of the gloom, they appeared at breakneck speed, thundering through the cloak of fog. Marianne screamed. They were on top of them, she and Monty were going to be trampled to death. In a flash, she scooped Monty into her arms, as a blur of heat hammered past, a hair's breadth away. She looked downwards. The horses' hooves had imprinted the sand where Monty had stood.

"Whoa," came a voice, muffled in the sound of hooves slowing, horses snorting. Another voice calling, "Hello, hello, you okay?"

She buried her face in Monty's fur. They were both trembling. She looked up, the riders trotting towards them, steam streaming from the horses nostrils, as they tossed their heads. It was Father Gregory and Franco Rossini. The priest was astride a beautiful, black hunter, Marianne had not seen before. He spooked a little when he saw them, but Gregory sat calmly, patting the horse's neck. Franco was riding

Father Gregory's chestnut mare, stocky and steady, yet thankfully, still nimble on her feet.

"Are you okay?" he asked the white-faced woman, rooted to the ground.

"Are you two mad?" She finally found her voice. "You could have killed us."

"We didn't mean to scare you, Marianne," Franco said, soothingly. "Didn't think anyone would be on the beach."

"How would you know? You can't see anything," she snapped back. "You were heading straight for us."

Gregory dismounted, leading the horse to where Marianne stood. He put a hand on her shoulder.

"Really sorry about that," he was trying to keep his voice calm, but Marianne could see he was shaken. "We started cantering on the far side of the beach," he pointed back from whence they had come, "hardly any fog there, but as we came round, it grew denser. We should have pulled up when we lost visibility. I truly am sorry."

Monty leaned out of Marianne's grasp to snuffle the muzzle of the huge, gleaming creature before him. The horse snorted loudly. Monty yelped in surprise, making the horse spook, rearing up. Gregory grabbed the rein, pulling its head down, hard.

"You didn't look like you were able to stop, from where I was standing," she said, eyeing the beast.

"We were fine." Franco gave her an indulgent smile. "Just two old men, playing *Cowboys and Indians*."

"You looked more in control than Gregory, here." Marianne scowled at the priest. "Galloping around in the fog, honestly." The colour was coming back to her cheeks.

"A nip of brandy for the fright," the priest said, offering her a hip flask.

She raised her hand. "No, thanks, a bit early and I've a long day ahead, we all have." She was bristly.

"Forgiven?" the priest asked.

"Just don't do it again, you ought to know better. That was bloody dangerous, especially with so many people on the island."

The horse started pawing the sand.

"New steed?" Marianne asked, as they started to walk back.

"He's mine," Franco said proudly, dismounting too. He patted its flank. "Something to ride out with Joey, when he takes to the saddle."

Marianne gave him a look. She had not missed him ferreting in his pocket for his pill box, slipping one discreetly through his lips.

"I think that's a while off," she told him, "and you'll need to revisit your ideas on health and safety."

He gave her a quizzical look. She pointed at his head.

"Riding hat, to start with!" She put Monty down, and strode off to continue their walk, to try and restore a little of the calm that had been so brutally disturbed.

Heading back to Weathervane, Marianne noticed a light in Maguire's. It was still very early for anyone to be up and about. She decided to call in. Pushing open the large, oak door, she stood for a moment in the dimness. The fire had been swept and laid, the bar gleamed, brasses shone. The whole place was hung with hearts of every shape and size, an assortment of candles adorned the surfaces. All was ready.

She could hear the familiar clunk of someone busy in the cellar. The door was ajar and a pale glow shone through. The clomp of footfall on the stone steps, signalled someone was on their way back to the bar. He came through backwards first, a huge crate of beer in his hands. He turned, she gasped.

"Padar Quinn! Look at you, back as if you never left," she gushed, rushing towards the burl of a man, sleeves rolled up, huge grin on his ruddy face. She threw her arms around him, beer crate and all. Sinead had phoned to say she was not going to be able to make it, her pregnancy was well advanced, and some special time with Bridget, just the two of them might be a good idea. Marianne, though disappointed, had agreed, but had forgotten to ask when Padar was arriving.

"Hasn't been that long," he said, eyes twinkling with merriment at Marianne's ebullient welcome. She stood back to let him offload. He bent down and took Monty into his arms, scratching him under the chin.

"That's a cold, ole mist out there, boy," he told him, "how about a nice drop of warm milk?" Monty wagged his tail, Padar was always generous in the treats department.

Marianne watched them, so pleased to see each other. She was suddenly back in time, back to the very first day she and the little terrier had arrived on the island. She had hired one of Padar's ancient 4x4s, taken it to look round the island and had come upon Sean Grogan. She had given him a lift back, he was grumbling as usual, there was a power cut and when they had come into the pub, it was aglow with candles, and the whole place smelled of peat. She remembered Padar, stomping up from the cellar, his reticence in stark contrast to his wife's effervescent nosiness. She could almost taste the delicious meal she had eaten, before she had fallen into bed in the cottage, which was now her home. So much had happened, in so short a time.

"I've missed you," she said, glancing around the bar, which looked better than it had in ages. Erin preferred more

practical projects, always wielding a ratchet or hammer
about the place. Brian was totally efficient when he was
there, but that was not very often, and when he was around,
Kathleen was always distracting him with some project or
another.

"I thought you were staying up at the pharmacy?" she
finally managed.

"Sure, he can't keep away. I don't think that business
in Cork is demanding enough. Look at the size of him," said
Erin appearing with Eve, the collie, in tow. The dogs greeted
each other excitedly. Padar pulled his stomach in, scowling
at her.

"Don't be messing this place up, you two," he told
them. They were both damp and out of breath. Eve shook her
coat, covering them all in a fine dusting of sand.

"Just took a run up to the big house. Even now I can
tell it's going to look amazing." Erin sounded enthusiastic.

"You didn't run into Gregory and Rossini, then?"
Marianne asked.

"No, but I heard them," Erin confirmed. "Galloping
around the place like a pair of teenagers let loose."

"Mr Rossini wasn't on one of Lily O'Brien's mad
feckers, was he?" Padar was concerned.

"No, Gregory was riding that, Franco had the good
sense to take the old mare," Marianne said. Eyeing the
optics, she would not mind a brandy now, the memory of her
near miss giving her goose bumps.

"Well, I hope he doesn't buy it," Erin said, pulling
off her scruffy tracksuit top. "That thing could kill
someone."

"Too late, he already has," Marianne told her,
thinking at the same time that, they had an awful lot of work
to do to get Erin looking glamorous for this evening. She

caught sight of herself in the mirror behind the bar. Not too pretty a picture there, either.

"Come on, Cinderella, we have work to do," she said.

"Really? Do we have to?" Erin pushed a mop of frizzy fringe out of her eyes. Marianne took her hand and tugged her up the stairwell. Erin stopped.

"Who's been in the cellar?"

"Why me, of course, there's only me here," Padar replied sharply.

"What were you doing down there?" Erin asked.

"What's it to you?" he bit back.

"It's not your pub anymore, it could be deemed trespassing," she sounded official.

"Hey, hey," Marianne made soothing gestures with her hands, "come on now, I'm sure Padar's just trying to help."

Erin shrugged. She and Padar were always having spats. Marianne pushed her up the stairs.

"Padar, will you feed Monty and Eve, please? God knows when they'll get a bite, with us all up to our eyes in preparations," Marianne called down.

"Yeah, I'll help myself to something too, it's already been a bloody long day," Padar said to himself.

It was a perfect evening, cold and crisp and still. Dusk had fallen quickly and soon the silent sky was filled with stars, a fitting backcloth to the house on the hill, sparkling with light. The coach lamps on the main gates had been polished and lit, the sweeping drive marked out with flaming torches, every few yards. Trees were hung with Chinese lanterns, and above the double Georgian doors, a huge, glass globe glowed.

Just visible as guests swung into the drive, was the terrace and the beach beyond. Vast beacons were ablaze along the curve of coast, guiding those arriving by sea; the old jetty had been extended to make space for extra mooring. The paddock beside the house had been turned into a car park, where aged farm trucks stood alongside supercars and elegant vintage models.

Above, on a flat piece of hillock, more beacons burned, so Scott, bringing the last of the VIPs over from the mainland, could land the helicopter in style. With his long ago SAS experience, he did not need any landing aids, but Scott was a showman, he knew his cargo of spoilt superstars would love the drama of landing on the island in a flame-filled frame.

"Ladies and gentlemen, here I am at the most glamorous event of the year so far," the pretty blonde anchorwoman said into the camera. "This is Innishmahon, one of Ireland's most remote islands, in fact, next stop New York if you head due west. I am in the grounds of a fabulous stately home," she indicated, as the cameraman panned out, "where you can see the stage is set for a truly sumptuous event of the grandest proportions." She started to sashay along the red carpet towards the entrance, ablaze with light.

"Champagne, cocktails, canapés, all is laid before us," she looked up, pointing at the helicopter hovering above, "with celebrity guests being flown in from the four corners of the earth. But let's go and speak to one of the organisers and find out what this is all about." She trotted in high heels to where Marianne Coltrane and movie star Ryan O'Gorman were greeting guests. Marianne was wearing a gown of molten gold, skimming her neat figure in a sheeny glow. She wore elbow-length, black evening gloves and a golden mask, edged with black lace. Her shoes were filigree on molten leather, finds from the attic in the big house.

Ryan complemented her perfectly; black dinner suit, black tie, a gold silk handkerchief at his breast pocket. He wore a matt black mask, his streaky hair brushed back. He looked slightly threatening, yet when he smiled, there was no mistaking it was him. No one smiled like Ryan, more dazzling than any spotlight the generator could produce, Marianne still thought.

The interviewer chatted easily, asking how much they hoped to raise, who was going to attend, what would the legacy of such an occasion mean.

"And I believe tonight will be yet another first," the reporter said, building the tension, "tonight will be the first time two *Thomas Bentleys* have ever appeared together, is that not so?"

Ryan grinned. "Rumour has it, but how will anyone know, in these masks?"

"Is it not traditional to remove the masks at midnight so you can see the identity of the person in your arms?" she asked, leaning in for Ryan's response.

"Indeed, but I'll be very surprised if I'm in the arms of the other *Thomas Bentley*," he pulled Marianne to him, "I'm hoping this beautiful girl is who I think she is," he teased.

"I'm sure it'll be a great night, and hopefully not too full of surprises," the reporter finished up, swishing away to interview the newest arrivals.

"The ballroom has not looked like this for over thirty years," Brian whispered into Kathleen's ear.

"Totally fabulous," she replied, eyes shining behind her mask; blood-red, the exact colour of her gown, set with rubies and crystals.

With all the guests seated, Father Gregory called upon the Bishop to say grace. The stout, elderly man coughed, he was not wearing a mask, yet his cassock and purple sash blended perfectly with the lavish costumes of the other guests.

He began, "In a world that expects reward without effort, riches without toil and success without humility, this little island has always bucked the trend, a strong sense of community, working together for the common good. Whenever Innishmahon needs anything, the people here just get on with it, no moaning or complaining about the hand they have been dealt. It is this fighting spirit, gumption and get up and go, which has made this island, and indeed, the whole of Ireland, great!"

"Oh dear," Kathleen hissed at Brian, "he's doing his 'state of the nation' speech." There was a pause, as the Bishop momentarily lost his place.

"Been at the communion wine again," Brian said, under his breath.

"So," the Bishop coughed, "in the words of *Freddie Mercury*, we are the champions, my friend," he wobbled a bit, "God bless you all, and if it's not too 'down with the kids', let's party on!" he declared.

Laughter and raucous applause followed, as wine was poured and the meal served. All the specialities of the island had been selected for the feast. Fresh crab salad, slow-roasted lamb with hearty winter vegetables, and a fruit-rich strudel laced with homemade plum brandy. The team of volunteer cooks had excelled themselves and the state-of-the-art facilities were more than capable of coping with the demands of such a large event.

Marianne checked her watch, quickly casting an eye over the programme of events. All running to schedule. The sale of sods of earth would commence after the main meal, during cheese and liqueurs. Simon Smith-Kavanagh, the local auctioneer, would handle proceedings. She scanned the room, she could see the top table. Franco Rossini flanked, not by frivolous starlets, but on one side her mother, animated and flirting, and on the other, her aunt Joyce, elegant in cornflower-blue, wearing a pearlescent mask, reading glasses perched on the end of her nose. She was listening intently to the man on her right, Franco's long-time friend, Roberto, no doubt regaling her with tales of the old country. Joyce had a great sense of history.

The furthest table away, nearest the kitchen was, being hosted by Dermot and Erin.

Erin had been the most surprising transformation of all, metamorphosing from a be-jeaned tomboy, brandishing a screwdriver, into a shimmering, gossamer butterfly, hair swept high and pinned with tiny pearls. She wore a sheath of palest pink, a translucent mask, with high-winged sides. Marianne watched her move around the table, her feline form, made more obvious beneath the clinging swathe of fabric.

Dermot who had left his seat, reappeared at the doorway; Marianne caught his eye. He had been watching Erin too.

"Alright?" Marianne mouthed at him. He made the okay sign with his fingers, giving her a grin. Plates were being taken away, Marianne's meal left virtually untouched. She went to lift the glass of champagne to her lips. A hand covered hers, a slight squeeze, it was Ryan.

"Relax, Marie," he said, his lips brushing her ear as he leaned into her. "Everything that can be done, has been done. Enjoy yourself now, it's a party."

231

"I know, but I can't help ..." she started.

"Being a control freak?" he offered, smiling.

She laughed. "You're right, I should just let go, roll with it."

"Even have some fun, yourself?" He pushed the pointed nose of his mask against hers playfully.

"Okay, okay." She took a large glug of champagne.

"Good, that's my darling girl, but don't wear me out with too much dancing now, I want to help you out of that beautiful dress later, and I want to do it, very, very slowly." She looked into the eyes behind the mask. She knew that look. He bent to kiss her mouth, deftly running his tongue across her lips.

"Delicious," he confirmed, and she knew whatever delights the Ball may impart, were nothing to the pleasures awaiting her when it was all over. She was grateful for the mask, as a deep blush rose up from the burn of anticipation in her chest; after all this time, Ryan could still do that to her. Yet there was something else, something even the promise of Ryan's exquisite lovemaking could not dispel. Deep down she was anxious, unsettled. Unsure of what she was worried about. She gave herself a little shake, as the waiter refilled her glass. There was a real buzz about the place, everyone was having a fabulous time, it was all going to be a huge success. The band struck up.

"Let's start the dancing," she said to Ryan, getting up.

"Thought you'd never ask," he replied, taking her by the hand to the floor, as the guests burst into spontaneous applause.

"How much do you think we've raised?" Erin was repinning loosened pearls into her hair, Dermot's dancing could only be described as vigorous.

"Well over anything we could have imagined," Marianne told her, reapplying her lipstick in the mirror they shared. The large first floor bathroom turned into the perfect ladies rest room.

"Everyone was so generous, it was quite moving the way they all rallied to support our little cause," Kathleen said, removing her staggeringly high heels and stretching out on the chaise longue.

"Half of them don't give a feck about the cause, sure they were only showing off to each other, the '*I've more cash to splash than you*' syndrome," Erin said.

Joyce, polishing her spectacles with the hem of her gown, tutted.

"You're too cynical, Erin," she reprimanded. "If you look at the guest list you'll see the majority of the names are Irish, they genuinely came to take back a piece of their homeland, their heritage."

"What a load of sentimental old tripe," Erin replied with a smile, "dreamed up by this one," she oiked a finger at Marianne. "The Queen of Spin, she could sell sand to the Arabs."

Marianne blinked. " I didn't ..."

"I'm not knocking it," Erin went on, "just saying, but I hope once this shindig is over, you kick back a bit."

"What do you mean?" Marianne asked.

"Stop coming up with ideas for this, schemes for that, plans for the other. Chill out, give us all a break." Erin snapped her bag shut.

Kathleen was spraying herself with cologne.

"I'm sure once the funds are in place, we can let the professionals get on with it and everything will be good and ready in time for the season," she confirmed. "I think we've done a marvellous job, and none of it could have happened without Marianne and Ryan, they've made a huge difference since they came to the island, giving so generously, time and money, only wanting to get things moving, make improvements."

"I agree." Joyce stood beside her sister, as they replaced their masks.

Erin sighed. "Yeah, yeah, but it would be nice to get back to normal as soon as possible."

"Normal?" Kathleen gasped in mock horror, hand flying to her throat.

"We don't do normal!" the sisters said together, descending the stairs, giggling like schoolgirls at what was clearly an old family joke.

The huge casement window on the landing was open to the elements and although the evening was clement for February, Marianne went to close it. The moon hung in the velvet night and the stars glowed; the scent of the sea mixed with burning peat from the beacons was delicious. Stopping to take it all in, she heard voices drifting up from the terrace below. Lovers, she hoped, making the most of this night of romance. She strained her ears to hear.

"And you've found out nothing?" a deep, male voice asked impatiently.

"Early days, I have a few leads, but nothing concrete yet," a younger man, accent indiscernible.

"And how long to do you intend to stay?" the other man asked.

"As long as it takes. I need to speak to the right people, get my facts straight, come up with some evidence if there is any, these things take time," the voice was calm, unpressured.

"Very well, but there must be no room for doubt. Time is not on my side, I'm not getting any younger. I don't want to die before you find out whether she really was killed by her own hand, or someone else was involved. I need to know." He gave a bitter laugh as he spoke, but his words were sad.

"If I can find out what happened, I will. Rest assured I'll leave no stone unturned," the other man replied.

Marianne leaned out a little, hoping she could see who was having this intriguing conversation. But the awning on the terrace hid the men from view, and the canvas muffled their voices. Who were they talking about? Was it Angelique? Or was that just her over-active imagination?

"Don't jump!" Someone grabbed her from behind, hauling her back into the room.

"Dermot, you eejit! You frightened the life of out me." She smacked his hand, playfully.

"Were you eavesdropping?" he asked. "Tut, tut, the women on this island are always listening in on that, interfering with this, you're all as bad as each other." He was smiling, leaning out of the window, himself. "Is it a lovers' tryst, a scandalous affair?"

"Just men talking boring business, as usual." She pulled the window closed. "Now talking of lovers' trysts, how are you and Erin getting on?"

Dermot shrugged. "Don't be matchmaking me with that one. Blows hot and cold, mainly cold." The door to the rest room opened and a very attractive blonde appeared. "Thankfully this one blows hot," he whispered to Marianne, who felt obliged to smack him again, but he ducked out of range, striding off to take Lily O'Brien by the hand. "Come on, it's the last set, I'm sure your dance card is marked," he called back, as they descended into the melee.

The band leader had everyone in a large circle, explaining the dance. A simple reel, the men stood still while the women danced through them, when the music changed, the girls danced with whoever was at their side. When the music changed again, it was the men's turn. As it was nearly the end of the evening, the idea was, when the band stopped playing, the dancers removed their masks and revealed themselves to whoever was in their arms. If they so desired, they were allowed to claim a kiss.

Kathleen, and Franco, as guest of honour, were to lead the dancing; Joyce took Roberto's arm and Brian escorted Erin. Marianne was delighted to see Larry and Lena link arms and take to the floor.

Larry, now almost acclimatised to the island, had been fretting about Lena's reaction to so remote, and by her standards, uncivilised, a place. But Lena had been charmed by it all, exclaiming the scenery bewitching, the food delicious and the company delightful. That said, Larry was relieved when asking her how long she intended to stay, she tapped the calendar on her tablet with a dark purple fingernail, saying, "I can't stay Larry, I'm in London day after tomorrow, Steven's got a whole heap to do, fittings, sessions with his dialogue coach and so forth. Have you seen the schedule? Gruelling ain't the word!"

He had indeed seen the schedule, but compared with Saggito, Ryan was easy to manage, nowadays. Larry adored his sister, but would be pleased to enjoy a few days peace and quiet on the island once everyone had disappeared back from whence they came.

'*Peace and quiet, now there's a notion,*' Larry thought to himself, as the bass drum beat them in and the fiddles started up.

The whole room shimmered and shone as the ladies twirled in their finery beneath the chandeliers. The men, elegantly be-suited, were standing in a circle, clapping along with the tune, each ready to pull a glittering, spinning jewel into their arms.

Adrienne Vaughan

Marianne followed Erin, first dance with Brian, then Franco, a jig with Father Gregory, a bit of a bop with Dermot, and then she found herself in the arms of Steven Saggito, who danced the same with every female, pulling them in close, taking a hand to his cheek and moving his hips slowly, no matter what tempo the music. He was tall, with masses of blue-black, wavy hair, square jaw, white teeth, good physique; what's more he smelled delicious. Marianne watched as even Erin, wilted a little. Saggito's technique might be crass, but there was no doubting its success.

The idea was, that everyone should finish up with their original partner for the final reveal and celebratory kiss. But some were slowing deliberately, to linger in the arms of a favourite and others were speeding up to avoid an unwelcome embrace.

With the room so full it was difficult to see who was where, and with the men all dressed more or less the same, hard to pin anyone down. Marianne spun and twirled and turned, and catching her heel in her gown, was just about to tumble to the floor, when she was gripped by the elbows and expertly propped back on terra firma. She leaned against her rescuer and, catching her breath, caught his scent, yet when she looked up, he was gone, disappeared into the dancing. She stood, momentarily still, as two strong arms wrapped round her. Ryan pulled her to him.

"Now I have you, I'm not letting go," he laughed, taking her hands and turning her in time with the music, the volume building, the crescendo upon them ... and ... *stop*. The band finished as one, the master of ceremonies spoke above the clapping and cheering.

"Ladies and gentlemen, reveal yourselves and claim your kiss!"

Marianne and Ryan lifted their masks. "Happy Valentine's Day," she said, and kissed him. Someone tapped her on the shoulder.

"May I have one of those?" The man was still wearing his mask, but his smile was familiar.

"Reveal yourself, Sir!" Ryan said, entering into the spirit. Paul Osborne pulled off his mask, eyes glittering with merriment.

"Paul!" Marianne exclaimed, throwing open her arms. Her former colleague bent and politely kissed her cheek. He turned to Ryan, shaking his hand, heartily.

"Good to see you," Ryan said. "Been too long."

"I didn't know you were coming." Marianne looked up into his face, still boyish, still handsome, but older, wiser, a little harder around the eyes.

"Nor did I till the last minute. I'm with Rossini's crew. I'm doing a series of articles about the making of a movie mogul, might turn it into a biography, you never know." Paul was staring at her, an odd smiled played about his mouth.

"That's my boy," she laughed, "still an old hack."

"Less of the old," he grinned at her. "It's in the veins, what can I say? You always told me that."

"Come on, you two, if you're going to start reminiscing, I need a drink," Ryan said, placing an arm around each of them and steering them towards the bar.

Chapter Twenty – Letting Bygones

The youngsters partied until dawn, enjoying a delicious traditional Irish breakfast on the terrace, beneath the dying embers of the beacons. Despite Brian's pleas to come home,
Kathleen partied with them, surprisingly with Joyce also in attendance.

"Who knows when we'll get another chance to dance the buckles off our shoes? Sure, if we're crippled with arthritis tomorrow, we don't care, the blisters will be well worth it," Kathleen told him, waving himself and Larry off down the drive.

She was sitting next to Joyce looking out through the French doors onto the beach, the silky dawn sliding in over the horizon, turning everything pearly. They were sipping coffee laced with brandy. Joyce pulled a sensible sheepskin over her gown; Kathleen was wearing an elderly mink.

"Were the rumours true, I wonder," she said, nibbling delicately on a sausage.

"Which rumours would they be?" Joyce was well used to Kathleen's late night ramblings. She had such a fanciful imagination. Joyce often thought, if her sister was a bit less like their mother, she would have had a far happier life, less dissatisfied, anyway.

"Our mother, the men, the freedom fighters, the way it ended," Kathleen's voice was small, jaded.

"She was a romantic, Kathleen, that's all. No real harm in her. Remember, it was an arranged marriage with our father. The families had a bit of adjoining land, it made sense to match the two eldest. But she didn't love him, not really," Joyce confirmed. "And when she was widowed so young, it was hardly surprising she fell for one of those handsome revolutionaries, all blood and bluster."

"And deep blue eyes," Kathleen said, dreamily.

"Well, we shouldn't judge her, is all I'm saying." Joyce was firm.

Kathleen pulled the coat tighter, it had been their mother's, but her perfume had faded, long ago. She looked down to the beach.

"I remember coming here, you know, I remember those beacons, burning in the night. Mother insisting we helped keep them alight, dragging logs and lumps of turf out of big baskets."

Joyce nodded. "So the men knew where to land the boats," she confirmed.

"What kind of cargo could only be landed in the dead of night?" Kathleen had asked this question many times. Joyce always gave the same reply.

"Who knows?"

"But you do know, Joyce, you know everything. You know who she was in love with and you know why it had to end." Kathleen was looking at her now, eyes blazing like the beacons she found so disturbing, bringing back memories she thought had been buried long ago.

"Not at all," Joyce said softly, patting her sister's hand, "sure I was too busy minding all of you to know what was going on. She always told me she was on important State business, and I was to keep everybody washed and fed until she got back. I just did what I was told."

Kathleen squeezed her sister's hand in return.

"You were a very good daughter, Joyce. We'd have been lost without you. Pat was only a baby, and you were no more than a child yourself."

Joyce shrugged and took a deep draught of coffee, the brandy warming her chest.

"I know she didn't love our father, but I did. I kind of hoped if I kept things going it wouldn't look too badly on him, dying the way he did." They were quiet for a while, gazing out to sea.

"I never thought we'd be back here, did you?" Kathleen asked Joyce.

"Never," Joyce replied. "And you, Mrs Maguire ... now that is something no one could have seen in the tea leaves." They chuckled.

"I know, imagine the old gossips, 'that flibberty-gibbet's daughter married the doctor's son, a scandal, that's what it is!'" Kathleen laughed.

"Even worse, 'the child she gave away came back!'" Joyce said.

"I never gave her away." Kathleen was serious.

"I know that, but imagine what they'd say."

"You're right," Kathleen agreed. "Far more scandalous than anything mother got up to!"

Joyce just nodded, still smiling. An icy blast blew in and they closed the doors.

"You must be tired, do you want to call it a night?" Kathleen asked, not admitting she was weary too.

Joyce was ready to leave, memories were stirring, time to go.

"Indeed, it's been a huge success, let's quit while we're ahead." And the two ladies rose to their feet, gathering their belongings to head back to Maguire's.

Paul and Larry were becoming reacquainted by the time Marianne arrived at Maguire's the following day. Larry had been far from impressed at Paul's treatment of his former boss in the past, spying on Marianne and Ryan at the beginning of their affair, and splashing salacious, revelations in all the gossip columns and celebrity blogs. Paul had redeemed himself by negotiating the rights to Ryan and Angelique's wedding with one of the better quality magazines for a hefty sum, so for Larry, he was both a necessary evil and a valuable ally. Although both Marianne and Ryan had forgiven Paul and made amends, to Larry's way of thinking, Paul only changed career once he had milked their association dry, valiantly taking himself off to deepest South America to bring the plight of peasant farmers enslaved to the drug cartels to the notice of the world's media.

Paul was in the throes of embracing Monty and reminding him of old times, when Erin arrived to distract him. They had danced together at the Ball and seemed to hit it off particularly well, if the conversation on the way home was anything to go by.

"I like your friend, Paul," Erin had told Marianne, as they walked back along Main Street, arm in arm with Ryan after the Ball. "He has that nice reserved Englishness about him, quite the gentleman."

Ryan stopped dead.

"Really? Quite the gentleman? Do you think we islanders are a bit too rough and ready for your sensibilities, Mistress Brennan?" He bent and made a fuss of kissing her hand, giving a full Regency bow. "I do hope neither of you delightful ladies would favour an Englishman over one of your own."

Marianne had laughed. "I recognise that little speech, one of your old TV dramas?"

"You're right." Ryan took them by the arm again. "I played a French highwayman, my lover was being married off to an English duke, must have been the mask made me think of it."

"Well, as far as I know, Paul doesn't have any blue blood, but you're right Erin, there is something about him. I was his boss once, we go way back," Marianne explained. "An interesting guy, not sure if he's single at the moment."

"I didn't say I wanted to marry him," Erin replied. "I just thought he was nice."

"How nice?" Ryan asked. Marianne squeezed Ryan's arm, hoping he would let the conversation drop. "You couldn't compare him with someone like Dermot, though. I mean, Dermot's a great bloke, he can be a real gentleman too when he wants to," Ryan continued, sticking up for his friend.

"I didn't see Dermot after the last dance. Was he staying for breakfast up at the house?" Marianne asked.

"He took Lily O'Brien home," Erin said matter-of-factly. "Not that it's any of my business, I'm not remotely interested."

"They're just friends, nothing more," Ryan confirmed, giving Erin a smile. She did not see his smile, her eyes were resolutely fixed ahead. They had walked on in silence.

Now, much later, with everyone changed and gathered at the pub, still buzzing with the aftermath of such a fantastic evening, Marianne could see Erin was in much brighter spirits.

"I was just thinking," Paul said, Monty in his arms. "Be nice if we all had dinner together, we're not here for long. I'd love to sample a bit more Irish hospitality, maybe go out on a boat if we could?"

"I'm sure that can be arranged," Erin fluttered at him. "I'm quite a good sailor, if I say so myself."

"But she doesn't have a boat, so you'd better come on mine." Dermot appeared through the pub door, shaking sand off his sailing boots.

"You've been home, then?" Erin said.

"Of course I've been home," Dermot replied, giving her a funny look; the penny dropped. "I only left a lady back at her house, the way any gentleman would."

"You don't have to explain yourself to me," Erin said airily, taking away the coffee pot to make fresh.

"How does tomorrow suit you?" Dermot asked Paul, taking Monty from him.

"Perfect," Paul replied, looking Dermot in the eye.

"Good, that's a date then," Dermot confirmed, glaring after Erin as she disappeared.

Larry stepped in. "Great idea, let's have today to recover, you guys go sailing tomorrow, and we can all have dinner together here after. It'll be our last night, so a perfect ending to a perfect Valentine's." Larry always abandoned his self-imposed regimes relating to diet when he was on the island, claiming he barely ate a morsel living the life of a lonely workaholic back in New York, although the tightness of the belt around his *Burberry* raincoat belied that declaration.

"I'm sure we'll be able rustle something up for the sailors return," Marianne said.

"Do one of your 'specials' Marianne, that delicious fish stew, haven't had one of them in ages." Padar smiled at her. "I'll make apple cake, it'll be like old times."

As if to underline Padar's sentiment, Sean Grogan pushed open the door, hopping to pull off his bicycle clips as he arrived.

"Good God!" he exclaimed, clambering onto his stool. "Have they run you out of Cork already?" He gave Padar an almost welcoming grin.

"Ah, it's yourself, Sean, the ray of sunshine this place has been missing since I arrived. Where have you been at all?" Padar asked good-naturedly as he poured Sean a pint of stout.

"Keeping out of the way of this crowd," he answered, squinting at those gathered. "I had enough of them the last time we had a fecking Festival. Drinking and carousing, music playing till all hours, the place covered in litter. No respect for locals trying to earn a living from a bit of fishing and farming. Townies and, worse, a crowd of rowdy blow-ins, that's all this lot is." He pulled a newspaper out of his pocket, unfolded it and started to read.

"We raised what we needed and more last night," Dermot told him. "So the crowd of blow-ins, as you all them, certainly came up with the goods."

Sean took a sip of his pint.

"Raised a load of money to give backhanders to people who should be doing the work anyway, did you?" he replied. "Well done, keep looking after the fat cats, that's what I say."

Dermot could see Paul was taking it all in.

"There's just no pleasing some people," he told him.

Paul excused himself and went to talk to Padar, but Padar disappeared as soon as he saw the journalist heading in his direction. He did not want to get involved with him again, Paul Osborne was bad news as far as he was concerned.

Marianne flashed a look at Larry. Larry nodded and quickly went to intercept Paul. Despite a goodly amount of champagne, delicious food and dancing until the wee hours, followed by an equally delicious devouring by Ryan,

Marianne had awoken with something unpleasant lurking in the depths of her mind.

It was the conversation she had overheard at the Ball. Voices she thought she recognised. Was the older man Italian? Roberto or Franco? Franco, it had to be, but the other voice, younger, accent indiscernible. *'You idiot!'* she had thought, *'only indiscernible because you lived in the UK for so long!'* The accent was English, educated. She had sat bolt upright in bed. Paul, of course, it was Paul Osborne.

Ryan had reached out for her. "Where are you going?" his voice full of sleep.

"Monty, a quick walk, see you in a bit," She had kissed his tousled head on the pillow, then grabbing jeans and a sweatshirt, hurried to May cottage, Monty cantering at her side.

Larry had been in the bright yellow kitchen, frying bacon, humming happily to himself. *'Oh, dear,'* Marianne had said to herself, *'I'm about to ruin his morning.'*

"I knew he would be up to no good." Larry had poured coffee as they sat facing each other across the breakfast table. "What do you suggest?"

"We have to tell him. Tell him the truth. I was with Angelique when she tried to kill herself. She accused me of ruining her life and then started popping pills like there was no tomorrow. We tried to stop her, but we had no idea she had already taken an overdose. You had to get her on the plane, she went into a coma, and that was it. It was no one's fault."

"But Franco knows all this, we've told him," Larry was stressing … did he have to go over all this again?

"He wants it verified. If there is any evidence to the contrary it will be here on the island. Franco wants to be absolutely sure her death was by her own hand, that neither I, Ryan, nor anyone else had anything to do with it."

Marianne had watched as Larry pulled himself round, smoothed his hair, focussed.

"Okay. How do you suggest we deal with this?"

"Later, the two of us take Paul to one side and tell him everything, straight. Let that be an end to it, no more suspicions, no more speculation in the media, in Franco's mind, or anywhere else for that matter." Marianne was firm. Larry had nodded, deciding Marianne was right, this needed dealing with, and they were the only people who could deal with it, because they had been there, witnessing the whole sorry story.

"And that's what happened," Larry concluded, looking directly at Paul as the three of them now sat in the snug in Maguire's.

Paul nodded, taking a sip of his pint. He looked at Marianne.

"I'm just doing my job," he smiled, turning on the charm. She was immune.

"Snooping around, spying on people is not what you were trained you to do." She glared back at him. "Just tell Franco the truth, Paul, please. There's nothing sinister or criminal to be found here."

"Okay," Paul said, not taking his eyes off her. "I will, for you."

"Do it for yourself, Paul," Marianne replied and left them to it.

Chapter Twenty-One – Rumours And Lies

Maguire's kitchen was the shiniest Marianne had seen it in a long time, gleaming range, work surfaces cleared and wiped, everything in its place.

"You've been busy," she told Erin.

Erin shrugged. "Padar, I think." She was filling the ancient coffee machine with freshly ground beans, the whole place smelled delicious.

"It's a shame Sinead and baby Bridget couldn't make it in the end," Marianne said from inside the vast fridge. "Padar's shown me some gorgeous pictures, she's the image of Oonagh, quite a character, I believe." She started preparing fish for the chowder ahead of tomorrow's farewell dinner.

"I'd imagine Sinead's getting big now, with the new baby coming. Too much for her, the journey and everything, especially if Bridget's a handful and Padar would be neither use nor ornament." Erin flicked the machine on.

"That's a bit harsh, he's been a great help since he came, with Brian busy organising all the catering up at the big house. It's like he's never left." Marianne was wistful, Maguire's did seem to have more soul with Padar at the pumps.

"Exactly, what's all that about?" Erin asked.

"Just being helpful, I suppose. They do have a vested interest in the place, the pharmacy is still on the market, they'll get a better price for it with the bridge and marina up and running."

"Yeah, a lot of people seem to have a vested interest in this place at the moment," Erin said.

"What do you mean?" Marianne was remembering the conversation she had overheard the night before. She wondered if Erin knew anything about it. "What do you think's going on?"

"Nothing." Erin shut up like a clam, loaded her tray and disappeared back into the bar.

Cogs whirring, Marianne carried on with her work. She was startled out of her reverie when Ryan came up behind her and grabbed her in an embrace. He bent to kiss her, but drew back.

"What is it, Marie? What's wrong?" he demanded.

She wiped her face, covered in tears, knife still in hand. She had been thinking things through, reminiscing, missing people.

"Onions," she said.

He gave her a soft smile. "I hear everyone's going sailing with Dermot, and then back here for the last supper. Nice idea, do you need a hand?"

She pointed at the shellfish. "You can prep that lot. How was your morning?"

Ryan started on the pile of fresh crustaceans.

"Interesting. I took Joey up to Lily O'Brien's to meet Franco and Gregory and see how they got on with the horses. Franco exercised his in the school. Looked good."

"And Joey?

"Hmm, not sure he's going to be a natural horseman. He was fine, until I sat him on the pony, then he squawked his head off."

"Oh dear, maybe a bit too young?" she offered.

"Not really, most professionals are more or less born in the saddle. Still if we take it gently ..." Ryan was an accomplished horseman himself, it went with the territory: fencing, shooting, horse riding, he was a professional, after all, he could even tap-dance if he had to.

"What did Franco think?"

"We sat Joey up with him, he still wasn't happy. Franco said Angelique was like that, had to be cajoled into doing anything remotely adventurous."

"I'm sure the poor child was terrified, up there on a big horse with a strange man." She scowled at Ryan.

"It was only for a minute or two, I soon took him back and put him on terra firma." Ryan was washing shells at the sink.

"Cajole is an interesting word, don't you think? I get the impression Franco is good at all types of cajoling. Some people might call it bullying."

Ryan put his hand over hers, feverishly chopping the onions.

"You think too much, you know that, don't you?" he told her. "Some people lead, others follow, the most important thing is choice, that's the ultimate freedom, to my mind anyway."

Marianne stopped what she was doing and looked at him.

"You've been spending too much time with Kathleen." She gave him a smile. "She has great theories, a real philosopher, yet sometimes she can be totally dismissive of everybody else's ideas and beliefs, despite declaring she's the all-welcoming, earth mother."

"Ouch, where did that come from? You get on so well with Kathleen."

"I do, but she's always having a go at Brian, and Joyce, for that matter. I don't necessarily agree with their politics, but let them have their ideology, they're hardly going to blow the world apart at this stage." Ryan went quiet, she could almost hear him thinking.

"You don't think either of them had anything to do with that cargo Dermot was tasked with intercepting awhile back, do you?" he asked.

Marianne frowned. "Not sure, Brian's great, but I can't help thinking there are very few men who would up sticks and traipse halfway round the world to take up with a love he left over a quarter of century ago."

"Romance, true love, that's why. You're such a cynic," Ryan exclaimed.

"Hmm, maybe. That highly valuable cargo might be at the bottom of the sea, but technically it's not that far away. If it's that precious, maybe it could be recovered?"

"No way, Dermot said the police divers checked it out. The yacht broke up, the cost of looking for what was on board would be astronomical, no one's going to fund that." Ryan was adamant.

"Still, an interesting dilemma. The arms ordered by one illegal organisation as a cover for the cocaine en route to another. If they clubbed together they could get their precious cargo back." Marianne shrugged.

"Like I said, you think too much. That's all water under the bridge." Ryan deposited discarded shells in the bin.

"If we had a bridge," Marianne replied, the onions diced to a pulp on the board before her.

An unseen hand was at the kitchen door, holding it slightly ajar, someone had been standing there for some time. The conversation reverted to the food they were preparing. The hand and its owner, slipped silently away.

Maguire's was filling up, most of the previous night's revellers were now hungry and in need of a 'hair of the dog'. Padar was in his element, pulling pints and serving wine. Marianne and Ryan turned their attentions to serving food, and Erin was despatched for more beers. Dermot did not need asking twice to follow her down the steps. She was standing in front of the pile of boxes they had pulled across the doorway into the secret cellar, her hands on her hips.

"It's been moved, then?" Dermot said, ducking under the single light bulb.

"Moved and put back. Maybe whoever it was, was disturbed, checked it's still there and left it at that. Coming back for it later."

"I've had a word with a few ex-colleagues, there's a huge market for illegal vodka. Easy to make, perfectly disguised in clear glass bottles with funny foreign labels and there's quite a haul here."

"Shipped in to be sold on?" Erin tapped her chin, pondering.

"Or made here to be shipped out?" Dermot said. He frowned. "Not Brian surely?"

Erin shook her head. "No, he's never here for longer than five minutes. Padar's back though."

"Do you …?"

"Not interrupting anything, am I? I heard you two were getting cosy." Padar was on the step, halfway down. Dermot lunged at Erin, enfolding her in a huge embrace, burying his face in her soft neck. She flinched, then melted into his arms.

"Thought so!" Padar exclaimed, clunking around the beer barrels. "I'll throw a bucket of water over the pair of you, if you don't stop." He was laughing.

Pleased they had deflected Padar's attention, Erin wriggled free and flew up the steps, back into the bar.

"Keep it between ourselves, will you, Padar? Early days, might not go anywhere and you know how everyone loves to gossip, spare us that, eh?" Dermot pleaded.

"Sure, it's none of my business, youse are free agents, not even my pub, do what you like."

"Thanks." Dermot patted him on the back. "What about you? How's things going?"

"Grand, why do you ask?" Padar was defensive.

"Just interested, Sinead and the baby, all okay?"

"Business isn't easy anywhere, as you know." Padar glanced around the cellar, packed with more stock than he could ever have afforded. "But if we manage to sell the pharmacy at a decent price, that will help. Put a bit behind us, you know, with two little ones to feed and clothe."

Dermot nodded. "Sure, that's a great problem to have, isn't it?"

Padar gave him a look. "Didn't think you had aspirations to be a family man, you never struck me as the marrying kind."

Dermot gave him an odd smile. "No, nor did I." Then humping up a large crate of bottles, he pushed past. "But you have to have something to work for, it can't all be beer and fishing, can it now?" And he went upstairs, leaving Padar to ponder.

"Will you have a pint, Paul?" Ryan emerged from the kitchen. Paul nodded. The Ryan he had witnessed since his arrival had changed since their last encounter; more relaxed; more gregarious; more everything good, really. Ryan pulled Paul a pint.

"Bet you've missed a decent jar, how long were you in South America?" Ryan handed over the drink.

"Long enough." Paul was non-committal.

"You look well, anyway. It seems to have agreed with you," Ryan pulled up a stool beside him.

"I was just thinking the same about you. You look good, living here on the island suits you, seems a good place to settle down, raise a family." Paul took a sip of his stout.

"Yeah, I think so." Ryan was thoughtful.

"Will you guys get married?" Paul kept his tone conversational.

"None of your damn business," Ryan replied, also conversational, a smile on his lips.

"I asked her to marry me once, you know," Paul said, smiling back at his old adversary. "She would have, too, eventually, if you hadn't showed up and scuppered my chances."

Ryan laughed. "You had no chance, after that."

"I thought I was in with a shout when you married Angelique, her being pregnant, and all," Paul continued. "But no, wasn't to be. Marianne still took you back, even though you were a two-timing bastard."

Ryan slid him a look. Despite all that had happened, he had never been unfaithful to Marianne.

"Only kidding," Paul told him. "I was quite close to the story at the time, I knew what was going on. Angelique was a wreck, you'd no choice but to marry her, you had to protect your son, get him out of that situation as fast as you could. Perfect solution for Marianne, you and a child, an instant family."

"It worked out," Ryan said, coolly.

"Yeah, even Rossini has given you guys his blessing. All just like one big happy family."

"This media type bothering you?" Dermot grinned, plonking the crate of bottles on the bar.

"Heard you've relocated here, too, Inspector." Paul gave the big man a casual salute. "On Lifeboat duty, marina manager, or something. This place is a magnet, I know more people here than anywhere."

"Career change. What about you? I thought you'd left all the showbiz stuff behind, heard you're a serious journalist now." Dermot joined them in a pint, it was the first opportunity they had had to sit down and talk.

"Special commission. A series about the *Thomas Bentley* franchise, appropriate timing given the latest developments, Ryan bowing out and all." Paul nodded at the actor.

"I heard Rossini might be retiring, too," Dermot said, under his breath. Both heads snapped round.

"No way, are you serious?" Ryan asked.

"Well, he's totally taken with the place, his great nephew, his new horse, and if I'm not speaking out of turn, Mrs Lily O'Brien," Dermot told them.

"He's after a married woman?" Paul was surprised.

"A widow, good-looking, former model or actress, back in the day," Dermot confirmed.

"Will you stop it," Ryan laughed. "You're playing right into his hands. Giving him loads of gossip and rumour to turn into 'exclusive' stories."

"No, no you're wrong, not my bag anymore," Paul insisted.

"It's total bullshit, anyway." Ryan clipped Dermot playfully about the ear. "Rossini will never retire, die in the saddle, we all know that."

"Yeah, you're probably right," Paul agreed, trying not to sound disappointed that Dermot's hint of an exclusive was probably a myth.

The scores of professionals and volunteers who had arrived to prepare for, serve and entertain at the Innishmahon St Valentine's Masked Ball, evaporated as suddenly as the sea mist that swirled restlessly about the island for the entire weekend. With everything ready for their visitors' last day, Marianne was grateful the sailing party had set off on their excursion and she could spend a few hours in Weathervane mopping up the PR following the event, answering queries, checking websites, making sure the rest of the world received good, positive messages about what had been achieved.

She had just sent her last email when someone knocked on the door. It was Joyce, her mother's sister, standing in the porch in her sheepskin coat and sensible shoes, weekend bag at her side.

Marianne was pleased to see her. With all that had been going on, they hardly had time for a proper conversation.

"I didn't want to disturb you, but couldn't leave without saying goodbye," Joyce said. Marianne stood back to let her in. Joyce removed her hat in the hall mirror, fixing her hair as she came through to the kitchen.

"I've just finished sending out the last press release about the Ball, one of the Sunday supplements is running a double-page spread, there's a gorgeous photo of you and Kathleen with Franco," Marianne said, taking the cake tin from the dresser.

"A lovely man, yet I would imagine quite ruthless, you don't achieve success such as his without steel in your veins, I wouldn't have thought," Joyce replied, looking about. "Are you on your own?"

"Yes, Joey's at kindergarten, Ryan and Monty have gone on the sailing trip with Dermot and the rest of them, it's nice to see you, glad of the company." She handed her aunt a cup.

"I wanted to congratulate you," Joyce said, taking a seat at the kitchen table. Marianne gave a quizzical look. "On the Ball, the fundraising, everything really, it was a huge success."

"Team effort," Marianne responded. "Loads of people helped, donating goods and services, giving their time, this is a great little community, we're very lucky."

"And we're very lucky to have you, Marianne. You've great drive, once you have a vision you go for it, single-minded, determined. I'm full of admiration and very proud of you. I wanted you to know that." Joyce sipped her tea, not taking her eyes off her niece. "Ever thought of a career in politics?"

Marianne's mouth was full of cake, she shook her head.

"You'd make an excellent councillor, senator, even, you could go right to the top, a minister ... think of it." Joyce put her cup down.

"I'm flattered you think so, but no, not my thing at all. I'm just an old hack, doing a bit of old-fashioned local campaigning, no more, no less."

Joyce strode to the end of the room and stood, hands behind her back, looking onto the little windblown garden leading to the lane and the sea beyond. She could just see a shiny sliver of water, the edge of the great Atlantic, teasingly lapping at the shore.

Marianne smiled at her aunt. "Maybe it's you who should be the statesman."

Joyce returned the smile. "I've always been a 'backroom boy' as they say. No, the country needs young blood, fresh ideas, people who know how things work and won't be swayed or distracted, who'll stick to their guns and get things done."

"An expensive and soul destroying business, the life of a good politician, I would say." Her words evoked an image of someone very dear, long gone; George the tireless, hardworking, 'play it by the book' politician. The lovely man Marianne thought she would spend the rest of her life with. Darling George, a dedicated, civil servant, whose vocation had been to selflessly serve, until his dying day. And so it had been. She closed her eyes, holding the image of his warm, crinkly smile, for just a moment.

"Well, give it some thought, not now, but maybe later, when you're done here and need a new challenge. I have contacts, friends in high places who would be very interested in helping you in a political career." Joyce fetched her hat.

"I'm all for a quiet life these days," Marianne laughed. "I've probably had more challenges than most people face in a lifetime."

"You could be right." Joyce made ready to leave. "You never know, you might get married and settle down, that would be its own challenge too." Joyce gave her a look.

"I …" Marianne did not know what to say. She already felt married and settled down, but in reality she was not.

"You'll be glad when everyone has gone on their way now, I'm sure," Joyce said. "Give you a bit of breathing space, ready for the new season."

"We'll be more than ready for that."

"And Kathleen tells me you have everything in place for *Oonagh's Project*, a manager appointed, youngsters lined up to come?"

"Yes, all organised," Marianne confirmed.

"And the big house, all cleared out and ready?" Joyce asked.

"More or less," Marianne told her. "A few of the attic rooms still need sorting, old boxes of papers and files, but we're nearly there."

"Good, give me a shout if you need me, it's a quiet time for me, too, over there on the mainland, I'll happily come and help. But I would heed Erin's policy, burn the lot, no good ever came of raking over other people's cast-offs."

"What do you mean?" Marianne asked.

"What belongs to another time is best left there." Joyce made her way out to the hall, she pulled on her gloves at the door, checking her watch.

"My taxi's due." She kissed her niece. "You take care now, Marianne, remember what I said."

Marianne waved her goodbye, wondering which bit she was to remember. Probably all of it, knowing Joyce, she surmised, going back to her desk and yet another list.

Chapter Twenty-Two – Sea Spirit

Ryan and Monty had arrived early at the jetty where Dermot's substantial launch, *Dream Isle* was moored. Dermot was already on deck, everywhere polished and gleaming, the tri-colour hoisted and fluttering in the breeze of a bright, February morning.

"What's all this?" Dermot asked, helping Ryan unload a large picnic basket from the back of the 4x4.

"Soup and sandwiches, coffee, whiskey and a slab of Padar's apple cake, Marianne had it all ready by the time I came back from dropping Joey off," Ryan told him.

"She's a marvel, that girl, make someone a lovely wife," Dermot quipped. Ryan ignored him. It was too early in the day for him to think what the future might hold; the time for decisions would come soon enough.

"Have you decided on the trip?" Ryan asked, once everything was on board and stowed away in the well-equipped galley. Dermot had a chart spread across the table.

"Weather's set fair. I thought a proper round trip, circumnavigate the island this way."

He pointed out the route. "Head south, come up the west coast, drop anchor in Cloudy Bay, have lunch, maybe a bit of fishing, then head back. What do you think?"

Ryan nodded. "Sounds like a plan. How many coming?"

"Five of us all told. Erin, Brian and Paul Osborne. That's it."

As if noticing he had been left off the list, Monty jumped onto the bench, sniffing at the chart.

"Not forgetting two sea dogs." Dermot scratched him behind the ears. "Monty and Eve, that silly creature never leaves Erin alone, she actually whines when she's out of sight." Dermot shook his head, smiling into Monty's big brown eyes.

"Pair of silly bitches, eh fella?"

On cue, they heard another vehicle arrive, and went to greet their guests. Dermot made a fuss of piping everyone aboard, while Ryan poured a welcoming cup of coffee with a slug of whiskey apiece. Only Erin declined, striding off to raise the gangplank and bring in the fenders ready to set sail, ably assisted by Monty and Eve, who trotted up and down the boat, wagging their tails, checking Erin had everything shipshape.

Once his guests had completed the 'official tour' as he called it, Dermot went onto the bridge to start the engine.

"All aboard?" he called to Ryan.

"All aboard," Ryan replied.

"Ready to cast off?"

"Ready," Erin called back.

"Cast off," Dermot decreed.

Quick as a flash, Erin slipped the knots on the bow and stern lines, as Ryan stretched over the rail to help her back on board. He clipped it secure behind her, as the boat pushed into the water, heading out to sea. The wind whipped up as they drew away from shore. Erin pulled up the collar of her sailing jacket, bright white against her cloud of dark hair flying out in the breeze. She stood gazing at the outline of the island as they left it. Ryan noticed she was wearing make-up, a smudge of lipstick, tiny crystals in her ears sparkling like her eyes. He wondered who she was making the effort for, maybe one of the men on board or just herself;

he knew Erin loved to be out at sea, loved it more than anything. She felt his eyes on her and turned to him.

"What?" She was smiling.

"You and the sea," he said.

"What do you mean?"

"Just love it, don't you? Being out on the water, like this."

She gave him a big grin.

"It's so free and exciting, just get in a boat and go, escape from everything, leave it all behind."

"It's that sort of place, isn't it? Innishmahon." Paul Osborne joined them. "Everyone's either escaping to it, or running away from it."

"I won't be running away, it's home for me now." Ryan was firm.

Paul was looking at Erin, he had been disappointed she had left the Ball without him the previous night, he had offered to walk her home, but she had just laughed and said it was hardly a walk.

"What about you?" he asked her.

She shrugged. "I was born here, ran away a few times over the years, but here I am back again. Who knows?"

Paul looked up at the cliffs, monolithic slabs of granite glinting in the sunlight, a natural fortress around the island's shore.

"I can feel the spell it weaves over you all, wherever you go in the world it calls you back, whatever nature throws at it, you all rally round to protect it, fight for it. It's amazing, really," Paul was wistful.

"Always been the same." Brian was standing beside them, holding the rail, shielding his eyes from the glare of the sun on the water. "My family has been connected to the island forever, there's always been a Maguire here. When I left, I thought that was it, the end of the line, the spell broken, the Maguire's all gone, and here I am, back after all this time, and to find I have daughter too, well that is magic, no doubt about that."

"Life jackets on, people," Dermot called down from the bridge. "Getting choppy." He nodded out to sea.

"Are we having a burn-up?" Erin asked, hoping he would push the launch to its limits once they were well into open water. Dermot gave her a look.

"You up for it?" he asked.

"Of course I am, come on, let's see what she can do," she egged him on.

"What about our guests?"

"A couple of native islanders, a super-spy and an investigative journalist, no namby-pamby land-lubbers on board, go on, it'll be fun."

"Buckle-up people, the lady wants to see what this old girl can do … are you ready?" Dermot shouted, pushing the throttle upwards.

As the boat speeded up, it rose onto the plane, skimming over the water like a stone, spray flashing out from its sides, a vast chasm of water sparkling in its wake. Erin and Eve climbed out onto the bow. Erin sat legs dangling over the front, she wrapped one arm around the bow rail and the other around the dog, cuddled up beside her as they raced through the water. She looked back at Dermot at the wheel, the wipers full pelt on the windscreen.

"Faster?" he called to her.

She pointed ahead. "Go!" she yelled, hair whipped back, biggest smile Dermot had ever seen her wear.

"Look at her, just look at her, she's like a kid, I've never seen anyone get such a kick out of a bit of a spin on the water," he said to Ryan, and Ryan did look at her, they all looked at her, she was alight and alive, a glowing, vibrant masthead, pointing out to sea, brave and bold and beautiful.

"That's it, full on," Dermot said, as the launch reached its pinnacle.

"Here, let me take over, get out there, feel it yourself," Ryan said, edging the captain away from the controls.

"Okay, just a bit longer though, then bring her back gently," Dermot said, as he climbed out to join the females. Paul and Brian were leaning out of the cabin, enjoying the ride. Monty was next to Ryan on the captain's seat, ears pricked, taking it all in as they sped on. Ryan watched Dermot clamber down beside Erin and the collie dog, fur fluttering in the breeze between them. He reached his arm across the dog to Erin. She gripped him in excitement.

"I've seen something, I'm sure of it," she screamed. "A dolphin, look, look. I can't believe it, look there!" She stretched out beyond the rail. It glimmered in the water, just below the surface, then leapt, a perfect arc, a rainbow of spray in the sunshine. "Oh my God, it's beautiful, just beautiful." She put her hands to her face, overawed. "I've never seen one in the wild before, close up." The dolphin flipped its tail, lifting itself out of the water, turning to look at them, it seemed to be smiling. It swam closer.

"Hello," Erin said. Bright, intelligent eyes shone into hers. "You are so lovely," she told it, stretching towards the creature, shining in the sunshine.

"Don't go too far!" Dermot shouted above the roar of the engine. She leaned out further and, as she did, caught her jacket on a shackle. She tried to free herself, just as the bow bounced off a wave. She lurched into the air, about to be catapulted into the water. Dermot lunged, grasping her sleeve as she began to disappear over the edge. Eve barked in alarm, then leaping forward, took the collar of Erin's jacket in her strong jaws. They hoisted her back on deck. Dermot threw his arms around her in a huge embrace. Eve was barking and licking her face, Erin was laughing. It was over in a matter of seconds. Ryan slowed the boat as smoothly as he could, careful not to jar the controls and cause his passengers, perched on the bow, to be flung into the water.

"Bloody hell, that was close," Dermot said, looking into her eyes.

"Not at all, I just slipped," Erin replied. "I can swim, you know." She shrugged it off, but her face was wet, spray or tears, he could not tell. "Did you see the dolphin?" She scanned the water for signs.

"Amazing, I've never seen one here before," he said, not taking his eyes off her. "You okay?"

"Totally." She bent and kissed Eve on the nose. "Thanks for saving me," she told the dog.

"What about me?" Dermot wrapped his arms around the two of them.

"Thank you, too." She looked up into his face, pale beneath his freckles, green eyes glinting down at her, a strange look, fear and something else, she did not recognise. "Come on," she wriggled free, "let's set our course properly, you can show me how to work all that new-fangled gimmickry you have on board."

Bereft of girl and dog, Dermot let his arms fall by his sides and followed them onto the bridge. Ryan had slowed the boat to a gentle tug.

"Alright?" he asked, as they appeared.

"Fantastic," grinned Erin. "Did you see the dolphin?"

"Only just, I was too busy watching you nearly going in the drink," he told her. Yet something had touched him when the dolphin appeared. A shadow from the past? A glimmer of hope?

"Ah, not even close, we got up some steam though, didn't we?" Erin laughed.

"She's brilliant, isn't she?" Dermot said, stroking the wheel lovingly. Ryan smiled, sure Dermot was referring to another female, one with wild dark hair and a penchant for speed; one almost as fearless as he was.

The next couple of hours on board were far more languid. Disappointed the dolphin had disappeared, Erin was fascinated by the launch. Fully equipped with the latest GPS and sonar, and given a fair wind and following tide, it neatly outperformed everything else on the island. It was comfortable, too, a well-fitted galley with all mod cons, impressive aft cabin, luxuriously appointed, mirrored wardrobes, soft lighting. She sat on the bed, running her fingers over the satin coverlet, wondering how many ladies had been entertained here, rocked to sleep by the movement of the water, wrapped in Dermot's warm embrace, having enjoyed his doubtless energetic lovemaking. She shivered, standing up, straightening the sheet she had disturbed.

"Here you are!" The clipped tones of an English accent. Paul Osborne pushed open the door. "Nice," he said, scanning the cabin approvingly, his gaze resting on her. She had taken off her jacket, it was warm down below. The soft V-neck sweater skimmed her neat curves, she had loosened her scarf, her throat bare. She felt a flush rise up from her chest. He stepped into the room, closing the door behind him.

"You look fabulous today," he told her. "You were pretty amazing at the Ball, too, I couldn't take my eyes off you …" He moved towards her, slipping his arm around her waist, pulling her gently towards him. She looked at him under her eyelashes, giving him a smile.

"You're very charming, Paul," she whispered.

"And you're gorgeous, Erin." He looked into her eyes. She knew that look, he wanted her, she wanted him too. Brushing against him, she could feel he was aroused. She swallowed. Her stomach fluttered. She leaned into him, breathing his scent. Suddenly his lips were at her throat, on her skin, she could feel the heat of his mouth.

"God, I want you, Erin, ever since I first laid eyes on you." He kissed her earlobe, then behind her ears, his breath on her neck. He lifted her sweater, running his fingers along her spine. She started to tingle. "Let me make love to you, please. Let me kiss you all over, lick you and love you, everywhere." His hands moved to her breasts. "I know you want me, too, I felt it when we were dancing, your nipples bursting through your dress, begging me to caress you, push my fingers inside you." He kissed her harder. She opened her mouth, his tongue soft and warm. She closed her eyes as desire seeped up from between her legs to her stomach. She felt again, that long forgotten rush of emotion, the need to be taken, devoured inside and out. She could feel the heat rising …

"Please stop," she said, the words barely audible. He paused, she trembled. He moved to kiss her again. She was a thread away from melting, all care for where they were, who she was with, right or wrong, evaporating. She lifted her gaze from his mouth, eyes awash with tears. He took a step back.

"Erin?" he asked.

"I'm sorry, I can't," she said, blinking a memory away. Confused, he fought his emotions, taking a deep breath. He swallowed.

"Hey," he said, pushing the fringe from her eyes with his fingers. "I'm sorry, sorry for being a stupid arse, coming on too strong." He put some more distance between them. She let out a gasp, her knees gave way, she collapsed onto the edge of the bed, relief, disappointment, she did not know which. She covered her face with her hands.

"Sorry," she whispered, unable to look at him.

"Don't be, please, I'm the one who's sorry, my mistake." He was Paul again, normal speaking voice resumed.

"Here you are!" The door to the cabin burst open. It was Ryan. Eve flew to Erin, tail wagging wildly, twisting her body in excitement at seeing her again. "She's been going mad looking for you, whining like a puppy," he told them, taking in the scene. "Everything okay?" He looked directly at Erin.

"Yes, why wouldn't it be?" she replied, getting up, arranging her fringe over her eyes.

"Just clearing up a misunderstanding," Paul told him. "I got something all wrong." He looked at Erin. She gave him a small nod.

"Good. Misunderstandings are best dealt with sooner rather than later." Ryan was brusque. "We're nearly there, time for lunch I'd say."

"I'll go and help," Erin pushed past. Paul went to follow. Ryan caught him by the arm.

"I hope you weren't trying anything on?" He looked his old rival in the eye.

"None of your business." Paul was defiant.

"It's all my business, Paul, remember that," Ryan warned. Paul gave him a bright smile.

"Sorry, forgot you're the self-imposed King of the island."

"Always making up headlines," Ryan replied, smiling back at the Englishman.

The galley smelled delicious. Brian was stirring soup in a large pot on the little gas stove. The table was laden with fresh soda bread, crab and rocket salad, ham hock and homemade apple chutney. Dermot descended from the bridge, rubbing his big hands together.

"I'm starving, even after all we ate last night," he said.

"Me too," Brian agreed. "What is it about being on a boat that heightens the senses? Makes you ravenous and everything taste absolutely delicious."

"That's true enough, always makes me feel frisky too," Dermot laughed, assembling a towering sandwich for himself. Erin took a mug of soup onto the bridge. She was looking across at the beach when Ryan joined her.

"Beautiful," he said, after a moment or two sitting munching his lunch companionably beside her.

"I love this side of the island. More remote, wilder somehow. It's not changed one iota since I was a child," she said.

"I remember it, too, fishing with my uncles. It always felt so exciting, being here, away from everything civilised and safe," Ryan agreed. "Will you stay, do you think? Stay for good?"

She shrugged. "Dunno. Not much for me here." They were quiet for a few minutes.

"It's what you make it, I suppose. Is there much for you anywhere else?" he asked. She gazed into her mug.

"I thought there was once, a long time ago. But no, I'd have to start again, pastures new and all that." She feigned brightness.

"Nothing wrong with a fresh start, we all need to make them from time to time," he assured her. "You can make a fresh start anywhere though. You don't have to keep moving away." Erin looked at him, how did Ryan know she was thinking about moving on?

"It's easy to do that when you're in my line of work. It's part of the job, on the road, a new role, a fresh start. Before you know it, you're no longer in your prime, with no home, no real family to speak of, no roots down. Need to be careful of that. Sometimes it's easy to miss what's right in front of you. Sometimes you just need to grab it."

She looked at him under her fringe.

"I hope you're not trying to give me advice, Mr Movie Star?"

"No way." He raised his hands defensively. "Just saying."

"Maybe you should heed your own counsel, as me granny used to say." Erin finished her soup.

"Such as?"

"Grab what's right in front of you. I know you want to marry Marianne, be a real family. Some people think that's old-fashioned, but if it's important to you, what's wrong with that?" She stood up.

"And what do you want? What's your dream?" Ryan put the ball back in her court. She shrugged. "Something similar?" he pressed.

"We were talking about you." She prodded a finger at him. "Make it happen!"

"Same as that," he smiled, prodding her back.

"Look, look …" a loud clatter of feet running along the deck. They jumped up, Brian was running towards them, pointing at the shore.

"What is it?" called Dermot, coming up from down below, perhaps the dolphin had reappeared.

"Horse, cantering along the beach," Brian replied, straining to look over the rail.

"Nice," Ryan said. It was a glorious day for a gallop across the sand.

"No, no. I can't see the rider." Brian was anxious. Dermot had the binoculars.

"You're right, all tacked up, no rider!" He handed the glasses to Ryan. "I'll get in a bit closer, see what's what."

Erin was at the anchor, lifting it. Paul joined her.

"What's up?"

"Loose horse on the beach. We're going in." She was matter-of-fact.

He put his hand over hers on the winch. "Okay?"

She gave him a brief smile. "Fine, honestly." And he smiled back, she meant it.

"Shit!" Ryan exclaimed. "It's Franco's horse. He went out with Gregory this morning," he called up to Dermot.

"Any sign?" Dermot called back, turning the wheel and *Dream Isle* skilfully towards the shore.

"Not yet."

"Keep a fix on it," the captain ordered. "Erin, get up here and check this sonar as we go. Rocks around here could ground us in a minute."

Erin fixed the anchor fast and flew up to the bridge to help Dermot. Paul stood scanning the coast. *If Rossini has been thrown from his horse and needs to be rescued by Ryan O'Gorman aka Thomas Bentley, rushing ashore in a speed boat, that would make a great story, even if I have to flush it out a bit, make it a bit more dramatic.* A yell broke his thought process.

"I can see someone, over there, by those rocks at the edge of the beach," Ryan shouted, pointing.

"Is it moving?"

"Can't tell," Ryan replied.

"We better go and find out. Help get the dinghy launched, we're going ashore. We can't get any closer on *Dream*, she'll be wrecked," Dermot explained, dropping the

271

engine into neutral. Brian was at the anchor, releasing it quickly, making the boat fast.

"Erin, will you stay with the boat? We'll need Brian with us, and Ryan, if we've to carry anyone."

"I'd like to go …" Paul started.

"No way." Ryan was firm. "Too many in the dinghy. We need Brian." Brian had found the boat's medical box, he was loading it into the dinghy.

"Erin, okay to stay here?" Dermot was the captain, his word was law.

"Take the two-way. You can tell me what's happening, what needs doing." She handed him the radio.

They climbed into the rubber boat and pushed off. The bay was calm, the water flat. They sped across the short distance to the cove, arriving just as another horse appeared on the horizon. This one still had its rider. The man waved down at them, then pointed at the body on the beach.

"Is that Gregory? I can't tell?" Ryan asked, shielding his eyes. The February sun hung low in the sky.

Dermot hopped into the water, immediately wet to his thighs. "We'll take the dinghy with us, current is deadly around here, it'll be washed away, we'll have no way of getting back."

The three of them ran together, carrying the dinghy between them. Brian had the first aid box tucked under his arm. As soon as the dinghy was safe, they raced to the figure splayed out in the sand.

"My God, it's Gregory, quick, fast as you can," Ryan shouted, racing ahead of the others. He fell to his knees. The priest was snow-white, his body crumpled and somehow twisted the wrong way. His eyes were closed, a small trickle of blood had escaped from the side of his lips. Ryan reached for his hand. Stone cold. He was patting it, calling his name when Dermot and Brian appeared on the scene.

"Shit, is he dead?" Dermot gasped.

"Dunno." Ryan was shocked. "It's not looking good."

Brian moved him gently out of the way. "Gregory, can you hear me?" he said loudly, feeling for a pulse. He lifted the man's eyelids with his thumb. He raised his hand for silence, although all could be heard was the soft whoosh of the waves against the shore. Taking the priest's wrist, he waited patiently to feel a pulse.

"Is he dead?" Dermot asked again.

"I hope not," came a hoarse whisper from the corpse. "Because I'm not in heaven if you feckers are here with me!" Gregory coughed, spat out some sand, then trying to move, groaned and fell back.

"Where does it hurt?" Brian asked. The priest pointed at his shoulder.

"Collarbone, I bet," Brian surmised. "Can you feel anything else?"

"It's more what I can't feel. No legs."

Brian started rummaging in the first aid box.

"What do you need?" Ryan asked him, grey with concern.

"Painkillers, a stretcher and a bloody miracle," Brian hissed under his breath. He had turned away so no one else could hear him.

They looked up at the sound of hooves approaching. Franco Rossini, riding Father Gregory's chestnut mare, was leading the gelding, the animal's flanks slathered in a froth of white sweat.

"Mama mia," he gasped, jumping from the saddle, striding quickly to where the priest lay. He knelt beside him. "Gregory, you hear me? We'll get you outta here, straight to the hospital, immediate." He looked at the men, then out to sea. "Thank God, you saw from the boat, and you have medical help."

Brian was trying to remember how much painkiller he could safely administer. Gregory was a big man, in a bad way, he needed a superhuman dose. Dermot was on the two-way radio to Erin, telling her who they had found and the state he was in. He kept it brief. Factual.

"We need the air ambulance, can you contact the Lifeguard. Over," he barked into the handset.

"On it. Over," Erin barked back.

Ryan was standing with Franco. The older man was pale beneath his sallow skin, he was sweating, eyes bloodshot, hands trembling. Ryan took the reins of the horses from him, leading them away from where Gregory lay. Franco was looking for something in his pocket. He pulled out his pill box, popped one into his mouth, struggling to swallow his mouth so dry.

"What happened?" Ryan asked.

"I ... I did not see," Franco's voice shook. "We were over there, beyond the cliffs." He looked up. "Walking together, talking, admiring the view. We'd swopped horses earlier because my stirrup broke, Gregory said his horse was safer and he would ride mine slowly back." He stopped, eyes scanning the hills beyond the cliffs, forming the backdrop to the beach.

"And suddenly, gunshot. The horses took fright, the gelding bolted, galloped ahead, we lost them."

"Gunshot?" Ryan was shocked.

Franco nodded. "Straight at us."

"Are you sure?" Ryan stared at him.

"Of course I'm goddamn sure, I know what a gun sounds like," Franco bit back.

"But why...?"

"Who knows? Thank God the horses took off, or we would both be dead." They looked to where Gregory lay. A dreadful silence hung between them.

"We're in luck," Dermot called to Brian. "Air ambulance not too far away, just off the coast on a training run."

"How long?" Brian asked.

"Ten minutes, they reckon," Dermot confirmed.

"Luck's nothing to do with it," Father Gregory murmured, smiling slightly now the painkiller was taking hold. "Sure, my boss is the main man, if he can't sort me out, no one can." He chuckled and closed his eyes.

Dermot looked at Brian, alarmed.

"It's just the drugs, he'll hopefully doze awhile. Let's cover him up," he said, pulling off his jacket. "Make him as comfortable as we can until they get here."

Chapter Twenty-Three – Conspiracy Theory

Totally unaware of events on the other side of the island, and with everything in place for the visitor's farewell meal in Maguire's that evening, Marianne was making her own voyage of discovery. She had never been to her aunt's guesthouse, she had heard how elegant the farmhouse was, how stylish the drawing room, the original works of art, the collection of *Waterford* crystal, but she had never visited.

She took a taxi from the ferry, the battered file she had thrown in the basket with the Christmas decorations, safely locked in an old briefcase. She wanted an explanation, there was a piece missing from this particular puzzle, the jigsaw puzzle that was her life and she felt sure her aunt was the only person who knew what it was, and where it should fit.

Joyce was totally unsurprised when she opened the large, Georgian door to find her niece standing there. It was the second time the women had greeted each other that day.

"Come in, I've been expecting you, for some time," she said, eyeing the briefcase.

Anxious to stay focused, Marianne barely noticed the beautiful hallway, tall mirrors, flowers everywhere, the solid staircase, walls filled with art. Joyce showed her into the morning room, the fire was lit, drapes drawn back, a watery sunlight played on the rich tapestry of the armchairs.

She sat, while her aunt brought coffee and shortbread.

"Well, what have you found?" Joyce asked.

"These." Marianne opened the file, spilling the letters over the coffee table.

She had read and re-read every single note, love letters from someone with the initial 'B', to someone only ever addressed as *'My love'*. The notes gave very little away, no dates, no times, nothing in detail; vague declarations of physical love, but nothing graphic or even erotic, letters from another time.

But this love was definitely illicit, maybe even adulterous, a third party was referred to, 'if they ever found out', 'if they were free would their love ever be permitted'. Every missive filled with passion and angst, love and fear. And then it stopped, ended as abruptly as it had begun. The last letter seemed to contain promise of a meeting, a secret rendezvous, word of 'great and glorious news to tell', 'a joy of joys' and then nothing. No letter of goodbye, note of regret, nothing.

Joyce barely looked at them. She walked to the window, looked out across the lawn.

"This is not a nice story, Marianne, but you need to know, what you choose to do with the information I am about to disclose is up to you. Just remember this is family, your family and no one but you and I will know this secret." Joyce continued to gaze outside. "My mother, Bridie, and Brian's father were having an affair. They were from different backgrounds, she, the widow of a farmer, he a married pillar of the community, the doctor. She was a Catholic, he Protestant. They had a common interest though, both were involved, rightly or wrongly with the IRA. He was highly principled, believing all of Ireland should belong to

277

the Irish, whatever their religion. She, a wild romantic. They were in madly love. It was not going to end well."

Marianne went to lift her cup, her hand trembled.

"How did she die?" she asked.

"No one really knows," Joyce said. "She disappeared one night, and a couple of days later she was found, on Horseshoe Bay, fallen from the cliff they said. They brought her body to the cottage and we prepared her for the Wake, then they took her away, buried her at sea."

"But you were only teenagers ..." Marianne was shocked.

"I had just turned twenty, Kathleen was younger, she didn't really know what was going on, says she can't remember, which is just as well."

"Why?" Marianne asked in a quiet voice.

"Brian's father ran the children for sale operation from the island. He checked the babies for diseases, gave them health certificates signed by himself, a doctor, ready to send to America. He did it as a sideline and anything he made, he gave to the cause."

"Oh my God." Marianne sat back in her chair, staring at the papers. "My own grandfather?"

"I'm afraid so. It wasn't long before Bridie found out what was going on, what was coming in off the boats along with the arms and the explosives; children, Irish children, being taken from their mothers and cleared for sale in America." Joyce had turned back into the room. Her face was hard and cold, Marianne had never seen her look so brittle.

"Shall I go on?" her aunt asked.

Marianne nodded.

"I remember arguments, huge rows. I'd put the others to bed, and sit on the stairs and listen, my mother crying, pleading for him to stop. Him saying it was the right thing to do, the children were better off, they would have good lives. And then he stopped coming, we never went to the big house again. Not long after that, they found her on the beach." Joyce was staring at the fire.

"Did she kill herself?"

"Who knows?" Joyce replied. "I heard, years later, she threatened to expose them all. It was around the time you were born, when she died. I know Kathleen thinks mother was ashamed of her, and wanted you given away, but it's not true, she was in a bad place. The Maguires sent Kathleen away to have you in the convent, but our mother loved us. If she could have found a way to keep us together ..." Joyce pressed her fingers to her eyes.

Marianne went to her aunt. She put her arms around her.

"I'm sorry, so sorry. I've stirred it all up again, all this bad feeling."

"No, don't think that, don't ever think that. You're a good thing, a good and precious thing. You see, you are the bridge, the bridge that was broken, washed away, the bridge between the Maguires and the MacReadys, the past and the future. That's why you're here, I'm sure of it." One of Joyce's guests appeared in the doorway. "Excuse me," she said, and left.

Marianne sat in silence, trying to take it all in. She looked into the fire, then at the love letters strewn before it. Letters that were neither good nor bad, but private, something from another time. And she realised, she had found her piece of the puzzle, Joyce was right, she was the bridge between the past and the present. Now it was down to her - the result of a love affair between a Maguire and a MacReady - to decide what to do with this dark family secret. Publish and be damned, it was the truth, after all, or leave them and their sad, sorry story buried in the past from whence it came. Marianne took a deep breath, then slowly and deliberately she took each sheaf, tearing the love letters into pieces before tossing them into the fire. The peat made a little sigh as the shreds burst into flames.

Joyce returned and watched expressionless as the last of the missives were flung on the flames.

"Will you stay for lunch, Marianne? I've lots of lovely, happy tales to tell you, tales I'd have told you every year of your life, if I'd had you with me." She was smiling at last.

"I can't wait," Marianne said, taking her aunt's arm as she led her out of the room.

By the time Father Gregory had been strapped to a stretcher and whisked away, Erin had radioed Kathleen and told her there had been an accident and to let Lily O'Brien know Ryan and Franco were walking the horses back, and they would be some time.

"Any idea how bad Gregory is?" Kathleen asked, fear caught in her chest like a fist.

"No word yet, I have to go, the others are back."

"Are they okay?" Kathleen was suddenly fearful for them all. Is this what she had been dreading? The line went dead.

Erin switched off the radio and went to help Paul haul up the dinghy as the rescue party came on board. Paul had kept a dignified distance while the others were away. Only asking if she knew who was injured, seeming mildly disinterested when he heard it was the priest. He sat quietly making notes on his tablet and Erin had been grateful for that. She was annoyed with herself for giving him the 'come on' at the Ball. Feeling guilty because Paul had not misunderstood the signals she had been sending, they were loud and clear and she was angry because after all this time, all this monumental self-control, a little bit of flattery and flirtation, with a suave, good-looking man had sent her into a tailspin. All defences down, she had dissolved into a spineless heap of desire at the merest touch. She hated herself for being so weak.

"I hope they protected you from any unwanted advances while we were away," Dermot grinned, pointing as the dogs trotted up to him in welcome. Erin gave him a look.

"Only trying to lighten the mood," Dermot said. "Come on," he handed them each a tot of whiskey, "no one's dead, and those guys back there were brilliant." He checked his watch. Brian had gone with the priest, he wanted to hear the verdict first-hand, be there for him when he came round.

"Could have been a lot worse, I guess. Was Mr Rossini ok?" Paul asked.

"A bit shook up, understandably, but fine I think," Dermot confirmed.

"Did the horses bolt? Did something spook them? Gregory is such a good horseman, I'm surprised …" Erin said.

"Well, here's the thing, Franco said they heard gunshot, that's what did it. No, wait a minute, it was more specific than that, he said they were shot at, that's what he said." Dermot poured himself another drink.

"Are you serious?" Paul was aghast. "Shot at?"

Dermot shrugged. "Like I said, he was pretty shook up."

Paul downed his drink. Erin looked at him, his eyes were alight with excitement, he seemed almost pleased with Dermot's news.

After Erin's call, Kathleen spoke to Marianne, who had not been home long, having enjoyed a long lunch with Joyce. Marianne was shocked, then stoical, saying how lucky it was they had spotted Gregory from the boat and that he was a strong, fit man and that Brian was with him, she was sure all would be well. Then Kathleen rang her sister, but Joyce had heard about the accident on the radio that very afternoon.

"How did they know so quickly?" she asked.

"Paul Osborne, the journalist more or less on the scene," Kathleen reminded her.

"Indeed, the English chap. I remember him from the Ball, had his eye on Erin all night, when he wasn't gazing over at Marianne." Joyce did not miss much.

"They've taken Gregory to a special unit in Galway, Brian's staying with him, sure, he has no one in the world."

"He has us," Joyce confirmed, aware that Kathleen was very anti-Catholic church when it came to issues like 'the three Cs'; clergy, celibacy and contraception. It would take only the slightest remark to set her off on a diatribe of why 'those feckers in Rome need to get with the programme' one of her favourite sayings. But for once she held her counsel, clearly too stressed to enter into a bit of sisterly banter.

"Try not to worry, I'll keep you posted," was all Kathleen said, replacing the receiver. Going through the beaded crystal curtain, into her inner sanctuary, she lit candles and placed fresh flowers before the Buddha and her favourite statue of the Virgin Mary.

"Give us a bit of dig out, will you?" she whispered to them both, by way of a prayer. She dressed lavishly. She was, after all, having dinner with three of her favourite men.

"Brighten up, now," she told her reflection in the mirror, as she clipped on earrings. "Nobody's dead." She pulled the door of the Post Office closed, marching down Main Street, pleased to see Maguire's ablaze with light, inside and out. She was not the only one making an effort for everyone's last night.

Erin and Padar were behind the bar and for some
unknown reason this was a comforting sight. In the light of
the day's events, there was little to celebrate until they had
news of their lovely priest.

Franco arrived down from his room at the same time as
Kathleen swished into the bar.

"I was watching for you," he said, embracing her,
kissing her on both cheeks. "You look bewitching,
beguiling, divine."

Kathleen's gaze swept over him. He, too, had made
an effort, beautifully cut midnight-blue suit, white shirt, silk
tie. He smelled delicious, citrus and amber. She stole another
kiss, to catch the scent of him again. Then grasped his hand.

"Today, how awful. Terrible for everyone, are you
frazzled to a thread?"

He gave her a look. Like Larry, sometimes Franco
had little clue what Kathleen was saying, beyond it sounding
vaguely English and highly entertaining. He patted her hand.

"A bad business, poor Gregory, I will not go until I
hear news, good news. You understand?" he said.

"I do, of course. Please God, it's not too serious.
He's in a marvellous unit, Brian says it's one of the best in
the world. He'll get the right treatment," she confirmed.

Padar was hovering. Even though it was no longer
his pub, he could not resist the challenge of a good night on
the till.

"A cocktail Kathleen, is it? Mr Rossini, what wine do
you want me to put to chill?"

"I'll see the menu first," Franco said, politely. "But
Kathleen, a White Russian tonight I think, you look like a
Romanov Princess, milaya moya."

"What did you say?" she fluttered.

"My sweet." He smiled, handing her the glass Erin produced in no time.

"Oh Franco, you're such a flirt," she told him, as Larry swung through the doors. She waved him over. "We're having White Russians, join us."

Larry shook hands with the producer.

"What can I say?" he shrugged.

"After such a night, to have a bad thing happen. We must hope and pray." Franco crossed himself.

With Brian at the priest's bedside on the mainland, Ryan joined Marianne and Erin in the kitchen. The delicious meal of Innishmahon king prawns, traditional Irish stew with potato and onion baked mash, followed by homemade raspberry ice cream laced with creamy whiskey liqueur, was ready to serve, but no one had much of an appetite; it seemed such a waste. Marianne was checking the dishes, listlessly. Erin was watching, arms folded. Ryan had poured them wine, but it remained untouched. The telephone rang. Padar called to Kathleen, it was Brian.

"It's the best news we could have, under the circumstances. A fractured vertebrae, it can be operated on, and if he makes good progress, with physio and exercise, a good chance he'll be okay," Brian told her.

"Able to walk?" She held her breath.

"Looking good on that front. We won't know for sure until he comes out of the anaesthetic and can be assessed properly. Time of course, he'll need time."

Relieved, Kathleen dropped the phone. Marianne ran from the kitchen door where she had been listening. "Mother, what is it?"

"Good news, if the operation is successful, and there's a good chance it will be, all will be well." Kathleen blinked tears away.

"Thank goodness." Marianne hugged the other woman. "To have such a brilliant weekend, tainted by something so awful."

"Come on, now, we're grand. It'll all be grand," Kathleen assured her, and herself.

The news spread through the pub in a nanosecond and the whole place visibly relaxed, the noise level increased, and little bursts of laughter could be heard, as conversation veered away from the terrible accident that had been foremost in everyone's mind.

Dermot was the last in, having moored up, swabbed down and dressed himself back in his tuxedo. Ryan laughed when he saw him, he looked good.

"Are you after my job again?" he joked.

"No, if they want an ugly fecker like you, that's their lookout." Dermot gave his chum a cheesy grin.

"You're not after my woman then, are you? You've no chance there, you know how good I am in bed." Ryan poked him in the ribs.

"Not through personal experience, I'm happy to say," Dermot laughed. "Sure, she'd have me in a flash, but no I just don't want to let the side down when there's a bit of competition."

Ryan gave him a quizzical look.

"That Paul fella, the journalist. A bit too *Hugh Grant* for my taste."

Ryan laughed. "Yeah, and you're probably a bit too *Liam Neeson* for his!"

By midnight, everyone, weary from the night before, and the day's dramatic events, was ready to take to their beds. Larry Leeson and Paul Osborne were travelling together to Knock airport the next morning, Paul back to London and Larry on to Shannon and then New York.

Blowing out the candles in the bar, Ryan scooped Joey up, fast asleep with a couple of Redmunds in the snug. Guessing she was in the midst of goodbyes, he waited for Marianne at the back door, Monty had left the hearth to join him, ready for his basket. Marianne was not saying goodbye, she was in the porch with Paul.

"Did you file the report about the accident?" she asked him.

"Of course I did," he smiled at her, "that's my job."

"Built it up a bit, didn't you? It was a riding accident, the newsreader made it sound more sinister." She was glaring at him under the light. Paul shrugged. He had intimated to his contact at the studio that there might be more to it. He had been pleased with the treatment, the newscaster hinting the incident might not have been an accident. Marianne was suspicious, she knew by the way the report was worded, there could be more to come.

"They were shot at," Paul told her.

"Not necessarily." Marianne stood firm. "A lot of shooting goes on here, game, vermin, the horses could have spooked at anything. What did Mr Rossini say when you interviewed him?" Paul remained silent. "I take it you did interview him? Check the story out?"

"Of course," Paul insisted. "All he said was he heard gunshot. I asked if it was aimed at him and he thought it was a possibility."

"A possibility? Is that what he actually said, for the record?" she pressed.

Paul lowered his gaze. "He wasn't sure. He said, the more he thought about it, it could have been someone out shooting, having a bit of sport."

"And that's precisely what it was. Mr Rossini was stressed and anxious when he made the first assumption. His companion had been thrown from his horse and badly injured. It's a dramatic enough story without you making it worse." Paul gave no reply. "We don't need any negative publicity, Paul. We need to get on with things, so the tourists will come back, can't you see that?"

He lifted his chin. "You wouldn't want me to hide the truth would you, Marianne, just to keep you and the island on track for a good holiday season?"

She looked him in the eye. "It was a riding accident, give over with the conspiracy theories or you'll have me to deal with, big time!" Nearly everyone had left as Ryan approached.

Paul beamed back. "You're just gorgeous when you're angry, you know that?" he whispered, as Ryan placed a hand on his shoulder.

"Coming back for a nightcap?" Ryan offered. "Be nice to catch up in private."

Paul could sense where this was going, a proper dressing-down from Ryan and Marianne for overstepping the media mark.

"No thanks," Paul replied, "Long journey tomorrow, much as I would love to enjoy even more of the island's marvellous hospitality, an early night is the wisest decision."

"Wise decision," Ryan agreed. "Good call all round." He shook Paul's hand, "Safe journey, come back and see us soon now, won't you?"

"I will," Paul replied, and although Marianne felt Ryan's invitation was not totally sincere, she sensed they had not seen the last of Paul.

Chapter Twenty-Four – A Fond Farewell

The fire glowed in the hearth, burning low as the night came to an end. Kathleen had long since removed her evening gloves to give Erin a hand clearing up, and nearly everyone had gone. Larry had also taken his leave, he needed to finish packing, and as he wrapped every item individually in tissue paper, it would be a lengthy process. He kissed Kathleen on both cheeks as he left, promising to see her in the morning so they could say goodbye properly.

Even Sean Grogan, who usually stayed for a couple of late ones, had called it quits, saying he was hoping for a good return on his day's work and would be taking the ferry early in the morning.

Franco Rossini seemed the most reluctant to leave, having taken up residence in the battered winged chair beside the fire after dinner. He had slung his jacket to one side, loosened his tie and was gazing, unseeing, into a squat glass of amber liquid.

"I'm done now," Erin called from behind the bar, "Eve's been out, so I've locked up. See you in the morning."

"Goodnight, love," Kathleen said, going to rouse Franco to his bed. He looked at her under heavy lids and patted the footstool beside him.

"Will you have a nightcap with me?"

Adrienne Vaughan

She shook her head. She had to be up early. However much Kathleen liked to party, the Post Office came first.

"I'll have coffee is all, Franco. Besides, you need your rest, you've a long journey ahead tomorrow. Far better I could persuade you to stay, surely you're not needed back so quickly, I believe you're not shooting the new movie till the spring?"

Franco took a sip of his drink, while she poured coffee.

"We may need to start sooner than we thought," he said.

"Oh, is there a problem?" she asked.

"A number of them … but nothing to worry your pretty head about."

"If I didn't know you better, sir, I'd bite your nose off for being so patronising, and demand you tell me who or what the problems are."

He burst out laughing. "I love you, Kathleen, I really do. You think it, and out it comes, so like my Sophia."

She gave him a smile, he had a twinkle in his eye, looked the best he had since the accident.

"Well?" she was insistent.

"Ah," he gave a gesture with his hands, "this and that, suffice to say the sooner we get the damn thing in the can the better."

"Is it to do with the backers?" she asked, her involvement in the insurance scam over Angelique's jewellery still vivid. It had been one of the most exciting episodes in her life. "Financial pressures? You need to start taking money at the box office to pay back the loans, the interest?"

"It's always good to start counting returns, but no, release dates are planned well in advance, this movie won't be in the theatres till next year."

"So, what's wrong?"

"I'm just thinking, while we're all well enough to fulfil our obligations, let's finish the movie and enjoy the fruits of our labour. I don't want to leave it too long," he said more or less to himself.

"You don't honestly think you were shot at today, do you?" She pulled her knees together to face him.

He shook his head. "Probably not, it felt like it at the time. I'm sorry for what happened to Gregory, feel like it's my fault, somehow."

"He'll be fine, you see. God doesn't want him yet, too good at his job. It was an accident, could have been a lot worse," she said.

"Too awful to contemplate." Franco pressed his thumbs into his eyelids. "To have come here, for a good cause, and something like that happen, to lose a good man, already a great friend."

Kathleen looked into the warm, brown eyes, tired now and emotional. She wondered how many real friends this wealthy, powerful man had. She put her arms around him.

"Come to bed, Franco, it's late, you're weary, we all are."

He gave her his arm as she led him to the staircase and his room above.

"Will Brian be back tonight?" he asked, as they ascended the stairs.

"Doubt it. He'll stay until Gregory starts to improve, if I know him," Kathleen replied.

"I wouldn't leave you for a moment if you were mine," Franco said. "I'd keep you beside me night and day, especially now, as we grow older and know not what lies ahead."

Kathleen gave him a look. "We don't know what lies ahead at any age." They were standing outside the door to his room. He looked into her eyes.

"You have a rare beauty Kathleen. I must confess I have fallen for you heavily. If I thought I could steal you away, I would. Wrap you in designer gowns, drape you in jewels, cherish you with my love." He held her hands as he spoke.

"You Italians," Kathleen rebuked him, gently. "What chance would a poor little colleen have against such passion? I could indeed be swept away," she joked.

"Would you make a lonely old man, desperately in love with you, happy, just this once?" he whispered in her ear.

"How?" she asked.

"Spend the night with me."

Kathleen took a step back, blinking at him in the half-light.

"Please, just lie in my arms, let me hold you, caress you, until I fall asleep. My last night here would be paradise." He lifted her chin and brushed her lips with his.

She swallowed, flattered, this attractive, powerful man wanted her.

"Stop it now." She gave him a playful tap.

Franco pulled her to him and kissed her, testing her. She did not withdraw. He wrapped his strong arms around her and, melting against him, she returned his embrace, kissing him right back. A light flashed on in her head. She stopped.

"Goodness me, what are we doing?" She was breathless. "Really, oh dear, I must go." Flustered, she lifted the hem of her gown, making to scuttle off. Franco caught her by the hand.

"Stay, Kathleen," his voice thick with emotion. He had opened the door to his room. "Please stay."

Her heart was pounding, her chest on fire, lips burning with his kiss. She closed her eyes, forcing the images in her mind away.

"Good night, Franco," she said, not turning back, terrified if she looked once more into that warm, brown gaze, she would fall into his arms and be lost forever. In matters of romance, Kathleen MacReady always did go for the *Mills & Boon* approach.

"Very well," he said, still holding her hand. "But I will never forget the passion I just felt between us, it has given me hope. You could be mine one day." He released her and she scurried away like a frightened animal.

She closed the door quickly, locking it, trying to calm herself, take control of her jangling emotions.

Erin had thoughtfully lit the lamp, turned down the bed, the bed she shared with her husband, Brian Maguire, the love of her life.

She pushed her shoulders back, walking across the room, her legs barely able to carry her as far as the dressing table. Automatically, she started to disrobe, unclipping earrings, unpinning her hair. She looked at herself in the mirror. Eyes bright as stars, a red rash of passion from her chest to her throat. She sighed, then started to chuckle.

"Kathleen MacReady," she wagged a finger at her reflection, "you hussy! Falling for a bit of flirtation and flattery at your age." She took off her make-up. "You've still got it, shedloads of it, now be a good girl and save it for your husband," she said, giving herself the biggest wink in the mirror.

She changed into a silk nightgown, brushed her teeth and, spraying lavender oil on her pillow, slid beneath the sheets. She was soon fast asleep. It had been a hectic couple of days, eventful, glorious, worrying and then hopeful. There was little could wake her, especially after such an emotionally exhausting end to the evening.

She was dreaming, she had forgotten to set the alarm, she could hear knocking. 'Bloody pensioners,' she thought, 'they'll just have to wait.' She turned over, but the knocking grew louder, someone was banging on the door, urgently. She half-opened an eye, she was not in the Post Office, she remembered, she had spent the night in Maguire's, in the room she shared with Brian. It had been too late to go back to the Post Office alone. Bleary-eyed, she padded across the room, turned the key and opened the door a sliver. She half expected Franco. It was Larry, staring eyes, face the same colour as his beige roll neck sweater.

"Come quickly," he hissed, looking along the corridor.

Kathleen pulled on her robe and followed Larry. It was dark in the room, she could make out a figure in the bed, still, silent. She ran to him.

"Franco, Franco, wake up, wake up," but she knew he was not asleep. "Larry, his pills, where are his pills?"

Larry did not reply, he just stood at the end of the bed, staring blankly at the figure in it.

"Here they are," she said, finding them in the man's clenched fist. She forced his fingers apart. Taking the pill box, she opened it, it was empty. "Where, where are your pills?" She threw the box on the floor. "Larry, help, get help." Again, Larry did not move. "Larry get help!"

"It's too late, Kathleen, he asked me to wake him early so he could get ready to leave. I came over, the door was unlocked, I found him like this. Gone, just gone," Larry said, monotone.

"Oh, Franco," Kathleen cried out. "Please don't go, please stay with us." She enfolded him in her arms, lifting his head gently to her breast. She started humming a low tune deep in her throat, a lullaby. Larry just stood there. Finally, she pressed her lips firmly against Franco's forehead in affirmation, a farewell kiss. She looked at Larry, eyes filled with tears, and nodded.

There was a clatter at the door. Voices. The room suddenly full. Hands, arms, reaching over, pulling, trying to take Franco from her.

"Resuscitation," someone said, "let's try. It's worth a try."

"Stop!" she shouted, then quietly, "stop, right now. There's nothing to be done. Let him pass in peace. Respect what is happening here, please." She turned on them and they shrank back.

"Kathleen, I ..." Erin said. Kathleen raised a hand.

"Not now, Erin. If you can ask the guests to go back to their rooms. We'll deal with this our way," her voice was steely. Erin ushered everyone out. Kathleen looked up as the door closed, Larry was still standing in the same place, staring at the man and the woman on the bed. They exchanged a long look.

"I'll go and fetch Ryan," Larry said in a small voice.

"There's nothing he can do," Kathleen replied.

"He needs to be here," Larry said. "Is there anything I *can* do?"

Kathleen continued to hold Franco in her arms. She remembered, after their goodnight kiss and she had gone to bed, someone knocking at her door, asking her to open it, in a breathless, muffled voice. She closed her eyes. She knew now, it had been Franco, needing her help, and she in her stupid vanity, thinking he had come again to woo her, told him to go away. She just turned over and went back to sleep.

"Kathleen?" Larry's voice was urgent.

"We'll need Father Cassidy bringing over from the mainland."

Larry wanted to ask why, but decided against it. "Would Dermot fetch him?"

"Yes, that would be best," she confirmed.

"Anyone else?"

"Joyce. Tell Dermot not to come back without Joyce. Tell her to bring her bag, whatever she needs."

"Her bag?"

"For the Wake."

"The Wake?"

"There'll have to be a Wake. He can't pass without one," she told him.

"Of course," Larry replied. He still made no move.

"Larry, please go, the sooner Franco is sent on his way, the better his passing. He's needed on the other side now, we can't keep him here, it's our job to help him move on." The next time she looked up Larry had left.

Ryan pulled the chair up to the bed, careful not to scrape it along the floor, as if Franco were sleeping. The sheet had a crease in it. Ryan straightened it, smoothing it with his hands. They were trembling, he sat back, clasping them together, not wanting to show any sign of weakness, not now. He gazed at the man before him. He looked better than he had in years, younger, freer. Smooth brow, thick eyebrows and long dark eyelashes, silky against his skin. His full lips, curved slightly upwards, the faintest smile. His hands were resting on his chest, rugged brown hands, with shiny fingernails. A peasant's Sunday hands, scrubbed clean of the working week, ready for Mass.

It was quiet in the room, the murmur of voices going about their business could be heard outside, the business of death. But inside the room, it was quiet and warm. The fire had been lit in the small hearth, the scent of peat mixed with the lavender and amber of Kathleen's candles was soft and soothing.

"This is another fine mess you've gotten us into," Ryan said, paraphrasing *Laurel and Hardy*. Franco loved the old time comedy duo. *Silence*. Shoving his hands in the pockets of his leather jacket, Ryan crossed the room. The bay window jutted out over Main Street. The weather similar to the previous day was bright and cold, the brittle ocean sparkling in the sun. Not twenty-four hours had passed and Franco was gone. Yesterday he had been alive, riding his horse out in the sunshine, having dinner in the pub, flirting with the women, laughing with the men. Today, he was gone. Leaving nothing but an empty space where his big, warm, and at times, frightening personality had been.

Ryan watched the scene outside. Cars and vans driving along the road, people bustling in and out of shops, children going to school. An ordinary day in the middle of the working week. No one seemed to know a great man had died. Not only a renowned film producer, a gifted visionary in the art of movie making, an innovator, a risk taker, some would say a genius. Not just a man who had a glittering and hugely successful career, but a man who had been a father figure to so many, a rock, a patriarch, the boss.

Ryan turned back into the room. All was serene. He went to Franco, resuming his position by the bed.

"I tell you what I'm going to do. I'm going to stay with you, all the way." He held Franco's hands in his. "I'm going to take you home to Sophia. I'll carry out your wishes to the letter, okay? And once you're there and settled and I know you're happy, do you know what I'm going to do then? I'm going to go off and make the biggest, most successful fucking blockbuster this planet has ever seen.

We'll break every box office record known to man, and guess what? When the credits roll, right at the end, do you know what it's going to say … this was a Franco Rossini film, in letters a mile high, you see if I don't do that, you see if I don't make you proud."

For some reason, no reason, Ryan had shoved the script under his arm when the call came from Larry earlier. He had known immediately, as soon as Larry spoke.

"Bad news, my friend, the boss," was all Larry said.

"On my way," and Ryan had replaced the receiver, quietly, knowing it was already too late. He had not slept and had been going over his part, sprawled on the sofa with Joey fast asleep in his arms. The script was still in his hand, he had dropped it on the end of the bed when he arrived. He picked it up now, turning to where he left off, he started reading aloud. He would come to a squiggle, a notation, and stop.

"How does that sound?" he would ask, then read on, "is that the right tone?" and reading again, "does that work?" Question after question, hanging in the air, as if Franco's spirit was still in the room and could give some guidance, a hint of how he wanted Ryan's final portrayal of *Thomas Bentley* played out.

"Ryan." Marianne shook him gently. He had fallen asleep, chin on his chest, papers dropped to the floor. He woke with a start, and for one millisecond thought he had dreamt Franco had died, there in Maguire's best room, overlooking Main Street and out towards the sea. Marianne was in his arms, holding him tightly. He buried his face in her hair.

"It's okay," she said, "it's all going to be okay." But it was not okay, not okay at all.

"Oh no, not a body bag, he can't go in one of those awful, bin liners. God no, I won't allow it."

"Calm yourself, Joyce," Larry whispered.

"She's right," Kathleen gripped her sister's arm, "we have standards, that man is one of our own."

"We can't dishonour him," Joyce said quietly, "we won't do that."

"He's Catholic, is he to be buried here?" The old priest was confused. The women looked at each other.

"No, he's to go to Sophia, his place is beside her," Joyce said.

Kathleen turned to Marianne, she could hear the cogs whirring from where she stood.

"I've an idea, it's a long shot, but worth a go. I need to see Ryan." She left her mother and her aunt lighting more candles, drawing curtains. They were going to lay out the body. Franco Marco Rossini would be given all due deference, the MacReady sisters would afford him every consideration, as they had been trained to do by the elder women in their family, as they had done for their own mother, on that terrible night, when she had been killed.

Chapter Twenty-Five – The Gun Cabinet

"I've a spare coffin," Padar informed them.

Only Larry was shocked. "A spare coffin?" he asked, flabbergasted.

"That's far better." Kathleen nodded at Joyce who was rummaging in her bag.

"Why?" Larry asked.

"For just such an eventuality," Padar confirmed. Kathleen could see the American's confusion.

"There's no funeral director on the island, we tend to handle that kind of thing ourselves. Sergeant Brody usually sorts out the death certificate, so we can get on with the other arrangements, providing things are straightforward."

"As in this case?" Larry was hopeful.

Joyce shook her head. "It appears so to us, but there will still have to be a post- mortem, then paperwork to get the body released and ensure the poor man has safe passage home." It did not strike anyone as strange to wish an already dead man a good flight.

"And where do you keep, the … er… spare coffin?" Larry was intrigued.

"With the hearse, of course," Padar told him. "I sold the funeral business to Brian, with the pub, I knew he'd have no problem pulling it in, only gets busy if we have a harsh winter."

"And the hearse?"

"In one of Sean Grogan's barns, under wraps, of course, immaculate condition, so it can be called into service whenever needed," Padar confirmed.

Larry looked at the door to the room where Franco's body was lying in state. He was not sure how the great man would feel about this particular turn of events. Would he be displeased, rain wrath upon them? Larry was finding it hard to come to terms with the sudden demise of such a powerful and controlling force in his life. He would not be surprised to find Franco risen up, requesting this, demanding that, ruling them all from not-quite-beyond the grave. Lena had not helped. After alerting Ryan to attend his boss' deathbed, Larry telephoned his sister, newly returned to Los Angeles after the Ball. She already knew Rossini was dead, the studio's press office had picked it up from the newswire following Paul's report. He had been surprised at her ambivalence.

"Yes, I know, that is sad news. Spikey old goat, but you always knew where you stood with him. May he rest in peace," she said, quite calmly.

"Is that all you've got to say?" Larry demanded.

"What else is there to say? He was an old man with a heart condition. He had a great life, a brilliant career, ended on a high. His latest movie is a smash hit, and because the next one will technically be his last, it will be huge too. Not a bad result, really."

"But what will happen now? What about Ryan? What about us?" Larry bleated down the line.

"Hollywood's very good at stuff like this. There'll be a memorial service, and everyone who so much as passed him on the sidewalk, will be there, declaring they loved him. They'll bring someone in to do his job and just get on with the movie. He was a pretty big cog in the scheme of things but the machine won't stop turning because Mr Rossini is no longer around. It'll be fine. Besides, they've decided to bring filming forward. So everything's pretty much set up already."

"Yeah, I heard that. I wonder why that is?"

"Sometimes, if you need a particular location or a certain actor, it just works out easier to reschedule. The only thing you don't want to move is the release date, you know that," Lena told him.

Larry heard voices in the background.

"I have to go, the PR people are here, we need to organise press statements, funeral, too I guess. How're you getting him home?"

Larry sighed. "That's a very good question," he replied, hoping Lena may be able to help; she was very efficient.

"You'll figure something out," she said, uncharacteristically giving him the responsibility. "How's Ryan taking it?"

"Shocked, of course, it seems too soon to be sad, but he will be, Rossini was a real father figure to him, they were quite close in some ways."

"I guess so. And there's the kid, don't forget, that kid is Rossini's flesh and blood. Could be worth millions of dollars if he's the heir. Hope the legal side of things is watertight. Be one hell of a headache if it ain't, is all I'm saying. Larry, I really have to go. Keep me posted, email me details."

"Email?" Larry wailed.

"Ask Marianne to do it. Larry, you really need to get with the programme."

Larry put the phone down. He could feel the beginning of a migraine behind his right eye. Get with the programme? He looked at himself in the mirror. He really

needed to get out of the business and concentrate on his
health. Rossini dying just like that, snuffed out, had really
floored him. He needed to change his lifestyle. Maybe take it
easy like Ryan, find someone to share his life with, get off
the treadmill. A loud banging broke his reverie. It was Ryan,
who looked far from enjoying a relaxed lifestyle.

"You ready to go?" he barked.

"Go where?" Larry replied.

"Airport, back to the states, home."

"Now? But ..."

"All sorted, tight window, though. Scott can come
and pick us up, next couple of hours, take us straight to
Shannon."

"Us?" Larry squawked. He could really feel that
headache now.

"Yep, you, me and Franco. We need to get him back
as soon as," Ryan told him.

"But Franco's in a coffin, isn't he?" Larry felt the
bile rise in his throat. He imagined the dead man on board
the helicopter. Seated between them, strapped in tightly, his
head lolling on his chest. He swallowed.

"It'll be fine. Get your bags. We'll have to cut the
Wake short and get up to the field behind the big house,
Scott will be here soon."

With the Finnegan twins away on the mainland, gigging for
the Valentine's Weekend, the Wake had to settle for a lone
fiddler to play a lament as the mourners followed the coffin
from Maguire's, up to the church for a blessing and onto the
makeshift airfield behind the big house. Scott was due to
arrive in the biggest helicopter he could lay his hands on.
The idea to call in the daredevil pilot had come to Marianne
when she remembered seeing a black and white photograph
by a renowned photographer. The coffin was on board a

helicopter taking the deceased back to be buried on an island just like Innishmahon.

At first, Ryan thought shock had deranged her, but when she went on the internet and found the picture, he called Scott immediately. Luckily, the ace stuntman, who had been instrumental in ferrying guests to and from the Ball, was 'resting' on his country estate in West Sussex, and having heard the news, had indeed been wondering how the island community was going to deal with this sudden turn of events. Checking the weather, the window of opportunity presented itself – the sooner the better.

By now, everyone on the island knew that the movie producer had died of a heart attack in the best bedroom in Maguire's. The pub was packed. Padar had made a special punch for the mourners, a spicy mulled wine with a good measure of dark rum, to warm them. The wind had turned bitter.

Marianne and Erin had cooked a huge ham, donated by a local farmer, and a couple of sea trout, which had mysteriously appeared on the table in the pub's kitchen. They decided to make trout pate and serve it on toast, when Dermot arrived with a crate of crabs.

"These any use to you?" he asked, plonking them on the table, casting about for a snack.

He had been sent up to Sean Grogan's for the hearse and, despite Padar's assurances, Dermot found an elderly black Mercedes covered in bird poo, with a flat battery. The coffin, which was to accompany him down from the mountain, was in much better fettle, polished and gleaming, having been put to good use. It stood upright inside the back porch of Sean's ramshackle cottage.

"What the …?" Dermot asked, running his hands over the mahogany, admiring the shiny brass handles and nameplate.

"Are you sure they want the coffin?" Sean was standing in front of it, protectively.

"Doesn't he just need a body bag? Won't he have his own coffin at the other end?"

Dermot shook his head.

"No, the women won't hear of it. He's to have full honours." Dermot looked at him more closely. "Why are you so keen to keep it? You're not planning on using it yourself just yet, are you?"

Sean pulled a face. "Not at all, I'm grand. It's just that it's very handy."

"Handy?"

"Yes, for keeping things in." Sean lifted the lid, hinged like a door, to reveal an eclectic collection of sporting equipment. A number of sturdy fishing rods, a couple of whips, he used for the pony and trap, and a good hunting rifle, all nestled comfortably in the pale, blue satin lining of the casket.

"Nice," Dermot said, taking out the gun and feeling the weight of it in his hands. He lifted it to his shoulder, looking along the shaft. "May I?" he asked.

"Go ahead," Sean replied, folding his arms. The rifle was tricky. He was hoping the ex-police officer would make a hash of things. Dermot was just another cocky blow-in, in his opinion. Dermot strode out to the yard. Sean pointed across to a tree stump in the distance.

"There's an old car door leaning against that, you'll hear it ping if you hit it," he told the other man.

Dermot lined the shot up, took aim and fired. But the rifle had a kick in it and he missed the door. He tried again, this time allowing for the merest flick to the left. He hit the target, spot on.

"I'm impressed." Sean had to admit, it had taken many hours practice to get used to the gun's flaw.

"Don't be too impressed," Dermot laughed. "I was a marksman in the force. But you'll have to give up your gun cabinet, it's needed for the purpose it was intended."

"Fair enough," shrugged Sean. "Will you need a hand lifting it into the hearse?"

"I will," said Dermot.

"I'd better come to the Wake, then. I'll be owed a fair few pints for storage and having to heave this yoke around. Always looking for something for nothing that Padar Quinn, and the other fella, Brian Maguire, he's no better. That pub will go to the dogs now he has it, you mark my words."

Dermot took the gun back into the kitchen. There was a large haul of rabbit skins hanging in the tack room, beside the stable.

"Do a lot of shooting, Sean?" he asked this reluctant helper.

"I do, especially in the winter, when the fishing is not so plentiful, why?"

"The rabbit pelts, what do you do with them?"

"Sell them, of course. Sell the meat too. Rabbits are the reason the islanders survived the famine, rabbits and fish, we were lucky."

"Didn't think you were that old, Sean," Dermot said.

"Don't be smart," Sean told him. "They were proper islanders in them days, not like now, a crowd of townies, letting on to be country people, buying horses, boats and pubs, haven't the first clue what to do with any of them."

Dermot was thinking about what Sean had said about the island surviving the famine. It seemed to have survived so much, a safe harbour, a good place to anchor your soul, hook up with another one, if there was another one that needed anchoring too. He leaned the gun against the range.

"Were you out shooting yesterday?" he asked.

"I was, why, what of it?" Sean was defensive.

"Just wondered. Where?"

"Over yonder." Sean pointed West. "The other side of the island, less people, more rabbits."

"Of course." Dermot smiled to himself. He had found Rossini's 'hitman'. The gunshot the movie mogul was convinced was meant for him, was nothing more than Sean Grogan shooting rabbits.

Marianne returned with the methanol from the pharmacy and gave it to her aunt. She had no idea the chemical was used in the art of embalming, until Joyce asked her to find some.

"Do you want to stay and help?" Joyce asked gently, as her niece paused at the door, watching her mother work efficiently at the man's body. Marianne noticed both women were wearing the same dispassionate mask, emotion suspended, while they carried out their task.

The journalist in her, wanted to say yes, so she could experience the ritual herself, learn about it, write about it. But Marianne, the woman, had grown fond of this man, and could not. It was too intimate a role for her, and for some reason she thought Franco would prefer Joyce and Kathleen performing this, his final ablution. He had connected with them both immediately, the mutual respect obvious, it was better done this way, she was sure of it.

"I think I'll help in the kitchen," Marianne told her.

"Is Ryan packed?" Kathleen asked, giving Franco's shoes a polish.

"Yes, he and Larry are going together."

"That's good, they will support each other. They've all been friends for many years. And Joey, will he come to the blessing?"

Marianne shook her head.

"It may give him an understanding," Joyce said.

For the first time since she had learned of Franco's death, Marianne felt tears rise up.

"He's so young. So many people have come in and out of his life already. Someone's always going somewhere." She was dismayed at how lost she suddenly felt.

"Island life. It's a fact of it," Joyce told her.

"You're right, love," Kathleen agreed. "Leave him with the Redmunds, he'll be totally distracted, and Ryan will be home before he knows it." Kathleen looked at Marianne, she did not seem remotely appeased. "What is it?"

"The movie, they're going to start filming sooner rather than later," Marianne said.

"Maybe that's not a bad thing. Get it over with, then Ryan's home for good, and if you have to go away again, you can all go together," Kathleen confirmed, checking she could see her reflection in the leather of Franco's shoes.

The bustle of the kitchen preparing for the Wake was enough to take Marianne's mind off Ryan's imminent departure, and whatever situation may or may not greet himself and Larry once they touched down at JFK. She sent all the details via email to Lena, and Lena in turn reassured her Franco's lawyer had confirmed the film producer's final wishes. Which included a full Requiem Mass in St Patrick's Cathedral in New York, followed by a private family internment, where he would finally be laid to rest beneath the white alabaster angel that guarded the grave of his beloved wife, Sophia.

Marianne was pleased he had made his wishes known, it all seemed fitting and appropriate. Lena said she thought the whole thing would take about ten days to organise, and they were using contacts and pulling strings to get everything sorted as soon as was humanly possible.

"Did you find the methanol for Kathleen?" Erin asked, cracking crab claws and scraping out the meat.

"I did, but I had to go down to the basement for it," Marianne replied. Padar looked up. "You'll have to get rid of all that stuff if you want to sell it," Marianne told him, arranging cakes freshly baked by the women of the town.

"What stuff?" Erin asked.

"Yes, what stuff?" Padar was giving the punchbowl a wipe.

"All that chemistry set stuff down there. It's a really useful space, make a great den for teenagers or a playroom for kids, but that laboratory set-up would put people off," Marianne said.

"Ah, that's what Phileas left behind. I don't think Sinead was too keen to go down there, you know, after he died." Padar took the bowl out to the bar. Dermot looked at Erin. She was already drying her hands, untying her chef's apron.

"We won't be long, Marianne. Just need to fetch something," she said, signalling Dermot to follow.

"How will we get in?" He jumped into the 4x4 beside her. She held up a huge bunch of keys.

"It seems everyone on the island leaves a spare key in the pub, there isn't anywhere I can't get into." She swung the jeep out of the car park, heading up Main Street towards the pharmacy.

"Are you thinking what I'm thinking?" Dermot asked her.

"I'm hoping, more than thinking," she said, eyebrows knitted into a frown.

"Hoping?"

"Yes, hoping we can at last find some concrete evidence, that someone has been making vodka on the island, find out who that someone is and arrest the bastard. That stuff is as dangerous as crack cocaine, it could kill someone." She pulled up outside the pharmacy.

"Maybe it already has," Dermot replied.

"Where are the other two?" Padar asked, when he finally made it back into the kitchen. Word was out they were having a proper Wake, people were arriving, the bar was busy.

"They've gone to fetch something." Marianne was checking all the food was covered up. It would be a while before it was served.

"Where?" Padar asked.

"Not sure." Marianne rearranged some of the cakes.

"Where?" Padar asked again.

"Probably the boat, I think they headed in that direction," she said, too busy distracting herself with menial tasks to notice Padar's growing anxiety. He went to the window of the kitchen, straining to look along the lane.

"Marianne, can you go out and manage the bar for a while? I've to sort a few things down in the cellar, don't want a riot on our hands if we run out of stout." He was already halfway down the steps.

"Sure," Marianne said, pleased to be given an actual job. Moving into the bar, she was surprised at how full the place was. A couple of locals were waiting patiently for a pint, so she went directly to the pumps, when she noticed a small queue of people going in and out of the snug. She realised that was where the beautifully prepared corpse lay, the coffin open for people to pay their last respects.

"He looks very peaceful," she overheard a woman tell an elderly man.

"I've never seen him looking as well," the man replied, "far better than the time he was interviewed by that fella on the film programme on the telly."

"I don't like him, do you?" said another woman, ladling punch into a glass.

"Oh, I think he's a great fella, some of his early movies were brilliant."

"No, not Franco, he's one of our own," she spoke as if they had been old friends. "The fella who does the interviews on the film programme, he was in a few movies, too, couldn't act his way out of a paper bag."

"I thought he was with the *Abbey*?" the man referred to Ireland's world renowned, national theatre company.

"Enough said," confirmed the woman.

Marianne found herself smiling for the first time that day. She loved how the Irish absorbed celebrity, the gifted were respected, but never revered; talent appreciated and enjoyed but not disproportionately lauded. You had what you had, did what you did, and if you made it big, fair play to you, and that was it, no more no less. She did like that about her native race.

Chapter Twenty-Six – The Booze Factory

B y the time Erin and Dermot had locked up the pharmacy and climbed into the 4x4 to head back to Maguire's, the town was deserted, everyone was at the Wake.

"How do you want to play it?" Erin asked Dermot, sitting grim-faced beside her.

"Do you think Padar was in on it?" Dermot was sure he was.

"Looks that way, how could he have not known all the liquor was stored in the cellar. Was he selling it? Did Phileas make it and Padar sell it on?"

"Sounds feasible," Dermot agreed.

"But Phileas is dead, who else would have known what was going on?" Erin pulled the jeep into the car park.

"Sinead?" Dermot wondered.

"There's a lock on the basement door. Phileas always made a big fuss of saying how secure the pharmacy was, how anything dangerous was well locked away. I'm guessing part of that was keeping everyone out, including his wife," Erin said.

"Let's get this morning's business over first and then confront Padar, see what he knows, before we go round accusing people of making lethal booze and selling it on the black market," Dermot suggested.

"Agreed," said Erin. "But we can't leave it too long. Padar's heading back to Cork, he wants to go home to Sinead and Bridget, he only stayed on because Brian had to go with Gregory to the hospital."

The hearse, now nearly as shiny as the coffin, was standing directly outside the main door of the pub. The villagers spilled onto the street, the cold wind coming off the Atlantic threw icy raindrops in their faces, the women were putting up umbrellas, men pulled caps over their ears, buttoning coats and jackets tightly.

Padar looked up, as Erin and Dermot pushed through the throng.

"Where the hell have you two been, we could have done with a hand around here?" he said narkily.

"It's fine," Marianne told him. "We all mucked in."

The MacReady sisters, showered and changed, now looked more like themselves. Kathleen had opted for maroon velvet, a hooded cape, floor-length skirt, silk blouse and her amethyst necklace. Joyce, a heathery tweed jacket suit, her good pearls evident beneath the *Hermes* scarf. They had hosted the Wake beautifully, chatting to everyone, serving food and drinks, encouraging Larry and Ryan to do the same. Although Larry just grew more agitated, the forthcoming helicopter trip tearing his nerves to shreds, and Ryan was monosyllabic throughout, finding it hard to play a part in this particular scene, unsure of his role, if he even had one.

Someone slipped their arms around him from behind, holding him tightly. He leaned his head back, Marianne's cheek was on his, he could smell her hair.

"It'll be alright, you see," she whispered into his ear.

"I know," he turned to face her, "I just feel so sad for him. To die alone, in a strange place."

"We're not that strange," she said, despite the crowd milling about. Ryan was right. Franco had died alone in a foreign land, without familiar faces and his own precious possessions around him. "None of us know when, how, or where it's going to end. But he had spent his last few days with people who cared about him. He'd had time with us and Joey, he laughed a lot, I don't think I've ever seen him laugh so much," she assured him.

"You're right," Ryan conceded. He pulled her close. She looked up into his slate-blue eyes, tears dulling the sparkle. His cheeks had hollowed, skin grey beneath his movie star tan.

"I want to die in your arms, at the end, that's where I want to be, in our home, our bed, in your arms." He pressed his lips to her forehead.

"Time to go," Dermot cut in. "Scott's on his way."

The lone fiddler followed the hearse at a stately march along Main Street. The mourners gathered around the car, as the priest gave a blessing in a loud voice, battling against the wind and the rain. Two altar boys were in attendance, one holding a gold dish containing Holy Water and the wooden handled brush placed in it. The other swinging incense, a little too vigorously. He clunked the vessel against the hearse a couple of times but no one noticed, the wind was so wild. They were all straining their ears to be the first to hear the beat of the helicopter blades, cut the Rosary short, send the man on his way and get the hell out of there. It was a terrible day.

"Here he is," yelled Dermot, hopping into the driver's seat, with Larry and Ryan behind, Marianne at his side. He slid the hearse slowly away, then turning left after

313

the church, put his foot down, rattling down the lane at speed to make sure they arrived as Scott swooped into view.

Scott's co-pilot helped the men load the coffin in a matter of minutes. Larry threw his bag on board and quickly followed it. Ryan, too, wasted no time, squeezing Marianne's hand in farewell as he left her.

"Come home soon," she called, uselessly as the noise of the engine and the gale took her words away.

The helicopter lifted off the ground, sweeping over the paddock and out towards the sea and was quickly just a grey dot, against an even greyer sky. Dermot looked at Marianne, her face had turned grey too.

"Let's get you back, you could do with a drink," he said.

"Not for me. I'm going to fetch Joey and Monty. We need to be at home," she replied, dully.

Unhappy to be away from her post and unwilling to spend another night in the pub without her husband, Kathleen packed her overnight bag after the Wake and returned to the sanctuary of the Post Office.

Brian had to wait for her to emerge from her bath before she answered the phone. He was anxious to have a long, reassuring conversation with her. She poured herself a nightcap and settled down to hear all his news, updating her on Father Gregory's condition. The operation was a success, the priest chirpy and once he was fitted with a corset, he would be allowed to make the arduous journey home.

She was relieved. It had been painfully obvious, during the whole of the Franco Rossini episode, that the one thing the entire scenario lacked, was the calm voice and measured reason of their own priest. Gregory always knew what to do, remembered everybody's name, he had a unifying influence that was badly missed, especially when the town needed to come together for a significant occasion.

She filled Brian in on all the details. He was well aware of the sisters' embalming skills, a tradition passed down through the generations, with the added benefit of more modern techniques, these days. For example they had learned how to inject the corpse with a chemical solution, to help the skin retain its natural colour, and to plump out the flesh as if blood still flowed through the veins. The MacReady women had always worked closely with the Doctors Maguire, sorting out the business end on behalf of the deceased.

"It's a long time since I heard of anyone undertaking the undertaking at home, if you get my meaning. You girls always had a fine reputation for it, he could not have been in better hands. You're marvellous, the pair of you," his soft voice and warm words filled her heart. She pressed the receiver closer to her ear.

"Come back soon, my darling. I've been long enough without you, to be left alone again," she said, and he heard the catch in her throat, biting down her emotions.

"On our way tomorrow, you've been amazing, hold out now till I get there. I'll be home soon, home to hold you in my arms," he told her, and she replaced the receiver as softly as a sigh. She looked in the mirror, her eyes a little brighter, the merest flush on her cheeks. Brian was coming home, all would be well. She pushed the dread away, taking another sip of whiskey.

After Scott swooped away, the mourners dispersed, everyone tired and ready to sit in front of their own hearth. Padar made the unprecedented decision to close the pub early.

Sean Grogan was the last to leave, grumbling at being thrown out before time, but as he had not bought a drink all day, Padar thought he would be doing Brian's profits a favour if he turfed Sean out into the night before he could get any more free beer down him.

Dermot bolted the door, as Erin finished clearing the tables. Padar called from the kitchen that he was making coffee.

A mug of coffee apiece, Erin decided to commence the interrogation.

"Padar, you know when you had the pub, where did you buy your spirits from?"

"Why, are you taking over that side of things too?" he asked her.

"Maybe," was all she said.

"Here and there. Wherever was cheapest, to be honest. Sometimes I got a good deal off the wholesaler in West Port, sometimes I'd have to go a lot further for a bargain, and then by the time I'd weighed up the cost of the fuel and my time away from the pub, sure I'd probably have been better off just using the regular supplier." He thought for a moment. "Is Brian running out of money, is that it? I did tell him, it's murder trying to make a place like this, pay in the winter."

"Did you ever buy spirits off, say, someone not a regular wholesaler, someone just selling stuff on?" Dermot asked.

"No way," Padar replied, putting his mug down. "Not worth it." He looked at Erin. "You know what the customs and excise are like around here. Not worth the risk, they'd love to make an example of someone like me running a pub on the island, sure they'd throw the book at me. I'd warn Brian against anything like that. I don't know what you'd get away with in New York but not here, no chance."

"What about poteen? There's always been a drop of the hard stuff around?" Erin pressed.

"Oh yes, true enough. I keep a bottle for visitors, tourists who want to try a brew made out of potatoes, sure everyone does that," Padar said.

"Isn't that illegal?" Dermot asked.

"Not if you don't sell it. You can serve it, but not sell it," Padar told him.

"Did you ever buy anything off Phileas?" Erin asked. Padar tried to hide his surprise at the mention of the dead pharmacist's name.

"Don't think so," Padar replied.

"Are you sure?" Dermot was staring at Padar's hands. Padar followed his gaze. His fingers were stained bright blue.

"What on earth?" Padar turned his hands over, examining them. He looked from Dermot to Erin and back, he moved to the sink and started washing vigorously.

"Would you like to come down to the cellar with us?" Erin asked him.

"What for?" Padar was scrubbing his hands with a brush.

"I think you know what for," Dermot said, moving to stand beside him. "Two choices Padar, the easy way or the hard way. Make your mind up." He towered over the other man. Padar looked at them both with stricken eyes.

Erin kicked open the cellar door.

"After you," she said. Reluctantly Padar went down the steps. When they arrived at the spot where the secret cellar had been hastily hidden, they could tell someone had been there, tampering with the boxes, pushing things carelessly aside.

"Here, give me a hand," said Dermot, hauling things away from the entrance. Padar swallowed, staring unblinkingly at the wall.

"The sooner we get this over, the better," Erin told him. She stood guard at the bottom of the steps, while the men removed the camouflage to reveal the entrance to the secret cellar.

"Open it," Dermot ordered.

"I don't know what it is," Padar stammered. "I didn't even know it was there."

"Yes, you did," Erin said. "The dye all over your hands shows you've been there. Old- fashioned booby trap."

Dermot grinned at her. "Works every time."

Padar forced air through his nostrils in temper and, reaching above the door, found a key, now also blue, and released the door. He flicked a switch. The boxes of illicit vodka stood stacked high, illuminated by the single bulb.

"Well?" Erin said.

"I've nothing to say," Padar replied. "This is Brian Maguire's pub, nothing to do with me, it's his problem."

"I don't think so," Dermot said into his face. "I think it's your problem and one of the reasons you were so keen to come back and 'help' with the Ball. You and Phileas had a right scam on the go. He made the stuff in the basement of the pharmacy and you, being in the trade, sold it on."

"Splitting the profits between you, no doubt," Erin confirmed. "But after the gun-running and the drug smuggling episode, the place was crawling with police. So you, with Phileas out of the way, decided to hole up the stock, wait for things to die down, then come back and make off with the booty. Classic tale, really."

"You probably have contacts lined up and waiting for it back in Cork. Big market for it amongst immigrant workers, I believe." Dermot had Padar pinned against the wall.

"Look here," said Padar, visibly shaken. "What's it to you two? You've both retired, no skin off your nose if a little bit of homemade vodka gets sold here and there. I was just going to load it up and take it away. I wouldn't want anyone getting into trouble over it. I was thinking of dumping it anyway. I've made a fresh start, we've a nice little business now."

"Yeah, right," Dermot said. "We've no choice but to call the guards, this is a lot more serious than a bit of home brew on the side."

Padar tried a laugh. "What makes you say that?"

Erin pulled out a broken bar stool.

"You'd better sit down," she told him. Trembling now, his face blotchy, Padar perched on the stool.

"Padar, did you ever put any of that vodka in the optics in the pub?" Erin asked, her eyes boring into his face.

"No way, never!" he said, angrily.

"Are you sure? Sure you never ran out of proper stuff and substituted this? Filled a genuine branded bottle with Phileas' home brew?"

Silence. They could hear the wind in the distance, the cellar smelled damp, unpleasant.

"Padar?" Erin tried.

"Oh God." Padar pushed his face into his blue hands.

"You did, didn't you?" Erin said calmly. "Was it when Angelique was here? I know she drank vodka, a lot of vodka. Did you run out and substitute the real thing with this?" She laid a hand on one of the white boxes. The red logo in fake Russian burned like a brand into his eyes.

He nodded. He remembered it all vividly. He had indeed run out, she had drunk the place dry. He had even used it, following Larry's instructions, to fill a hip flask for the movie star to take on the plane.

"We know you did, because I drank it, too." Erin tapped the box. "I had a couple of vodkas at Christmas and fell dangerously ill. Dermot was with me. Thank goodness, he knew what to do."

Padar looked at them both.

"I never meant anything. It was an accident. I wouldn't ..." he was devastated, his face seemed to have caved in on itself.

"We guessed as much," Dermot confirmed. "But we just couldn't risk this going onto the market. Christ knows how many people would have been taken ill, died, even."

"We needed to know who was involved, if it's a big commercial operation, then we would have no choice but to bring the guards in," Erin announced. "As it stands, Dermot and I need to discuss how we want to play it. We may be retired but you can't live all your life by a code and then assume once you hang up your uniform, you can hang up your conscience too."

"I understand that," Padar said, annoyed at being patronised. "But I haven't done anything wrong. I didn't even sell the stuff, sure it was only stored here, what did I know?"

"Angelique died, Padar," Dermot said sternly. "And Erin could have died too. What you sell, serve or give away over your bar is your responsibility."

Erin closed the door to the secret cellar. She was still wearing her catering gloves. She locked it and pocketed the key.

"How did you find out?" Padar's voice was a whisper.

"We found the cellar a while ago and decided to sit on it, see who showed up. Dermot came up with the invisible dye plan, a bit schoolboy for me, but it worked." Erin told him. Padar looked pityingly at his hands.

"It was when Marianne went to fetch the methanol from the pharmacy. It's used in embalming, and I remembered it's also used to make vodka. So when she came back and berated you for not clearing out the basement before putting the pharmacy on the market, describing it as a homemade laboratory, we knew we'd found the booze factory. You were the missing piece of the jigsaw," Erin said.

Padar struggled to his feet, he looked pleadingly at Erin.

"Don't call the guards, Erin, for the love of God. Think of all the trouble it will cause, digging up all that stuff about Phileas. They would want to interrogate poor Sinead, who's already worn out with her pregnancy and what about little Bridget, your own flesh and blood? What will happen to her in all of this? They could lock me up."

Erin glared back at him. "Don't try and blackmail me into letting you off the hook, Padar Quinn. You've always been the same, dodgy MOT certificates for the vehicles, cash deals wherever you could. I know you sold photos of Ryan and Marianne to the media when they came here first."

"What? I never knew that." Dermot was disgusted. He glared at Padar. "You're a right little shite, aren't you?"

Now steadier on his feet, Padar pushed past Erin and up the steps.

"Hey ..." Dermot made after him. Erin laid a hand on his arm.

"Let him go. He needs to lick his wounds." She gave him a half-smile. "Well done, Inspector Finnegan, you're good, you know that?"

Dermot beamed back at her. Her eyes were shining, her smile broadened, completely transforming her face. She had the most beautiful smile. He bent and kissed her. He withdrew quickly, expecting a slap, a rebuke at the very least. But she was still smiling, smiling and twinkling her eyes at him. He was sure of it.

Chapter Twenty-Seven – Making Plans

Marianne was curled up with Joey under one arm and Monty under the other, when the shrill ring of the phone pulled her from her slumber. It was only seven in the evening, but by the time she had finished feeding her little gang, bathing first Joey, then Monty, and dealing with the latest emails from the *Lost Babies* website, she was exhausted. She lifted the extension, Ryan's latest attempt at modernisation. She hoped it was him.

"Hey, gorgeous, how're all my best guys doing?" Ryan's languid Irish-American lilt was like a lullaby.

She brightened, realising he had just come from the very public event that was Franco's funeral, no space for private feelings, he was in the spotlight again.

"How did it go?" she asked, gently.

"Full house, glorious music, great turn out, every movie star and actor who could be there, was. Some great tributes, too."

"How did your contribution go down?" she asked. They had written the eulogy between them by email over the last couple of days, mindful to include Joey's perspective, what his great uncle would come to mean to him, as the years went by.

"Rapturous applause. I think the people who were close to him appreciated it especially. Roberto told me afterwards that Franco would have loved it."

"Good work. Larry okay? Lena?"

"I'll see them tomorrow, we're having lunch after the meeting."

"Meeting?"

"Reading of the Will and then a run through the schedules, a calendar full of locations and shoots."

"Choose somewhere nice and hot for us to visit on location, will you? It's not stopped raining since you left and it's so cold."

"It only feels like that because you're missing me," he told her, a smile in his voice. "The Will should be interesting, though, no hints yet, all very respectful, just waiting to see what the big man has decreed will be his legacy, how he's going to keep tabs on us all from beyond the grave."

"And the post-mortem, throw any light on things?"

"Apparently he's had the heart condition for years, even before Sophia died. Always ignored it, refusing to have surgery, saying it was God's will, and when he was taken he would be happy, because he would be joining Sophia. His only concession, the little pill he used to take when he had a pain in his chest. He refused to change his lifestyle, just didn't see the point."

Marianne was quiet for a moment. "I get that. The person he most wanted to spend time with, no longer here, why shouldn't he do what he wanted, not necessarily to hasten his death, but refuse to take steps to lengthen his life, his time without her."

"I think I know how he felt," Ryan said, and Marianne could feel it too. A sense of loss, the void of loneliness. Joey stirred. He had heard Ryan's voice. He slid across Marianne and put his ear to the phone.

"Your son wants to speak to you." She held the receiver for the little boy.

"Daddy? Daddy, you long away?"

"Yes, son. In America, saying goodbye to Papa Franco."

"Maryan says he's going to heaven."

"Yes, Joey, it's time for him to go."

"Long away?"

"Very long away."

"Can he see me?"

"Yes, I guess he can."

"That's good. Tell him I'll ride my pony."

"I will, Joey. That's good news, I needed a bit of that."

"Home soon, Daddy?"

"Home soon, son."

"Good, Maryan sad, Monty sad, too."

"Make them happy till I get back, will you Joey? Do that for me?"

"Okay." Joey thought for a minute. "I'll give them biscuits, with choccie on."

Ryan laughed. "That should do it." And Joey put the phone down, leaving Ryan smiling, ahead of what was going to be another grim day.

The news that Franco Rossini was more or less broke did not come as the biggest shock to his close friends. The movie industry had been tough for years, and after investing in a couple of box office flops, Franco had hocked nearly everything he owned to fund the *Thomas Bentley* franchise. What remained, he left to his great nephew, Joseph Rossini O'Gorman; the ranch in upstate New York; some paintings and a vintage *Lamborghini* he had bought for Sophia when they first married. There was another legacy too; a good-sized cash sum, invested in a special trust fund which had to be used for charitable works. He had left this to Marianne Coltrane, together with a personal letter, marked Private and Confidential and for her eyes only.

When Brian arrived by taxi into Maguire's car park the next day, he was unsurprised to find Kathleen decamped to the Post Office and Padar Quinn gone without so much as a 'by your leave'.

Erin was padding about the kitchen in her bare feet, closely followed by Eve who was hoping some of the toast her mistress was carrying, might fall to the ground and serve as breakfast. They were both pleased to see him.

"I've left Gregory up at the presbytery with Joy in charge, she was serving him bacon and eggs but I'm afraid the medication he's on, means he hasn't much appetite. Still now he's home, he'll soon be on the mend."

"I'll nip up and see him later," Erin said. "Bring him a couple of bottles of *Budweiser*. Can he have a drink with his painkillers?"

"Not really." Brian smiled. "But that's never stopped anyone, has it?"

Erin went to pour coffee.

"Not for me, Erin, I'm just on my way …" But before he had finished his sentence, Kathleen had burst into the room, furs flying, earrings jangling, arms spread wide.

"Brian, Brian, I saw the taxi go by the window, why didn't you stop? You knew I'd be at my job," she gushed, running into his arms, kissing his face repeatedly with frosted pink lips.

"Ah, the fragrant Mrs Maguire. Good to be home." He grinned at her, holding her chin in his fingers so he could look into those sharp, shiny eyes. "You okay?" He could see dark circles beneath her make-up, her mouth tight at the corners.

"Grand, absolutely grand now you're back." She sank into his embrace, a relieved smile on her lips.

"Let's have lunch together, and catch up properly," he suggested.

"That's a great idea. I'll go back and sort out the next collection, get it on the ferry, then I can take the afternoon off. See you here at one?" She was already through the door.

"Looking forward to it," he called to her. "And Kathleen, don't overdress!"

She stopped. "What on earth do you mean?"

"Well, I won't be able to keep my hands off you as it is, so don't wear too many layers, is what I mean."

"Brian Maguire, you're outrageous!" she exclaimed, and fluttered out.

"Ugh!" Erin snorted. "That's gross!"

"Not when you're in love, Erin." Brian gazed after his wife. "No, not when you're in love."

Erin was alone in the bar later that afternoon when Dermot called in to check if Brian was back and to see what Erin wanted to do about the stash in the pub's cellar.

"Padar's gone," she said flatly, joining him on a stool on the other side of the bar.

"I know," Dermot confirmed. "I saw him this morning at the marina, he took the first ferry back to the mainland. I get the feeling we won't be seeing him again."

Erin nodded. "Perhaps no bad thing. Padar's just one of those guys who can't walk in a straight line, know what I mean?"

"I do. Not a real criminal, but not completely honest. Always something slightly underhand going on somewhere."

Erin agreed. "What do you think we ought to do with the vodka?"

"Leave it where it is? Hole it up again?" Dermot was all for dealing with it there and then.

"I think we should dump it," Erin said. "Rather be safe than sorry."

"Fair enough." Dermot was happy to go along with whatever she suggested. "How and when?"

"Take it out on the boat and pour it into the sea, job done."

"Good idea, it'll take us ages though, just the two of us, and we'd have to go a long way out, too, just to be sure."

"I know, but it can only be us two, really. Involve anyone else and there'll be questions. Nope, us two, out on a fishing trip, safest option."

"You'll have people talking," he teased. "Won't we need a chaperone?"

"It's not a date, Dermot, it's a job, our duty." She gave him a brief smile, but he had unnerved her. "Serve yourself if you want a drink, I'm off out." And calling Eve to her side, she pulled on her jacket and disappeared.

Ryan had arrived home late the night before, and the occupants of Weathervane had welcomed the opportunity of a long, lazy morning. It was, in fact, mid-afternoon by the time Marianne unfolded herself from Ryan's embrace, and, pushing feet into slippers headed downstairs to the hall door. Monty was running round in excited circles, so she knew the, as yet unseen, visitor, was a friend.

She opened the door slightly, to find Erin and Eve standing there. Erin was in running gear, panting slightly, as Eve pushed her nose through the door at Monty.

"Problem?" Marianne asked her friend.

"Question," Erin replied.

327

"Coffee?"

"Herbal tea?" Erin asked. Marianne knew she had stopped drinking alcohol, but wondered how far she was going with the health kick, Erin was painfully thin these days.

They were at the table in Weathervane's sunny kitchen, two mugs of tea and a plate of hot, buttered teacakes between them.

"Dermot and I have a job on, and the thing is, we could do with a hand. It won't take long but it would be much quicker and safer with four of us at it," she explained.

"No way," came Ryan's voice. He was standing at the top of the stairs, hair on end, sporting the beginnings of a beard. "The last time I did Dermot Finnegan a favour, I broke my arm, he got shot and you guys were more or less kidnapped." He went to make coffee.

"Ah, Ryan, you exaggerate. Anyway, no one else is involved. We just have to go out on the boat, a good distance away from the island, and get rid of some stuff," Erin told them. Marianne, as usual, was curious.

"This stuff we have to get rid of. Is it stolen?"

Erin shook her head.

"Is it your stuff or Dermot's stuff?"

"No one's, really."

"Is it dangerous stuff?"

"Not at the moment, could be, in the wrong hands though."

"That's why you have to get rid of it?"

Erin nodded.

"Is this stuff stored in the cellar by any chance? You seem to spend an awful lot of time down there," Marianne pressed.

Erin nodded again.

"Would the police be interested in this stuff?" Marianne asked her.

"Best not to involve them. Too many questions. People could end up in trouble, we want to avoid that."

"How long will the trip take?"

"A couple of days. A fishing trip, stopover on the boat, then back." Erin sipped her tea, looking from one to the other. Ryan had not said a word.

"Ryan?" Marianne tried.

"No way!" Ryan exclaimed, again. "Absolutely no way. Sorry Erin, you and your boyfriend will have to deal with it yourselves, we're not getting involved, okay?" He grabbed a teacake and left.

"He's not my boyfriend," Erin called after the baggy, track-suited bottom of one of the world's most fabulous movie stars. "Padar's gone," Erin whispered to Marianne.

Marianne raised her eyebrows. "I see."

It was great to see Gregory home and typically keen to be back in the swing of things, calling a meeting of the committee organising the bridge and marina project not long after his return.

They were in the study, walls lined with ancient tomes, the lives of the saints, a large section on Irish history and Gregory's personal collection of books on horse riding and rock 'n' roll. The regular chime of the grandfather clock in the hall gave the place a cosy solemnity, while the squeals of laughter from the children playing in the garden – it was a bright, sunny day and Joy had the kindergarten out in the fresh air – gave everything a feeling of hope for the future, a promise that spring was on its way.

Marianne was late. She burst through the door, apologising, with Monty hot on her heels.

"I'm sorry, I got caught up in emails and phone calls from early this morning, I was still in my pyjamas five minutes ago."

Her mother's gaze swept over her. Unruly auburn hair haphazardly clipped up, jeans and walking boots and an old sailing jacket she was far too fond of, for Kathleen's sartorial taste. Yet she looked fabulous, vibrant, excited, happy.

"Have you news?" Kathleen passed her a cup.

"I have," Marianne replied, and Gregory laughed.

"It obviously can't wait for 'any other business' so come on, spill the beans," he said.

"You know I've appointed a manager for Oonagh's project, ready to start ahead of the first guests arriving in May?" They nodded. "Well, part of Franco Rossini's legacy was for me to set up the *Lost Babies* as a charitable trust, with a director and some paid staff to run it." She drew breath.

"Makes perfect sense. It's grown far too big to be handled by one person, and so many people are coming forward, looking for long lost relatives. You're working day and night, hardly any time for your own family," Kathleen confirmed.

"Well, the new manager at the project heard about the vacancy, and not only would he like to help with the *Lost Babies Trust*, but his partner has all the relevant experience for the position of director, worked for an animal charity for years. If we like each other, they're going to come here together on a six-month trial." Marianne was thrilled.

"Do they know the island?" Father Gregory was cautious. The island could be paradise for some, hell on earth for others.

"That's the best bit," Marianne grinned. "They were both here as students, at the Marine Biology Unit, they love the place, can't wait to get back."

"That is good news," Brian agreed. "A bit of new blood, always a good thing."

"So what's next?" Gregory was handing out the agenda, moving stiffly around the table because of the back brace he had to wear while he healed.

"I'm going to meet them in Dublin, hopefully confirm all the details and we'll be good to go," Marianne said.

Kathleen tapped her clipboard with her pen.

"Better get on with this then," she smiled. "Let's agree the build programme, now all the funds are in place and get this show on the road. We could do with lots of new blood heading here. Let's go for it and make sure we have the best season ever. What do you say, Brian?"

"I'm up for it, I've already started the refurbishment on the pub," he said. Marianne and Gregory raised their eyebrows. "Oh, don't worry, I'm not modernising it, just making improvements. It'll be exactly the same, only better, if you know what I mean. I shall start at the bottom and work my way up. Kathleen has some brilliant ideas."

Kathleen beamed at him. "I do love a project," she said.

They got down to business. After a couple of hours, they had everything agreed, tasks allocated and deadlines set.

"Have you everything you need, Dermot?" Gregory asked, as the big man rolled up plans, putting papers away.

"Really keen to get going now, chairman," Dermot said. "Need something to get my teeth into, been bitting and bobbing long enough."

"Good man, and the Lifeboat, still on schedule?"

"It is, once the station is up and ready to take it. Having a Lifeboat based here will make a huge difference to the whole area."

"I agree," Gregory said. "You're not just running the project, taking delivery of the Lifeboat then leaving us, are you Dermot? Surely you'll stay longer than just the season?"

"Not sure." He was thoughtful. "I'd like to stay, I love it here, but I need more than a job, if you know what I mean. I've had a career all my life, came here because I wanted a bit more."

The priest stood up slowly. He was a big man, as tall as Dermot.

"If it's for you, it won't go by you, as they say." He looked the younger man in the eye. "But sometimes you have to give it a shove, a great big, bloody shove, if you take my meaning." Dermot gave him a quizzical look. Riddles, most of the people around here talked in riddles half the time.

"I do," he said, not really sure he did at all.

The little committee, fired up and raring to go, gathered up their belongings and went to collect their coats. Kathleen stopped Marianne at the cloakroom door.

"Any other news?" she asked, but she could tell by how animated her daughter looked, that she had no knowledge of the letter Ryan had received that morning, the letter from the consultant's office.

"Nope, think that's it." Marianne smiled at her.

"I was hoping I'd hear of a wedding," Kathleen changed tack. "Any news on that front?"

"No, and if you're talking about myself and Ryan, there won't be, so scratch that off the agenda, if you please," Marianne said, perfectly pleasantly with steel behind her eyes.

"Only, a girl I know recently lost her partner, they had children, too, she wasn't the marrying kind, but he had always wanted to get married. Killed outright, on his motorbike. It was very sad, and to not even be a widow, a cruel blow," Kathleen's mouth was a thin line of pain. "To not even have the dignity of that, most unfair, I'll be having words." Her voice broke as she cast her eyes upwards. Marianne looked at her closely. She gave the older woman a hug.

"Let's have a drink later," Marianne said, leaving Kathleen in the hallway.

As they came out of the church gates and Dermot made to cross the road towards the site office at the marina, Marianne stopped him.

"What about the stuff in Maguire's cellar?" she asked.

"What about it?" Dermot replied, taken off guard.

"Erin told me you need to shift it."

"Yes, and she told me you and Ryan don't want to help. He's turned into a right wuss now he's going back to the day job." Marianne ignored the slight on her beloved. Ryan did have a point, Dermot's jobs were always tricky.

"Well, you heard what Brian said, he's refurbishing the pub, starting from the bottom."

Dermot just looked at her.

"The cellar, Dermot. Sounds like Brian's going to pull the place asunder, whatever needs disposing of, needs getting rid of sooner rather than later."

"You're right! What's the plan then?" He looked hopeful.

"Leave it with me," she said. Dermot bent and kissed her on the head.

"I love you, Marianne Coltrane," he told her.

"So you should!" she replied, breaking into a run. She was sure she had just spotted Erin and Eve on the beach, she needed to talk to Erin first, check out what really needed to be done.

Chapter Twenty-Eight – For Her Eyes Only

66What's up?" Brian was polishing glasses idly behind the bar. He had employed Mary from the supermarket to help with the cleaning and he had started making improvements, Maguire's would be a much more attractive establishment once his refurbishment plans were complete.

"Nothing," Ryan replied, turning the glass in his hand, gazing into it.

"Really? Whatever is it, the answer's not in there," Brian said, good-naturedly. "Is it the job? Marianne? Joey? What?"

Ryan knocked the whiskey back, handed the glass to Brian for a refill. It was only ten in the morning.

"Spit it out, man," Brian said. "Maybe I can help, maybe I can't, but you know what they say, it's good to talk."

Ryan felt inside his leather jacket, pulled out an envelope and placed it on the bar.

"This came this morning, don't know what to make of it. I thought I was okay."

"May I?" Ryan slid the expensive vellum across the bar. Brian opened it, read it quickly, then again, slowly.

"When did you find out about this?" he spoke quietly.

"When I had the medical for the movie, we all have them, part of our contract for insurance. They spotted it then." Ryan was still looking into his glass.

"You've been for tests?" Brian asked.

"Yes, just before Christmas."

"And everything was okay?"

"The results came through in the New Year, saying everything was fine. Then I got a call, saying they wanted me back, more tests."

"Did you go back?" Brian asked.

"Well, how could I? There was the Ball, and then Franco, the funeral. It's all been a bit manic to say the least." Ryan's eyes flashed angrily at Brian, he hated being put on the spot. "Now, they've written, saying it's urgent."

"Surely you're not too busy to ignore your own health? Ryan this is very serious, you know that." Brian watched him take a sip of his drink, and waited.

"But if it is what they think it is, what's the point? I'm a dead man anyway, aren't I?"

Brian came out from behind the bar. He sat down beside Ryan.

"Not necessarily. Try and think rationally about this. Firstly, it may not be what they think it is. Secondly, if it is, there are various types of tumour, some aren't even dangerous, they're benign, just stay there in the brain. They need to be checked, but very often they don't change, don't make any difference and people just lead normal lives." Brian looked the younger man in the eyes, he knew what he was talking about. "And then there are ones which can be operated on, often with a good chance of full recovery." He was using his medical voice, calm, reassuring. Ryan looked back at him. His eyes were hard, hard with fear.

"And then there are the ones they can't operate on. The ones that kill you and all the time you know that

336

something inside your own brain, something that can't go away, is killing you, quickly or slowly, it makes no difference, your own body is killing you stone dead!"

Brian reached out and put his hands over Ryan's clenched fists.

"You don't know what it is yet. It could be nothing, or something they can cure. It's not knowing that's worse. Let's get that out of the way first."

"Let's? There's no let's about it. This is my problem, my business. I'll deal with it my way. I only told you because I know you've taken the *Hippocratic Oath* and you can't tell anyone. No one at all, do you hear me?" He jumped from the stool, knocked back the remains of his drink and left.

Brian stayed where he was.

"You're wrong there, Ryan," he said to himself. "You told me for a whole other reason. You told me because you want me to help, and don't worry son, you came to the right place." Brian already knew Ryan had a serious problem, Kathleen had told him. How Kathleen knew, Brian preferred to ignore, her intentions were always good, however dishonourable her methods.

After making arrangements with Erin to dispose of Padar's illicit vodka as soon as possible, Marianne took Monty for a punishing walk. Marching along Main Street, she took the track to the beach and on to the invisible opening in the cliff leading to Horseshoe Bay. She paused for a moment at the top of the natural stone staircase winding down to the sand. The perfect sweep of gold, the deep, dark blue of the ocean, the surf breaking the shore. She took a long breath, scanning the horizon.

She could see a small boat anchored off the bay. Sean Grogan was making the most of the weather and doing a bit of fishing. He looked up, saw her, easy to identify with Monty at her heels. She gave him a wave. He lifted his hand back in recognition. Marianne smiled to herself. Despite all the positive things she had tried to do since her arrival on the island, she was still unpopular with Sean. He hated what he called 'blow-ins', interlopers relocating to the island for a better life, escaping the rat race, taking everything down a gear. To Sean, far better the new bridge was never built. He wanted things left the way they were. Except for *Sky* that is, he loved *Sky*.

Chasing Monty along the shore, they took a sharp turn and started to climb upwards, onto a hill and then onwards up the cliff face. They were heading to one of her favourite spots. The clearing on the cliff top, overlooking the beach and the sea beyond. An eagle's perch, where she and Oonagh had shared wine, sandwiches and secrets. When the cliff became too steep to walk, she started to climb, using her hands. She had lived on the island long enough to know not to take chances with the terrain or the weather. But by now she was fit and sure-footed, not quite on par with Monty, but close.

She dragged herself upwards to the ledge and, hauling herself over, arrived face down in the clearing where the bench and picnic table stood. Monty, taking his own route, gave himself a shake and trotted over to her, tail wagging. It was one of his favourite places too.

Marianne sat on the ledge, her legs dangling over the edge. She pulled a tinfoil package of sandwiches out of her sailing jacket, a small bottle of water and a hip flask. Dog biscuits and a chew were placed before Monty to take his pick. She took a drink of water, shared it with the terrier, opened her lunch and took a bite of delicious home-cooked ham. Chewing contentedly, taking in the view, she then ferreted about in her inside pocket and withdrew an

envelope. It contained the handwritten letter from Franco
Rossini. The one marked, *Private and Confidential,
Marianne Coltrane, for her eyes only.* Ryan had brought it
back from New York with him, intact. Only she had read it.
After explaining the proposal to turn the *Lost Babies* into a
charitable trust, with enough money to pay staff, she told
Ryan there were also a few comments in the letter she would
rather keep between herself and Franco. He respected that,
said it was good his boss had been so fond of her.

Ryan was secretly delighted Franco had seen fit to
help in this way. Freeing Marianne to spend more time with
Joey, doing fun, family things, instead of constantly
working, endlessly tired, continually worrying about people
desperately trying to find each other and being upset that
selling babies for profit still went on all over the world, even
in Ireland.

She unfolded the letter. There was something in it
that was puzzling her, something she was not sure about. She
needed to read it again, alone.

My dearest Marianne,

*If you are reading this then I am no longer around. I
pray my ending was far less gruesome than the many I
bestow upon the villains in my movies. I hope this finds you
well and happy – despite the no doubt devastating sorrow of
my demise – and that you, Ryan and Joey, and Monty, if he
too is still around, are building a good life together on
Innishmahon, surrounded by your family and all those lovely
people, I have recently come to know, admire and in some
ways, also love.*

*I have tried to have this conversation with you
several times and hoped that you have heard my words and
taken their meaning to your heart. But now I have your full*

attention, and more, I am able to give you the wherewithal to carry out my wishes and yours too, if you are honest.

I have left you a charitable trust, with enough funds to staff and manage your Lost Babies campaign. Add to this a year's fees for lawyers and accountants to set you on your way, and to help guide you wherever you want it to go. This, with the management team running Oonagh's project, will leave you free – freer anyway, because you will always be involved in something – to spend time with Joey and take care of him.

You don't have to be a mother to feel a mother's love. There is no formula that connects one soul to another, the invisible thread, as delicate as a spider's web, as strong as steel, you have that in you, Marianne, give it time and space to grow.

Take care of yourself and cherish your little family. Something I was always too busy to do, and I have been left lonely, grumpy and sad. I wouldn't want that to happen to you.

And then, there is Ryan. Has he told you yet? Probably not, knowing him. Press him, you need to know, you need to be there for him when he needs you, as he will for you when your time comes, and it will, such is life.

And my last piece of advice, which is also my dearest wish. Marry him, Marianne. Marry him and make him your own. He needs that old-fashioned stability in his life and so do you. Marry and be happy, you are both amazing people, go and be truly spectacular together, as man and wife.

God bless you, Marianne, treasure the precious gifts I leave in your care, a boy who is a grandson to me and a man who is the son I never had.

I'll be there, helping if I can.

Franco Marco Rossini

She let the missive fall from her fingers. It was as if Franco was sitting beside her, she could hear his voice so clearly in these written words. And then there was the puzzle. Ryan, what had he to tell her? What did Franco know that she did not? And if it was something Ryan did not want her to know, how was she ever going to find out? Ryan was stubborn. She smiled, he often described her the same way.

Refolding the letter, she put it back in her pocket. Unscrewing the top of the hip flask, she took a sip of whiskey. Although the day was beautiful, there was a nip in the air, particularly there, high on the cliff above the Atlantic. What would Oonagh do, she wondered; be direct, ask him outright, maybe even show him Franco's letter. Erin, what would she do? Ignore it, probably bin the letter, saying if he wanted her to know something he would tell her eventually, probably none of her business anyway. And Kathleen, what would she say, surely she would have an opinion, offer some advice?

The gulls circling above, cried out. What an idiot she was! Kathleen already knew, of course she did, saying they ought to be married, saying it would be a terrible thing *not* to be a widow, what was that all about? Franco had probably told her, they were close. She took another quick swig of *Powers* and scrambled to her feet. She looked up to the new road, the shiny black stretch of tarmac that snaked to the village.

"Come on, Monty," she called him from sniffing vigorously under a rock. "Let's go and see Miss MacReady, Mrs Maguire, Kathleen, my mother, or whatever she's called. I've a couple of questions for her, and I'll be extremely surprised if she doesn't have all the answers."

Monty looked up. His mistress was already striding along the road, muttering to herself. *Now what? We only came out for a quiet walk*, he thought, as he cantered to catch up.

Kathleen threw open the door. "Come in, come in, when you said a drink later, I didn't know whether you meant here, Maguire's, your place or what?" She was wearing a turquoise cocktail dress, diamante clips at the neckline. Of course, Marianne thought, it's Monday.

"Have you arranged to see Brian?" Marianne asked, shrugging off her jacket. It was always exotically warm in the Post Office, one of the reasons Kathleen managed to get away with so few clothes.

"Do you think you'll ever call him father?" Kathleen asked.

"I don't know." Marianne was taken aback. "I never thought I'd call you mother, but I do."

"Sometimes, yes," Kathleen acknowledged. "But only in private and usually an admonishment."

Marianne gave her a lopsided smile.

"I don't mind, I don't mind at all," Kathleen fluttered. "We're blessed, we're so close, how many mothers and daughters who know each other all their lives are as close as us? Very few, mark my words." She reached for her fur wrap.

"Do you mind if we have a drink here?" Marianne asked. "I'm exhausted and don't fancy the pub tonight, I either feel obliged to help or make conversation. I'd like a night off."

"No problem," Kathleen said. "I'll ring Brian and tell him I'll be down later. You fix the drinks, love. *White Russian* I think for me tonight, in honour of Franco, he'd approve of that."

Marianne had no idea what she was on about, but followed the recipe, and had organised the drinks by the time

342

her mother tottered through the beaded curtain into the sitting room. She moved a pile of *Vogues* off the chair and waited for her to sit down.

"Times like these I could murder a cigarette," Kathleen announced. "Those electronic yokes are only fresh air, a complete waste of money if you ask me. You never smoked, did you, Marianne? Tell me, has Ryan given up? I mean completely given up, I hope he has, he's more than just himself to think about these days."

"He has the odd one," Marianne said, keeping an eye on Kathleen who seemed agitated, almost nervous.

"He must stop!" Kathleen declared. "What about his health?"

Marianne sipped her drink. "What about his health?"

"Just saying, none of us is getting any younger."

"What about his health?" Marianne asked again. She knew Ryan had a large amount of post that day; not unusual, fan mail, letters from all over the globe. He did not always deal with it straight away, so if Kathleen thought anything looked particularly important, she would stick a yellow post-it on it. One such letter had been received that very morning.

"Another drink?" Kathleen had drained her glass.

"Mother, was there something in that letter to Ryan this morning, something you think I should know about?"

Kathleen was at the fridge, fetching ice. It was worse than just the letter, she thought to herself, the consultant's secretary had telephoned earlier. Kathleen had put the call through to Weathervane. Ryan had made an appointment for the week after next. Kathleen knew all this because she had listened in on the conversation. She could not admit this to Marianne. It was too humiliating, disgraceful, dishonest. If anyone found out she would be sacked on the spot. Yet it was how Kathleen had always operated, everyone knew that, and when it came to it, everyone knew she was the soul of discretion, only ever interfering if she really had to, and this situation was close, very close. She took a fresh drink back to the sitting room.

"Marianne, don't press me because I can't tell you how I know, but I have reason to believe Ryan has a medical condition which needs attention."

Marianne put her glass down, slowly. "What do you mean, a medical condition?"

"He's to see a consultant, he's had some tests and they want to see him again, that's all I know."

"He's told you this?"

"Not exactly."

"What kind of consultant? Why hasn't he told me?" Marianne picked up her jacket. Monty was already at the door.

"Wait, wait a minute." Kathleen raised her hand. "Sit down!" she commanded. Marianne did as she was told. "He may not be ready to tell you yet, but I'm sure he will. I imagine with Franco's funeral and everything, he's just biding his time, you've had so much on, the pair of you. I can understand why he doesn't want to burden you with this too."

"But I'm his partner, we share everything."

"Give him time, he only got the call today," Kathleen said, then wanted to bite off her tongue.

"They phoned him? It must be serious then, oh God." Marianne turned pale.

"Did you ever hear the story of the West Wind and the Sun?"

"What?" Marianne exclaimed, already exasperated by her mother's recalcitrance.

"The West Wind claimed he was stronger than the Sun, so he picked on a man walking along the sea front wearing his top coat, and bet the Sun he could get the coat off the man the quickest."

"Give me strength," Marianne groaned.

"Hear me out," Kathleen insisted. "So he huffed and puffed and blew as wild and fierce as only the West Wind can, and what did the man do? He buttoned and belted his coat as tightly as he could, turning up his collar, wrapping a scarf around his neck. The West Wind was so angry, he blew the man over, but he could not get the coat off him. My turn, says the Sun, and out it came, warm and shiny and turning his full heat on the man, in no time at all the man was down to his shirtsleeves, rolling them up."

"So?!" Marianne was really agitated now.

"Use warmth, coercion, womanly wiles to find out what's wrong, to get your man to open up to you," Kathleen's words were soft, but her eyes were boring into her daughter's face. "You young women seem to have forgotten how to use charm to get what you want, far too direct in my opinion, slowly, slowly catchee monkey," Kathleen concluded.

"Stop with the analogies, for heaven's sake," Marianne cried. "Yes, and if all else fails, open his confidential mail and listen in on private telephone conversations!"

Kathleen gave her daughter a haughty look.

"Stealth. Just another weapon in the armoury," Kathleen confirmed, going off to find nibbles, leaving Marianne smarting on the sofa.

Chapter Twenty-Nine – Burning Ring of Fire

Dermot checked the weather with the Met office and although Innishmahon seemed to have its own microclimate, apart from some potential squalls, it was set fair. He had *Dream Isle* loaded with equipment and provisions for a four-person fishing trip, moored up awaiting its cargo and crew.

They had timed the expedition to coincide with Brian and Kathleen's trip to Galway. Brian wanted to visit a couple of recently-refurbished pubs, and Kathleen was going to choose fabrics and light fittings. She had a good eye, she kept reminding him, although he viewed some of her suggestions with trepidation.

Erin and Marianne had spent a couple of evenings in the cellar at the pub, under the pretext of clearing out old stock and abandoned furniture, so they could open up the hidden cellar, and see precisely how much illicit booze they needed to shift and make a plan how to do it.

Marianne's idea of just loading vehicles in the car park in broad daylight seemed the most sensible. Moving boxes of spirits around a pub car park would not be seen as out of place, if anyone questioned the quantity, they would say the wholesaler had over-delivered and they were merely returning the stock.

When the two old 4x4s rattled up to the quay, having completed the final trip, Dermot was staggered to see how many boxes of bottles remained to be loaded.

"When you see it like this, looks like a fairly serious commercial operation to me," he said, hands on his hips. "I hope we don't sink!"

"I know, where was it all going? And how many families would have been devastated by the damage it could have caused?" Marianne looked ruefully at the bright white boxes with the extravagant red lettering *'Genuine Russian Vodka – Export Quality'*- a veiled promise of sophisticated, exotic, intoxication. She shuddered. Looking up, she saw Ryan and Monty coming towards them. He had taken Joey and the Redmund boy for their riding lesson up at Lily O'Brien's stud earlier. Monty always knew when Joey was going to the stables, he could tell by the scent of his clothes and was pleased to escort him, keeping him as safe as possible, until he had to leave him astride one of those long-legged, un-dogs. He ran to greet the gaggle at the gangplank. Eve barked with joy at the sight of him, by now, two old sea dogs, together.

"Everything okay?" Marianne asked as Ryan joined them.

"He's delighted with himself, a full day at the stables, stop-over with the Redmunds, and crabbing with Papa Brian tomorrow, he tells me." He gave the girls a kiss. "I can't believe I've been roped into this," he called to Dermot, preparing to load the boat.

"Ah, come on." Dermot gave him a grin. "It'll be fun, always is."

"There's an awful lot of it. How far do you think we'll get before we sink?" Ryan asked the captain. Marianne gave him a frown. "Only kidding," he said, lifting a box onto the trolley Erin had purloined from the pub. But Ryan was not sure if he was kidding. He was hoping Erin and Dermot's superior knowledge and experience would ensure this was as uneventful a trip as possible.

"Don't worry," Erin told him. "I'll keep an eye on the plumb line while we're loading, make sure we dissipate the weight on board so she still sits safe enough in the water. It's fairly calm out there, we'll be grand."

By the time Erin was satisfied, they had been at it for hours, the sun was out, and they had worked up a decent appetite for lunch.

"All aboard," Dermot called. "Let's get out on the water and enjoy some of this glorious day."

Erin and Ryan cast off. Marianne had already taken in the fenders and settled in a sunny spot, below deck, with Monty snuggled beside her. As they set sail, Erin and Eve scrambled to take up their favourite position at the bow, with Erin dangling her legs over the side. Dermot was getting used to seeing them there, from his position at the wheel.

"Add to the scenery, don't they?" Ryan said, following the captain's eye. Dermot smiled, but made no comment.

Dermot was taking no chances, he kept *Dream Isle* moving at the same steady pace, keeping her well away from the rocky shoreline and in deep water. Halfway up the coast, towards Widow's Peak and well out to sea, they dropped anchor.

Erin and Marianne had been on duty that week in Maguire's kitchen, so the boat trip was benefitting from the pub menu of stilton and broccoli soup, with chicken liver pate on toast for lunch and the promise of dauphinoise shepherd's pie for supper. They squashed in beside the vodka boxes and after they had eaten, spread the charts out on the table. Although *Dream Isle* had all the new-fangled gadgetry on board, Dermot still liked to check his course the traditional way.

"Once we're over Widow's Peak and beyond Cloudy Bay, I think we head west and really push out into the Atlantic."

Ryan pointed at the map. "Is that Monks' Mound? I haven't been there since I was a kid." He was pointing to a tiny island, right out in the ocean, sitting between Cloudy Bay and the next stretch of coastline known as Ragged Sands.

"Yeah, you're right, what's on it?" Dermot asked.

"Just a ruined monastery as far as I recall," Ryan told him.

"It's a bird sanctuary now," Marianne said. "With the Marine Biology Unit here," she pointed at the promontory jutting out before the land swung back on itself, "it's a natural haven, a perfect place for all kinds of research."

"Lonely, though," Ryan said.

"Perfect for a few students and a couple of nutty professors, I'd say. Keep them holed up here, away from civilisation, where they can do less damage." Dermot had little respect for academia.

Marianne was quiet. Her adoptive parents, the Coltranes, had worked here, their research was still cited as ground-breaking in universities all over the world. She looked across the water, she could just make out the squat building that served as the research centre. No wonder they liked being alone, just the two of them, immersed in their work and each other. No wonder she had always felt surplus to requirements whenever she was with them. She felt someone lay an arm casually around her shoulders. It was Ryan, she nestled into him.

"So, what are you thinking, captain?" he asked Dermot.

"I think we plough on, get beyond Monks' Mound, dump the vodka this evening, head to Cloudy Bay and spend the night there. Take a leisurely route back to port the following morning."

Ryan agreed.

"What about the tide?" Marianne asked, looking back to the coast. "We don't want it taking whatever we're dumping on shore, there's marine life to consider, too, don't forget."

"I've thought of that," Dermot said, "there's a strong undercurrent here, a slipstream, it should take everything away quick as a flash."

Erin was clearing up, she was far tidier on board then she was ashore.

"Besides, I know we think we have masses of vodka on board, but we haven't really, pour it into the sea and it will soon dissolve, be too weak to damage anything. It's not a tanker or an oil rig now, is it, spilling millions of gallons into the ocean and completely upsetting the ecological equilibrium?"

"True enough," agreed Ryan. But the proximity of the research centre had unsettled Marianne.

"We will go miles out, won't we, Dermot?" she asked.

"Course we will, it'll be fine," he assured her.

It was a black starless night, the water slightly choppy, causing Dermot to check and double- check the anchor was secure. They planned to position the boat at various points around the western side of Monks' Mound, to give their insidious cargo a better chance of disappearing without trace.

"What changed your mind?" Dermot asked Ryan, as they passed boxes to one another.

"What about?" Ryan's thoughts had been somewhere else entirely.

"The fishing trip, giving us a hand."

"Bridget," Ryan replied. "Marianne told me the whole sad, sorry tale. Phileas making vodka in the basement and Padar selling it on."

"We don't know that for sure," Dermot replied, opening bottles and tipping the contents into the water.

"I think we do," Ryan said. "Padar was always after a fast buck. I reckon he had all this lined up, ready to go and then with Oonagh so sick, he had to take his eye off the ball, his sidelines had to be sidelined."

"But why did Bridget sway you?" Dermot was curious to know what the little girl had to do with things.

"She's our godchild, mine and Marianne's. One of the things that really welded us together, made me realise I wanted to spend the rest of my life here. I was determined to keep Joey with me, I'd have hung onto Bridget, too, if I could. But she's better off with her real father, and Sinead is a good woman. I wouldn't be happy about Padar doing time. He's more of an eejit than a criminal." Ryan stood next to Dermot, pouring the vodka into the sea.

"I've read about this stuff, apart from being illegal, it's dangerous, and being in the cellar of a pub, anyone could have mistaken it for the real thing. Served it, drank it." Ryan stopped. He stared at the bottle in his hand. "My God, Dermot! Angelique! You don't think …?"

Dermot shrugged. "Who knows? She was so screwed-up, could have been anything and was probably everything."

Ryan was quiet for a minute. "If this stuff could be linked to her death, it would be the end for Padar."

"Yeah, that's more or less what Erin said. I was all for turning the little shite in, I'd no idea he'd taken photographs of you guys and sold them to the papers, and then this!"

They both fell silent; the water sloshing against the boat; vodka glugging into the sea.

"Best leave it as it is," Ryan said, sadly. "Water under the bridge."

"Vodka poured into the sea, more like." Dermot gave a rueful laugh. He changed the subject. "What about the journalist-fella, what's his name, Paul Osborne, what was he doing sniffing round? Wouldn't trust him as far as I could throw him." Dermot was lining up the bottles.

"Nor would I," agreed Ryan. "These days though, I think he's trying to play a straight bat, his reports on Franco's death, the funeral, and all that stuff, were okay. But he's always looking for an angle, a conspiracy theory where there isn't one."

"But why?" Dermot was bemused.

"Fame, money, glory?" Ryan was crushing the boxes. "Who knows? It's a crap job, days, months, years of hard work, ending up in the recycling the day after it's published."

"Bit like being a movie star?" Dermot offered.

"At least I know my lines are made up, I don't put words in people's mouths and claim they actually said them."

"True enough. I think his problem's jealousy, plain, insecure, old-fashioned jealousy," Dermot said.

"Jeez, that's very profound for you, Dermot, what's brought this on?"

"I think he made a pass at Erin."

"No way!"

"I think he was letting on he fancied her, trying to see if Marianne would react, if she still had any feelings for him, that's what I think." Dermot sounded convinced.

"Well, you could be right about that. Erin quite liked him though, he's a good-looking fella."

"A bit too foppish if you ask me," Dermot said, bending his broad back to lift another box.

"Maybe he and Erin did get it on, we don't know."

"Oh, we do. I sent you down to the cabin to interrupt them the day we found Gregory on the beach. Good job I was distracted or he was going to get a punch on the nose."

"Who?" Ryan was confused.

"That Paul Osborne."

"Why?"

"It's my boat, any carrying on with women on my boat is down to me."

Ryan burst out laughing. "You're a total *Neanderthal,* Dermot, you really are."

"Do you know what I think you should do about that Paul Osborne fella? What I did with troublesome, smartarses when I was in the force."

"What was that?" Ryan asked.

"Get them on side, put him on the payroll. Rather have him with you then against you!"

Ryan thought for a minute.

"Bloody hell, Dermot, that's brilliant! Make him head of PR. We need somebody like him, Marianne's always tied to deadlines, writing blogs and press releases. He'd be perfect, and as you say, he'd be on our side, he'd soon scupper anyone trying to have a go at us in the media. I'll go and tell her now, she can email him, he'll be up for it if Marianne asks him, she's his old boss, after all, no worries."

It was past midnight and they still had about a third of the cargo to offload. A pale moon hung behind a veil of cloud, the remaining sky resolutely starless.

"Let's call it day," Erin declared. They were all hungry and exhausted. "We'll grab a snack and hit the hay, we can finish this tomorrow."

"We agreed to do it at night," Dermot told her. Erin had insisted all lights were extinguished at dusk, so the boat could not be spotted.

"I don't think there's anyone about, do you?" Marianne asked, desperate for sleep.

"I know the Gardaí are supposed to patrol the entire coastline, keeping an eye out for nefarious activity, but I never see them," Erin confirmed.

"Ah, those two eejits wouldn't recognise nefarious activity if it fell on them." Dermot was disparaging, he and Erin knew the local constabulary well.

"Unless, like so many, they're paid to look in the opposite direction," Ryan said. No one commented, but they all thought he had a point.

Dermot had been gracious and given Marianne and Ryan the main cabin. He was touched how grateful they had been at this simple gesture, they seemed closer than ever, exchanging looks, little signs of affection. When he looked in on them to say goodnight, they were wrapped together so tightly, he could not see where one began and the other finished.

Erin declared she did not care where she slept, a bed of nails would do her at this stage, as she zipped herself into a sleeping bag and settled down on a bench in the salon. Dermot took the opposite bench and sat for some while, watching his roommate slumber. The cloud of dark hair spilling onto the pillow, the rise and fall of fabric wrapped around her neat little body.

He was just drifting off when he heard her sigh and roll over, her arm fell free, hand draped on the floor. It was cold in the cabin. He reached over to take her arm and place it back beneath the quilt. He touched her hand and like a reflex, she grasped his. He was just about to pull free, when he decided against it, and as uncomfortable as it was, he left his arm there, holding Erin's hand, keeping it warm while she slept.

It was later than they had planned by the time they were underway the next morning, they had woken to a thick mist sitting on top of the water, an eerie stillness, broken only by the cries of sea birds, calling through the gloom. When they did catch sight of land, the unfamiliarity of the landscape made the whole place feel even more mysterious, the task ahead more daunting with the lack of visibility.

"I've an idea," said Ryan, as Dermot and Erin re-examined the charts, and Marianne passed around mugs of coffee. "Let's drizzle the stuff over the side as we go. If Dermot takes the helm and just tugs along slowly, we can get rid of the rest of the vodka a bit at a time."

Agreeing this was the best plan, they each donned multiple layers and took up their positions. The fog was dense and it was cloyingly cold on deck. As much as Dermot would have preferred to speed around to the far side of Monks' Mound, dump the cargo and get back to a peat fire and a plate of stew in Maguire's as soon as possible, he had no choice but to pootle along at a snail's pace, while the rest of the crew, gritted their teeth against the dank, and got on with the job.

By early evening they had circumnavigated the tiny island, and the last boxes of the invidious liquid they had all come to loathe, were on deck ready to be poured into the water.

Erin had radioed to say *Dream Isle* and its crew would be back the following day. With Kathleen away, Joy was on standby and took the call, saying the whole area was swamped in fog, they had better wait till it lifted anyway.

Their odious task finally completed, the mood on board *Dream Isle* brightened and as dusk fell, Dermot dropped anchor and gave Ryan permission to turn up the lights.

"Sure, anyone would be mad to be on the water in this," he said. "And if they are, at least they'll spot us before they crash into us."

With charts put away, the table was laid for supper, and wine poured. It was soon warm and cosy down below and with a good portion of delicious shepherd's pie apiece - including the dogs – the whole world looked a far more amenable place.

"You're off filming soon, then Ryan?" Erin asked the movie star.

"Couple of weeks, a bit of business in Dublin first, and then away. Lots of cities feature in this one, the criminal mastermind plans to shut them all down at the same time and blackmail every government for billions."

"Don't tell me the story!" Dermot exclaimed. "I love those films, you'll spoil it."

Ryan laughed. "Surely you don't remember the story, Dermot, it's all about the action."

"And the romance, don't forget the glamour and romance," said Erin dreamily, the wine having kicked in.

"Dublin?" Marianne asked. "Business?"

"Just final costume fitting, stuff like that, which now I think about it ..." Ryan pushed his plate away, patting his stomach. Dermot picked it up, ladling Ryan's leftovers into his own dish.

"Mind if I join you? Haven't been to Dublin in ages, I've a few things to do, myself," Marianne said.

"I'll be working," Ryan told her.

"I know, I won't interfere, but I'm sure we could find time for a little farewell dinner before you leave." She leaned across the table and whispered something in his ear. He gave her a glance, eyes sparkling.

"Well, if you put it like that," he said, his lips almost on hers.

"Get a room!" Erin and Dermot shouted in unison, and everyone burst out laughing.   "Well, if this is our farewell dinner, my friend, I think it calls for a toast." Dermot rummaged in the freezer and presented an ice cold bottle of vodka."

"Argh!" Erin groaned.

"Now, come on, has to be. It's good stuff, mind you, the real deal. Let's just have a shot each, straight back, the Russian way," he said in a terrible Eastern European accent.

They toasted each other royally and, finally, Marianne and Ryan, followed by a yawning Monty, slipped away to their cabin, leaving Dermot and Erin arguing good-naturedly about *Led Zeppelin* albums.

Lying snuggled together as the boat rocked gently, Marianne closed her eyes, trying to imagine what could be wrong with this gorgeous creature in her arms. She ran her hands delicately over his skin, surreptitiously checking for lumps, bumps, any changes. He moaned.

"You okay?" she whispered.

"Hmmm, go to sleep," he murmured. She pressed her ear to his chest. Could she hear anything, was he breathing normally? She placed her hand on his forehead, did he have a temperature?

"Marianne," Ryan said through gritted teeth. "Go to sleep, for godsake." He clamped her arms to her body in an embrace. He guessed what she was up to, she suspected something, she had been checking him out. Well, let her suspect. Until he knew what was going on himself, he was keeping schtum. End of.

Dermot and Erin were dancing. He had found an old CD, not rock and roll but *Barry White,* the king of sexy, get down and dirty, come to bed with me, soul. Erin was in hysterics.

"Dermot Finnegan, trust you. Is this part of your seduction routine?" she asked him.

"How did you guess?" he grinned, taking her in his arms and twirling her around. Eve, stretched out under the table, gave a grumble but wagged her tail anyway.

"Well, get a bit closer, we're supposed to bump and grind to this one."

"Don't need asking twice," Dermot said, clasping her to him in a bear-like embrace. The music ended.

"Can I walk you home?" he asked.

"Don't think so, you're not my type." She looked at him under her fringe.

"I could be. I was an actor in my youth, what type do you want?"

She smiled at him. She did have a lovely smile.

"A big, handsome, bruiser of a fella, who'll love me and only me till the day I die."

He smiled too, but he could see she was serious.

"I could do that, I'm a natural, you see." He fell to his knees. "Look at me, a big, handsome bruiser of a fella, who'll love you till the day you die," he declared, over-acting dreadfully.

"Ah, Dermot, I'm too long in the tooth to be play-acting with come day, go day, fellas, like you." The old Erin was back.

"What do you mean?"

"You've never been in love with anyone in your life except yourself," she was dismissive.

"That's not fair!"

"True though."

"Not necessarily. Anyway, what about you, who've you ever been in love with?"

Silence.

"Come on, who?"

"No one, none of your business, now stop it. Get in your sleeping bag and leave me alone." She started putting glasses in the sink, tidying up. Dermot went to stand behind her.

"Care to join me?" he said, softly at her neck, lips on her skin. It tickled.

"Where?" she asked.

"In my sleeping bag?"

"Dermot Finnegan, you're incorrigible!" she laughed. Eve barked, making them jump. "What was that?"

"What?"

There was the soft chug of an engine outside; water sloshing against the boat.

"Ahoy, ahoy there," came a shout. Dermot and Erin looked at each other.

"Ahoy, is there anyone on-board?" A voice through a megaphone.

Dermot and Erin scanned the cabin, empty vodka boxes everywhere. Monty had started howling next door.

"Shit, it's the guards," Dermot hissed. "Quick wake the others, get this lot hidden away."

Marianne and Ryan were already awake.

"Just coming," called Dermot, as the other three scurried in the small space, shoving box after box into the cabin Marianne and Ryan had just vacated.

The police launch was alongside. Dermot was surprised, he did not recognise the two Gardaí on board.

"What's the problem, officer?" he called to them. Monty and Eve were on the deck, growling gently.

"Just routine, is this your boat, sir?" the policeman asked. Dermot confirmed it was.

"How many on-board, sir?"

"Four of us, and the two dogs here, why?"

"Just routine. Pleasure trip, is it, sir?"

"Yes, fishing and the like."

"The like?" The guard pushed the peak of his cap back.

Dermot pointed to the binoculars. "Wildlife."

"Looks like there's a bit of that going on, alright." The guard nodded at the cabin window, where he could see a number of scantily-clad bodies writhing energetically. Dermot stepped back and hit a switch, throwing below deck into darkness.

"You woke us, is all," he said, giving the guard a steely look.

"What's up?" Ryan now in jeans and sweatshirt joined him.

"Nothing, just routine," said the policeman, again. "Have you seen anyone else on the water this evening?"

"In this?" Dermot asked, the fog was even thicker.

"Just checking, we have a report of a vessel drifting around Monks' Mound, weren't sure if anyone was stranded, engine trouble, you know."

"We're not stranded, just anchored for the night. Off again in the morning, hopefully this will have lifted a bit."

"And you haven't seen anyone?"

"Nope," Dermot confirmed.

"Not meeting another vessel, hooking up with someone else, who might be stranded, lost even?"

"No, just us, out fishing." said Dermot folding his arms. Ryan did the same. "Where's Sergeant Brody?"

"On leave, sir."

"And Garda O'Riordan?"

"Off sick, sir, why?"

"Not your usual beat, we were just wondering what you guys were doing, out on a night like this, making 'routine checks'." Dermot was glaring at them.

"Who's your boss?" Ryan asked.

"Why, sir?" The sergeant was looking surly now.

"Just wondering if my friend here knew him, being an ex-inspector himself."

"Inspector Regan, sir."

"Seamus Regan? We were at the academy together. Give him my best regards won't you, he'll remember me, I was a better shot than him," Dermot said, coolly. "Have you finished disturbing our sleep now, lads?"

The sergeant nodded at the guard. He started the engine.

"Good night to you both." Dermot saluted as the police launch pulled away.

"Isn't that fella, the actor, you know *Thomas Bentley*, international superspy?" they heard one say to the other, the words travelling through the silence of the fog.

"Are you mad? What would a multi-millionaire movie star be doing on a little fecking boat like that floating in the middle of nowhere, off the Irish coast?

"I swear it was him, I swear it!"

"Yeah and I'm *Pierce Brosnan* on me weekends off … mind them rocks, ya eejit!"

"What was that all about?" Ryan asked.

"A couple of chancers," Dermot said. "Hoping they found someone up to no good, so they could get a backhander to say nothing about it."

"Really?"

"Happens all the time. If they'd have caught us, we could have given them a couple of bottles of vodka to keep quiet and that would have done the trick," Dermot confirmed.

"Good job it's gone then, probably would have killed them," Ryan joked.

"Yeah, there is that," Dermot confirmed, solemnly. He had always been in the zero tolerance camp where bent coppers were concerned.

Magically the fog had disappeared by the time *Dream Isle's* sleepy crew had arisen. The sun was seeping over the eastern horizon and the sky was already pale blue. With most of the provisions devoured, they shared a breakfast of leftover pate on toast, cheese and yoghurt, with Eve and Monty enjoying the last of the soup poured over their biscuits. Everyone was in good form, congratulating each other on a job well done, praising Dermot's nautical skills and speculating about the Gardaí's impromptu visit the night before. Everyone except Ryan, he was both eager and reluctant to return to Innishmahon. Eager to see Joey and sleep in his own bed. Reluctant because he would have to leave again very soon, to attend his appointment in Dublin, an appointment to find out what life did or did not have in store for him.

"I'll just take my coffee on deck," he said, leaving the others preparing for the homeward trip. Marianne and Monty watched him go. He had been awake for hours, just lying there, staring at the ceiling. She knew this, because she had been awake for hours, too.

Deciding he did not want coffee after all, Ryan tipped it away and rummaged in an inside pocket of his jacket. He pulled out a lone cigarette, battered but not broken. He dug deeper in the pocket, his fingers finding the slim, gold lighter Franco had bequeathed him. He read the inscription, translating it in his head. 'Reach for the moon, if you fall you'll land on the stars.' He lit the cigarette, taking a long drag of the sweet, rich tobacco. He looked out across the water, the bold, brash Atlantic that led to America, the promise of fame, glory and untold riches. He looked back towards Innishmahon, soaring cliffs, emerald green hills, wrapped in a sweep of golden sand. His home. The place where his heart and soul were so grounded, so solid with love, he had wings, wings to fly above and beyond anything bad or sad ever again. Whatever this was, he would beat it, well and truly. Nothing was going to take away what he had now, what he had known deep down he had wanted all his life.

"Penny for them?" she said, sidling up beside him. He went to throw the cigarette away, like a schoolboy caught in the act. "Don't, finish it, maybe you needed it." She looked into his eyes. He gave her a grin, but she could see beyond it. She pushed her arm through his, "I've been thinking." He groaned. It was a routine they had developed. She was always thinking. "You know that marriage thing? Why don't we give it a go?"

He kept his eyes fixed on the horizon.

"What's brought this on?"

"Nothing, like I said, I've been thinking. I've been feeling, too, feeling that it's right, the right thing to do."

He slid her a look. But instead of bright, sparkly eyes, shining at her in anticipation, there was a cloud of confusion.

"My turn to have a think about it then," he said. She frowned. "Is that okay?" he asked.

A strange emotion rattled through her. She gripped the handrail. Monty whimpered and tucked in between their legs. She bent and picked him up, holding him to her, burying her nose in his fur.

"Sure," she said, giving Ryan her brightest smile. "You have a think about it. It is a good idea though, I have the ring and everything." She turned and wiggled her bottom at him, making him laugh. He took once last draw on his cigarette and flicked it far into the ocean, turning to follow her below deck. He heard a hiss, then a low boom. Turning back, he stopped dead, something had ignited in the water, there was a pool of fire a few metres away. Marianne stopped.

"What on earth …?"

The fire began to leak out of the pool, running along what looked like a track of fuel, oil or something, the water bursting into flames around the boat. Dermot looked down from the bridge. The fire was moving towards them, across the water, he could feel the heat.

"Christ! The anchor … away… anchor away…" he roared, starting the engine. Ryan was there in a flash, hauling on the chain, Marianne ran to help him. Dermot revved the engine.

"Hold on!" He pulled on the throttle, launching the boat into the air. He swung the boat round, desperately looking for a gap in the circle of fire, a space he could power through, clear of the flames, which could ignite the fuel tank and blow them all to Kingdom come.

Monty and Eve were running up and down the deck, barking.

"Find me a gap!" Dermot yelled, as Erin ran to the bow, Ryan to the stern. The flames were spreading, a double circle of fire now, trails of burning water snaking off in every direction.

"There, three o'clock, there's a gap at three o'clock," roared Ryan above the engine.

Dermot spun the wheel, the vessel lurched as he pointed the nose of the boat at the space in the fire, growing ever smaller by the second.

"Hold on!" he yelled again, and with one almighty push, shoved the engine into gear and leapt across the water and out through the other side of the flames. Not even looking behind to see if he had cleared it, he powered on and on through the waves, charging *Dream Isle* forward, driving her like the chariot she was.

Finally, with the promontory of Widow's Peak in view, he slowed the engine and started to breathe again. He could hear his crew moving about behind him, he turned to see, three greenish-grey faces smiling at him. A couple of waggy tails endorsed the smiles.

"What was it, what happened?" Marianne was the first to speak. "I've never seen anything like it in my life." Dermot edged the boat round so they could look back. As far as the eye could see, the whole area was a mass of flaming circles and trails of fire, literally burning water, the smoke drifting up to form a toxic cloud sitting above the ocean. It looked like a scene from a major sea battle. They stood in bemused silence and watched as the methanol in the vodka burned itself out.

"Now will you give up?" Dermot said to Ryan.

Chapter Thirty – Erin's Secret

Barely twenty-four hours later, Brian telephoned to tell Marianne the bad news that Erin Brennan, only a few months into her role as manager of Maguire's, had handed in her notice, with immediate effect. She was going to England, she had contacts in Manchester and was going to cover maternity leave at an insurance company. Marianne was crestfallen, why had Erin not discussed this with her? They were friends now, Erin did not appear unhappy, she was in better spirits than ever, far less snarky than when she first came.

"Will you wait till I speak to her before you fill the position?" she asked Brian.

"I can't see anyone rushing to join us," Brian told her. "We're hardly an attractive career proposition at the moment, the season is still some time away."

"I thought you wanted a career break, you were fed up with the rat race you, told me." Marianne busied herself at the sink, surprised at how upset she was at the news Erin was planning to leave. "Or is it just the pub you've had enough of?" She crossed her fingers under the water, hoping it was only her work as bar manager Erin was fed up with and that they could sort something out.

"I like the pub," Erin replied, taking a bottle of wine from the fridge.

"Not vodka?" Marianne slid her a look.

"Never again," Erin smiled grimly, then waving the bottle at her colleague, "just one?" They rarely drank on duty these days. By now they were a good team, each knew the other's strengths and weaknesses; it worked.

"Go on, then." Marianne glanced at the old school clock on the wall. "We've time."

Seated at the large oak table, a glass apiece, Marianne was hopeful Erin would tell her what was on her mind. But Erin just hid beneath her fringe, staring glumly at the wine.

"Well, if you like the pub, what's the problem?" Marianne asked.

"Ah," Erin said, leaving a long silence hanging between them.

"Ah what?" Marianne pushed.

"It's this place, it never changes, a small island, filled with small-minded people. For some reason I'd forgotten that." Erin was dispirited.

"Come on, it's not that bad." Marianne took a sip of wine. "Every community has good and bad, even in big cities, you can find plenty of small minds."

"Maybe so, but you can get lost in a big city, you don't have to listen to a load of ole shite."

"Who's been giving you a load of old shite?" Marianne asked.

"Lots of people, they talk about you and Ryan all the time, repeating crap out of the newspapers. It sickens me." Erin sighed and took a big gulp of her drink.

"Pay no heed, it's fine, honestly. While he's in the public eye there will always be rumours, innuendo and downright lies. Just roll with the punches. It's usually the work of some saddo trying to make a name for themselves, searching for the big exclusive, their '*Freddie Starr ate my hamster*' moment." Erin gave her a quizzical look.

"Desperate for a headline with their name attached to it," Marianne explained.

"That's sick!" Erin said.

"That's why you can't worry about it, can't take it seriously. But that's not why you want to leave, surely? It'll all be over soon, Ryan will be back for good, his new life waiting for him here, all the scandals of today, tomorrow's chip paper. What's really up?"

Erin shrugged.

"Come on, tell me, it's not fair if you go without telling me. I thought we were friends?" Marianne reached over and touched Erin's hand, clamped in a fist on the table.

Erin took a deep breath.

"I'm getting too attached if you must know." She took up her glass and swallowed.

"Really? To what? To who?" Marianne asked.

"Ah, you know." Erin shrugged again.

"No, I don't know, tell me!" Marianne almost shouted.

"Someone on the island."

"Who? Don't tell me it's Eve or I'll brain you, she doesn't count as a someone, and I can't see you going anywhere without her, so spill the beans, who is it?"

"Not saying, someone anyway." Erin finished her wine.

"And that's a bad thing?" Marianne was at the fridge, she pulled out another bottle of wine, she was going to get a name out of Erin if she had to drown her in drink.

"Wouldn't work, bad scene." Erin offered her glass up for a refill.

"How do you know? You could give it a try. He's not married, is he?" It was a smokescreen. Marianne was sure it was Dermot, but she played along with her friend.

"No!" Erin was emphatic. "But a total bachelor, you know the type, loads of women, past and present. Anyway, best if I just head off, back away."

"Before he breaks your heart?" Marianne asked.

"No way, no one's going to get that close." A long silence. Marianne kept staring at Erin. "What?"

"Again. That's that word I'm waiting for. 'No one's going to get that close again.'" Marianne poured more wine.

Erin let out a big sigh. "Yeah, maybe you're right." Silence, while they drank.

"Was it the guy you went off to Dublin for?" Marianne asked after a while.

"No, that was all in my head. When we got to Dublin he wasn't interested in me at all. A hick from the sticks. He had a fiancée, the wedding booked, everything. His future was all mapped out and that's how he wanted it."

"Well-educated? Well-to-do?" Marianne asked.

Erin nodded. "He did me a favour though. I took a long, hard look at myself and went straight back to school, achieved as much as I could, as quickly as I could. Then I landed the job with the Gardaí and I must have shown some sort of promise, because I moved swiftly up the ranks and my career was set."

"You're a very bright, hardworking young woman," Marianne told her. "I hope you're proud of what you achieved. Cheers." They chinked glasses.

"Was he a guard?" Marianne knew she was on the right track. Erin nodded. "Gorgeous?"

"Deadly. A great big bruiser of a fella, handsome, great company, amazing sex." Erin looked up from her wine, eyes clouded with memory.

"Married?" Marianne asked.

"Very," Erin replied. "And only to the Chief Superintendent's daughter. I was on a hiding to nothing."

"What happened?"

"Usual story. I fell pregnant. He dropped me like a stone. Said if I ever told anyone I'd lose my job and never work in Ireland again, let alone Dublin. I believed him, too, he was quite frightening, riled."

"The bastard, you poor thing." Marianne poured more wine. "And?"

"I had an abortion."

"In Ireland?" Marianne was shocked.

Erin nodded. "Belfast. He arranged it, paid for it, the lot."

Marianne went to put her arms around her, but Erin pulled away. Marianne sat back down.

"I'm so sorry, that's a tough call." She squeezed the other woman's hand.

"It wasn't straightforward. There were complications, I ended up in hospital back in Dublin. I was really ill, there were questions asked, but it all got dealt with and swept under the carpet. So anyway, that was that, done. He had me transferred and I hated it, so I left to work for the insurance company. I had fantastic references, as you can imagine, the Gardaí were glad to see the back of me in the end."

"You earned those references, you were brilliant at your job." Marianne could not believe the change in the girl before her. The brash, straight-talking female she had come to admire, crumpled and shrunken, all confidence and vitality ebbed away in the telling of the tale, a sad, but not uncommon story. "But you're a vibrant young woman, outgoing, fun to be with, surely you had other boyfriends?"

"Nope," Erin replied.

"But why not?"

"Ah, it put me off."

"Did Oonagh know?" Marianne wondered if this was something that might have contributed to the sisters' estrangement.

"God no! I was terrified she'd find out, one of the reasons I stayed away," Erin confirmed.

"But why? Oonagh would have understood, she would never have been judgemental."

"I don't know about that." Erin was unconvinced. "But it was more my fault, my guilt. I knew she and Padar were desperate to have a baby. I knew she thought she had left it too late and she very nearly did."

"But what difference could you have made?" Marianne was bemused.

Erin was quiet. "I could have given her mine. She could have had my child, called it her own, if I hadn't killed it."

"Erin, no!" Marianne was on her feet, horrified. "Stop this immediately. Stop thinking like that. It's total nonsense. You had no choice, you were forced to go down that road, bullied into it. It was nothing to do with Oonagh, she had to make the decisions that were right for her and Padar."

"D'ya think?" Erin was a bit slurry now. "Well, if I'd have given her my baby, she wouldn't have had to have all that treatment, which probably gave her cancer, and now she's dead." Erin banged the table with her fist, fighting her tears.

"Come on, Erin, the treatment didn't give Oonagh cancer, they found out she had it, because of the treatment. They did their best."

"Well, it wasn't good enough was it. She's dead and it feels like my fault." Erin was angry now.

"It's not your fault, it's no one's fault, and it's wrong that feeling like this is stopping you having a relationship, a

371

good relationship with a good man." Marianne kept her voice calm.

"Ah, what would you know about it? You've never been pregnant, lost something that could have been perfect, could have changed your life, something that could stop you feeling all twisted up inside." Erin slumped back in her chair. Marianne pushed her glass away.

The door opened and Ryan appeared. He could tell there was an atmosphere.

"You guys on a break?" He eyed the wine.

"Yep, just chatting, you know." Marianne replied.

"Sorry to hear you're leaving Erin, need a hand with anything, let me know. Brian said you want to get over to England quite quickly, have you a job lined up already, or just a fella?"

Marianne glared at him.

"Tell you what, I'll help out here in the bar then, while you two have a chat, break, whatever ..." He backed out of the room.

"We're talking about you, not me," Marianne said to Erin coolly. "You're being too hard on yourself, you were young, you got pregnant by the wrong man, it happens, happens a lot, actually."

Erin was staring at the table. "I should have helped Oonagh."

"You had no choice, it seems to me. You're living a life of regret for no reason." Marianne was dismayed, her head exploding with all this information, the room heavy with grief. But Erin was not finished, the floodgates had been opened.

"When it went wrong, the operation, I thought I was being punished for having the abortion, for destroying the baby. But I got through all that, I was on my own, but I did it," her voice barely a whisper, eyes brimming with unshed tears, "and then Oonagh died, and we weren't even on speaking terms, and the only family, friend I had in the world, was gone. And I realised that was my punishment. So you see, it was my fault, all of it, really."

Marianne sighed. She went to make coffee. They needed it.

"So, there's been no one since?" she asked. Erin shook her head. "And now there could be, and you don't want to risk it?" Erin was silent. "You don't want to risk being happy?"

"I can't be happy, how can I be, when deep down inside, all I feel is hollow, no warmth, no love, nothing?" She turned her eyes on Marianne, they were so dull with the pain of loss, it made her stomach clench.

"Maybe if you let that someone get a bit closer, he could help untwist things. Because that's what you've done, you've got all these thoughts and feelings knotted up in your head and you've been carrying around a big clump of guilt and it's doing you no good, no good at all." She placed a mug of coffee in front of Erin. "Anyway, what about him? Are you going to deny him the chance of happiness with a gorgeous, warm, loving woman?"

"What woman?" Erin asked.

"You, you eejit!" Marianne gave Erin's shoulder a thump. "Now, blow your nose and drink your coffee. You're going nowhere. You're going to stand your ground and face your feelings. But you'll have to be brave. Falling in love is not for sissies, I know that for a fact," Marianne said.

Erin gave her a half-smile.

"You sound more like Kathleen every day," she told her. Marianne was not one-hundred per cent sure whether that was a compliment or not. "You won't breathe a word of what I've told you, will you?" Erin looked pleadingly at her.

"Of course, not," Marianne confirmed, "you have my absolute word." But deep down, Marianne was not so sure. If keeping Erin's secret meant two people destined to be together would be torn apart, then that would not be right, not right at all. She went to open a window, to let some of the angst out of the room.

Marianne did not sleep well, she twisted and turned all night. Erin's confession, her terrible admission of guilt was driving her to distraction. What on earth could be going on in the head of a perfectly sensible, well-educated, intelligent young woman to even imagine such nonsense could be remotely true? Why did she feel responsible for her sister's happiness? Why did she think what she had been forced to do would mean she could never be happy, herself? Why did the world do this, why could life not just give women a break? It was the crack of dawn, and she was about to do something she had not done for a long time, head for the decanter and a long talk with George's paperweight resting in her desk, next to the box containing Ryan's ring.

As she padded downstairs, she could hear Monty snuffling at the door. There was something whining, piteously outside. She threw open the door, it was Eve. The collie turned forlorn eyes up to her. The phone started ringing. Before she even picked it up, she knew it was Dermot, she knew Erin had gone.

The 4x4 bounced over the road as they sped off the ferry and on towards the airport. Marianne gripped the back of the passenger seat, she could feel every pothole as Dermot drove like a demon, with Ryan attempting to navigate at his side.

"Sooner that fecking bridge is built, the better."

Dermot smashed through the gears.

"Then when someone takes a fargarie, we can get after them a bit quicker, stop them before they ruin their lives altogether."

"Slow down, for godsake, Dermot," Ryan pleaded, hanging on to the dashboard. "None of us will make it at this rate."

Swinging into the airport, Dermot ignored all the signs and barriers and drove right up to Departures. He dumped the jeep outside the doors, jumping out of the vehicle, barely able to wait the couple of seconds while the sliding doors opened.

"I'll park it, no worries," Ryan called to him, climbing into the driver's seat. But Dermot did not hear, he was already racing through the airport. Checking the departures screen, making sure the flight to Manchester had not yet left. Casting about, he caught a young steward by the sleeve.

"Manchester, which gate?" he demanded.

"That's already boarding, sir. I think you're too late."

"Please, which gate?" Dermot begged.

"Follow me," replied the young man, heading off at such a pace, Dermot found it hard to keep up.

"There, sir." He pointed across the mezzanine at the top of the stairs. Dermot spotted her, a cloud of dark hair, disappearing down the walkway towards the plane.

"ERIN! ERIN!" he called. But she did not look back. He ran to the gate, a steward blocked his way.

"Boarding pass, sir. I can't let you any further without a boarding pass."

"But ..." Dermot ran to the window. Knock was a small airport, he could see Erin's plane, barely visible through horizontal sheets of rain. He hammered on the glass, calling her name. People were looking at him, tutting, assuming he was drunk, demented, or both.

"Sir …" The kind young steward was at this elbow. He swivelled his eyes downwards. Dermot frowned. The steward tried again. Dermot followed his glance. Emergency exit doors, opening onto the apron where the aeroplane stood. Dermot kissed him.

"Thank you, thank you," he called, charging downstairs as fast as he could.

Shaking out the umbrella, Marianne and Ryan had just arrived. Dermot flashed past them, pushing open the door, and out in one movement. He ran through the rain to the aeroplane, he could just see her at the top. The steps were packed with people trying to get on as quickly as possible. It was hopeless, he could not get by.

"Erin!" he yelled, cupping his hands over his mouth. "Erin, wait!"

A murmur through the crowd. He saw her stop, turn around.

"Erin, it's me, Dermot!" he was jumping up and down, waving his arms at her.

"Wait!"

She turned to board the plane.

"Please wait." The passengers murmuring on the steps, fell silent. "Come back, Erin, please. We can work it out, I know we can."

The crowd looked from the man pleading in the rain, up to the girl near the top of the steps.

"I'm sorry, I can't," she barely whispered.

"What did she say?" someone asked.

"She can't," someone else said.

"What was that?" another voice.

"She said, she can't," replied another. They passed the message down the line till Dermot heard.

"Tell her we can work it out, tell her it will all be okay," Dermot told the man at the foot of the steps. The man blinked at him. "Go on, pass it on."

The man passed the message onto the next person and up it went, up the line to Erin at the top.

"It won't," came the answer via the line of people standing in the rain.

"Tell her I'm in love with her, pass it on," Dermot tried again. He waited. Then a flutter, as a message came back down the line.

"She says she's falling in love with you, too."

Dermot beamed. "Tell her ..."

"Oh, tell her yourself," shouted the man, "we're all getting soaked. I want to go home, bloody country, all it does is rain." He stood back to let Dermot up the aeroplane steps. People started moving sideways, letting him through. Erin was standing with the stewardess, she still had her boarding pass in her hand. She looked round as she heard the commotion. Dermot was standing at the top of the steps.

"Give it a chance," Dermot said, water streaming down his face, his clothes stuck to him. "We're worth a chance."

"But ... but I'm falling in love with you. It's bound not to work." She was hiding behind her fringe, he could see tears in her eyes. He dropped to his knees and threw open his arms.

"Fall ... please fall," he begged.

The stewardess nudged her. "Go on," she said in a warm northern accent. "Give it a go, love, you'll never know if you don't give it a go."

The door to the flight deck sprang back.

"What *is* the problem?" demanded the captain. "We need to get this plane airborne. Can those boarding, please board!"

"You're right," Erin told the stewardess and threw herself into Dermot's embrace. He closed his eyes and held her as tightly as he could.

"Really!" the captain exclaimed. "Always some sort of drama in this place, I don't know, must be the influence of that weird shrine or something."

"One passenger disembarking," the stewardess announced pleasantly. "Everyone else on board now please, come along, we don't want to miss our slot." She hurried the other passengers up the steps, as Dermot carried Erin away with him.

Ryan and Marianne watched the whole episode through the plate glass window. Marianne pulled off her coat and wrapped it around Erin's shoulders. Dermot's total wetness had soaked her through to the skin.

"Put this on before you start shivering," she instructed.

"Don't think I'll ever shiver again," Erin said, giving her a huge grin.

Ryan gave Dermot a look. "Good work, didn't think you'd follow my advice to the letter though."

"You took advice?" Erin was incredulous.

"Well, he is the world's most devastating romantic hero, isn't he?" Dermot smiled.

"Not now, he's not," Erin replied, standing on tiptoe to kiss Dermot on the chin.

"WOO HOO! WOO HOO!" Dermot yelped, and everyone in the vicinity moved deftly away, he really did look like a total madman at this stage.

Chapter Thirty-One – Friday The Thirteenth

The movie star and his attractive ex-journalist partner were becoming a familiar sight at Knock Airport. They had been there only days before when a friend had boarded the wrong flight to Manchester and the lovely staff at the airport had put everything on hold to make sure she disembarked safely, while another of friend of theirs had something like a seizure in the departure lounge, but it was all okay, he had just forgotten to take his medication.

Ryan folded the newspaper. "We're certainly keeping Paul busy with stories at the moment."

"It's working though." Marianne sipped her tea. "Having him as press officer, don't you think?"

"Working like a dream, I've never had such positive PR, and every time anybody steps out of line, he's on them like a ton of bricks, well worth the investment."

"Well, he is classically trained," she beamed at him. "Do you think you'll be tied up for long in Dublin? I would like us to spend some time together."

"I'll check the diary against whatever Lisa has set up for me, and we'll take it from there. Is that okay?" He had his brusque, business head on. "Now, do you mind if I read the paper?"

Leave it, she thought to herself, he's stressed, just leave it.

"Sure, no worries." She continued sip her tea and hatch her plan.

"Right, I have everything, I just need to send it special delivery so it's all there for when Marianne arrives." Kathleen was in full postmistress mode, glasses on the end of her nose, small stud earrings, pale pink nail varnish, this was serious business; this involved not only the State but the planets, the angels and possibly God – whoever he or she was.

"Have they given her a time yet? Can you book it like a hair appointment?" Erin asked, rubbing, first Monty, then Eve, dry with a towel, they all needed to look their best.

Kathleen pondered this. "Do you know, I'm not sure. I know Ryan has a very important appointment on Friday. What date is that? Oh Lord, it's Friday the thirteenth, now I never know if that's a good thing or a bad thing. What do you think, Erin?"

Erin pulled a face. Not being remotely superstitious about anything, she had no clue what Kathleen was on about. The bell pinged and Father Gregory strode in.

"Goodness Gregory, you're looking very well, did they take that ole brace off you yet?" Kathleen said.

"Not yet, but I am moving a lot better. I'll be riding again next season, you mark my words." Kathleen admired the priest's spirit, but nothing would ever entice her to bestride a horse, she did like the clothes though, in fact she was sure she had a riding habit somewhere.

"What's in the package, looks very official?" He nodded at the beautifully wrapped, multi-labelled parcel in Kathleen's hands.

"If I tell you, I'll have to kill you," Kathleen replied, and she was not joking. "What do you think, Gregory, as a priest, is Friday the thirteenth lucky or unlucky?"

Gregory laughed. "Depends on whether the horse wins or not."

Kathleen rolled her eyes.

"Number thirteen," called the clerk. Marianne checked her ticket, but she knew she was number thirteen, how could she forget that? She went to the little glass window.

"I think it's all here." She handed the man the envelope. He peered at her over his spectacles.

"Well, it needs to be, we cannot proceed without every piece of documentation required, it's the law you see, we can't mess with law, it says here quite clearly on my checklist what I can and cannot accept." He pulled everything out of the wallet. Marianne knew her mother would have lovingly checked and rechecked, every item. She was thorough, it had to be said. He examined everything and then pressed a button on his desk. Marianne heard a buzzer sound. A door opened and a young girl appeared.

"This is Miss Coltrane," he said to the girl. "You can take her through now."

Marianne looked askance.

"The Superintendent Registrar needs to see you," the girl had a lilting Donegal accent. All Marianne heard was a harsh whoosh, it made her reel.

"There isn't a problem, is there? I mean, everything you asked for is there," Marianne felt her throat constrict. *Don't do this to me, God, please don't.*

The Superintendent's office was a vast, modern room, huge windows, a massive desk. There was no one at it. She heard a loo flush, and a small man appeared, wiping his hands. Her insides flipped, she wondered if her whole future was about to go down the pan too.

"You're Kathleen's girl, aren't you?" He gave her a big toothy grin. "I can see a likeness, I really can. Please sit down."

She swallowed. She might have known everyone in Dublin of a certain age, in a position of authority in the civil service would know her mother. The girl gave her a chair, Marianne felt her knees give way.

"As you know, this is highly irregular and we have had to pull some strings, speed a few things up, but all is in order, even your partner's poor wife's death certificate and their marriage certificate ..."

Marianne swallowed again, she had no idea what he was talking about.

"We have everything. Now, will Mr O'Gorman be joining us to sign his statement of consent." The man looked around her, as if there was a chance, Ryan, all six feet of him, could be standing behind her. She had been expecting this.

"No, I have it here, we've both signed." She bit her lip. It was Kathleen's idea to put the form under a pile of mail Ryan was signing to go back to Lisa and the fan club. They just followed the imprint of his signature with his fountain pen. Stroke of genius, that was.

He took the document. "Well, I'm afraid I can't let this go, can't let this go at all," he told her.

"What do you mean?" She was definitely going to be sick.

"A world famous movie star's autograph, and I've to put it in a dusty old file! Such a shame, I bet I'd get a good few euro for it if I put it on *eBay*." He roared with laughter at his own joke, and popped the form into the file with the big No 13 on it. "There we are, Miss Coltrane, all done and dusted. All we need is you and Mr O'Gorman, twelve noon, on Friday." He came out from behind his desk to shake her hand. "How many guests will there be, no don't tell me, I know, a private family affair here, and then a huge party in the Shelbourne Hotel, is that it?"

"You look rather gorgeous," Ryan told her. "You've had your hair done." He lifted her hand, "Nails too, good, you should treat yourself. Wait a minute, are you going on the pull as soon as I get on the plane?"

He was forcing jollity, she could see that, because tomorrow was the day, the day when they would know what the future held, good or bad. But of course, she did not know that was the case, she was still in the dark, as far as Ryan knew.

"I wanted to look nice on our last date," she cringed as soon as the words came out, "together, before you have to go to away. What time's your flight on Saturday, do you know?"

"Lunchtime. What time will you go back to Knock?" He was picking at the delicately grilled calves' liver on his plate, his favourite, the one he always said he would choose for his last meal. She put her knife and fork down, she could not eat, either.

"I'll go on Monday, I'm having lunch with the couple taking on *Oonagh's Project* on Sunday, they're all signed up and raring to go. I thought it would be nice to start to get to know them." She could not care less about *Oonagh's Project*, the *Lost Babies* charity, the bridge, the marina or World War III breaking out right this second in the middle of Grafton Street.

"Hey," he took her newly manicured hand in his, "you seem a bit down, we're supposed to be having fun up here in the big city, what do you want to do, go to a show? See a movie? Shop?"

"Not really in the mood," she tried to smile.

"Missing Joey? Monty? Fecking Sean Grogan?" he asked, giving her his lopsided grin.

"Not really, an early night would be good. I think we're both tired," she said.

"Okay, is that a real early night, or a *real* early night?" he flashed her his best Hollywood beam. If she was honest, she did not really care, once she woke up in his arms and he was still Ryan, still with her, still alive.

"Come on, come on Friday the thirteenth, get up, get out there, get walking under some ladders, stepping on cracks in paving stones, don't let Lady Luck down!" He was out of the shower, shaking wet hair in her face. She opened her eyes a crack and looked at the clock.

"Christ! Look at the time, how could I have overslept, today of all days!" she yelped, hopping out of bed, squealing because she stood on his hairbrush.

He turned the hairdryer off. "What's today, then?" He looked at her through the mirror.

"Friday the thirteenth, you said it!" she quipped back. She knew his appointment was at half past ten, she knew his doctor was a senior consultant at Dublin's neurological institute in Eccles Street, she had no idea how long he would be there, but she also knew it would take a good thirty minutes to get to the registry office on the other side of the river, and even if he agreed to go with her, and there was no guarantee, they would be cutting it fine, really fine.

He pulled on his jeans, a white t-shirt and his battered leather jacket.

"Is that what you're wearing today?" she asked.

"Er, that's why I've put it all on. Why?" He was puzzled.

"Very casual, a bit dressed down, I'd have thought."

"For what, a Friday?"

"Shoes, put your good shoes on, makes everything look classier, I always think, don't you?" She was putting on make-up, she needed to get a move on.

"Okay, whatever the lady says." He put his deck shoes back and took out his shiny, black *Church's*.

"Are we meeting for lunch today?" She was drying her hair.

"Dunno, see how this morning goes, eh?"

"Oh yes, you have a meeting." She left it at that, she did not want to force him to lie to her, that would be unfair.

"What are you up to?" He picked up his everyday aftershave. She ran to the dressing table and handed him *Chanel Pour Homme*. "This one?" She nodded.

"I think I'll buy flowers or something," she said. He opened the door. She jumped up to kiss him goodbye. "I love you."

"Who wouldn't?" his stock answer.

"Good luck," she beamed at him.

"It's Friday the thirteenth, Marianne. What are you like?" He made to leave.

"Ryan," she called, pointing at his shoes. "Can you run in those?"

He closed the door, and despite the sword of *Damocles* hanging over his head, entered the lift, chuckling. She was up to something, up to something big time, she never put her make-up on before she dried her hair.

She had to leave her hair wet, it was the only way she could follow him. She flew down the sweeping marble staircase, into reception and out through the highly polished rotating door. She had opted for the sea-green, satin dress with pale silk underskirt, far too flimsy for a bright March day, but with her *Barbour* over it, she was warm enough, and if it rained, as it so often did, she would still be reasonably dry. She had forgotten her full-length, cream wool coat with the fur collar, she was so delirious with worry about the outcome of Ryan's tests, she had hardly packed anything at all. She had nothing for her head, and she knew her hair would be a total frizz, but it would have to do. At least she had remembered her lipstick, the bright orangey geranium red, it reminded her of Spanish sunshine, even on the blackest of days.

At the bottom of the stairs, she caught sight of a woman going into the Horseshoe bar. For one second, she reminded Marianne of her mother. Smart, busy, sexy. She loved Dublin women of a certain age, spunky, that was the word for them. The brass glinted in the sunlight as she sailed through the door, the porter raised his top hat at her.

"Taxi, ma'am?" he said.

"I would if I knew where I was going." She stopped, she remembered, she had written the street down, the consultant's name, it was Murphy – easy, she would find him. She hopped into the cab.

"What number is it, love?" The taximan asked.

"I don't know, I just know it's … he's a doctor, a consultant, Murphy and its Eccles Street."

He looked at her through his mirror. "We'll try love, there are lots of consultants around here. What does he do? Gynaecologist?"

She gave him a wry smile. "Neurologist, I think."

It was just past eleven, she was panicking when she told the taxi driver to give up and she would try the rest of the street on foot. She paid him, pulled the collar of her *Barbour* up and started marching along the street. Door after elegant Georgian door, shiny paint, gleaming brass nameplates, they all looked the same, nearly every one had some sort of *Murphy* listed.

She was about to despair when she saw a small group of women outside one of the buildings. They were gathered at the foot of the steps, they seemed to be holding something, in their hands, pens and notebooks, some had flowers. Students? No, too old… or… autograph hunters!

"Who are you waiting for?" she asked a large, flamboyantly dressed redhead.

"Yer man, Ryan O'Gorman, the film star, is in dere," she told her.

"Great, lovely, thanks," Marianne said, and pushed past them up the steps and in through the large, surprisingly jolly, primrose yellow Georgian door. It was quiet in the hall. Classically tiled in black and white with a sweeping ornate staircase carpeted in pale green. She checked the name board. Mr Orphileus Murphy, consultant neurologist was on the fourth floor. She cast about, no lift, no matter. She ran up the stairs and found the door which led to Mr Murphy's consulting rooms. She poked her head in. An elegant administrative type was on her *iPad* at the desk.

"Is Ryan O'Gorman still with Mr Murphy?" she hissed at the woman.

"Who wants to know?" the woman hissed back. She had clearly batted off the fans earlier, and by the way she was dressed, looked like she was paid a small fortune to play *Hydra* at the entrance to her boss' inner sanctum.

"Me," Marianne tried. The woman removed her glasses.

"I know who you are, his partner. Why aren't you in there?" she nodded towards the door.

"He's a man," Marianne said.

"I get it," *Hydra* said. "He shouldn't be too long now, Mr Murphy is teeing off at two, and it's a schlep to Killiney. Do you want to wait?" She indicated a seat.

"I'll wait outside, thanks." Marianne withdrew, and hid around a corner. She took out her phone and started to text.

'Not long ago you asked me to marry you, I was less than enthusiastic. I want you to know why I said no, it's because I'm stupid and stubborn and always know best. What am I trying to prove, why do I have to insist on being totally independent, in control, in charge of everything, what's wrong with me? Ryan, I'm so sorry, and if you could bear to forgive me, bear to give it a go, then this is my proposal, please, please marry me. If I lose you, I lose everything. You've no idea what my life was, before you, no idea how empty and pointless and just bloody crap it was, before you. Please Ryan, please say yes, whatever is out there, we can face it together, whatever life throws at us, we can make it. I want to be your wife, please say yes and marry me, please. Marianne X.' *Send.*

She heard a door open, no words, it closed. She held her breath. Then a thud, a groan, she thought she heard someone crying. She peeked out from where she was hiding. Ryan was collapsed against a wall, head in his hands, covering his face. She ran to him and threw her arms around him. He jumped and then, realising it was her, embraced her. His face was wet with tears. He was shaking. She held him, just held him, and held him …till he found his voice.

"It's okay," he told her. "It's going to be okay. Benign, benign tumour."

She collapsed into him. "Thank you, God, thank you, thank you. Oh Ryan, you're not going to die."

"Not today, Marie," he said, wiping his face with his hands. "Not today."

The grandfather clock at the bottom of the stairs struck. She checked her watch. It was quarter to twelve.

"Fancy getting married instead?" she said.

"What? Are you crazy, you just can't …"

"Come on, I'll explain on the way." She grabbed his hand and started pulling him down the stairs. "Why you never read your texts, I don't know. Could be really important, you know!"

Ryan told Marianne to slow down or his head would explode, at least three times in the taxi, he gave up in the end. She was trying to explain how she, her mother, and probably everyone else who knew them, had managed to arrange a wedding, in the Dublin registry office, for twelve noon on Friday the thirteenth. The only person who did not know about it was the groom, who happened to be himself.

The gaggle of fans, who had been waiting outside, overheard Marianne ask the taxi driver to take them to Lower Grand Canal Street, as fast as possible. They hailed the next cab and jumped in.

"Follow that cab!" Demanded the redhead, "I've always wanted to say that."

"It's the registry office, isn't it?" said one of the others.

"Of course," said the redhead. "That was a lovely dress she had on under her coat."

"Her hair's a right mess, though," said the other one, holding the starburst lilies meant for Ryan.

"He doesn't seem to mind," said the redhead, and they all laughed.

The bride and groom were ten minutes late, but this was Dublin so that was fine and everything was ready and waiting. They were ushered into a beautiful room, a stained glass window adorned with doves of peace, glowed above a large table on a raised platform. Vases filled with tulips and freesias filled the air with fragrance, as a well-dressed man and elegant lady, showed them to their seats.

Ryan smoothed his hair back with clammy hands. He had been in this situation before, many times. Dozens of wedding ceremonies as an actor and once before as an actual groom, but this time it was different, this was for real, this was for life.

"And your witnesses?" the well-dressed man asked.

They looked at each other. *Silence.*

"And your witnesses?" the man said again, much louder.

The double doors burst open. "SURPRISE!!!" came the cry, and a very mixed bunch burst forth into the rarefied atmosphere of this formal yet cheery establishment.

All were present and correct. Kathleen, dressed to kill in scarlet from head to toe, just like the woman in the upmarket hotel, rushed to her daughter's side. She slipped something out of her bag, it was her most precious treasure, the *Romanov* tiara, a delicate circlet of pearls and tiny diamonds. Marianne bent her head as her mother twisted her hair, placing the jewels firmly on top. Ryan's fans had shuffled into seats, but not before the redhead tapped Marianne on the shoulder, passing her the bouquet of lilies.

"For luck, love," she told her and they shared a look.

Once Kathleen was happy Marianne was ready, Brian wanted a minute with his daughter before the service. He took her hands and looked deep into her eyes.

"May I have your permission to give you away?" he asked solemnly.

Marianne gave him a broad smile. "I'd be delighted, father."

Larry stressing, kept checking his watch until Joyce, dressed in pink silk and wearing more pearls than she ever had in her life, took his hand as she went to sit beside him.

Dermot and Erin, quite the couple now, with Erin training to join the Lifeboat crew and Dermot helping regularly at the pub, were suited and booted. Erin had her hair up and Dermot had flattened his down. Kathleen hoped they might buy an engagement ring while they were in Dublin, recommending a number of jewellers she knew personally. Father Gregory, a little late, had been to the bookies, delighted to be at a wedding and not on duty.

"No speeches, I shall have a few pints so," he told Ryan.

"No speeches? At a Maguire wedding? Never been known," declared Kathleen and they all knew they would all have to do their party pieces at some stage.

The last to enter was Joey, trotting into the room with Monty on a shiny new lead. They had been sitting, patiently, in an antechamber with Joy Redmund and some of her brood. He ran and threw himself at their legs, Monty running round in circles of joy. The registrar, finally called order and the proceedings commenced.

Despite the room being filled with some of the biggest personalities on the planet, when Marianne and Ryan came to say their vows, there was no one else in the world, let alone in the room.

Ryan had no voice and asked for a glass of water, he smiled at his bride, "I'd be fine if it were just a script."

Trembling, Marianne held Ryan's hands in a vice-like grip, until the crucial question. "Who has the ring?"

Her hands flew to her mouth. "I've forgotten it, Ryan the ring, it's not here."

But Kathleen had found it in the desk when she was looking for Marianne's birth certificate, she took a punt on it being a wedding ring. It was Friday the thirteenth, after all.

A small voice piped up.

"We have it," Joey said. "Me and Monty has the ring."

The little boy bent to the terrier's collar and, untying a ribbon, placed a sparkling circle of gems in his father's outstretched hand. Ryan held it in his palm, the light from the window made the stones shine. He rolled it in his fingers as he watched Marianne see, again, the colours of the island, their home, the place they fell in love and would be part of, heart and soul for always.

He placed the ring on Marianne's finger and, finally, they were man and wife.

"At last," he said, and bent to kiss her mouth.

"And forever," she whispered, giving him the biggest smile, before kissing her brand new husband right back. Because that's who he was, not *Thomas Bentley*, the suave, sophisticated superspy; not even Ryan O'Gorman, world famous, movie star; he was her husband, just a man, who loved her more than anything else in the universe. And Marianne knew, from that moment on, whatever lay ahead, they would face it together, and it was going to be alright, more than alright, it was going to be amazing, a real love story, now and forever.

THE END

Epilogue

"Come on, come on, hurry up, they're here." Brian flew out of Maguire's, the big old oak door had never looked so grand, brasses gleaming, steps polished, a new sign – exactly the same as the old one – graced the front of the building, overlooking Main Street. Pots filled with flowers were scattered about the refurbished courtyard, baskets hanging from the new 'old style' street lamps outside.

A horse-drawn carriage stood at the entrance, six horses in full livery, coats gleaming, swishing their tails, anxious to be off. The street was filled with bicycles, riders and ponies, a couple of vintage cars. Everywhere, people were in fancy dress, tweed caps, waistcoats, white shirts with stiff collars, ladies in long skirts, mutton-sleeved blouses, some in traditional Irish costume, it was a fascinating sight. The place had a real buzz to it, a feeling of triumph, celebration and sense of achievement, oozed out of every corner, seeped along the beach and raced up the street. For today, the people of Innishmahon had a right to be proud, extremely, happily and justifiably proud.

"Ryan, are you ready?" Marianne smoothed her skirt, fixed the pins in her hair.

"I am, Mrs O'Gorman, what d'ya think?" He twirled his stuck-on moustache, so handsome he would look good with a bin liner over his head. They raced downstairs, collecting Joey and Monty at the bottom. They were taking a

394

carriage ride, with Brian and Kathleen, Father Gregory, and all the Redmunds. They were going to drive the horses across the new bridge, and everyone had dressed for the part, commemorating the date the very first bridge to the island had been built.

The carriage smelled deliciously of leather and oil, and as they trotted regally across the vast stretch of road forming the new bridge, they heard the maroon boom out, which could have spooked the horses, had Lily O'Brien and her new man, not been in charge of the reins.

First they heard it, then they spotted it. The Lifeboat, the new Lifeboat that had come all the way from Salcombe in South Devon. This glorious grand lady of the sea, gliding into the harbour under the new bridge, sending sparkles like fairy lights out into the dark dramatic Atlantic. They waved madly out of the carriage windows, and Dermot at the helm, waved wildly back, with Erin and Eve at the bow as usual, giving them all a proper salute.

There was only one dissenter, a local man, never been much for progress, his name Sean Grogan, a farmer, a fisherman and lover of *Sky*. He was standing outside Maguire's, arms folded. The pub was shut. It was a disgrace, that's what it was. The notice on the door gave the opening time, just after the official ceremony, when the whole village was welcome for a free drink and barbecue.

A tourist, just off the ferry was standing beside him.

"They won't be long, and a free drink to come that's nice, isn't it?" the man said, in a foreign accent. Sean looked him up and down. The carriage was clattering down Main Street, and the Lifeboat had sailed into the marina, people were spilling along the road towards the pub. Marianne jumped from the carriage, and taking Joey in her arms, raced across the road to the beach, with Ryan and Monty in hot pursuit.

"You can't catch us, we're going in!" she declared, and the woman and the little boy ran straight into the sea, fully clothed. The dog and the man followed suit, screams and barks of joy drifted across the road, as all four jumped up and down in the waves, the humans clapping their hands and shouting, "We did it, we did it!" The little white dog, making as much racket as he could.

The tourist was smiling at the family and their obvious exultation in celebration of the day.

"A local family, I think?" the man asked of Sean.

"Yes," he said, rolling his eyes. "I'm afraid they are." He made a twirling movement with his finger at his temple. "Mad as March hares, that lot. We're not all bloody mad though, no, not by a long chalk and we don't want any more flippin' blow-ins, either!" He said, scowling at the man, before banging on the door in search of his free pint.

The landlord, Brian Maguire, opened the door, smiling broadly at the man.

"You've met Sean, then, head of the local welcoming committee?"

Adrienne Vaughan

Acknowledgements

People say being a writer is a lonely business, not for me, solitary at times but never lonely. Apart from all my characters, who are great company, the following, are all great characters too, without whom Secrets could not have been 'told'.

Grateful thanks to my stunning editorial and production team, namely my mentor and earth-angel, June Tate; beta-reader Natalie Thew; copyeditor Jan Brigden, formatter and technical guru Sarah Houldcroft and cover designer Paul Burrows.

Always right behind me, the New Romantics 4, three wonderful writers, June Kearns, Mags Cullingford and 'headgirl' Lizzie Lamb. For medical research, Jennie Findley, Anna Bergmann, Madeline Poole and Reta Wrafter; agricultural assistance, Nicola Langton and Lizzie King; marketing department, Marion Wrafter, Dee Cotter Daly, weather expertise, Deric O'Hartigan, one's Aunts and cousins, with a special mention for, Joann Smith. All my unsung naggers and pushers-on, and of course, my good

friends in the **Romantic Novelists' Association**, a
truly amazing organisation.

And finally, my love and grateful thanks to my husband,
Jonathan, for words of wisdom, his sublime vocabulary,
unerring faith and great tea.

Adrienne Vaughan

Check out the latest novels published by
The New Romantics 4

Boot Camp Bride
By Lizzie Lamb

20's Girl, the Ghost & All that Jazz!
By June Kearns

Twins of a Gazelle
By Margaret Cullingford

an indie
publishing group

www.newromantics4.com

**AVAILABLE FROM AMAZON
FOR DOWNLOAD AND IN PAPERBACK**

Secrets of the Heart